LOVE
IS IN
THE AIR...

CONTENTS

LOVE IS IN THE AIR

BY
ROSALIE ASH
ANGELA DEVINE
BETTY NEELS
JENNIFER TAYLOR

MILLS & BOON LIMITED
ETON HOUSE   18–24 PARADISE ROAD
RICHMOND   SURREY   TW9 1SR

First published in Great Britain 1993
by Mills & Boon Limited

© Rosalie Ash 1993
© Angela Devine 1993
© Betty Neels 1993
© Jennifer Taylor 1993

Australian copyright 1993
Philippine copyright 1993
This edition 1993

ISBN 0 263 77962 9

Set in 10 on 12 pt Linotron Times
80-9302-104185

Typeset in Great Britain by Centracet, Cambridge
Made and printed in Great Britain

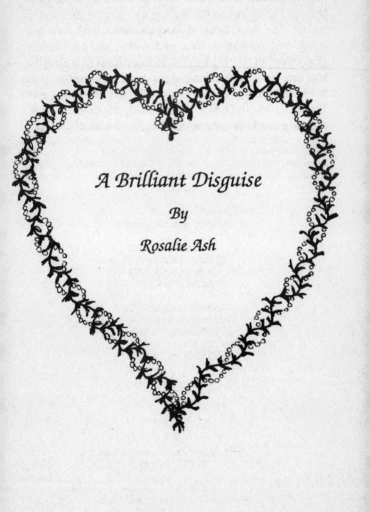

A Brilliant Disguise

By

Rosalie Ash

Having abandoned her first intended career for marriage, **Rosalie Ash** spent several years as a bilingual personal assistant to the managing director of a leisure group. She now lives in Warwickshire with her husband, and daughters Kate and Abby, and her lifelong enjoyment of writing has led to her career as a novelist. Her interests include languages, travel and research for her books, reading, and visits to the Royal Shakespeare Theatre in nearby Stratford-upon-Avon. Other pleasures include swimming, yoga and country walks.

CHAPTER ONE

'HELLO, Jenna.'

Until the shock of hearing that particular voice again, a deep, arrogant voice she'd know anywhere even if she were brainwashed or struck down with amnesia, Jenna Nancollas's eyes were peacefully closed.

She was relaxing in the hot bubbles of the Jacuzzi, and her thick gold-brown lashes formed a soporific sweep against the smooth olive of her face. But the sardonic greeting was like a brutal shot of adrenalin into a main artery.

Large eyes, as brilliantly green as winter wheat, flew open, then, in spite of the warmth of the water, coldness began to creep from the tips of her feet, to her knees, to her stomach, slithering its icy way up into her heart. Relaxation forgotten, she recoiled into a defensive ball as if an alligator had surfaced near by.

'*Ross!*'

'Full marks. For remembering who I am.'

He was sprawled nonchalantly against the opposite side of the Jacuzzi, muscular hair-roughened arms spread out along the rim. He was regarding her with ruthless derision from narrowed, black-fringed, icily grey eyes. Their crystalline grey was intensified by the hard Celtic darkness of his face. His expression was as cold and frightening as the Atlantic in winter, when it crashed against the nearby North Cornish cliffs. Treacherous, mesmerising. She checked her wayward thoughts with a catch of her breath, threads of the past whipping out of some dark corner of her mind and threatening to strangle her. . .

Squeezing her eyes shut, she opened them again in growing panic. She was practically hyperventilating, she registered with grim self-mockery. Calm down. Breathe deeply. Compose yourself.

'What are you *doing* in here?' she bit out furiously, withdrawing her arms to clutch protectively around her naked breasts. Did he *know* she had no swimsuit on?

'I could ask you the same question.' It was a cool taunt.

Jenna glanced wildly around for incriminating evidence of her embarrassing state, and her heart sank. The sight of the brief slip of yellow Lycra lying discarded on the green-tiled surround told its own eloquent story.

For the last ten minutes, believing she was quite alone, she'd been relaxing beneath the hot foaming bubbles of the Jacuzzi, her long, heavy Titian hair caught up on the crown of her head with an outsize tortoiseshell clip. Until now the only problem marring her euphoric state of floating semi-consciousness had been a niggling awareness that fingers and toes were starting to wrinkle like walnuts with the overdose of hot soaking.

'It should be fairly obvious. I'm relaxing in the Jacuzzi and I wasn't expecting company!' She forced herself to cool down, to control the thudding panic in her heart.

Why was she feeling so. . .dizzy with panic? She'd had five whole years to get over Ross Trenwith, hadn't she? And, since Kevern's death, plenty of time to anticipate his eventual return to Lantressa.

There was no excuse for this melodramatic urge towards hysteria.

But Margot Trenwith had told her Ross wouldn't be coming back to Cornwall before the end of the month. If she'd had the remotest inkling that he'd march in here this afternoon, she'd hardly have risked taking her regular weekly swim and Jacuzzi in Lantressa's pool. . .

'I'm intrigued,' Ross said abruptly, apparently highly entertained by her inner struggles. 'The last thing I expected to find was my family fraternising with the enemy.' The grey gaze was merciless on her clenched figure beneath the bubbles. 'A Nancollas borrowing Trenwith leisure facilities?' The piercing gaze narrowed still further. 'Or. . .let me see, now. *Are* you still a Nancollas, I wonder?'

Colour flared in her cheeks.

'You know the answer to that better than most, Ross!' she said in a low, frigid voice. 'I'd like to get out of here. Will you just *go* while I——?'

'Ordering me out of my own Jacuzzi?' he grinned lazily, clearly enjoying her acute embarrassment. 'And I haven't been back five minutes?'

'You've been gone five years!' she spat shakily. 'And frankly five hundred years wouldn't be long enough for me!'

'Great welcome home.'

'*Home*?' she sneered, goaded unbearably by his taunting, privately wondering if the entire surface of her skin was prune-like by now. 'Don't be such a hypocrite!'

Ross slanted an enquiring eyebrow, as thick and dark as his wavy ink-black hair. His gaze was dispassionate.

'A hypocrite. Is that what I am, Jenna?'

'You never wanted to be here at Lantressa. You made that *abundantly* clear to everyone, didn't you?'

Wise or not, the reproaches seemed to pour from her. While she certainly hadn't envisaged its taking place in such a compromising situation, it was as if she'd been unconsciously rehearsing a scene like this, ever since Kevern's death and the reluctant acknowledgement that Ross would come back, that he'd *have* to come back. . .

'. . .no time for home, or family, or loyalty. Don't try to pretend you had. The big city lights were more important. There was nothing you wouldn't do to spite your father, was there? Absolutely *nothing*. . .'

Ross held her accusing green gaze in silent battle, and then he gave a soft laugh.

'Oh, quite,' he agreed, quietly sarcastic, 'I recall similar accusations being slung at me five years ago. Everything I did was to spite my father. Or to spite *your* father. Or maybe even to spite you?'

'Wasn't it true?'

There was a long, loaded pause. Ross sat forward, moved deliberately closer. She felt the brief brush of a coarsely textured leg against hers, and fought down the urge to scream. She felt paralysed, locked in tense anger.

'What do you expect, Jenna?' he murmured, resting a long, casual arm behind her, overwhelming her by his nearness. 'A full confession of my *vices*, after all this time?'

'Ross. . .' With a supreme effort, she began to speak very levelly, fighting for control. It was essential to retain control. Otherwise. . . 'Ross, will you just. . . *go*? I want to get out of here, and. . .'

'And you're feeling too shy to climb out?' he suggested, relentlessly amused. 'Don't mind me, Jenna. We know each other well enough to cope with a spot of nudity, don't you think?'

She shuddered, her pulses drumming. The colour deepened, then drained from her face. Resolution returned. She was damned if she'd let him reduce her to begging.

She felt another brush of his leg against hers. It was the last straw. If he touched her. . .*really* touched her. . .

She was trembling all over. Every nerve-ending had jerked into agonised life. In a frantic cascade of bubbles, she surged to her feet, shaking with indignation and banked-down fury.

'OK, I'll prove that at least *one* of us has grown up this last five years!' she said unsteadily, clambering towards the steps and silently cursing the foaming water which made a dignified exit virtually impossible.

Summoning composure, she made it as gracefully as she could on to the green tiles, beneath the high, domed glass Edwardian ceiling. Her heart was thudding in anger. She hardly dared think of the spectacle she presented, stark naked under Ross's mocking scrutiny, breasts and thighs pink from the hot water, face scarlet with mortification. If she could die, right now, she'd be grateful, she told herself numbly. And she hated Ross, even more than she'd hated him all these years for the way he'd treated her. . .

'Pointless asking you to be *gentlemanly*, and look the other way, I suppose?' she ground out.

'Pointless,' he drawled tauntingly. 'This is too good to miss. Venus rising from the waves.' The deep voice was edged with laughter and something else, something much, much more alarming. . .

Before she'd fumbled with her towel and managed to drape it in place, the grey gaze had slitted to a glittering male appraisal. His eyes flicked boldly over the high thrust of her breasts, nipples taut at the centre of dusky-bronze aureolae. When the flinty gaze roamed lower, lingering on the flat plane of stomach and then on the curls of red-gold at the junction of her slender thighs, it felt as if he was touching her, making love to her with his eyes. . .

'*God*, Jenna, it's been a long five years.' It was a thick masculine growl, electrifying the atmosphere, a potent assertion of desire. 'There should be a law against females with bodies like yours!'

Her knees were infuriatingly shaky.

'There should be a law against womanisers like you! Go back to New York, Ross!' She was furious, but her voice sounded disappointingly husky, as if her emotions refused to toe the accepted line of outraged hostility.

Shivering, she retrieved the yellow swimsuit, swathed the copious emerald folds of her towel around her as tightly as she could, and aimed unseeingly for the door to the changing-room. Before she got there, out of the corner of her eye she saw Ross standing up. He rose from the swirling pool in a lazy, powerful unravelling. The hard planes of lean, darkly tanned muscle were potently male and infinitely threatening.

But if she'd had a subconscious dread that he too

might be naked, she registered with a mixture of relief
and confusion that at least he wore close-fitting black
swimming trunks.

'Go back to New York? No chance,' he rasped, his
eyes following her retreat with a smoky air of speculation. 'Too many challenges here. I've a couple of
projects I need to talk to you about. Possibly a proposal
to make. . .'

'Well, I don't want to talk to you. And I don't want
to hear any of your proposals. About anything!'

He caught her as she tried to slip through the door.
His hold on her soft upper arm felt vice-like.

'You may not have any choice,' he purred softly, his
voice tipped in venom.

'What is *that* supposed to mean?' His touch was
sheer torture. The pain he was causing her was nothing
to the physical turmoil he was provoking. . .

'Jenna, sweetheart, it's hard talking when all I have
on my mind is flattening you on these tiles and making
violent love to you.' The brief endearment, the bold
intimacy of the words were belied by his tone. It was a
laconic drawl. Bitter and cynical. But for a few mesmerising seconds, heart pounding, throat drying, she
feared he was going to carry out the threat.

'Ross, *please*. . .'

With his free hand he twitched the tortoiseshell clip
from the top of her head, and her heavy mass of red
hair tumbled wildly down her back, partly hiding her
face. He dropped her arm and raked her derisively
with his eyes.

'It's OK.' He handed her the clip and she took it
with trembling fingers. The hard mouth twisted drily.
'I'm quite civilised these days. Have dinner with me

tonight. I'll call for you at eight. We'll talk about "old
times". . .'

'*No!*' Her vehemence provoked a sardonic grin.

'All right. We'll talk about why I need your help.
And about a plan for turning Lantressa Cove into a
theme park. . .'

A *theme* park? In tiny, quaint, historic Lantressa Cove?
The place where she'd grown up, where she now
earned her living running her very own Cornish
museum, packed with lovingly assembled relics of a
bygone age? The last mocking phrase had alarmed her
even more than his veiled sexual threats. It echoed in
her mind, all the time she was pedalling her bicycle
downhill at reckless speed, away from Lantressa
Manor.

She'd been visiting Ross's widowed mother Margot
for her weekly tea and gossip, something which would
have been impossible to do while her own father and
Ross's father were alive.

At least, she reflected, swerving to avoid a frantically
darting rabbit, that was one good thing to come out of
a lot of bad—the ridiculous feud between generations
of Nancollases and Trenwiths had finally been laid to
rest along with those last two patriarchs.

Unless you counted the secret, bitter, far more
modern feud still being conducted beneath the surface
between herself and Ross, of course. . .

The family feud had consisted of a series of clashes
over land, and slate quarrying, and fishing, and in a
nutshell had arisen because, according to her father at
least, the Nancollas family were traditionally more
liberal and soft-hearted with their tenants and employ-

ees, more concerned with their welfare and well-being, whereas the Trenwiths were harder, uncaring, oblivious to the human suffering under their patrician noses. . .

Whatever the specifics, the general effect had been undisguised hatred between her father and Ross's father, and their fathers and grandfathers before them. And an unspoken assumption that Nancollases did not associate, in any way, with Trenwiths. Which in part, she supposed, forcing herself to address something she'd conveniently swept under the carpet these last five years, could have partly contributed to the unhappy state of affairs which now existed between herself and Ross. . .

She was heading back towards her own little stone-built cottage and museum on the slipway down to the beach, the cool breeze lifting her hair behind her, the dramatic cliffs dropping away to the sea on her right.

The unexpected, deeply disturbing meeting with Ross had unnerved her to such a degree that she was in dire danger of wobbling right off the cliff path and plunging down to the dizzy black rocks far below. She clung on to the handlebars grimly. The predatory glitter in his eyes as he inspected her naked figure just now returned to sweep heat into her face, a mix of embarrassment and raw anger. . .

Ross Trenwith was capable of anything, of course, on bad terms with his own family, as well as with the Nancollases. He was the archetypal 'black sheep' of the Trenwiths. Even Margot, his mother, unexpectedly sweet and humorous as Jenna had recently discovered her to be, spoke of him with sad resignation. The elder son who had refused point-blank to accept his inheritance of the entailed house and lands, and quarrelled bitterly with his father, leaving the running of the estate to his more dutiful younger brother while he sought independence and self-generated wealth with his own international computer business.

It was disturbing to recall the fact, but she and Ross had known each other, on and off, nearly all their lives. Summers surfing on this coast's gigantic Atlantic waves, beach parties, midnight barbecues, teasing kisses in the moonlight, a prolonged sequence of minor events had combined to produce the most powerful of teenage crushes.

Nearly all her childhood memories seemed to consist of falling secretly, fearfully, painfully in love with Ross Trenwith, and hiding such an unthinkable possibility from her father.

It was odd, but until coming face to face with Ross again just now she hadn't realised how much the past five years had felt like an elaborate charade. Even her father's death, last year, hadn't ended it. In fact, it had made everything seem so much worse. Highlighted all those deceptions, all those disguised emotions, never confessed to him while he lived.

Jenna wheeled her bike thoughtfully into the garage, and then walked on down the steep lane to the shingly fishing cove, with its scattering of tar-stained boats and tangle of nets and lobster baskets, its sharp exhilarating smell of salt and seaweed.

She waved and smiled to people she'd known all her life, a slender figure in tight denims and emerald anorak with a familiar bouncy walk, her red hair blowing in the breeze. Lantressa Cove was quiet in April. Locals mainly, at this time of year, before the

influx of visitors. Soon it would all change. Soon she'd
open her little museum again, and be back behind the
desk taking entrance money, and politely explaining
how the exhibits were on two floors, with a reconstruc-
tion of a turn-of-the-century Cornish cottage on the
second floor, as well as displays covering just about
everything from shipbuilding to granite quarrying, right
down to the village blacksmith, shoemaker, fisherman
and farmer.

She walked to the sea's edge, and sat down on an
upturned boat. Her thoughts jangled discordantly.
How typical of Ross. To come back and threaten. . .
come back to try and disrupt the established order. . .

The tide was out, waves breaking over the distant
rocks. The sky reminded her of a water-colour artist's
palette—washed with pale blue, grey and gold seeping
into each other. Three gulls swooped high, their
mournful cries sending a shiver along her spine.

She didn't want Ross Trenwith back here, stirring up
trouble. Lantressa Cove was peaceful, unspoiled. Her
home. Now Ross was calmly planning on turning the
village upside-down. Turning her *life* upside-down. . .?

Did he mean it? A *theme park*? *Here*?

And he'd said something about a proposal. . .what
proposal was he talking about? And· he wanted her
help? That was no doubt one of his dry jokes.

The thought of having dinner with him tonight filled
her with foreboding, and a deep, smouldering anger.
But, if she wanted to find out what he was up to, she
supposed she'd have to go.

She felt trapped, pressured, a feeling she hated. She
dug her teeth into her bottom lip so hard that she
tasted blood, but scarcely noticed.

CHAPTER TWO

'IT's quite simple.' Ross leaned back laconically in his chair, his dark face angular even in the soft golden candlelight. 'You're a historian. You're an expert on Cornish history. You can advise me on the design of the project. . .' The deep voice was cool and mockingly bland.

'You're mad!' Jenna clenched her hand round the stem of her wine glass so tightly that there was a risk of breakage. 'Do you think you can just *waltz* back here and. . .and click your fingers and get everyone enthused over one of your manic money-making schemes?'

Over their meal, Ross had outlined the plans. A time-warp rail-journey relating the history of the 'Cornish story', a pleasure-dome to lure in summer visitors—commercial nightmares to Jenna, which would swamp tiny Lantressa Cove with cheap gimmicks, destroy its identity. . .

'Did I say everyone? Just you will do.'

'I'm not interested. In fact that's an understatement. Quite honestly, if you're serious, you can count on my total opposition. Along with most of the locals, I should think. . .'

'Jenna. . . Jenna. . .' The soft repetition of her name was purred with such taunting patronage that she stifled the urge to throw her wine at him. 'It won't be as bad as you think, I promise. Haven't you learned anything, these past five years?'

'I've learned lots. Like, not to trust anyone, no matter what they promise.' She took an agitated gulp of the rich red Bordeaux, and replaced her glass with elaborate care on the crisp white damask cloth.

She gazed around her, wishing Ross had brought her anywhere but here, in the kind of setting which created an irresistibly intimate, pervasively *romantic* atmosphere. The ancient Fisherman's Restaurant, right on the Melyn River a few miles inland, boasted every luxury—solid silver, cut-glass, fine linen. Its thick stone walls had withstood scything Cornish winds for over four hundred years. A massive fireplace was full of blazing logs. Vivaldi's 'Spring' trilled discreetly and elegantly from hi-fi speakers concealed behind centuries-old beams.

Ross sat forward, resting his elbows on the table, his grey gaze ruthlessly speculative. They'd finished melon with *langoustines* and salmon with fennel and lemon meringue pie with cream. Coffee and Stilton had been laid on the table between them.

The meal had been exquisite, true, but Jenna had hardly tasted any of it. Her throat seemed to be permanently choked. She ached with the pain of seeing him again, being with him again, and feeling this wild mixture of hatred and resentment and. . .fear?

Ross's intent appraisal was unnerving. Lifting a hand to the neck of her peach silk blouse, she absently fingered the brooch. A cameo, left to her by her mother. Distractedly she slid her hands across her hair, checking that the bronze combs held its heavy waves in place, away from her face. The stretching movement drew Ross's eyes to her breasts, outlined clearly beneath the silk. She dropped her arms abruptly, and defensively crossed them instead. Her cheeks felt warm. She hated him for the way he could make her squirm in her seat. . .

'How did you know this place was so good?' she queried briefly, thinking of his long absence from the country.

'An old friend recommended it. Last month, after Kevern's funeral.'

'Oh. Yes.' Jenna dropped her eyes. She'd been in Greece for a fortnight, with her friend Amy who ran the pottery in the village. It was their annual winter break, before gearing themselves up for the new tourist season. Meanwhile Kevern Trenwith, Ross's younger brother, had apparently had one too many tots of Southern Comfort, staggered out on to the lawn to shoot moles, and ended up not merely shooting himself, but falling into the lake.

The whole sorry saga had erupted and been neatly tidied away by the time Jenna and Amy returned. And Ross had appeared briefly for the funeral and gone back to New York again.

'As I said earlier,' he resumed calmly, sinking even white teeth into a wedge of cheese, and demonstrating the tricky social art of speaking and eating with complete confidence, 'nothing stays the same. Lantressa Manor needs a lot of cash to keep it in repair——'

'It seems to have fared perfectly well while Kevern was alive! And at least Kevern stuck around and shouldered his responsibilities, while you took off to further your own interests. . .'

'Don't rake all that up again,' he said shortly, his

eyes clashing with the brilliant green of hers across the table. 'Freedom of choice was at stake, Jenna. No one, not even my own father, was going to tell me how to run my life!'

'Apart from Cheryl?' Jenna cut in sweetly, reaching for some more coffee, watching the black liquid swirl into her cup with a sensation that she was plunging headlong into the darkness herself. 'Cheryl and her father were allowed to run your life, weren't they?'

Ross's dark face hardened. She couldn't be sure, but she imagined she could even see a surge of angry colour along the high Celtic cheekbones. His mouth twisted into a humourless smile, and Jenna shivered. In spite of his immaculate and thoroughly modern attire, grey-stripe designer suit, the contrasting whiteness of his shirt, the soft pearl silk of his tie, he reminded her of some pagan god, a dark warlord. . .

'I'm surprised you care enough to remember Cheryl's name,' he countered, with distaste. 'You made your choices, Jenna. You had the same freedom I had——'

'*No!*' The denial burst from her, low but fierce. Heads turned their way. 'That's just it, Ross, I didn't! I wasn't free. My father needed me. . .'

'And I didn't?'

Her heart was thumping frantically against her rib-cage. Sipping some coffee, she spilt it on the cloth and replaced her cup in trembling desperation.

'Not enough. And not as much. . .'

'I doubt that.' The three words were so bleakly spoken that she darted a searching gaze at his face, hardly believing he could be so devious.

'Ross, let's get this straight,' she said slowly, lacing her hands against the soft cinnamon wool of her skirt.

'You've spent your entire life exercising the freedom of the totally selfish. You don't care whom you hurt, whom you betray, as long as you can be as free as a bird——'

'Jenna——' The interruption was gratingly harsh, but she ignored him.

'It doesn't matter what you say, Ross! You can't change what happened! Within days of making that. . . that *sham* commitment to me, without even telling me you were going you'd flown to New York to feather your nest with whatever darling Cheryl and her father could offer you!'

'I seem to recall asking you to come to America with me.'

'Dad was ill! I couldn't go, and you knew that.' She glared at him, burning with resentment. 'Besides, considering what I found out, I should think you were relieved! I'd have cramped your style. You'd hardly have been able to set up that cosy little love-nest with Cheryl Lange with me tagging along——'

'That's enough.' It was a curt command, not a suggestion. Ross had gone very still, outwardly relaxed but radiating a coiled, pantherish tension.

'Don't give me orders! I'm not one of your subordinates!'

'I went to America to build up my computer business. You know that.' He sounded dismissive, as if he'd heard it all before and was tired of defending himself. 'I chose independence over the cosy, stifling inheritance I was expected to accept. I wanted you there with me. You chose not to come. Let's consign the rest to history, shall we? I'd rather concentrate on the present.'

She regarded him scornfully over the rim of her wine glass.

'Can't you see? *History*, Ross, happens to shape current events! I'd rather save a killer shark from drowning than help you now!'

The hard mouth twitched.

'Killer sharks don't drown, Jenna. Water is their natural habitat.'

'Well, *your* natural habitat is the cut-throat business world. The sooner you go back to it the better.'

'Wrong. Lantressa is my home. It's where I choose to be now. You can't say my roots aren't here. So let's talk about how you're going to help me, shall we?'

'I'd be fascinated to hear it!'

'As I said, it's quite simple. Advise me on the plans, come up with some constructive advice, and I may give some thought to preserving your precious little museum.'

At her sharp intake of breath, he shrugged in mock apology.

'Otherwise, since you rent both museum and cottage from the Trenwiths, the changes may have to be slightly more. . .radical.'

'Are you *blackmailing* me, Ross?' Her throat had gone very dry. The words came out on a husky whisper.

'Something like that.' His sudden grin, in any other circumstances, would have knocked the breath out of her. The ice-grey eyes crinkled in genuine amusement for the first time. The white slash of teeth against the swarthy skin conjured everything male and arrogant.

'I see. *That's* your "proposal", is it? Was there anything else?' Her voice was bitter with sarcasm.

'As a matter of fact, our "deal" depends on your

agreement to something else as well. Another proposal I wanted to make to you,' he added, reflectively, his gaze moving up and down her in a speculative, highly insulting manner. 'But it'll keep. I think that's enough to be going on with, don't you?'

To say she'd spent a bad night would be understating the case, Jenna decided, cycling up to Lantressa Manor in the morning with leaden legs. Confronted with Ross's arrogant suggestion last night, she had seemed to have no choice but to go along with him, for the time being. She rented her museum and cottage from the Trenwiths. Ross Trenwith was back at Lantressa with an awful lot of power on his side. . .

Nothing new, of course. A Trenwith holding the trump cards. Over the generations, by fair means or foul, the Trenwiths had prospered and the Nancollases foundered. So much for fortune smiling on the right-eous. If her father's version was to be believed, fortune smiled on the 'parcel of rogues' who owned Lantressa Manor and most of Lantressa Cove. The Trenwiths' power and wealth in the county had been founded on the iniquities of their ancestors, which, according to the sourest of the Nancollases, reputedly encompassed smuggling and wrecking. Jenna considered this to be stretching the truth to embroider an old grudge. But whatever else might be the case, it was certainly true that when her father died he'd left very little. The old family tin-mining interests were long gone, properties sold or used as collateral to borrow from the bank to fund new business ventures which duly foundered in their place. Teudar Nancollas had left a pile of bad debts. Sometimes, though she missed her mother furiously, Jenna felt glad she'd died ten years earlier, before she saw Teudar's bitter self-pity, which Jenna had had to cope with for the last few years of her father's life. . .

She was quietly proud of her own small achievement in the village. The Cornish museum had been entirely her own idea. Armed with a history degree and a burning passion for her subject, she'd rented the old barn and begun with exhibits begged or borrowed from the older families in the area. Now the museum was a regular tourist attraction. She'd never be a wealthy woman, but she had job satisfaction. . .

It wasn't just her own interests at stake. Protecting her museum from Ross's vandalistic plans was just the tip of the iceberg. It had occurred to her during her sleepless night that if she buried her pride and got involved she'd at least have some control over the fate of Lantressa Cove. She'd at least have some say in the eventual outcome of whatever glitzy monstrosity Ross had dreamed up in his exile in New York. . .

But it was like a bad dream. She couldn't recall ever feeling quite so helplessly furious. Not since that fiasco five years ago, when she'd lowered her defences, admitted her feelings for Ross, and reaped the miserable consequences. . .

She paused, out of breath, halfway along the cliff. Gulls circled, spray foamed up in the distance where the Atlantic crashed against Hendra Head. The landscape was awe-inspiring, primeval, the massive hogsback cliffs curving green then shearing dizzily away to the rocks below. Sometimes she thought only the beauty and power of this place kept her going. Otherwise the bitter frustration in her life so far would have smothered her completely. . .

She leaned on her handlebars, tears pricking her eyes as powerfully as the memories jostling for position in her mind. Five years ago, she'd been filled with such secret joy, riding high on the heady belief that Ross, her childhood idol, the only man who'd ever set her pulses racing and her heart thudding, seemed miraculously to return her feelings.

She'd been twenty, that summer when everything had peaked then disintegrated. She'd been about to take her finals, a year younger than most of her contemporaries after a brilliant school career, sailing through O and A levels a year ahead of her peer group. Ross had already graduated, two years ahead of her, gaining the honours degree in maths and computers which he'd ruthlessly set his sights on. Basing himself in Cambridge, with valuable contacts made during his degree course, he'd begun laying the foundations of his own computer software empire, his business ambition as diamond-sharp as his apparent determination to win Jenna's love, against the odds of family hostility.

For a brief spell everything had been sublimely, supremely good. And then abruptly everything had been unbelievably, cruelly bad. From the pinnacle of happiness, she'd plunged into an abyss of despair.

But, while that summer had been the watershed, it had all started, really started, further back than that. Had it started when she'd arrived at Cambridge University, a naïver than average first-year history student, with Ross in his final year?

No, before that, even, if she were totally honest with herself. Right from those earliest days when she'd suppressed her fierce adolescent attraction for Lantressa's notorious heart-throb, terrified in case her father found out and berated her for disloyalty. A sudden vivid image of Ross at seventeen, the summer before he went to Cambridge, sprang to mind. Ross, standing on a sunbaked Cornish beach after giving her brotherly, teasing surfing lessons, talking and joking with friends, drinking Coke from a tin, carelessly devastating in a black wetsuit unzipped to the navel, soaked black hair clinging to his head. She'd been nearly fourteen, tolerated on the fringe of that charmed circle of admirers, snatching the odd smile as if it were a crock of gold. To her he'd seemed everything she could ever want; he'd filled her dreams.

Even so, ending up at the same university had been entirely coincidental. Being offered a place at Cambridge, after all, was too glamorous to turn down. And she'd convinced herself it would simply be pleasant to have a familiar face from Cornwall to ease the break from home. But then the magic had begun. Despite a circle of friends and admirers very reminiscent of Cornwall, Ross had sought her out, filling her fragile heart with such tender hope that she'd almost held her breath for the duration of their relationship. It had begun platonically enough, but when she and Ross began seeing each other frequently, joining the same clubs and societies, going to films and theatres together, pooling meagre resources for pizzas and Chinese meals, the pretence had crumbled.

After he had graduated, he was away for months on end in America, but he had bought a flat in Cambridge and returned frequently. When he was away, she'd found studying the only way of relieving the grey endless agony of separation. When he came back, the sun had shone again, life sprang back into Technicolor. Throughout her three years at university, she'd had no real idea of Ross's feelings for her. He'd seemed content to play a waiting game, waiting for what she wasn't sure. They had spent hours together, getting to know each other so deeply that she sometimes felt impossibly close to him, a secret soul-mate. But he had had hosts of friends in Cambridge. There was almost a female fan-club, fellow undergraduates who'd fallen victim to the rakish Trenwith charm. Jenna had tried to interest herself in other boyfriends, but they were like pale shadows, mere substitutes for the real thing.

Then in her final year, when he had singled her out for every dance at the May Ball, wickedly, headturningly gorgeous in his dinner-jacket, annihilating the hopeful young escort she'd arrived with, she'd felt like Cinderella must have felt in the arms of Prince Charming. Floating around in strapless emerald taffeta, her red hair rippling wildly down her back, she'd been secretly melting with longing and love. All those stolen teenage moments, the forbidden times when she'd guiltily revelled in Ross's company, back at Lantressa Cove, the frustrating uncertainty of the last couple of years of cat-and-mouse courtship whenever Ross was back from the States, it had all come together in one huge, cataclysmic infatuation.

Wildly and unwisely, she'd whispered to Ross that she loved him. The dazzling light of triumph in his eyes had jolted her like an electric shock.

That night Ross had made love to her for the first time, with fiercely suppressed hunger which had halted only briefly at the discovery of her virginity. That point had seemed a silent triumph. Her novice status had been devoured possessively, victoriously, guilt and self-consciousness banished with one glittering smile from those ice-cool, reckless grey eyes.

Had he merely been scoring points, even then? Seducing Teudar Nancollas's daughter, chalking up petty victories for the Trenwiths?

But at the time, in the aftermath of that wondrous, heartstopping experience, the emerald taffeta discarded with the jumble of tuxedo and bow-tie in wild abandon on the floor of Ross's flat, like trail-markers to the bedroom, her softness beneath his hard masculine need, it had seemed that all her dreams were coming true.

The only cloud on the horizon had been Cheryl Lange.

Cheryl had been an American student in Ross's year, studying in England for twelve months. Art Lange, her father, was an immensely rich, successful businessman. Cheryl had given Ross the introduction to her father in New York, which had led to the meteoric rise in his career. . .

Cheryl Lange. Staring at the seagulls executing perfect arcs above the cliffs, Jenna realised that, even after all this time, she could still visualise Cheryl Lange in perfect detail. Chic black hair, endless legs, long smoky violet eyes trained hungrily on Ross whenever he entered or left a room. . .

A sick jolt in the stomach. She didn't want to think about Cheryl. She squeezed her eyes shut, blocking out the unwelcome memories. Time hadn't healed, but dulled. And now, everything was being stirred up again, and it hurt, it hurt so much that she wanted to scream it into the sky, the way the gulls did. . .

Ross was in Lantressa's big book-lined library when his mother showed her in, with two men Jenna recognised from the estate office—Ben Jasper, the deputy land agent, and another man. Plans were spread out on a massive Sheraton desk. They all straightened up, and eyed Jenna's long, jeans-clad legs and cloak of wavy Titian hair with keen interest as she approached. After brief greetings, the others melted discreetly out of the room.

'I'll send coffee in later,' Margot said calmly, giving Jenna an affectionate smile before she closed the door.

Propped against the desk, casual but dangerously attractive in rough denim shirt and tight jeans, feet in soft tan suede boots crossed casually at the ankles, Ross folded his arms and scanned her rigid, hostile figure. His wavy black hair was tousled, as if he'd recently come in from the wind. There was a wry expression in his eyes.

'Good morning,' he mocked. 'Just seeing you makes my day, Jenna.'

'Cut the smarmy remarks,' she told him flatly, 'I'm here to render assistance, as ordered! So let's look at the plans. What do you need my advice on?'

'Slow down. Relax, lady. You're too uptight.'

Mutinously, she glared at him, her hands thrust hard into the pockets of her jeans, her red hair glowing like a furnace above her loose golden mohair sweater.

'Are those the plans for your precious "theme park"?' she queried, stiff-lipped.

'More or less. . .come here, Jenna.'

'Ross, there is no way I——'

The protest was cut short as with tigerish accuracy he reached out a lazy arm and captured her, pulling her to him with a jerk.

Galvanised, panic-stricken, she fought his superior strength, punching and kicking.

'Stop it, you little firebrand——'

She was slammed against him in punishment, aware in every pore and cell of her body of his lean, whipcord strength. Her struggles were inflaming everything. Belatedly, she recognised the amused darkening of his eyes, detected the whiff of masculine desire.

She stopped fighting, stood like a statue in his arms, crushed against his hard chest. Her breasts were prickling with reaction, her nipples tight beneath the mohair. Her stomach seemed to have vanished completely. Her knees were in the process of dissolving into water.

'That's better. What a little hellcat.' The deep voice taunted, but there was another layer of emotion beneath.

'Don't call me *little*, you patronising bastard,' she grated unsteadily, her heart hammering like a piston. 'I'm five feet five, and I'm only three years younger than you. . .'

'Four,' he corrected, narrow grey eyes mocking her. 'Four years younger, seven inches shorter. That entitles me to call you "little" if I want to. . .'

She was opening her mouth to retort, when he bent his head and kissed her full on the lips. The heat was engulfing, like a flow of molten lava trickling from her head to her toes. Ross drove his tongue between her teeth, plundering the warm softness of her mouth. With lazy insistence, he ran his hands up her back to the nape of her neck, tracing the tender line of her jaw with lean, spatulate fingers, then swept the caress back down to her hips, outlining the high jut of her buttocks with a possessive intimacy which shook her to the core.

'That's better,' he murmured again, lifting his head and watching the turmoil of reaction in her eyes with a glint of unholy triumph. 'Feeling more relaxed? Because I've got another proposal to make to you. I'm sure you'll be happy to agree, since you're feeling so amenable this morning, Jenna.'

With an effort, she wrenched herself out of his arms, fixing him with a glare of such venom that he made a wry grimace, jokingly putting up his hands in self-defence.

'Don't tell me—let me guess!' she spat softly. 'A "roll in the hay" for old times' sake? I'm not *that* desperate for sexual gratification, Ross!'

'Nothing as crude as that,' he reproached, with an unrepentant grin. He was laughing at her, but behind the laughter was a watchful wariness.

With a fresh burst of rage, she recognised he was finding her fury highly entertaining.

'Well? *What*?'

'I need someone to pose as my wife for the weekend.'

There was a resounding silence. The library itself seemed to shimmer with tension. Above the glass-fronted bookcases, dark portraits of long-dead black-haired Trenwiths with pale, watchful faces stared down, impartial observers of the small drama unfolding beneath them.

'Your *wife*?' Jenna breathed. Colour had rushed to her cheeks and then drained away, leaving her ghostly white. 'You're asking *me* to pose as your *wife*?'

There was a merciless glitter of laughter in his eyes. He tilted her small chin with his forefinger, inspecting her shattered appearance dispassionately.

'If you care enough about your museum and the village, you'll say yes,' he said with calm audacity. 'I knew you'd appreciate the irony, Jenna. And incidentally, how's your French?'

CHAPTER THREE

'APPRECIATE the *irony*?' Jenna echoed, beginning to tremble all over. Her voice sounded quite unlike her own. She felt as if she'd just got in a lift which was hurtling downwards out of control. 'What sort of a sick joke is this, Ross?'

'It's not a joke at all.' The amusement lingered in his eyes, but his deep voice resonated with arrogant certainty. She shivered, gripping her hands together in front of her.

Ross's voice was one of the things about him she'd always found fatally attractive. She hadn't been alone. That husky bass growl lured females like a magnet. With a voice like that he could have been born Quasimodo and women would still have fainted with desire at his feet. . .

Instead, she admitted bitterly, glaring at him with shocked green eyes, he had it all. Dark, rugged good looks, perfect white teeth, the lean, flat muscles of an athlete.

But heart-stopping good looks and a sexy voice weren't everything, she reminded herself, gritting her teeth. Inside that irresistible outer appearance lurked the black soul of a highwayman. . .

'Go to hell,' she whispered. Her lips felt stiff. She felt numb all over. Swinging away, she stalked furiously to the door and escaped into the hall, closing the door with elaborate care behind her.

Stumbling out to her bicycle, she tried to climb on to pedal away, then thought better of it. Walking was safer, with her knees infuriatingly refusing to function as knees, and her hands shaking so much that the handlebars wobbled precariously.

Wheeling the bike beside her, she made it halfway down the cliff-top path, then abandoned her bike against a wind-bowed hawthorn tree and struck off down the steep, narrow track which wound down to the beach far below. She had to think. She had to be alone to think. She began the descent fast, her anger driving her on, almost oblivious of her steps. She was so confused and angry that she hardly noticed the route she was taking. From up here, the whole of Lantressa Cove was visible, an ancient weathered inlet hewn into the rocky magnificence of the North Cornish coast. Unspoiled, unchanged for hundreds of years. How *dared* he coolly propose ripping it all apart to create a theme park? How *could* he? This was his heritage, his home, as much as it was hers. . .didn't he care at all?

The path zigzagged through brambles and bracken, and then began to fall very steeply indeed. So steeply that she slowed and then halted, and looked around uncertainly. She'd taken the wrong path. She could see that now. At least, she could just about see that now. With one of the quick-change acts of Cornish weather, the wind had dropped and the thin April sun had vanished behind a patchy sea-fret. It was quite misty, as she neared the halfway down point. And the path she should have taken was a little lower, to the right.

Glancing back the way she'd come, she felt her heart sink at the climb needed to retrace her steps. If she was agile enough, she could rejoin the right path by a spot of mountain-goat cunning, and scramble over the rocks just to her left. . .

Seconds later, her trainers slipped on the damp rock, sending a shower of small stones scattering ominously down the cliff face. Adrenalin pumping through her, she clung to what felt like loose scree with her finger-nails. Unbelievably, she was stuck. . .

The sound of Ross's voice, echoing up from below, came as such a shock she nearly fell.

'Jenna, what in hell's name are you doing?'

'Climbing down the cliff! What does it look as if I'm doing?' she yelled back furiously.

'From here it looks as if you're trying to kill yourself.'

'I took the wrong path, that's all. . .'

'You're way off the path. Heading for the overhang!'

Her voice seemed to dry in her throat. Drawing a deep breath, she worked hard at not panicking.

'Ross. . .'

'Stay put. Don't move!' The tone was peremptory. 'I'm coming up. . .'

'There's no need for that!' she managed to shout defiantly. 'I've climbed up and down this cliff enough times. . .'

'Just for once, will you do as you're bloody well told?' Ross roared furiously. Jenna capitulated in mor-tified silence. Clinging grimly to the rocks, she listened to the thud and scramble of someone ascending the cliff, at what sounded to her like reckless high speed. Surefooted as a seasoned rock-climber, he appeared a few feet from her.

'Is this a melodramatic protest about my proposal just now?' he queried drily. With casual expertise, he was easing her shivering limbs into a nerve-racking step by step descent to the safety of the path below. 'I'm not sure even I could live with a suicide on my conscience!'

'Don't be ridiculous!' she snapped, clutching on to him in terror as another rattle of stones plunged seawards. 'If you imagine I'm the kind of defeatist idiot who jumps off a cliff under stress, then you're——'

'No. I don't think that. Watch where you put your left foot—that's it, nearly there. . .' They were down. Her heart was nearly bursting in her chest. 'But now I come to think of it,' Ross was continuing blandly, 'you were always prone to silly impulses. . .'

'Thanks a lot! So were you! Now can we just——?'

'In a minute.' Ross was shrugging off the loose suede bomber jacket he wore over his denim shirt and jeans, wrapping it round her shoulders, then drawing her down to the small hummock of grass beside him. Until then, she hadn't registered how much she was shivering. The jacket was warm from Ross's body. It sent uneasy *frissons* of awareness skittering through her nervous system. She didn't want to be reminded of Ross in any intimate way. Yet she found herself perched halfway up the cliff, Ross's muscular arm round her shoulders, pinning her against him. The tide was well in, she realised belatedly. The sea was crashing against the rocks far below. She'd been too distraught to notice, but she wouldn't have been able to get down to the beach in any case. . .

'Just as well you were wearing that bright gold sweater,' Ross said abruptly, turning to inspect her white face with a twist of a grin, 'or I might not have spotted you.'

'I suppose I should be grateful?' she managed at last, through gritted teeth.

'I save your life, and that's all I get?'

She crouched there in seething silence for a few seconds.

'Ross, this may be your idea of the perfect setting for a chat, but. . .'

'Why did you rush off like that?' he queried lightly, ignoring her. 'Was it something I said?'

'Very funny!' She glared at him impotently. 'Did you really think I'd just nod and smile and agree to everything? What kind of a bastard are you, Ross?'

'A solid twenty-four-carat-gold bastard,' he conceded, his gaze on her tense face.

'And you think this shabby little blackmail is going to work? What possible reason can you have to come back and torment me like this, Ross?'

'I think you know the reason.'

His soft words echoed in the misty air. She stared at him, then dropped her eyes, focusing blindly on the white leather of her trainers.

'No. I'm afraid I don't. . .' Inside, she was screaming, mentally crashing around in panic. How come she was outwardly so calm?

'I'm feeling nostalgic.' He was mocking her ruthlessly. With bold insouciance, he slid his hand beneath the suede jacket, investigating the taut plane of her diaphragm through the fluffy mohair jumper before moving up hungrily to the soft jut of her breasts. She caught her breath, outraged, and he smiled slowly, his eyes narrowing to a mesmerising brilliance as he met her stormy gaze.

'I just remembered something,' he said huskily, his

fingers teasing the sensitive tips of her breasts, feeling the nipples harden and grow, even while she was rigid with shame and fury. 'I've rescued you from this cliff before, remember?'

Shutting her eyes, teeth clenched, she dimly registered that he was right. She'd got stuck up here with a friend, when she was twelve. Ross and Kevern had been passing in their boat.

'Yes! I remember!' she hissed, writhing as Ross abruptly dispensed with the modesty of her sweater, skimming expert fingers beneath to find warm, trembling bareness. Her stomach hurtled downwards while her body stayed motionless. Warm honey was invading her thighs and her groin. There was no sense in it. She was fired with outrage, yet she couldn't move a muscle.

'You have the most delectable breasts,' Ross murmured, his deep bass voice thickening, vibrating with male arrogance as he stroked and explored. 'Sweetheart, when I touch you, you respond. Physically, you respond. I still want you, Jenna. And you still want me. . .'

'Really? Whatever gave you that idea?' she managed, a touch hysterically. With superhuman control, she managed to quell the roar of the furnace inside her. If she struggled, the situation could escalate. Besides, struggling halfway up a cliff suggested a death-wish which, present problems accepted, she was very far from feeling.

'I remember your heroic rescue,' she forced a light, uninterested voice. 'You jumped off your boat, and scaled the cliff like the man in that chocolate advert. . .'

To her horror, she heard herself burst into slightly

hysterical laughter. 'My *hero!*' she said weakly. 'I think that was when I first——'

She stopped abruptly, feeling Ross's arm tense round her shoulders. The exploring hand slowly withdrew from its audacious caresses beneath her sweater. He drew the warm mohair down again, and pulled the suede jacket closer around her.

'When you first. . .?' he prompted, a husky note of amusement in his voice.

'I. . . I was going to say. . .' she swallowed on a painful lump on her throat '. . .when I first fell in love with you. Calf-love,' she explained shortly, heat flooding through her despite the chilly exposure of the cliffside. 'Just a passing phase! Most girls go through it. You were tall, dark, and handsome, you had a wild reputation, and you were forbidden territory. Every little girl's dream, in fact. . .'

'I can recall a sixteen-year-old thinking you were every little boy's dream, too,' Ross said, weighing his words slowly, 'but I didn't realise how special you were, until I saw you with other men. At university. It took me a while to work out what was causing the acute pain in the gut whenever I spotted you with someone else. . .'

'Indigestion?' she suggested caustically, her pulses drumming frantically. 'Ross, I think I've enjoyed the view for long enough now. If you don't mind I'd like to go back up and retrieve my bike and——'

'Jenna. . .' He held her there with effortless strength, twisting her face round to his. 'Let's be honest, shall we? These last five years, I've just been too damn proud and bitter to come back and force a showdown! How about you?'

Her shivering had little to do with coldness of her body, she realised dimly. The hard intensity, the hunger in the deep voice had taken her by surprise. The shiver of reaction seemed to reach right down into the centre of her body, and light a small tentative fire there. . .

'Are you planning on keeping me prisoner here all day,' she said unsteadily, 'as well as forcing me to play the dutiful wife next weekend, with your crass threat of destroying Lantressa hanging over my head?'

'Jenna, stop fighting me,' he breathed roughly, half amused, half angry, twisting his fingers in her hair. 'We'll have a good time in France, sweetheart. . .'

Taking her completely by surprise, he moved his head and covered her lips with his mouth, muffling her protest in her throat. His tongue traced the outline of her lips before invading the warmth of her mouth.

Abruptly, fiercely, with a sort of despairing anger, she found herself kissing him back, parting her lips to his hot invasion, clutching her arms around him as tightly as she could. The uncomfortable, precarious surroundings were forgotten. Shocking, burning desire ripped through her stomach. Even there, halfway up the bleak cliff, she had an unthinkable, wild yearning to feel his weight and strength against her, feel him naked against her, rough and male and urgent, feel him inside her, and more, much, much more. . .

As if sensing her inner turmoil, Ross drew back a fraction, assessing the dilation of her pupils, velvet-black in brilliant green. With a soft growl of masculine triumph he moved to roll half on top of her, one strong thigh thrusting between her legs, separating her thighs, rendering her abruptly powerless beneath his weight.

She'd heard of people being kissed senseless, Jenna acknowledged numbly, but she hadn't appreciated that the phrase had any relevance in reality. Now, with the drugging, explosively arousing sensation of Ross's hard lips on hers, his tongue probing the intimate recesses of her mouth, his hands forceful and determined as they sought to claim possession of her slender body, she began reluctantly to acknowledge some relevance.

'God, sweetheart, you're driving me crazy. . .' It was a rough groan against her lips. 'I've missed you like hell. . .'

Shuddering with emotion and physical arousal, she fought for control. But her brain was temporarily out of action. He tasted so wonderful, his tongue arrogantly exploring inside her mouth, forcing his way in, mimicking the ultimate sex act with a hunger which ignited a flame inside her. He felt even more wonderful, the hard strength of his body braced and tensed against her own soft curves.

With an abrupt quickening of desire, she closed her eyes, sinking into despair at her body's ability to trick her. The stroke of the lean fingers on the swollen jut of her breasts, the smooth indent of her waist, the curve of her hips, sent her temperature soaring. And then her control slipped still further, as Ross slid his hand down between her thighs, eased them wider apart, raked hungrily expert fingers back up over the sensitive mound at their apex. Even through the protective chastity of her denim jeans, she gasped and flinched as if he'd burned her with an electric probe. . .

'You still want me, sweetheart. . .I can feel you do. . .'

She was shaking her head, speechless with shame

and anger, powerless to shrug off this consuming lethargy. How could she want him so, after all this time? After the way he'd treated her? After his ruthless behaviour since he'd returned?

Letting her senses take over was reckless, emotional suicide. This slow-burning, sensuous smoulder inside was unravelling her brain. . .

'Admit it?' he probed thickly against her ear.

'Ross, this isn't fair. . .'

'I'll be honest for both of us, shall I? Just as well we're halfway up a cliff in a cold April mist.' The deep voice had thickened with desire, half mocking, half desperate. 'Or my control would be long gone, sweetheart. . .'

She could feel his swollen hardness against her thigh, sense the massive control he was exerting over his sexual need. The foolishness of her response to him suddenly overwhelmed her. The wildness, the urgency singing through her bloodstream abruptly receded. Cold reality flooded back. With a shudder, she pushed him away. This time he wryly allowed himself to be pushed.

'Ross, it's no good. . .' She spoke on a choked sob, lurching distractedly to her feet. 'It's just. . .hopeless! It could never work out between us, if that's what you had in mind! Not after all that's happened. . .it's all too complicated. . .'

Whirling away, she began to stumble up the path away from him, slipped and fell, bruising her knees and grazing her hands. Ross caught her from behind, set her gently on her feet again. Tears were blurring her vision.

'Calm down,' he murmured wryly, his voice still

thick with emotion. 'All I have in mind is a little masquerade in France. You play Mrs Trenwith, I play Mr Trenwith. Happily married newly-weds. What could be less complicated than that?'

'Astrophysics, maybe?' she shot back unsteadily. 'Nuclear magnetic resonance?'

He took her hand, felt her convulsive trembling, and his mocking amusement faded.

'Come on,' he said firmly, easing past her with her hand crushed tightly in his. 'You're not running away from me again. We'll take the path back up to the top. And I think I should lead the way, don't you?'

CHAPTER FOUR

'HERE, you'd better wear this,' Ross murmured, as they stepped off the plane at Bordeaux airport. The sun felt unseasonably hot, reflecting off the glass in the reception building, dazzling Jenna's eyes. The rest of the disembarking passengers swirled past them, leaving them standing alone in the middle of the tarmac.

Almost unseeing, she turned to stare as Ross pulled a small black velvet ring-box from his pocket, extracting a heavy gold band. The expression in his eyes was darkly shadowed as he took hold of her left hand, and slid the band on to her third finger.

'Ross. . .' There was an infuriating break in her voice, and she clamped her throat fiercely closed again. She would not cry, she would not show him even for a fraction of a second how agonising she found this stupid charade of his, how the sight of the ring drove a spear of pain into her heart.

'"With this ring, I thee wed",' he mocked softly, catching hold of her as she made to swing blindly away, wrenching her against him with merciless strength, the heat of his body swamping her beleaguered senses. '"With my body, I thee worship. . ."'

'*Ross!*'

In response, he kissed her swiftly on the mouth, overwhelming her furious protest in his usual arrogant fashion.

'What's wrong, Jenna?' He searched her white face,

45

his eyes deadpan as he lifted his head. 'Don't you like playing at being husband and wife?'

Mutely, she shook her head. With a slight mocking frown he bent to study her face, detected the tears smarting the backs of her eyes.

'Tears, *Mrs* Trenwith?' With one hand at the nape of her neck, he twisted her averted head back towards him, smudging an escaping tear roughly with his thumb. 'Could these be tears of happiness, I wonder?'

She stiffened, her throat so choked that she simply couldn't speak. The breeze toyed with the red strands of hair escaping her elegant topknot. She closed her eyes, fervently wishing herself elsewhere, *any*where but here, acting out this sick pretence with Ross. . .

'I suppose it's conceivable that brides might weep tears of happiness on their honeymoon,' Ross was musing with relentless irony, steering her towards the airport buildings with an iron arm round her shoulders, 'although our story goes that we've been married several months, haven't we, sweetheart? Tears of joy as you gaze into your husband's eyes might be a little melodramatic. Familiarity breeds contempt, don't they say?'

'In our case, the familiarity was unnecessary.'

'Careful—we're conveying marital bliss, remember? That's the deal.'

'I'll do my best,' she retorted sharply, twisting out of his sheltering arm, disguising her ragged feelings as best she could, 'but it's an alien state to me, I'm afraid!'

She still found it hard to believe this was happening. The last few days had progressed in a stressful blur of warring emotions. She had yet to stop stinging with resentment. But. . .there were reasons why she was doing this, weren't there? Reasons of her own. Reasons unassociated with Ross's contemptible blackmail. But those reasons were too complex, too tangled. Suffice it to say she was here. Protecting her beloved museum, even martyring herself for the sake of the village. . .?

The last notion brought a bitter smile to her lips. That was going a bit far. Because, while she had no doubt that Ross was devious and ruthless enough to implement his threat to destroy her museum—past experience had taught her as much—she doubted if her pride would allow her to be manipulated like this purely on that basis. . .

Ross had another hold over her, one she couldn't deny. . .

Oh, if only she could *change* the past. If only she could wipe out that idiotic *brainstorm* five years ago. If only she'd had the courage to do something about it since, instead of playing ostrich, hiding behind her duty to her father, playing her childhood wishing game and hoping all her problems would vanish into the Cornish mist. . .

'Ross, Ross, honey! Over here!' The vibrant female voice abruptly cut across Jenna's thoughts.

With a disbelieving jolt in her stomach, she glanced across the crowded airport hall, caught sight of the voice's owner, waving enthusiastically among the swelling throngs, and shut her eyes in a wave of pure shock.

She wasn't hallucinating, then. It *had* been Cheryl Lange's voice, remembered as clearly as if she'd spoken to her yesterday. Abruptly, she realised that Ross was being even more devious than she'd suspected. . .what on earth was he up to?

'Hello, Cheryl.' Ross's deep voice was easy and

assured, his grin unrepentant as he exchanged formal kisses on the cheek.

Nothing had changed, it seemed. The dark girl's eyes still held that smoky, possessive gleam for Ross. There was still that shimmer of sexual awareness between the two of them. Jenna stood back a fraction, tense as a reed in her lovat-green suit and tan court shoes, clutching her bag like a shield in front of her.

'Ross, I was so *glad* when Daddy told me you'd agreed to come to the wedding! You've no idea how much I've missed you! I thought I'd come and meet your flight, darling. . .'

Cheryl seemed unable to drag her gaze away from Ross to acknowledge Jenna's presence. Jenna had always felt like a dispensable extra, right from that first meeting when Ross had introduced them in his rooms in Hall at university. . .

'You remember Jenna?' Ross was saying easily, stretching out a laconic hand to haul Jenna closer, his grey gaze shuttered as he watched them cautiously shake hands. He looked very cool and implacable, tall and dark and saturnine. The puppeteer manipulating. . .

'Hi, Jenna,' Cheryl purred huskily, eyeing her thoroughly up and down, a small smug smile on her lips. Turning to Ross, she tossed back her short black fringe, smoothing her palms sensuously along the silky mauve material of her smart shirt-dress. 'Daddy didn't mention Jenna was invited, honey.'

'No?' Ross's tone was deadpan, as they began to walk towards the exit. 'I see too little of my wife as it is. Pressure of work, you know. A romantic weekend seeing Art remarry at his French château seemed the ideal way of making up a little lost time, didn't it, Jenna? We might treat it like a second honeymoon.'

Cheryl's suck of breath was clearly audible. A frigid, shocked silence was followed finally by a light, masking kind of laugh, bitterly lacking humour.

'Oh, I see. I'd no idea. How perfectly *sweet* for you both!'

Jenna's emotions felt battered. She kept her eyes straight ahead. Nothing in the world could have made her look across at Cheryl, because she knew only too well what pain and anguish she would read there and she couldn't bear it. Fury at Ross came second only to a searing *pity* for Cheryl. Whatever Ross's twisted motives for this charade, he was treating Cheryl with what appeared to be the most unbearable cruelty. If she'd had any idea of his intentions, she'd have dug in her heels and point-blank refused to play along with this. There would have been alternatives to achieving the same goals. She could have rallied the village, perhaps, gained local support in opposition to Ross's plans, staged a massive protest, *anything* as an alternative to playing a part in this sadistic ploy to rid Ross of an unwanted lover. . .

Digging her nails into the palms of her hands, she followed them to a glamorous metallic burgundy Bentley. A uniformed chauffeur was in the driving seat, resplendent in dove-grey and burgundy. He leapt out and opened the boot, took their cases, ushered them inside.

There was ample room on the wide back seat for the three of them. Ross sat in the middle, relaxed but lazily alert, like a large panther contemplating his next victim. Cheryl had recovered her poise remarkably quickly. Her sophistication had always far outstripped Jenna's. Now it came to her rescue, it seemed, enabling her to keep up a steady flow of animated questions, throughout the drive south.

Jenna made minimal responses, confirming only the details Ross had briefed her to confirm. That they'd married on the spur of the moment, at a register office. That they'd had to spend some time apart since, through Ross's business commitments in New York and her own business commitments in Cornwall. That, until they could be together more frequently, they'd kept the marriage quiet because of their feuding families, and their wish to avoid the resultant pressure of local disapproval and censure. The conveniently tailored lies and half-truths tripped off her tongue, lashing her with guilt and distaste. She hated Ross for this, she decided coldly, watching their journey through the tinted Bentley window.

They were driving through rolling wine country, dotted with glimpses of fairy-tale castles, their fat round turrets soaring majestically into the blue sky above hills striped with young green vines. It was beautiful here. But it was wasted on her. The wedding-ring seemed to burn like acid on her finger, and the weekend seemed to stretch ahead like a cruel, potentially fatal obstacle course.

As the beauty of their surroundings sped past, she sat in an invisible cocoon of pain, fists clenched in her lap, her stomach tense, her heart aching.

'How *could* you, Ross?' The high, panelled door to their room was safely closed behind them. But she doubted if even the centuries-old thickness of carved

wood would be adequate insulation for her to express
her feelings unheard. She was quivering with resentment and indignation.

'How could I what?'

Ross had deposited the cases on a wide oak stand,
and had clicked both open. It took her a little while
before she realised he was riffling through *her* case,
with a wry smile on his face.

'How could you deliberately deceive me over this
weekend?'

She marched across the wide, high-ceilinged bedroom as she spoke, and snatched her white Victorian
nightdress from Ross's interested inspection.

'And how dare you go through my things?'

'Just checking on my wife's weekend wardrobe,' he
demurred, 'and may I say how much I'm looking
forward to seeing you in these?'

'*Stop* it!' She gave an outraged yelp as he snatched a
lacy satin bra and suspender belt from the case, and
held them high in the air. 'Oh, for heaven's sake, Ross!
That's the kind of behaviour I'd expect from a. . .a
playground bully!'

'Hush, sweetheart.' The deep voice shook with
laughter as he lowered the offending articles, and slid
his arms around her rigidly protesting figure. 'You'll
frighten the other guests. I'm only doing what any self-
respecting husband would do—fantasising about his
wife in skimpy underwear.'

'*Fantasise* is all you'll do!' she snapped furiously,
retrieving the scraps of satin and thrusting them back
into her case with trembling fingers. 'I've agreed to
pose as your wife in public only, remember?'

'I confess I've got a lousy memory. And what are

you so uptight about, Jenna?' Ross's hand cupped the nape of her neck, as she bent over her case to hide her scarlet cheeks, his thumb rhythmically stroking the delicate hollows exposed by her upswept hairstyle. 'You've got a lovely body. It's selfish not to share it.'

Summoning all her control, she spun round to stare up into the icy grey gaze trained mercilessly on her. Her own eyes were burning with contempt.

'You're totally amoral, aren't you?' she began shakily. 'What's more, you're a coward! This business with Cheryl—I'm not surprised you conveniently forgot to mention *who* we were seeing this weekend. If I'd had any idea you intended playing me off against her, I'd never have come. . .'

'Expand on the "coward" accusation, Jenna.' Ross's fingers still circled the sensitive back of her neck, and she shivered at the warning darkening of his eyes. The pupils had dilated, dark tourmalines in glacial grey.

'You *are* a coward! Otherwise, you'd have the guts to end your sordid liaisons all by yourself! You wouldn't need to hide behind someone else!'

'Jenna——'

'You *use* people, Ross! That doesn't rate you very high in my estimation!'

'Oh, I know how I rate in your estimation, Jenna.' Ross's voice was arctic. 'You made that crystal-clear five years ago, didn't you?'

'I don't know what that's supposed to mean, but——'

'Yes, you do.' The stroking fingers had begun tangling in her hair, and she winced as his fingers dug into the tightly pinned pleat at the back of her head and wrenched it free to tumble down round her shoulders.

'You couldn't wait to duck out, could you? You latched on to the first excuse you could find!'

'If you're talking about my father's illness, I hardly think that counts as an *excuse*!'

'I was talking about that letter I got, Jenna. Three weeks after I went to New York without you. The letter with its extraordinary contents and its sick little accusations. . .'

'Could you deny them?' she fired at him, shaking from head to toe as he slammed her closer to his hardness. 'Could you?'

'There didn't seem much point, as I recall.' Ross had cupped her hot face between his hands, his gaze dispassionate on her fiery cheeks, and furious emerald eyes. 'I came back, and was accused of everything from infidelity to petty revenge. I was as black as you wanted to paint me, wasn't I, Jenna? It struck me you'd made your choice, and I came a poor second to misplaced family loyalty.'

'Even if I'd wanted to come back with you to New York, Dad had been ill—he was terrified of being left alone!' She could hardly believe she was having this bitter fight, so long after she'd assured herself it was water under the bridge, long forgotten. 'If you'd loved me, if you'd *ever* loved anyone but yourself, Ross, you'd have told me your plans! You'd have *shared* them with me! But you just grabbed what you wanted. . .'

'It's always tempting,' he agreed darkly, taking the last step towards her which brought their bodies so tightly against each other that she could feel his powerful thigh thrusting between hers. 'If you want to know my philosophy these days, Jenna, it's grab what you really want, whether or not the means justify the end. . .'

'You're despicable——' she began hotly, but then her head was jerked back, Ross's hands entwined in her hair, and he was kissing her as if he were dying of hunger and she were a gourmet meal. . .

Mindlessly, she found herself responding. It was a physical necessity, utterly separate from moral or spiritual truth. Ross lifted his head from her lips, caught her up in his arms and swept her over to the vast bed, then came down after her with ruthless strength to crush her to the elaborate brocade bedspread, his eyes narrowed as he expertly flicked at the buttons of her suit jacket.

'Ross, stop this. . .' The strangled protest came out weakly, and she loathed herself. The buttons were all dispensed with, the wrap fastening of the white silk blouse beneath was roughly pulled apart. A sinking, melting feeling had begun in her stomach and thighs as Ross's lidded gaze roamed speculatively over the jut of her breasts, barely concealed beneath a smooth white lace bra.

'I can't stop this. . .' he murmured thickly, his gaze teasingly devastating as he lowered his dark head to trail a burning path of kisses across the firm swell of flesh, one knee pinning her to the bed while he reached to unfasten her bra. He lifted the lacy wisp away from her skin, and her nipples seemed to spring up to meet him, goose-bumps covering her skin as his investigating hands smoothed possessively, his palms warm and indescribably arousing in their intimate movements.

Slipping his hands up to trace her slender neck, he tangled his fingers in the red mass of her hair, and with a low throaty exclamation he bent to take one pink nipple between his teeth, circling its aching point with his tongue, then sucking gently before sliding his lips to the other breast and repeating the process all over again. . . Jenna gasped in frantic denial, squirming from side to side, but all that happened was that the short skirt of her suit rode up her thighs, and Ross discovered her penchant for suspenders with a crow of sensual triumph.

'Oh, Jenna, Jenna,' he chided mockingly, assisting the upward movement of her skirt to reveal the lacy triangle of panties and suspenders, the silken olive of firm thighs and groin. 'So defensive, yet so. . .seductive. Are you playing games with me, sweetheart?'

'Ross, I warn you. . .'

'Is this moral outrage just a brilliant disguise for what you *really* want, Jenna?' The husky probing triggered heat, coursing through her from neck to knees, overwhelming her defences. She was shivering so violently that she felt feverish.

'Now that we've come this far,' Ross murmured assertively, tearing impatiently at his tie, flinging it off and ripping at the top button of his shirt with similar haste, 'we might as well go the rest of the way, don't you think?'

'*Ross*. . .' She was drowning in sensation. Anger was still there, outrage and indignation, all the emotions she needed to fight him. But they were weighted down, somehow. Deactivated and treacherously sinking in some dark quicksand of blind desire.

The dark head had moved boldly downwards, his caresses had become directional, lifting her hips and sliding the wisp of lace from her groin, splaying her trembling thighs, rediscovering the warm, honeyed secrets which nestled beneath the silken gold at the apex of her thighs. With a sureness which shot red-hot arrows of reaction radiating from its centre, his tongue found the small nub of desire in the soft shell-like pink, his hands firmly forcing her wider, more widely open, more utterly surrendered to his power, and Jenna's trembling became volcanic; she had no fight left inside her, only molten fire consuming her.

'Oh, Ross, please, please, *please*. . .' She hardly knew what she was saying, her voice sounded unlike her own, throaty and choked, shaking with emotion.

'It's all right, sweetheart.' Ross's voice ached with rough hunger. 'You don't have to beg. I'm so hot for you, I'm in flames. . .'

Their clothes were flung off, thrown to the elegant Aubusson carpet, landing anyhow in discarded tangles. Their coming together was almost primeval in its intensity and reckless haste. Jenna was sobbing, almost without realising it.

'Hush, darling. . .hush. . .this is no crying matter, for this we'll drink champagne tonight. . .'

When he thrust powerfully deep inside her, she let out a muffled scream, and Ross suspended movement for a moment, his narrowed gaze on her face, as if her tight hotness took his breath away too.

'Jenna. . .' he groaned. 'Jenna. . .' He began to move again, fiercely, possessively, his rough hardness a sensual dream against her silky skin, his hoarse cry of fulfilment echoing round the lofty bedroom as he reclaimed what was rightfully his. . .

It was all over at last. After the blinding heat of passion, Jenna lay, still trembling, but this time from stunned regret. So much for her high ideals. Past infatuation died hard. Physically, she'd surrendered without so much as a fight. What a complete *fool* she was. How on earth was she going to survive the entire weekend, after feeding Ross's outsize ego within an hour of arrival?

CHAPTER FIVE

'AH, Ross! So *this* is your beautiful little wife!'

Art Lange was out on a wide gravelled terrace, formal gardens descending in layered perfection as far as the eye could see. White doves wheeled above them from an ancient golden stone dovecot. The evening sun was warm, the air sweet and fresh with the heady scent of early spring.

Spotting them approaching, he spun round from the elegant little group of guests he was talking to and strode to meet them, a tall grey-haired American in formal dinner dress, still lean, tanned and attractive in his late fifties.

As he pumped her hand enthusiastically, Jenna couldn't help responding to his warmth. This was Cheryl's father? This was the man who'd lured Ross to America five years ago? The millionaire who'd made his fortune in computers and who'd given Ross the foothold to do likewise? Smiling reluctantly, she stared at him. The only resemblance between father and daughter lay in their eye colour—Art's were that curious purple-blue too. But whereas Cheryl's habitually held a competitively feline gleam, Art Lange's expression was open and friendly.

'Ross told me about you, Jenna. You've landed yourself a darned good man. As for Ross. . .'

The dark blue eyes roamed over Jenna's Titian waves and simple fitted sheath dress, the apricot silk delicately complimenting her clear olive skin, and he gave an appreciative laugh. 'Let me tell you, if I weren't marrying Marie-Hélène tomorrow, I'd be a jealous man!'

'Back off, Art,' Ross murmured wryly, sliding his arm around Jenna with a forceful determination. 'I have sole rights.'

Stiffening, she turned wide green eyes on Ross, tempted to blurt out her precise reaction to that arrogant statement. The sardonic lift of his eyebrow silenced her. In his dark dress suit and snowy white shirt, he did unspeakable things to her stomach.

'Let me get you a drink. . .' Art was laughing, his gaze approving on the tinge of colour in Jenna's cheeks. A passing uniformed maid was hailed, champagne dispensed. Cheryl detached herself from another group and appeared at Ross's side, sleekly sensual in purple taffeta with a vast amount of creamy cleavage exposed at the plunge V-neck.

'Hello again,' she purred, linking her arm through Ross's, dismissing Jenna with one comprehensive sweep of her eyes, 'Have you everything you need in your room, Ross darling?'

'Honey, he has *Jenna* in his room,' her father teased gently. 'What more could a man ask for?'

Cheryl's long violet eyes glinted with anger. But she carried on smiling.

'Daddy, I was meaning *luxuries*—the little extras that make for a *really* good weekend,' she said silkily, her cerise-tipped fingers moving hungrily along Ross's dark-clad arm. 'You will let me know, Ross? If you need anything to. . .spice up your stay?'

'Mirrors on the ceiling?' Ross drawled lazily, tight-

ening his arm around Jenna's waist, and dropping his
amused eyes to her incensed green glare. 'Well, I'll be
frank, Cheryl. Things don't need spicing up so much as
cooling down. A fire extinguisher might come in handy,
don't you think, Jenna, sweetheart?'

Cheryl wasn't the type to blush. In fact, as her own
cheeks burned in mortification, Jenna detected instead
a slight blanching of the other girl's complexion. Beginning to feel like a pawn in some invisible chess game,
she forced a cool smile on to her lips. It was high time
she made an effort to drag her wits together, attempted
to take some control over the situation.

'Ross, for heaven's sake,' she said firmly, flicking her
eyes briefly skywards, 'you're embarrassing Cheryl.
Not everyone shares your peculiar sense of humour!'

Swinging free from Ross's encircling arm, she
glanced up at Art, giving him the benefit of her fullest,
most dazzling smile.

'This château is quite wonderful,' she told him
warmly. 'How long have you owned it?'

'Couple of years now. Magical, isn't it?'

'Do you own these vineyards too?'

'You bet. Along with my partner here!' Art nodded
at Ross, who sipped his champagne with a deadpan
insoucience.

There was a short, intrigued silence. Cheryl was
staring at Jenna as if she were a specimen in a test-
tube.

'Ross hasn't told you much yet, has he?' she queried,
cut-glass in her voice. 'How long did you say you'd
been married?'

'Long enough,' Ross cut in smoothly, seeing Jenna

struggling for an answer, 'to communicate on the most important level.'

Jenna had had enough. There was only so much she could take of Ross's insufferable smugness, his unbelievable arrogance. He was passing her off as some kind of mindless bimbo!

'I haven't really had a chance to look around, but history is my subject,' she said to Art, glueing a social smile on her lips. 'I'd adore the chance of a guided tour when you've time! It's no use asking Ross to guide me—he's a complete ignoramus where past civilisations are concerned. He wouldn't recognise "culture" if it hit him in the face!'

'Honey, we don't dine until nine here! I've all the time in the world!' Art grinned, proffering his arm, which Jenna neatly circled with her hand. 'Excuse us, you two?' He shot a wicked wink towards Ross, adding, 'I can never refuse a beautiful lady!'

Glancing back as Art led her away, Jenna saw Ross gaze after her with a darkly ironic gleam in his eyes, then turn to Cheryl, bending his head to listen more closely to something she said. Cheryl's fingers slid up to his collar, moved to weave intimately into Ross's thick black hair. Ross put his hands on Cheryl's shoulders, moved with his back to Jenna. Over his shoulder, she caught sight of Cheryl's long violet eyes watching her departure. A smile curved the cerise-painted lips.

Abruptly she switched her gaze away from them. There was a sick thumping in her chest. Confusion and anger kept her from hearing Art's friendly conversational gambits as they looked over the château. What kind of a double-bluff game was Ross playing? His body language with Cheryl shrieked intimacy, sexual awareness. . .

Jenna tried frantically to concentrate on talking to Art, but there was a cold knot of pain forming deep in her heart. . .

The bedroom door opened, admitting a brief shaft of light, then clicked shut. Jenna tensed beneath the bedclothes, swathed defensively in the white Victorian nightdress, her pulses racing. After dinner, she'd pleaded a rather unoriginal headache, and escaped early to bed. Ross could flirt to his heart's content with Cheryl. He could proposition all the other female guests too, if he liked. He could play Casanova and bed-hop all night. She felt emotionally unable to compete with it all. And besides, she didn't care what he did. The flare of passion earlier had been an aberration. It wouldn't happen again. She'd rather die than let it happen again. . .

Ross came over to the bed, squatted down at her side.

'I can see you're not asleep. Are you all right? Not ill? Just sulking?'

The harsh mockery cut deep.

'Go to hell, Ross.'

In the shadowy moonlight she heard him expel his breath through his teeth, wryly amused, controlling his anger.

'If there's something on your mind, let's talk.'

'I don't want to talk. I don't want to talk to you. I just want this whole. . .*grubby* charade over with!'

Her voice was husky, muffled. Ross reached to pull the crisp white sheet back from her face. He touched her cheek with one thoughtful finger, found the heavy plait of her hair and pulled it out from the covers, weighing it contemplatively in his hand before dropping it like a Titian rope on the gold brocade bedspread.

'What's going on, Jenna? Didn't we have a deal? You shouldn't let Cheryl Lange upset you——'

The cool reproof acted like salt on a wound.

'*Upset* me?' She sat up in bed, goaded out of any pretence of sleepiness. 'Why on earth should that. . . that voracious *man-eater* upset me?'

'Is that what she is?' Ross's deep voice shook with laughter.

'I'm surprised she hasn't gobbled you up entirely!'

'I'm a little too tough for that.'

'Ross, why did you bring me here under this pretence?' she demanded shakily, reaching to click on her bedside light. She blinked in the sudden brightness. Ross stared hard at her face.

'You've been crying?' he queried abruptly. 'What the hell have you got to cry about, Jenna?'

'Answer my question, Ross! Why did you need me to pose as your wife this weekend? For a start, it must look very suspicious to your old friend Art! He's no doubt wondering why you married in such secrecy— why you didn't ask him to the wedding?'

'Did he say that to you?' Ross looked thoughtful.

'No. . .but he implied it. What have you said to him?'

'Exactly what we said to Cheryl. That we married on impulse, in secret,' Ross's eyes were unnervingly level on hers, 'and kept it quiet because of family opposition. It's a good story. It could almost be true. Don't you agree?'

With a shiver of emotion, she dropped her eyes away from that wry, challenging gaze.

'I just can't see any advantage for you, having me along this weekend! Apart from *revenge*? To. . .to humiliate me?'

'I told you,' Ross explained patiently, his dark gaze amused, 'I needed protection—against the embarrassment of extricating myself from a very persistent female whose father happens to be a close friend and business associate. . .'

'Whom you conveniently forgot to *name*! Because you knew I'd never agree to come if you told the truth! And as for needing "protection", it looks to me as though you'd be only too happy to take advantage of everything dear Cheryl has to offer! Just as you were in New York!'

Ross regarded her in steely silence for a few moments.

'Since you never bothered to come to New York,' he said finally, his tone ominous, 'how the *devil* do you know what happened there?'

'I heard!'

'Ah, yes, you *heard*. You wrote in your letter how you *heard*, didn't you?' He raked a hand abruptly through his black hair, his eyes kindling with anger. 'My little brother Kevern came to stay with me in New York, then came back to Cornwall and told you I was living with Cheryl Lange? Correct?'

'*Yes*. . .! Ross, I don't want to go over all this——'

'And you believed him.'

'He seemed fairly sure of his facts!' she said woodenly, hating Ross's cool interrogation. 'And after all, he had no axe to grind! He didn't know about us. . .'

She shuddered in memory. Kevern had imagined he was passing on a snippet of gossip. He'd innocently dropped his pebble in the pool and been unaware of the ripples. He'd had no idea of the shock-waves radiating out from his casual words. . .

'Whether he knew about us or not is irrelevant. You chose to believe the worst. You couldn't *wait* to believe the worst!'

'I had good reason to, remember?' Her voice was choked with fury. 'You'd already cheated. . .deliberately deceived me about going to America, when you knew damn well I couldn't go!'

'Couldn't or wouldn't?' Ross stood up, and turned away. He strode to the window, and reached through the open glass to fold back the shutters. Night scents drifted in, cool and green. The breeze billowed the long voile curtain inwards.

'Couldn't you understand, Jenna?' he said, a savage undertone in his voice. 'I *had* to succeed! There was no way on earth I could have come back to Cornwall before I'd achieved what I vowed I'd achieve! Sure, I've got a damn big ego! But after the row with my father I swore I'd prove him wrong. I'd show him I could make it on my own. My big mistake was you. How the hell was I green enough to think you meant to keep those promises you made to me, that day in Cambridge?'

Pain tore through her. This was unfair, cruel, an underhand attack she hadn't expected. . .

'How convenient, to claim it was all *my* fault!' she shot back bitterly. 'You're so selfish, there's no getting through to you! Oh, I don't want this all dragged up again! There's no point!'

'The point, *Mrs* Trenwith,' Ross said with suppressed violence, returning in long angry strides to grasp her cruelly by the shoulders, 'is that I begged you, on my bloody *knees*, to come back to New York with me, five years ago. Even after you'd written me that priggish little letter telling me what an unprincipled lout you considered me to be! Our break-up was your choice, all along the line! It's high time we resolved our differences, once and for all. Unless you think we can drift on for another five years?'

She glared at him, wildly, rigidly resisting in his punishing grip, her heart hammering uncontrollably in her chest. Fear lanced through her, with a sudden intensity which shocked her.

'No!' she whispered fiercely. '*No*! We can end the whole sorry mess, as soon as you like! The minute we get back to England, in fact! But *you* can go, not me! You don't want Lantressa, you never wanted it! Let Margot sell it to the. . .the National Trust, or something! At least they'd be sensitive to the surrounding area. At least *they* wouldn't submit plans for a tacky great *theme park* to raise money!'

'You really hate me, don't you.' For some reason, the flat statement vibrated with pent-up aggression. For a frightening moment, she thought Ross was going to harm her physically, harsh anger was etched so intensely on his dark face.

Instinctively she shrank back. There was a flicker in his eyes, and he expelled his breath sharply, pulling her closer, crushing her against him so tightly that she could feel the thick thudding strokes of his heartbeat beneath the starched white of his dress-shirt.

'Stop looking like a frightened fawn,' he advised her,

his deep voice rough. 'I'm not going to strangle you. But I'm damned if I'm giving in without some dirty fighting!'

'Ross, don't you *dare*. . .' Her voice rose on a furious command but was stifled by his mouth on hers. His kiss was hard and punishing. One strong hand grasped the plait at the nape of her neck. As his lips plundered her mouth, the other disposed of the buttons at the bodice of the nightdress, exposing her breasts to his hungry gaze.

'"Who dares wins",' he teased hoarsely, tugging at the pintucked, lace-trimmed cotton. 'This is very demure,' he growled. 'Very prim and virginal. . .'

'Ross. . .' She gasped as he peeled the white broderie anglaise down, a thousand unwelcome sensations rippling through her nervous system as his mouth moved down to her taut nipples, his tongue tantalisingly warm and wet against her heated skin.

Shivering, she arched instinctively against him then withdrew in panic, pushing frantically to free herself before the familiar sensual lethargy drained the fight from her limbs.

'Sex is your answer to everything, is it?' There was a melting sense of inevitability about this physical contest between them. . .

'Only to some things. . .'

'Ross, you have no *right*. . .'

Savagely, she was flattened along the bed, with Ross's lean hardness pinning her still. His hands ran arrogantly along the full length of her, then lifted the hem of the nightdress, bunching it in his fingers to jerk it forcefully upwards. The cool air from the unshuttered

window touched her bare thighs, before the hard
warmth of Ross's hands stroked and explored.

'Oh, I have every right, *Mrs* Trenwith,' he murmured
raggedly in her ear, tearing at his own dark evening
clothes to free himself, tossing each garment to the
floor and coming down hard and male against her,
extracting a gasp of shock as he prised her knees apart
and made a place for himself against her trembling
body. 'My ring is on your finger. We're talking *conjugal*
rights here, aren't we, sweetheart?'

'*No!* Stop playing sick games with me, Ross! In any
case,' she shivered violently as his hands roved beneath
her to cup the soft jut of her buttocks, lifting her
ruthlessly against him, 'that's not even legal any more,
is it? Not even a husband has the right to. . .to. . .
force his wife. . .'

'Who said anything about force?' The deep voice
was mesmerising against her hair as he scored his hands
back up to unweave the plaited strands, running his
fingers through the heavy tresses spread on the pillow.
'By the time I've finished with you, my darling, you're
going to beg me to love you. . .'

She was burning up inside, hot waves of desire
searing through her. The provocative words dashed
against her like hail on a window. Dragging a shuddering breath into her lungs, she forced herself to freeze
beneath his hungrily seeking hands and lips. Lying like
a statue, she stared up at the dark face above her. His
shoulders and chest rippled with lean muscle. His body
felt rough and hard, lacking tenderness, brutally men-
acing against her.

'All right,' she spat with soft violence, 'you've proved
you're stronger than I am. Go ahead. Do what you

want. Just don't expect me to beg you to *love* me. I don't want your love. It's not worth having, Ross.'

She felt him tense. Slowly, deliberately, he lowered himself on to her rigidly trembling body, his weight pinning her down. The kiss he dropped on her lips was ferocious, plunging deep inside her mouth, but brief. Then with a short laugh he rolled free of her, stood up.

'That's why you threw it away?' he quipped bitterly, bending with elaborate mockery to twitch her night-dress down over her nakedness, his eyes black with suppressed desire. 'Your loss, sweetheart.'

'Just. . .*leave* me alone, please.'

Turning her head into the pillow, she snatched the covers to hide herself, aching and shivering all over with frustrated need, bitter denial. Her heart felt shattered, in a million jagged pieces.

When Ross returned from the bathroom, the bed dipped as he climbed in. She tensed, but he didn't try to touch her.

'Goodnight. Sweet dreams, Mrs Trenwith.'

Ross's softly mocking voice was followed by a fraught silence in the dark. And then, utterly maddening and humiliating, by the unmistakable slower, deeper breathing which signalled that he'd fallen swiftly asleep.

CHAPTER SIX

THE huge pink and white marquee was completely unnecessary, in Jenna's opinion. The great hall in the château could have accommodated the hundreds of guests at the wedding breakfast with ease. But it added an extra touch of charm and luxury.

Outside it seemed to hover like a giant hot-air balloon on the sweeping green lawn, dwarfed only by the immense spreading cedar trees studding the vast estate. Inside it was a warm hubbub of chatter and laughter and champagne drinking. The jewel colours of expensive silks and crêpe de Chine contrasted with the elegant grey of morning dress.

'Try to look as if you're enjoying yourself, sweetheart.' Ross appeared at her side, tall and dark and devastatingly good-looking in grey tail-coat. 'Sartorially you're a success,' he added tauntingly, his eyes assessing her neat three-piece suit in heavy gold silk, wide-brimmed navy boater and matching court shoes. 'Facially, you're a potential disaster.'

'*Ross*! Will you just give it a *rest*?'

'This is a wedding reception, lovey, not a wake! Have some more champagne!'

'Why don't you go and find Cheryl?' Jenna retorted between clenched teeth. 'Press *her* to a drop more champagne?'

'I prefer to spend time with my *wife*.'

She winced, starting to turn away, and he caught her

chin between his fingers, twisting her back, his eyes hard on her flushed face.

'You *are* my wife, aren't you, Jenna?'

'Not for much longer, I promise you!' she hissed, jerking away from him.

Art and Marie-Hélène came by, smiling, arms linked, their love radiating in the air around them.

Jenna felt her throat tighten, as she smiled and kissed the beautiful dark-haired French girl, admired the soft cream taffeta wedding dress, recalled the poignant ceremony at the church in the village. Art clearly worshipped his younger bride. And from the soft starry looks she was directing at her new husband, the feeling was mutual. Her own sham 'marriage' made her heart ache.

Disguising her inner turmoil, she talked and laughed, but she longed to escape. The lengthy sit-down feast loomed ahead like an insurmountable hurdle.

'Enjoying your second honeymoon?' Cheryl was chic in a shocking pink coat-dress with huge gilt buttons. Her mocking violet eyes were regarding Jenna from beneath the thick dark fringe.

'Yes, thanks. . .' Jenna glanced round for Ross, but he'd been caught up in another group of friends.

'You don't look as if you are.' Cheryl's full, curving pink lips held more than a twist of malice as she inspected the other girl's pallor.

'These things are always a bit tiring,' Jenna countered warily, searching Cheryl's face for some sign of normal human emotions, 'don't you find?'

'Not really. I'm a party animal. New York, London, plenty of life and action. Ross is the same. He and I have *so* much in common.'

Jenna regarded the dark girl with a stab of intense dislike, bordering on hatred. Beneath that brittle exterior, she decided, lay an even harder core.

'Marie-Hélène seems a lovely person,' she said, making a last effort to be civil. 'You must be very happy for your father.'

'You think so?' Cheryl's eyes narrowed a little. 'I'm not a naïve little romantic. I don't go for the pink hearts and lucky silver horseshoe routines. She's married him for his money. I give them six months maximum.'

'*What*?'

'Which, Jenna, darling, is more than I give you and Ross!' Cheryl smiled, taking a sip of her champagne. 'If ever I saw an ill-matched couple, it's you two. *Your* motives have a lot in common with Marie-Hélène's, I'd guess. But what he sees in a little country mouse beats me. . .'

'Are you suggesting I married Ross for his money. . .?' Jenna was so stunned by the other girl's vitriol that she found it hard to string the words together. She made a huge effort to collect her wits.

'You bet! He's made a fortune out of his software business—quite a catch now, isn't he? But it won't last, honey. He'll be back for a much more interesting city feline. . .'

'What's this about felines?' Ross had appeared at Cheryl's shoulder, his expression bland, but his grey eyes deceptively alert.

'It's OK, darling,' Jenna heard herself saying coldly, taking advantage of the other girl's fractional hesitation, 'Cheryl and I were just discussing New York's cat population.'

With deliberate emphasis, she stepped close to Ross's side, and lifted her face towards his, adding expressionlessly, 'And Cheryl was just flexing her claws.'

Before either Ross or Cheryl could speak, she'd lifted on tiptoe to kiss him, the angry glitter in her half-closed eyes triggering an abrupt, hungry response. Ross took possession of her mouth with a sensual need which melted her bones. He slid a hand to her nape, holding her still while he kissed her more deeply. Suddenly oblivious to her surroundings, Jenna shut her eyes, let the hot shaft of desire scorch through her as Ross grasped her shoulders, pulling her closer still, the firm male lips moving urgently on hers. . .

When they broke apart, breathing raggedly, she vaguely registered that Cheryl had disappeared. They were left standing alone, locked in private battle, while guests strolled past in a general drift outside to sit down at the countless long, white-clothed tables ranged along the lawn in the shade of the cedar trees.

'Very impressive, Jenna,' Ross murmured huskily, his eyes wryly guarded as he stared down at her. 'Was this little performance for real? Or just play-acting?'

'Just scoring a rather petty victory, I'm afraid,' she whispered shakily, dampening down the smoulder of need inside her.

'That's all?' Ross mocked softly.

'*And* keeping my side of the bargain,' she snapped, 'to make sure you keep yours!'

'Mine?' Ross tilted an infuriating eyebrow, his gaze darkly amused.

'To tone down your *stupid* plans for Lantressa!' she prompted furiously, 'Don't pretend you've forgotten what this nightmarish weekend is supposed to be about!'

'Ah, yes. Thanks for jogging my memory.' Ross's smile was ruthless as he extended his arm. 'Shall we go and have lunch, Mrs Trenwith?'

At least the food was delicious, Jenna thought, tasting course after sumptuous course, even if her appetite had maddeningly deserted her. Whether by accident or intent, the feast seemed tailor-made to Ross's tastes. Covertly watching him relishing rare beef, red wine, ripe Californian peaches and ripe Brie, strong black coffee and after-lunch cigar, she felt jolted back to the past. She knew him so well. Just as he knew her. . . passing the sliced tomatoes which he hated but she loved, proffering cream for her coffee, remembering she adored marzipan *petits fours* but loathed coconut. . . she had the uneasy sense of slipping into a time-warp, switching back to those years of discovering one another's tastes, delighted to find a shared love of such trivia as pepperoni pizza and pistachio ice-cream, wind-surfing and hill-walking, the Beach Boys and medieval church music. . .

Stop it, she ordered herself ruthlessly. There was no mileage in harping sentimentally on the past. She should concentrate on the present. Be happy for Art and Marie-Hélène, forget her own silly mistakes. . .

There was a delightfully rustic air to the celebrations. Wine flowed, the decibels of talk and laughter swelled. The dappled sunlight through the trees lent a magical touch, as if someone had breathed life into a painting by Monet.

'Before I sit down again, I'd like everyone here to

drink a very special toast.' Art had finished his brief speech, and was waving his champagne glass with a smile. 'To my old friend Ross Trenwith, sitting just along here on my right. . .'

Jenna felt herself go very still. Heads were turning, glances of undisguised female approval levelled at Ross.

'Ross and I have been in business together now for several years. He's not just an astute businessman, he's a friend. In fact, I sometimes find myself thinking of him as the son I never had. No offence to my gorgeous Cheryl here. . .'

Jenna squeezed her eyes shut. She had an awful premonition of what Art was about to announce. Her stomach had clenched into an iron knot of horror.

'. . .and today, he has something to celebrate as well,' Art was saying genially, his fingers on his new bride's creamy shoulder as he spoke. 'He and the divine Jenna here recently married in secret. And I think they deserve a little of this fanfare and hoopla surrounding *me* today!'

Ross was like a granite statue, at her side. She could feel the tension radiating from him.

'So raise your glasses, my friends, to Ross and Jenna Trenwith. May their love for each other grow with the years. . .'

There was a warm murmur of assent, a rumble of their names and a clink of glasses. Jenna felt a hot wave of panic sweeping up through her body. The panic gripped her so tightly that it almost blacked out her vision, held her rigid in the grip of such agonised trembling that she felt sick and ill.

She couldn't go through with this pretence any

longer. She couldn't play-act the happily married couple, when Art and Marie-Hélène were glowing in the joy of the real thing. She couldn't publicly claim Ross's love when he'd never had any to give. The knowledge hit her so hard that it was like a physical blow. Stumbling numbly to her feet, she pushed her chair back so violently that it crashed to the ground.

'No, *no*! Art, I'm so sorry but. . .don't. . .don't *tarnish* your wedding-day!' She was too beside herself to care what she said. 'Be happy with Marie-Hélène, I'm so happy for you both, but I don't belong here, I don't belong with Ross. . .'

'Jenna, for God's sake. . .'

Ross had risen abruptly to his feet, his deep voice agonised, edged with fury, but she turned and fought her way defiantly past him, marched blindly, determinedly up the sloping lawn, leaving the bemused wedding guests staring after her.

'You can't live in the past forever, Jenna.'

The cool male voice from the doorway made her jump violently. She hadn't heard anyone coming up the stairs.

'For heaven's sake, Ross! You frightened the wits out of me!'

She straightened up, wiping grubby fingers down her jeans, and glared at the interloper with mixed but mainly angry feelings. Lost in concentration, in the gloomy twilight of the museum, she'd been moving the waxwork figures around in the nineteenth-century Cornish cottage display. The small family group was now reassembled into a more authentic huddle. She was quite pleased with the effect. There was a fake, battery-lit fire, a blackened range.

'Redesigning my museum hardly constitutes living in the past! And what do you want?' She added, with scant politeness, 'If you've come to rant on about France, you're wasting your breath!'

'I'd have every right to "rant on" about it, if I wanted to.' Ross leaned back against the door-jamb, laconic in denim shirt and jeans, arms folded, suede-booted feet crossed at the ankles. 'You staged a scene worthy of a Hollywood audition, left me looking a complete fool, ruined Art's wedding breakfast. . .'

'No! That's not fair! One small outburst from me wouldn't have ruined Art and Marie-Hélène's day, Ross!'

The grey gaze was merciless.

'You call that a "small outburst"?' he taunted, an amused gleam in his eyes. 'I'm surprised you didn't throw the ring down on the table, up-end your wine over my head and punch me on the jaw, for a little more dramatic effect.'

Jenna stared at him bleakly, her emotions tightly wound inside her, her face a tense white oval in the shadowy room. The dusty air seemed to vibrate with unspoken conflict. She'd been back in Cornwall only forty-eight hours since her abrupt departure from Art's château. Ross had stayed on in France, grimly furious. He had no intention of cutting short his planned visit, he'd informed her ominously. And as far as their 'deal' was concerned, she could consider it null and void. . .

'I wish I *had* done all those things, when you put it like that! But I didn't stage a scene deliberately! I tried to go through with it all, but I couldn't stomach it! I left your ring in the bedroom at the château,' she added shortly. 'Did you find it?'

Ross's mouth twisted. 'Cheryl did. But that's another story.'

Cheryl? In their bedroom? The pain tearing like a knife through her stomach couldn't be *jealousy*, she thought numbly. Because jealousy would imply she still cared for him, and that was unthinkable, despite that passionate coming together in France. Sexual desire was a separate issue. It bore no relation to loving, caring, yearning to spend your life with someone. . .

'She didn't waste much time, did she?' she heard herself say coldly. 'Look, if you've come to gloat, and threaten, and generally throw your weight around as usual, I'm warning you that you're in for a fight over those plans of yours——'

'I've come with a message from my mother,' Ross interrupted wryly, as motionless and impervious as the waxworks. 'I'm to tell you not to stop coming up to Lantressa to see her just because I've come back.'

Jenna swallowed what felt like a lump of lead in her throat.

'Does she know?' Her voice was annoyingly husky. 'Have you told her. . .about us?'

'Would it matter if I had?'

She felt hot colour suffuse her face. A dizzy wave of anger swept over her, and she struggled for control. Ross seemed intent on goading her. She shouldn't give him the satisfaction of a reaction.

'I've grown very fond of your mother,' she said slowly. 'I've only really got to know her since Dad died, and frankly the last thing I want is to involve her in our sordid little affairs, hurt her in any way. . . That stupid feud between our families has a lot to answer for as it is. . .'

'You're damn right it has.' The ironic inflexion was strong. 'It broke us up, didn't it?'

She caught her breath, her temper flaring beyond control.

'No, that's just not true. . .it might be more convenient to blame family hostility for what happened, but *you* broke us up, Ross! You, because you were too selfish and. . .*arrogant* to come clean about your plans!'

'Just a minute——'

'Because you just assumed I'd go off to the other side of the world with you, without even asking me first! And because then, when you found I couldn't come, you couldn't even stay faithful to me for a few weeks! Presumably you thought I wouldn't find out— that what you did in New York couldn't affect your interests in Cornwall! Or maybe you just didn't care who got hurt?'

Her shallow, angry breathing turned to a gasp as Ross sprang abruptly from the doorway and captured her roughly by the arms, giving her a furious shake.

'I wanted you in America with me, more than anything in the world!' he said forcefully, anger darkening his eyes. 'I didn't tell you beforehand because I was frightened of losing you! I was wrong, I admit that! I was a stupid bloody fool, but I loved you so much! I couldn't face life without you!'

'You expect me to believe that. . .?'

'I'm long past expecting you to believe anything I say!' Ross ground out, his fingers digging painfully into her arms through the yellow fabric of her sweatshirt. 'You claimed to love me, but you'd have trusted a rabid *wolf* sooner than trust me!' He shook her again. 'Wouldn't you, Jenna?'

'You're hurting my arms.'

He dropped his hands, turned away.

'You were very quick to give the ring back,' he said after a long, motionless silence. 'Does wearing it make you feel so bad?'

'*Bad* doesn't even begin to describe it!' she whispered bitterly, shivering, wrapping her arms round herself. 'And frankly, as of tomorrow I'm putting things in motion to end *everything* between us. . .'

'So you never loved me?' He swung round slowly, eyeing her with a curiously shuttered expression. His voice was flat, expressionless. 'Tell me, Jenna. I need to know.'

'Of course I loved you!' she shot back, huskily. 'You *know* I did! And I went on loving you, even after you deserted me, and betrayed me, but thank God time puts everything in perspective!'

'Time hasn't put *this* in perspective. . .' Reaching out with almost casual strength, he caught her to him again, crushing her so hard against him that he knocked the breath out of her, tangling his hands in her hair, his voice a deep masculine growl of hunger. 'When I kiss you, Jenna, you kiss me back. . .when I touch you, I feel you responding. . .you still want me, sweetheart, just the way I still want you. . .we proved that in France, didn't we?'

Heat erupted as he bent his mouth to cover hers. She briefly fought, then was swamped by the tidal wave of sensations created by Ross's warm male body, the seeking demand of his lips. Trembling violently, she shut her eyes, forced herself to stand motionless under the onslaught.

With a husky exclamation, Ross slid his hands beneath the yellow sweatshirt, his fingers moving warmly and urgently against the smooth skin of her back. When he heard her small intake of breath as he traced the swell of her breasts, he drew back slightly, gazing down at her with heavy-lidded eyes as he very lightly skimmed one finger along her jawline and neck, around the nape and then down her spine to slide boldly along the tight cleft of her rear, crushing her hard against him with a hunger which frightened her with its savage intensity. . .

'Jenna. . .*Jenna*, can't we stop this, sweetheart?' The ragged words were breathed hoarsely into her hair. She wasn't even sure she'd heard them correctly. Convulsively she slid her arms round him, clinging despairingly to his strength and vitality, as if he could somehow bolster her own. . .

The footstep on the flagstoned floor downstairs only dimly registered, but then a male voice called out, and she stiffened, dropping her arms to her sides, and Ross reluctantly released her.

'Mr Trenwith? Ross?'

'Coming, Ben.'

With a long, kindling look at Jenna's devastated face, Ross turned abruptly away to go downstairs. As she slowly followed, Jenna saw that it was Ben Jasper, the deputy land agent from the Lantressa estate office, who stood there, mousy-haired and smiling in tweed jacket and twill trousers. A clipboard and a green folder were clutched under his arm.

'Thought I'd lost you,' he grinned at Ross, nodding cordially to Jenna. 'Amy at the pottery next door said she'd seen you come in here.'

'Let's get on with it, then, shall we?' Ross sounded tense, his voice clipped as he waved a hand to encompass the solid stone walls of the museum. 'Under the proposed plans, this whole row of cottages would have to come down. Agreed?'

Ben extracted a pencil from behind one ear, nodding thoughtfully as he prepared to write something on his clipboard.

'I'd say so. To accommodate a development on the scale shown would need fairly radical site clearance. . .'

Jenna felt as if her skin was being stretched tight all over her body, her anger and indignation were so intense. Wide-eyed, she stared at Ross.

'You're really going ahead?' she demanded incredulously, coldness growing in her heart. Was Ross really capable of this? Trying to seduce her one minute, talking of bulldozing her livelihood the next? 'You'd really consider demolishing half a village like Lantressa, just to make way for your *appalling* money-raising scheme?'

'Did you think I was bluffing?' Ross was deadpan, his grey gaze narrowed on her scarlet cheeks.

Heart hammering, she spun round to Ben Jasper, who was looking uneasy.

'What do you think?' she asked wildly. 'Surely someone must have some. . .some common sense? Some *integrity*?'

'It's not for me to say, Miss Nancollas, but——'

'I thought *hate* was the worst feeling I could have for you, Ross,' she said shakily, switching back to Ross, uncaring of Ben's rueful presence, 'but I've discovered *contempt* is much stronger!'

'I said I wanted your advice, Jenna. As a local historian. If you'd calm down, discuss things rationally, we might make some headway.' Ross seemed infuriatingly unruffled.

'You're not interested in discussing things rationally!' she exploded, green eyes sparking flames as she glared at Ross's dark face. 'All you want is destruction, and. . . and *revenge*! At the expense of this village, this whole environment. . .'

'You're getting hysterical. We need to examine various possibilities, before we accept or reject them. We have to live in the real world.'

'And you think *your* cheap, tacky, tasteless plans reflect the *real* world, do you, Ross Trenwith?'

'Unlike you, I never dismiss any new idea out of hand.'

Ross's mocking coolness was like petrol on flames. Catching her breath to flare back at him, Jenna was interrupted by Ben Jasper.

'With respect, Miss Nancollas,' he sounded diffidently apologetic, 'I think Ross is just giving Kevern's plans a fair and impartial hearing. He wants to see if they're the right way forward or not. It's the only fair approach, in my view. . .'

'I don't really care about your view,' Jenna began furiously, blind to civility in her burning fury, 'so keep out of. . .' Ben's words were abruptly sinking in. She stopped short, bewildered. '*Kevern's* plans? I'm sorry. . .*what* did you say? The theme park proposal was *Kevern's*?'

Ben glanced at Ross, with a helpless shrug. Jenna jerked an accusing stare in the same direction.

'He'd had them drawn up a few months before he died,' Ross agreed imperturbably. 'Ben and his colleagues have been trying to convince me of their viability.'

'But you deliberately made me think they were *yours*!'

'Did I?' The ruthless, teasing light was back, fanning the heat of her temper. 'Didn't you just *assume* they were, and start hurling abuse right from word go? Maybe I was interested to see how good you still were at jumping to the wrong conclusions? How red-hot keen to think the worst of me?'

Ross's dark face was implacable as he watched her angry confusion.

'I've proved my point,' he added dismissively. 'As far as *trust* goes, nothing much has changed in the last five years, has it, Jenna?'

CHAPTER SEVEN

'CAN I come in?' Ross stood outside Jenna's cottage door, his dark height illuminated by the storm-lamp. There was a charged silence before she swallowed her pride, stepped back to let him in. In equally charged silence she led the way into her tiny beamed sitting-room, and gestured towards one of the wing-chairs by the fire.

'Sorry,' she said, stiffly formal. 'It's rather chilly in here. I've only just lit the fire. I was washing my hair. . .'

'So I see.' Ross sat down and looked very much at home. To the denim shirt and jeans he'd added only a soft tan suede jacket. His black hair was slightly ruffled, as if he'd walked down from Lantressa Manor in a stiff sea breeze. He looked rough, tough, and devastatingly desirable. He sprawled back in the brown velvet chair, narrowed eyes taking in her tousled mass of damp Titian hair, the tightly belted apple-green silk robe, and Jenna had to clench her fists at her sides to suppress the urge to fly at him like a vengeful harpy.

Zombie-like, she sat down in the opposite chair, and gripped her hands in her lap.

'We have to talk,' Ross said flatly.

It sounded ominously final. Her heart seemed to squeeze inside her chest. Her stomach felt hollow with suppressed anger and despair.

'I suppose we do,' she managed icily, when Ross

continued to observe her in disconcerting silence. 'Now that you've had your *fun*, and made a complete fool of me, I suppose it's high time we sorted things out. Then we can both be free to get on with our separate lives. . .' She was trying hard to disguise her bitterness.

'Is that what you want?' Ross's deep voice held a rough hint of suppressed emotion.

'It's the logical outcome, isn't it?'

'And we have to be logical?'

'What else?' Tensely, she wound the belt of her robe around her fingers. 'So. . .since you're *not* planning to bulldoze Lantressa for a theme park after all, what exactly *are* your plans, Ross?'

'I've amassed enough capital to revive the old place without going to the lengths Kevern was proposing.'

'Vindication for sticking to your guns over your career?' she suggested lightly. She was avoiding his eyes. There was a disturbing light in the cool grey gaze, a penetrating quality which threatened her fragile composure.

'In a way,' Ross agreed shortly. 'I'll admit I was out to prove something. That there's more to life than a pat on the head and automatic inheritance.'

'And your ambition paid off.'

The bitterness was audible now. She couldn't hide it.

'Only in one direction.' Ross's voice was compelling. 'My wealth and status rocketed; personal happiness took a nose-dive.'

'Why? You've had the devoted Cheryl, poised to supply every need?'

'I've never wanted Cheryl.'

'What a pity you never seem to have told her!' Her voice shook with pent-up anger.

'Cheryl is the product of a very rich, doting daddy.' Ross sounded ominously patient. 'What Cheryl wants, Cheryl gets. She still hasn't figured out why all her scheming and conniving and mischief-making hasn't succeeded in getting me.'

'How very gratifying for your grossly swollen ego!'

The fire was licking into life in the hearth. Jenna fixed her eyes on the sporadic flames, willing Ross to say what he had to say and go. Ross's arrogant point-scoring over the origin of the plans had left her feeling slightly ashamed of herself, but wildly resentful. How *dared* he wind her up like that? Deliberately lead her on, then casually deny any intention of carrying out his threats? She felt keyed up to the point of dementia. If this went on much longer, she'd end up screaming and throwing punches. . .

'Why did you rush from Art's and Marie-Hélène's wedding breakfast, Jenna?'

The question was put with a quiet intensity which touched a buried chord inside her. To her horror, she felt her tenuous composure crumble.

'*Why*?' she echoed incredulously, jumping to her feet, all the violent emotions she'd felt at that crisis point in France flooding powerfully back. The room itself seemed to pulsate in turmoil.

'You need to ask me that? You're even more insensitive and. . .and *brutish* than I thought! How could I sit there, listening to Art proposing a toast to our happiness, to our love for each other? Knowing our "marriage" wasn't just a cheap sham, but a *double* sham? Knowing we really *were* married, but deserted each other five years ago? Knowing you really *were* my husband but that you couldn't care *less* about me?'

She finished on a choked sob, pressing her knuckles to her mouth, fighting desperately for control. She didn't want to break down completely, in front of Ross. That would be the final humiliation.

Ross didn't move. Motionless in the chair, he radiated coiled tension. But he could have been carved from granite. The pagan warlord, sitting in silent judgement.

'Is that what you think?' he queried finally, his voice unrecognisable, elaborately polite but suppressing smouldering anger. 'That I couldn't care less about you? That I've forgotten you really are my *wife*?'

Abruptly, she recoiled from the pain of the confrontation.

She couldn't face any more. She felt shaky and exhausted by the force of her own angry emotions. She sat down again.

'Ross, I'm tired and I——'

'So am I. I'm tired of playing games. Tired of pretence. Tired of these brilliant disguises we wear when we're together.'

She lifted her head slowly, and stared at him, the hard edge to his voice sending shivers along her spine.

'I'm tired of it too,' she said miserably.

'So let's take the masks off,' he said, leaning forward abruptly to take her clenched hands in his, the warmth of his fingers emphasising the coldness of hers. 'Tell me the truth, Jenna. When we made love in France, you couldn't seem to get enough of me. When I touch you, you tremble. I can feel it, right now. When I kiss you, you're warm and responsive. . .physically it's far from over, Jenna. You're still mine. I want it to stay that way. I want you back. . .'

She stiffened, trying to retract her hands.

'*Why*?' she burst out, fresh anger and resentment erupting passionately inside her. 'Just so you can boast a one-hundred-per-cent success rate? Tie up all those annoying little loose ends in your life?'

'I hardly think patching up our *marriage* could be termed "tying up loose ends", do you?'

The harsh words felt like forcible blows, as if he'd flung some tangible missile at her.

She wrenched her hands free, trembling violently in the grip of intense emotional turmoil.

'Patching is the right word! Like papering over the cracks, you mean? The cracks are too big, Ross. The whole thing would just tear apart again. . .'

Ross stood up slowly, pulling her up with him, his broad-shouldered height dominating the small room, dominating her.

'Not if we still love each other. Not if we've done enough growing up in the last five years to climb down and admit we were wrong.'

She stared at him in fraught silence, flinching as he reached to take hold of her shoulders, pulling her nearer to him. The brilliance of the grey gaze was vaguely hypnotic. So was the deep, wryly husky voice.

'Jenna, sometimes I wonder if I dreamt it. Once upon a time, there was a warm July day in Cambridge. The most beautiful girl in the world stood by my side, wearing something long and floaty in creamy silk, with a straw hat on her long red hair, with cream flowers round the brim. She recited the solemn vows of marriage. She promised to love me, and stay with me forever. . .and afterwards we made love all night long, to seal the promise. . .'

Ross had drawn her so close that she could feel his body heat through the rough denim shirt, almost hear the deep thud of his heart.

'Did I dream it, Jenna?'

Her throat was so choked that she couldn't speak. The emotion firing her senses was a heady mix of pleasure and pain, overlaid with a fiery indignation.

'No!' she said, with quiet intensity. 'You didn't dream it, Ross. But *you* made those promises too! Then a week later I discovered you'd tricked me! You're so arrogant, so utterly *convinced* you're always in the right, I don't see any future for us. . .'

'I didn't intend to trick you,' Ross's voice was hoarse with emotion suddenly, his gaze darkening on the fierce green of her eyes in the tense whiteness of her face, 'but I admit I was arrogant. Wrong, stupid, selfish, anything else you want to throw at me. But I *had* to go to New York, Jenna. The opening was there. My business success depended on it. After the row with my father, my pride depended on it. But I *had* to have you, too. And I had a terrible fear that you wouldn't come with me. . .'

'Just like a spoilt little boy?' she countered relentlessly. 'You wanted everything your own way. So you married me, and *then* told me where we were going to live! When you knew my father was alone, and ill in Cornwall. . .'

'Be fair. I didn't know *how* ill he was. Neither of us did, until later.'

'No. But you still went to New York without me. . .'

'Only to set up the deal I was involved in,' Ross reminded her, the restraint on his own anger beginning to show, 'but by the time I was due to come back, your

"Dear John" letter arrived, complete with wedding ring!'

There was a tense pause. The heat building up between them was dispelling the coolness of the room. Jenna shut her eyes, trying to blank out the unsettling effect of Ross's overpowering closeness. That final showdown between them, here in Lantressa, had sprung back on to the screen of her mind in unpleasant Technicolor. The need for secrecy had lent the whole thing added drama and tension. They'd met on the beach, around the rocky headland, out of sight of the village and their respective families. It had been a hot early September day. They'd been in beach gear, swimsuits, bermudas. The few holidaymakers left within earshot would doubtless have enjoyed eavesdropping on Ross's white-hot rage, as he demanded an explanation of the letter and the returned ring. Her bitter accusations about Cheryl. . .

And then Ross's arrogant ultimatum—come back to New York with him right away, or forget it. . .that had stuck in her memory, like a weapon lodged in her heart.

'Jenna. . .' Ross gave her a slight shake, bending his head to see her expression, his own eyes very bright. 'I told you the truth five years ago. Cheryl and I have never been lovers. . .'

'Then why did Kevern think. . .?'

She stopped, the wry cynicism in Ross's eyes suddenly communicating itself to her.

'Cheryl. . .?'

'I think between them they managed to stitch us both up quite neatly.'

'Are you saying Kevern deliberately made trouble for us?'

Ross shook his head. 'No. Kevern wasn't malicious. I'd told no one about our marriage. He couldn't have realised exactly what Cheryl was up to.'

'You mean she told Kevern you were lovers? Knowing he'd come back and tell me?'

'Something along those lines. When I got out to New York, initially dependent on Art for my business contacts, Cheryl was very excited about the situation. She felt powerful. She knew you and I had been serious in Cambridge. But in New York she was on the spot, and you weren't. And with Daddy's leverage, she aimed to keep it that way.'

'You knew what she'd done?'

'Later. Too late for it to alter the dead-end with you.'

'So you weren't even living in the same apartment?'

'I rented one of Art's apartments for a while. Unfortunately it was right next door to Cheryl's.'

Jenna was wrestling with years of bitter jealousy and resentment. And with the fresh perspective of maturity, of seeing people the way they really were. Finally, she levelled a steady gaze on Ross's bleak face.

'You say you never intended to trick me, five years ago. But you're still just as. . .as *devious*! What about the theme park plans? And this weekend in France?'

Ross pulled a wry face. He had the grace to look slightly sheepish, she detected, her heart in shreds.

'Top of my list of faults is pride,' he admitted flatly. 'I genuinely wanted your opinion on Kevern's plans. But you flung insults at me before I'd had a chance to explain. . .'

'And omitting to mention who we'd be staying with in France?'

'Crude opportunism,' he confessed solemnly. 'It was true. . .I did need a wife for the weekend. I hadn't seen Cheryl for months. She'd finally taken the hint that I wasn't interested. I didn't want to trigger the whole thing off again with an enforced weekend in her company at Art's château. It could have been very embarrassing. . .'

'So you used me, coldbloodedly. . .'

'No! I thought it might give us a chance to get together again, sort out our differences——'

'By *blackmailing* me?' she burst out incredulously. 'Pretending to have leverage over me? Threatening to desecrate the village, pull down my museum. . .?'

Ross held her fierce gaze for a long, expressionless moment, and then dropped his arms away from her shoulders. With a despairing shrug, he sat down again heavily on the chair by the fire, raked a hand through his black hair and fixed a watchful, brooding grey gaze on the expressions flitting across her furious face.

'Do you want a divorce?' he asked at last, his voice totally unlike his own, deep and rough with banked-down emotion. She had the feeling it had cost him dearly to ask the question.

'Not. . .not necessarily. . .' She could hardly speak, her throat felt so choked.

'Is there someone else?'

'*No!*' Rage was abruptly blazing through her, illogical in its intensity. 'What do you think I *am*? Do you think I'd have let you make love to me like that in France if I cared for someone else?'

There was a loaded silence. She thought her heart

was going to burst, her pulses were juddering so frantically.

'And do you think I could have made love to you like that,' Ross echoed bleakly, his gaze dark, 'if *I* cared for anyone else?'

'It's different for a man——'

'You think so? If I just wanted convenient sexual release, I could click my fingers and several willing females would doubtless come running. . .those that haven't started to half believe my interests lie in another direction entirely, that is. . .'

'Modest as ever. . .' Her head jolted up suddenly, meeting the ironic gleam in Ross's eyes. '*What* did you just say? You don't mean you've led women to believe that you're. . .?'

'Gay?' he supplied with a strained, but wicked grin. 'Not entirely. Just with a penchant for a celibate life. . .'

A heat was beginning to suffuse her whole body beneath the silk robe. A disbelieving flip of reaction contracted her heart.

'Ross, are you telling me that all this time you've stayed. . .stayed. . .?'

Words failed her, and she felt her cheeks grow hotter.

'Faithful?' he suggested with biting irony. 'As I wasn't interested in meaningless flings—the answer's yes. Purely through choice, sweetheart. I've sublimated my baser instincts in my work. Plus, I've been too bitter and twisted to give much love to anyone else. I didn't think the female population deserved the kind of vengeance I was likely to wreak. I've been torturing myself, waiting to receive some cold solicitor's letter, demanding your freedom. The longer the silence went on, the more I fantasised about us somehow rebuilding our relationship. But the longer the separation, the less I could imagine how. . .'

'There's been nobody else for me, either.' She closed her eyes, thinking of the various would-be suitors who'd come and gone in the last five years. Not one of them coming close to Ross's devastating magnetism. . .

'So. . .is that why. . .in France. . .?' Her voice trailed away as the full force of what he was saying hit her squarely.

'I fell on you like a beast from the forest?' He raised a self-deprecating eyebrow. 'Not really. I'm quite capable of controlling my sexual urges, darling. I didn't make passionate love to you because I was starved of sex. Making love seemed the most powerful way of demonstrating how good things could be between us. . .'

'But you can't build a marriage purely on physical desire, Ross. . .'

'And you can't accuse me of only wanting you for your body,' he countered drily. 'We had months—no, years getting to know each other inside out before the night of that May Ball. The last accusation I wanted thrown at my head was that I'd seduced and discarded you just to spite the Nancollases. I'd vowed to myself I'd do the decent thing, wait for you to finish your Finals before I took you into my bed. But that night you were so bloody beautiful and desirable, like a green-eyed goddess. Seeing you with that keen young escort nearly drove me to homicide. All my good intentions vanished into starlight. . .'

He stopped, gazing at her through lidded, intent grey eyes.

'You are my one and only, Mrs Trenwith. I love you. I've always loved you. Always wanted you. Even when it wasn't even legal to. Ever since I taught you to surf, when you were thirteen going on eighteen. . .'

The wry note broke, his voice cracked slightly. Digging her teeth painfully into her lower lip, she caught her breath. Suddenly, she felt dizzy, her head whirling with the force of her feelings, feelings she'd denied for so long that she'd almost forgotten how deep, how complete, how devastating they were. . .

'And I love you!' she said on a slight, self-conscious laugh. 'Truly, I do! Stupid, isn't it? All these years too proud to contact each other. But I've never stopped, Ross. There's been no one else. There never will be. I don't think there ever could be. . .and I'm sorry. I know I should have said that before, but I'm sorry I didn't trust you! I was so angry at you over going to New York, but I'd have come, I'd have left Dad when he was well enough, if only I'd trusted you about Cheryl. . .'

'Jenna. . .' It was a deep, ragged groan. 'Will you stop twittering like a demented seagull and come over here?'

She stood up blindly and went to him, pushing herself into his lap and pressing her face against his chest. His arms tightened round her with a sudden, convulsive strength which conveyed a powerful surge of emotion. A small, persistent core of joy buried deep inside her was sending out tremors of happiness.

'I'm sorry too, sweetheart,' Ross said hoarsely into

her hair. 'If I could wipe out the last five years, start all over again, believe me, I would. . .'

'Ross. . .about the ring,' she whispered doggedly, lifting her eyes and meeting such brilliance in Ross's grey gaze that she caught her breath involuntarily. 'You said Cheryl found it. . .?'

'*After* I left,' Ross said with a soft, teasing laugh. 'The green-eyed monster doesn't lie down and die so easily after all! Cheryl rang me last night to say she'd put it in the post. Accused me of pretending to be married, threatened to stir up trouble with Daddy unless I admitted it was all a bluff. . .'

'And. . .?'

'I suggested she take up a dangerous sport. Preferably paragliding with an adverse air current.'

'*Ross*!'

'Will it cause a major stir in the village if I spend the night here?' he demanded unevenly, raking his fingers abruptly into her damp red hair, and dropping a devouring kiss on her parted lips.

'Probably, but. . .'

'On seconds thoughts. . .' He drew back a fraction, his eyes kindling on her flushed face and tumbled hair. 'I've got a strange, ascetic urge to behave like the perfect gentleman from now on. . .'

She shot him a disbelieving glance, her eyes dancing with scepticism.

'*Really*?' she teased softly, reaching to trace the dark lines of his face. The blissful freedom to touch him, love him, express her feelings without fear of destruction was almost too much to bear without crumpling into incoherent idiocy. . .

'I'd like to make my wedding vows to you all over

again, sweetheart,' he nodded, his grey eyes warm with
rueful humour at her disbelief, 'in Lantressa Church,
instead of a faceless register office. With all our friends,
and all surviving approving relatives. With choir, bells,
a solemn vicar in surplice and cassock, all the ancient
trappings of permanent commitment. . .'

He pulled her down with him on to the soft Chinese
rug in front of the fire, and rested on an elbow while
he searched her face hungrily with his eyes. Her heart
thumping, she smiled up at him. The brilliance of his
gaze was like a brand of possession.

'Well? What do you say? Will you marry me all over
again, Jenna? Live with me at Lantressa Manor? We
can install Margot in the Gatehouse Cottage, whatever
you want. You can be a lady of leisure, or open six
more museums, whatever you want. Have babies, as
many as you want, whatever you want. . .' The wry,
husky words of commitment did unthinkable things to
her heart.

'Ross, there is nothing in the world I'd rather do
than marry you all over again. . .'

She raised her lips to kiss him, lingeringly, tenderly,
on the mouth, and as she drew gently away again the
edges of the silk robe had slipped apart a little. The
silken curve of her throat and breasts gleamed like
mother-of-pearl in the soft lamplight, and, bending his
head, Ross buried his face against her, inhaling the
perfume of her skin, his touch sending her senses
haywire. Against the soft curve of her thigh she felt his
body quicken and harden, and her insides began to
melt into jelly.

'Jenna. . .sweetheart. . .I'd better go,' he murmured thickly against the thud of her heart, sliding his

hands possessively over the fullness of her breasts before pulling the robe closed, beginning to move away from her, 'if I'm to keep my good resolutions, my delectable little wife—my self-control goes only so far. . .'

Lifting her arms to him, she took hold of his shoulders, and lay back on the rug with an exultant laugh, shaking her head.

'You're not going anywhere,' she asserted softly, drawing him determinedly back down. 'We've wasted five long years apart, Ross. And if you want my opinion of this belated gallantry of yours, I can tell you—it *stinks*!'

His eyes narrowed, alight with amusement as he poised above her.

'Does it, now?' he breathed, a touch raggedly.

'Don't misunderstand me,' she added serenely, sliding her fingers into the thick black hair and shivering with combined happiness and excitement at his answering shudder of desire. 'The choir and the bells and the renewal of vows, I like. The bit about living at Lantressa, and having your babies, I like. The bit about the ascetic, perfect gentleman, I don't like. . .'

Flames now licked brightly in the hearth, throwing warmth and light and shadow over Ross's granite darkness, turning her hair to a copper-gold cloud on the rug.

'So you'd feel happier if I acted a little more. . .in character?' The rough emotion in his voice, and the dark tilt of the eyebrow as he lowered his mouth to hers made her tremble like a reed in his arms.

'I think we've donned enough disguises, don't you?' she agreed breathlessly, gasping as his warm lips found the taut jut of her breasts through the silk, sending shafts of hot desire streaking down to her thighs. She tangled her fingers deeper in his hair, then slid her arms down to cling as tightly as she could to the strength of his body, cradling him with a deep surge of love and need. 'I love you. You love me. I want you, you want me,' she breathed shakily. 'We've wasted far too much time for high-minded self-denial, Mr Trenwith. . .'

'Shameless, Mrs Trenwith. . .' he growled forcefully, peeling the silk robe aside and appraising the glorious curves and hollows of her exposed body with gleaming, humorous, darkening eyes, 'but you're right.'

Then there were no more words. Only their love for each other as they lit their own private universe with undisguised brilliance.

Floating on Air

By

Angela Devine

Angela Devine grew up in Tasmania surrounded by forests, mountains and wild seas, so she dislikes big cities. Before taking up writing, she worked as a teacher, librarian and university lecturer. As a young mother and Ph.D. student, she read romantic fiction for fun and later decided it would be even more fun to write it. She is married with four children, loves chocolate and Twinings teas and hates ironing. Her current hobbies are gardening, bushwalking, travelling and classical music.

To Liz and Ian Shuey of 'Balloon Magic'.

CHAPTER ONE

'OHH, typical Tasmanian weather!' Sarah Marlowe groaned as she turned her mini-van into the quaint Battery Point street where she lived.

Although it was November and supposedly late spring, the morning's glorious sunshine was fast vanishing under the chill approach of ominous charcoal-grey clouds. Wind whipped down from the dark blue flanks of Mount Wellington, setting the peony bushes and daisies tossing like waves in the cottage gardens that lined the street. As Sarah parked the car in front of her home, the first plump spatter of raindrops began to fall. Jumping out, she ran to the rear of the van, dragged out a large box and staggered towards the garden gate. A moment later she was nudging open the front door of the tiny cottage with its brightly painted sign 'FLYING HIGH: BALLOONS FOR EVERY OCCASION'.

'Whew!' she exclaimed, dropping the huge box of balloons and sweeping the rain out of her tangled red curls. 'It's starting to pour out there, Howard! Just as well that birthday party this afternoon is indoors and not in a park.'

Her fiancé came forward to meet her. The internal wall of the cottage's front parlour had been knocked out to make a display area for Sarah's business. Now the only remaining vestige of the room's original style was the fireplace with its carved cedar chimneypiece.

The old-fashioned wallpaper had been stripped from all the walls and replaced by huge photographic murals showing Sarah's designs. Most of them included larger-than-life blow-ups of Howard. There were photos of Howard crooning into a microphone beneath a ceiling of scarlet and purple balloons, of Howard helping a toddler to blow out birthday candles on a table decorated with balloons, of Howard and his fellow singer Charlene Page dressed in nothing but bunches of purple balloons as they opened a new winery. Sarah had always thought that photo rather vulgar, but whenever she said so to Howard he simply smiled slyly at her and called her his sexy little puritan.

He was smiling now. That slow, dazzling smile that sent creases down his cheeks and displayed teeth which had once starred in a toothpaste advertisement. The smile that Sarah had always found utterly irresistible. Yet for some reason it now gave her only a deep feeling of foreboding.

'What is it?' she asked sharply. 'Is something wrong?'

Howard's green eyes kindled mockingly. He ran his hand through the silky blond hair that fell over his forehead and gave her the slow wink that always drove the teenage girls wild at his concerts.

'Wrong?' he drawled. 'No. Nothing serious anyway. It's just that I'm afraid I can't make it to your grandmother's party tomorrow.'

'What?' cried Sarah in dismay. 'But Howard, you promised!'

Howard shrugged.

'I'm sorry,' he said with rather less charm. 'I have to work.'

'Again?' exclaimed Sarah incredulously. 'But that's

outrageous, Howard! Every time we've planned to go to Swansea and visit my family, you've had a lousy concert to do. Twice now I've had to ring my mother and cancel and it's Gran's fiftieth wedding anniversary this weekend. Well, it's just not good enough! Why couldn't the bookings manager at the hotel let you off this weekend? After all, we told him about the party in plenty of time.'

Howard smiled wryly. 'I know, sweetheart,' he murmured caressingly. 'And, believe me, I'm just as upset as you are. But Alan says there's no way round it. The way my contract is written they can make me sing at a moment's notice and there's not a damn thing he can do about it.'

Sarah's chin went up and her blue eyes flashed.

'We'll see about that!' she said, marching across to the sideboard where the phone sat. 'I'm going to tell him exactly what I think of this!'

Howard's hand closed over hers. 'No, don't do that!' he cried.

Some undercurrent of alarm in his voice must have warned her. As she stared into his green eyes, Sarah wondered why she had never noticed how shifty Howard's expression was sometimes.

'Why not?' she asked softly.

He gave a forced laugh. 'Well, he's not likely to be there at this time of day, is he?' he demanded heartily. 'Besides, you know how muddled old Alan gets sometimes.'

'Oh, does he?' murmured Sarah. 'I can't say I'd ever noticed, but do tell me about it, Howard.'

'Well—um—remember that time that I was booked for Launceston and Alan really messed it up? I had to drive back two days late with Charlene Page and you thought——'

Sarah bit her lip, feeling suddenly tired of the whole absurd business.

'And I thought you'd slept with her on the way,' she said hoarsely. 'Yes, I remember, Howard. You don't need to go on.'

But Howard did.

'Pretty silly really, weren't you, darling?' he demanded playfully. 'I mean, if you live with someone in the public eye, you just have to accept that his work will come first sometimes.'

Sarah stared at him with cool blue eyes. 'Oh, come off it, Howard!' she exclaimed in exasperation. 'I don't believe you're working tomorrow. Why don't you just tell me the truth?'

Howard's lips set in a sulky line. 'I am telling you the truth,' he insisted. But Sarah raised one eyebrow and his self-control evaporated.

'Oh, all right, then, Miss Goody Two Shoes!' he shouted. 'You asked for it! I'm not coming to your grandparents' pathetic little party because I'm taking Charlene Page to Melbourne for the weekend. There! Are you satisfied now?'

Sarah stared at him in horror. Once as a ten-year-old child she had fallen out of an elm tree and lain stunned and winded. Now, as she fought for composure, that incident came hurtling back with sickening vividness. It was fully half a minute before she could move or think.

'I don't believe you,' she whispered at last.

Yet she did. That was the awful thing. Looking back now, she saw that there had been hints, signs that she had ignored because she trusted Howard. Those late-night rehearsals, the phone calls that were wrong numbers when she answered, the scent that was heavy on his coat when he came home from concerts. . .

'This has been going on for weeks, hasn't it?' she cried accusingly.

'Well, what if it has?' challenged Howard, his green eyes shifting away from hers. 'Look, Sarah, you must realise that I'm a man and men need a bit of variety. But there's no need to stand there looking as though somebody has died. Charlene's just a bit of fun, that's all. It's not as though it changes anything between you and me.'

'Oh, doesn't it?' breathed Sarah unsteadily. 'Well, think again, Howard, because it certainly changes things for me! I'm not prepared to marry a man who thinks he can go to bed with other women just for. . . for fun!'

She caught her breath on a low, tearing sob.

'Oh, for heaven's sake!' exclaimed Howard in exasperation. 'Why do you have to carry on as if all that marriage business really meant something? It's just a bourgeois hang-up that you've picked up from your stupid family. If you ask me, they're still living in the nineteenth century and you're just as mid-Victorian as the rest of them!'

'You leave my family out of this,' said Sarah in a dangerous voice.

'Great!' agreed Howard. 'Just what I always wanted to do. No more trips up to Woop-Woop to help Granny celebrate her two hundredth wedding anniversary. No more fluttering about what Mummy's going to say if she comes to Hobart and finds her precious darling

Living With A Man. Just you and me living together the way we have done for the last year. Suits me fine.'

'Yes, sure!' whipped back Sarah. 'You and me and Charlene. And any other groupies that hang around after your concerts who take your fancy. No, thanks, Howard. I may be mid-Victorian, but I'm not stupid. You can spend the rest of your life frolicking around naked in a bunch of purple balloons with Charlene if you want, but I won't be here to see it. I'm leaving!'

'Good for you,' said a deep, masculine voice approvingly.

Sarah gave a gasp of horror and swung round. The man who stood behind her must have come in through the open front door so soundlessly that neither of them had heard him. He was as tall as Howard, but with a breadth and muscularity that Howard would never achieve. Where Howard looked boyish, the newcomer was about thirty-five and gave the impression of tough, rugged manhood. There was no film-star prettiness here. His hair was dark and wavy with a few threads of silver at the temples, his features were harsh and brooding, relieved only by the keen intelligence in the silver-grey eyes and a hint of grim humour around his mouth. And, in spite of the expensive charcoal-grey suit, white shirt and red tie, there was a hint of wildness about him.

'Who the hell are you?' demanded Howard furiously. 'And what do you think you're doing here?'

Thick, dark eyebrows rose mockingly. But it was to Sarah that the newcomer addressed himself. With a formal nod, he handed a crisp white card to her.

'My name is Niall Morgan,' he said. 'You've been

very highly recommended to me and I think we can do business together.'

The black lettering swam before Sarah's startled gaze:

'Niall Morgan. Van Diemen Festival Director.'

But she was far too overcome with embarrassment to wonder what it meant. Only one thing concerned her at the moment, and her cheeks flushed to a wild rose-pink as she framed her question.

'When did you come in?' she asked in an agonised voice.

'Let me see,' he murmured thoughtfully. 'Ah, yes. "I'm not coming to your grandparents' pathetic little party because I'm taking Charlene Page to Melbourne for the weekend". Does that sound right?'

There was a hint of cold amusement in his grey eyes as he looked Howard up and down. And the expression on his face made it plain that he was not impressed by what he saw.

'You bastard!' seethed Howard. 'You can take that smirk off your face right now. What the hell do you think you're doing intruding into a private conversation anyway?'

A steely gleam appeared in Niall's eyes.

'I was under the impression that there was a business being run from these premises,' he replied silkily.

'Well, the business is closed as of now,' snapped Howard, striding forward and thrusting his face towards Niall. 'Is that clear?'

'No. Wait!' cried Sarah, pushing her way between them. 'Look, Mr Morgan, I'm very sorry that you've come at such a bad moment, but if you need anything in the way of balloons I'd be happy to help you.

Perhaps you'd like to look at my folder of past projects to see if——'

'Shut up, Sarah, and get out of the way!' snarled Howard.

And, seizing her by the shoulders, he pushed her out of the way so violently that she went spinning against the wall and banged her elbow.

'I've got something I want to say to Mr Clever Morgan,' continued Howard threateningly.

'Stop it!' cried Sarah, darting forward to try and prevent a disaster.

In spite of his boyish physique, Howard had learnt Aikido and she knew that he wasn't averse to showing it off. But this time he met with a surprise. Wearing a faintly bored expression, Niall blocked the attack, side-stepped and twisted Howard's arm painfully behind his back.

'You can say whatever you like to me,' he said pleasantly. 'But first you'll apologise to the lady for pushing her. Won't you?'

Howard gave a faint whimper of pain and then nodded. 'Sorry, Sarah,' he muttered.

'Well done,' smiled Niall.

Then he marched his captive briskly to the rear of the cottage, booted him out into the shrubbery and locked the door behind him. Dusting off his hands as if he had just finished carrying out the rubbish, he nodded to Sarah.

'Right,' he said calmly. 'We obviously can't do business in this madhouse and you look as if you need a brandy. I'll take you to lunch.'

Ten minutes later Sarah found herself in the casually elegant ambience of Mure's Fish House on the water-

front. Reflecting wryly that arguing with Niall Morgan
was rather like arguing with a steamroller, she begged
five minutes to go and tidy herself up. After a quick
trip to the loo, she stood in front of the large mirror
with a hairbrush in her hand and tried to make sense
of all that had happened to her. She felt shaken and
humiliatingly ready to cry. After all, she had been
passionately in love with Howard and the realisation
that he had betrayed her came as a devastating shock.
It was as if her whole world had fallen apart around
her.

Well, she hadn't been brought up to believe that
misery was a good excuse for avoiding work. And she
had work to do. With a final sniff, she splashed a
handful of cold water in her face, scrubbed her eyes
with a paper towel and stared at herself in the mirror.
In spite of all the drama, she still looked very much as
usual. Long, tangly ginger hair, a dusting of tawny
freckles and deceptively fragile features gave her an
ethereal air, but she had inherited her grandmother's
determined chin and there was a militant light in her
blue-grey eyes. Fighting down the ache in her throat,
she tried to look like the sort of career woman Niall
Morgan would want to meet. The first genuine flicker
of interest sparked inside her. Why did he want to talk
to her? Well, there was only one way to find that out.

Picking up the brush, she dragged it through her hair
with long, scouring strokes and then drew a defiant
outline of red lipstick around her mouth. In a moment
she would have to go out and confront him and for
some reason her heart thudded violently at the thought.
Careful, Sarah, she warned herself. That man is pure
dynamite.

Yet he looked as harmless and relaxed as a drowsing panther, sitting by a window overlooking the water with a glass dangling negligently from one hand. He looked up and smiled at Sarah's approach. Then, setting down the glass, he stood up and helped her into her chair. As he did so his hand brushed against her arm.

'You're still shaking,' he observed. 'I think you'd better drink that brandy and soda I've ordered for you. Unless you'd rather have something else?'

Sarah picked up the glass of reddish liquid and stared unhappily at it.

'Won't you have to pay for it anyway?' she protested.

He chuckled. 'I suppose so. Does it matter?'

'It does to me,' replied Sarah. 'I'll drink it.'

She took a large gulp and almost choked at the potency of the mixture. Heat seemed to run through her veins and her ears rang.

'That's awfully strong,' she gasped.

'I thought you needed it,' said Niall. 'Anyway, I'm glad it wasn't wasted.'

Sarah blinked, wondering if the top of her head was about to lift off.

'Oh, my Scottish thrift is far too ingrained to waste good brandy,' she replied.

'I thought you said your name was Marlowe,' remarked Niall. 'Is that Scottish?'

Sarah looked baffled. 'I've no idea,' she admitted. 'But McKenzie certainly is and my mother's family were McKenzies who came out from Scotland in the 1830s. Oh, sorry, I'm babbling. I didn't mean to tell you my family history.'

'No, please go on,' insisted Niall. 'It will calm you

down and anyway I'm genuinely interested. Tell me more about them.'

Sarah paused, trying not to recall the look of malicious satisfaction on Howard's face when he told her about Charlene. Trying to think of something else. Anything else.

'W-well,' she stammered, 'the McKenzies thought that the colonies were the right place for people of industry, frugality and high moral tone to prosper.'

She rolled her 'R's vigorously as she named the three virtues and Niall gave a low growl of laughter.

'Well, you're an impudent wee lassie to make fun of them like that, aren't you?' he demanded. 'But tell me about these moral paragons who produced you.'

Sarah sighed, unable to keep up the pretence of light-hearted humour.

'They haven't changed much since the 1830s,' she said gloomily. 'They're awfully sweet and I love them dearly, but they don't really approve of me. And right now I'm not sure I blame them.'

'So you're the black sheep of the family, are you?' asked Niall, giving her a shrewd glance.

'Well, off-white anyway,' agreed Sarah. 'They're always wishing I'd settle down and get a bit more sense.'

'And what exactly have you done to convince them that you haven't any sense?' demanded Niall.

Sarah was saved from answering by the arrival of a waiter bearing the menu and wine list. This gave her thoughts a new direction and she hovered for two or three minutes in indecision before making her choice.

'Seafood chowder, followed by Kashmiri curry

please,' she said. 'I'll think aobut the raspberry ice-cream afterwards, too.'

'Would you like some wine with it?' asked Niall.

'No. Just some lemon mineral water, thanks.'

'And a glass of the Chablis for me,' added Niall, handing the menus back to the waiter.

He settled back in his chair, pressed his fingertips together and scrutinised her thoughtfully. Sarah was so unnerved by that relentless silvery gaze that she glanced hastily down at her blue and green plaid dress. Had she spilt something on it? But it seemed perfectly clean. Looking up again into those amused eyes, she found herself beginning to blush and stammer.

'H-how did you hear about my balloon business, Mr Morgan?' she asked, taking another hasty gulp of the brandy and soda.

She choked again as the fiery liquid surged into her bloodstream, making her feel as if she were about to float up into the air like one of her own balloons.

'Call me Niall,' he ordered.

'All right. How did you hear about my balloon business, Niall?'

'Word of mouth,' replied Niall, still watching her closely. 'Always the most reliable form of recommendation in my opinion. You did a birthday party for the daughter of one of my business associates. Ken Lewis.'

'Oh, yes,' recalled Sarah with a flicker of pleasure. 'Little Hayley Lewis. Her mother Chrissy went to school with me. And they were pleased with the decorations, were they?'

'Ecstatic,' agreed Niall drily. 'Chrissy showed me five pages of photos from the party. But I must admit you seem to have a genuine flair for colour and design.'

Sarah turned even pinker with pleasure.

'Thank you,' she murmured.

'So,' said Niall briskly, reaching into the inside pocket of his jacket. 'To business. I've been asked to take over the directorship of the Van Diemen Festival at short notice, since the previous director has resigned. Most of the work has already been done, but I'd like to add a bit of razzmatazz. Now do you think you could handle the opening ceremony for me?'

Sarah's mouth fell open. It was a bigger project than anything she had ever dreamt of tackling and for a moment her only response was pure terror—followed by an adrenalin-surge of excitement. For the moment she completely forgot about Howard.

'What do you have in mind?' she breathed.

'What do *you* have in mind?' countered Niall, pushing a sheet of paper covered in drawings across the table at her and gesturing with a silver pen. 'We're having the opening down here on the waterfront tomorrow week. The Lord Mayor will be here, the band will be over there, the spectators here and I want something colourful and dramatic to kick off the festivities. We'll be relaunching the old sailing ship, the *Lady Franklin*, at the ceremony too, if that gives you any ideas.'

Sarah's eyes shone with anticipation. For a moment she sat gazing out at the water which was now dancing brightly in a sudden burst of sunshine. A colourful image rose before her eyes.

'How about a balloon release from the decks of the *Lady Franklin*?' she suggested. 'Say a thousand helium balloons all rising into the sky at the same moment? Not white, because that wouldn't show up well enough,

especially if it's cloudy. But rainbow colours. Or all
red. That would look superb against the sea and the
sky.'

'Sounds great,' applauded Niall, making a note on
the paper. 'Are you sure you can handle it?'

Sarah felt a momentary qualm. Could she?

'Yes,' she said firmly.

'Right,' agreed Niall. 'I'd suggest a fee of——'

And he named a sum which staggered her.

'You mean I've got the job?' she croaked. 'Just like
that?'

He grinned at her astonishment. 'Yes,' he said. 'Just
like that. But on one condition.'

'What's that?' asked Sarah warily.

Niall's mouth hardened and his eyes took on a
dangerous gleam. 'That your good-for-nothing fiancé
Howard has nothing to do with the project.'

Sarah's face shadowed.

'Ex-fiancé,' she corrected him with a catch in her
voice.

'I'm glad to hear it,' he retorted grimly. 'But are you
sure you can handle the project without him?'

'Yes,' insisted Sarah.

'And what was the business arrangement between
you, may I ask?'

Sarah looked down at the tablecloth.

'Well, the business is all mine,' she said with a sigh.
'But Howard talked me into renting his front room as
office space. He inherited the cottage when his mother
died, but he always seemed to be short of cash. You
see, a singer's pay is rather irregular and he never
could seem to budget very well. So when we started
going out together he thought it would be a good idea

if I used his house. He found the money useful and we could see more of each other that way.'

A stormy expression glinted in Niall's eyes.

'I see,' he said repressively. 'But you'll need new premises now, won't you?'

'Yes, but I can handle all that. Don't worry.'

Niall scribbled something on the back of his paper and looked across at Sarah with a frown. 'Were you by any chance living with him in that cottage?' he asked thoughtfully.

Sarah coloured. 'Yes,' she admitted in a choked voice. 'But I don't see——'

Niall waved her objection aside and wrote something else. Twisting her neck into an imposible contortion, Sarah was horrified to decipher two completely unexpected memos: 'Find Sarah new business premises. Find Sarah new home.' She stared at him in outrage.

'That won't be necessary!' she said indignantly. 'I can look after my own life, thank you very much!'

Niall grinned mockingly at her. 'Can you?' he taunted.

Sarah held on to her rising annoyance with an effort.

'Look, I suppose you mean well,' she muttered in low, rapid tones. 'But I'm twenty-seven years old and I don't need a nanny.'

'I was only trying to help,' said Niall reproachfully.

Sarah stared at him, aghast. She might be grateful to Niall Morgan for offering her such a wonderful business opportunity, but that didn't give him the right to take over her private life as well.

'I'm surprised you didn't write down "Find Sarah new fiancé" while you were at it,' she flung at him.

'Good idea,' murmured Niall.

And, to her horror, he uncapped the pen and added the words Find Sarah new fiancé to the back of his plan. Sarah uttered an incredulous gasp of rage, but fortunately at that moment the waiter arrived with their first course. For the next hour and twenty minutes they were both fully occupied in doing justice to the food and Niall chatted harmlessly and very amusingly about an astonishing range of subjects: politics, films, agriculture, foreign countries and Sydney theatre ventures. Sarah was stunned by the breadth of his knowledge.

'Goodness! I can't believe all the places you've travelled to and all the things you've done!' she exclaimed, as they sat back with port and coffee. 'Did your parents put you on a jet when you were three years old to start you off?'

Niall smiled bleakly and tossed down a gulp of port.

'Far from it,' he said. 'I was born to an unmarried mother in a Sydney slum. She ran off with another man when I was six years old and I was put in a series of foster homes. By the time I was fifteen I had dropped out of school and was living on the streets.'

Sarah winced.

'Oh, heavens. I'm so sorry,' she breathed.

Niall shrugged.

'Don't be,' he retorted. 'I believe it's supposed to be character-building.'

'Character-building?' echoed Sarah. 'More like character-annihilating, if you ask me. I've seen those poor kids and how they live. . . But, Niall, if you were a street kid, how on earth did you get from that to this?'

Niall summoned a waiter with a practised lift of the eyebrow. Barely visible even to Sarah, the gesture carried enough authority to bring the waiter gliding rapidly across the room.

'More coffee, please,' said Niall with a smile. Then he turned back to Sarah. 'How did I make the transition? It was easy actually. I had the good fortune to encounter a very dedicated social worker who taught me the one important lesson that every human being should learn.'

'What's that?' asked Sarah blankly.

'That you can have anything you want, provided you want it passionately enough,' said Niall.

His voice was low and vibrant and a visionary flame seemed to blaze up in his eyes. Sarah caught her breath, shocked by the extraordinary magnetism of the man. At that moment he seemed to radiate an urgent sense of vitality and purpose. Her whole body tingled with awareness as she noted the way his silvery grey eyes were narrowed and his mouth was set in a determined line. She was suddenly, achingly aware of the powerful muscles rippling beneath that elegant business suit. What would it be like to be loved by such a man? she wondered. An involuntary shiver went through her at the thought.

'I—it sounds a bit ruthless,' she protested, feeling distinctly uncomfortable at the reactions she was feeling.

Niall shrugged impatiently.

'I didn't say you had to trample on people to get what you want,' he retorted. 'Only that you had to want it passionately.'

'And what did you want passionately?' wondered Sarah aloud.

His lips twisted into a reflective smile.

'To escape poverty,' he said. 'So I started to climb and kept climbing. I went back to school, then university and did a masters degree in business administration. I tendered for some government contracts in supply and got them. Gradually more and more work came my way as I discovered that I had a flair for organising things.'

'I think I've heard about you, actually,' she said thoughtfully. 'Didn't you arrange food drops for refugees after one of those volcanic eruptions in the Philippines?'

'Yes,' replied Niall with a shrug. 'But never mind that now. Tell me more about you—what sort of person you are, what *you* feel intensely passionate about.'

Sarah stretched slightly and gave an embarrassed laugh.

'Oh, dear. You do ask the hardest things,' she protested. 'And I doubt whether there's anything on earth that I feel intensely passionate about. But my background is straightforward enough. I grew up on a sheep farm near Swansea and I have a brother Tom, who's two years older than me, and a sister Fiona, who's three years younger. Both married. I went to the local primary school until I was twelve and then came to boarding-school in Hobart. After that the general family plan was that I should study agricultural science at university, then go back home, marry a local farmer and breed merino sheep and babies.'

Niall chuckled. 'But?' he prompted.

'But I didn't want to!' wailed Sarah. 'You've no idea how boring that sounded to me.'

'I can guess,' replied Niall drily. 'So what did you do instead?'

Sarah looked guilty. 'Threw a lot of prima-donna tantrums until they let me come to Hobart to art school,' she confessed. 'I really wanted to go to Sydney and study stage design, but Dad put his foot down. He said it was too expensive, too far away and too decadent. He was afraid I'd get involved with all kinds of weirdos.'

Niall snorted. 'Instead of which you got involved with the admirable Howard,' he remarked. 'And now you've found yourself high and dry with a relationship over and your pride in tatters?'

Sarah's shoulders dropped for an instant.

'Yes,' she admitted. Then her eyes flashed. 'But it won't be like that forever, I can assure you. The balloon business is doing really well and I'll make it do even better. And one of these days when I can afford it I will go to Sydney and do stage design. You don't have to pity me!'

'I wouldn't dare,' replied Niall mildly.

'All the same,' added Sarah, gritting her teeth, 'this break with Howard couldn't have come at a worse time. It's my grandparents' golden wedding anniversary this weekend, you see, and everyone is looking forward so much to meeting Howard at the party.'

'Your family have never met him before?' asked Niall in surprise.

Sarah smiled ruefully.

'No. None of them has. Swansea is only ninety miles away, but it might as well be on the other side of the moon as far as my family is concerned. They hardly ever come to town. Besides, I only got engaged a

month ago. And the really awful thing is that my
brother Tom phoned me last week to tip me off that
Mum had a wonderful surprise waiting for me at Gran
and Grandfather's party.'

Her expression was so gloomy that Niall gave a
hoarse chuckle.

'What's the surprise?' he asked. 'Death by firing
squad?'

Sarah shuddered. 'Worse,' she assured him. 'Mum
decided to make it a double celebration, so they're
throwing a surprise engagement party for me!'

Niall whistled softly. 'That is awkward!' he admitted.

'Awkward?' groaned Sarah. 'It's appalling! Can you
imagine how everyone will feel when I show up without
a fiancé? Honestly, I'm almost tempted to ask someone
to stand in for the weekend. You're not free by any
chance, are you?' she enquired jokingly, thinking if she
didn't laugh she might just cry.

'What a good idea,' Niall said slowly. 'I'll do it.'

Sarah stared at him in horror.

'It was just a joke,' she said. 'A crazy one.'

'But a good idea nevertheless,' retorted Niall. He
leaned across the table with a gleam of unholy amusement in his eyes. 'Look, Sarah, it's simple. Your
grandparents are old and this is one of the biggest days
in what remains of their life. Obviously you want it to
be a happy occasion for them, don't you?'

'Well, yes,' muttered Sarah in consternation.
'But——'

'And everybody's going to turn up with presents and
good wishes for you and your fiancé, aren't they?'

'Yes, but——'

'But nothing!' insisted Niall. 'If you arrive tomorrow

and tell them the engagement is all off, it will spoil the whole day for everyone,' concluded Niall. 'It would be cruel to do that, especially when it's so simple to avoid it. I'm perfectly willing to act the part of your fiancé for the weekend and you must admit that it will keep your family happy for a while.'

Sarah began to feel as if she were sinking rapidly in quicksand. A wave of temptation flooded through her, but she made a desperate attempt at resistance.

'And what about after the party?' she demanded. 'What do I tell them then, when they ask about our wedding plans?'

Niall cast her a smouldering look that sent an uncomfortable thrill of excitement sparking through her.

'Tell them we quarrelled,' he said with a shrug. 'Tell them I was an overbearing swine and I bullied you too much.'

Sarah gave a gasp of laughter. 'Well, that's certainly true!' she cried.

'Good. Then it's settled,' said Niall with satisfaction.

And, taking out his pen again, he put a neat tick next to the third item on his paper—Find Sarah new fiancé.

'Now,' he murmured. 'What about your other two problems? New business premises and a new home?'

'Wait a minute!' cried Sarah in outrage. 'Nothing is settled! You've just ridden right over me, that's all! I haven't said I'll do it.'

'No, but you will, won't you?' challenged Niall, giving her a slow, provocative smile. 'You'll fuss and fume and carry on and throw a few prima-donna tantrums. But in the end you'll come round to my point of view, won't you, Sarah?'

Sarah stared at him in dismay, but those unblinking grey eyes held an almost hypnotic power.

'Why should I?' she demanded.

'Because it would hurt your family if you didn't, and that's your weak spot, isn't it, Sarah? You can't bear to hurt people?'

Sarah let out her breath with a faint shudder.

'You're right, of course,' she said bitterly.

Niall continued to smile. For a brief instant the feral gleam of a hunting panther lit his eyes, then he was brisk and practical again.

'I think we'll leave the new business premises till Monday,' he announced. 'But you'll certainly need somewhere to stay tonight. Well, that's simple enough. You can sleep at my place. I'm renting a house from friends and there's plenty of room.'

'Don't be ridiculous!' she cried. 'I don't even know you.'

'Oh, don't worry. I'll move out for the night, if you like. But I suppose you want a character reference and, really, that's only fair. Waiter, could you please bring me a mobile phone?'

While Sarah was still reeling with shock, Niall accepted a mobile phone, punched in the numbers and smiled genially.

'Hello, Chrissy. Niall Morgan here. I've got a friend of yours, Sarah Marlowe, with me. I've just invited her to spend a night at my house. In my absence, I hasten to add. Would you be good enough to tell her that I'm perfectly safe to associate with?'

As Niall handed her the phone, Sarah heard an explosive chuckle from the other end of the line.

'Safe?' exclaimed Chrissy. 'That's the last word I'd use to describe Niall Morgan, Sarah. He's dynamic, totally unconventional, wickedly good-looking and hell-bent on having his own way. He'll turn your life upside-down, if he hasn't already done it, but he'll never, ever hurt you. Will that do?'

Sarah's gaze travelled down over Niall, his glossy, dark hair, the grey eyes alight with mischief and devilment, the twisted smile that somehow set her heart hammering against her ribs in the most uncomfortable way.

'I suppose it will have to,' she said unsteadily.

Two hours later she found herself on the front doorstep of a luxurious beachfront house in Lower Sandy Bay, feeling rather as if she had been through a whirlwind. In the intervening time Niall had helped her blow up balloons for a children's birthday party, removed all her possessions from Howard's cottage and signed her up as a festival employee. Now he stood looking down at her with an expression that made her feel strangely breathless.

'I've never been engaged before,' he remarked. 'I must say I rather like the sensation. Well, goodbye, Sarah.'

He leaned down towards her and her heart lurched violently. Oh, lord, he's going to kiss me, she thought in panic. Instinctively she shrank from him and saw the flash of amusement in his eyes. With agonising certainty she realised that he had only intended a friendly brush of his lips on her cheek. Colour flooded her face.

'I-I'm sorry,' she babbled. 'I wasn't. . . I thought. . . I didn't realise. . .'

His arms came round her reassuringly. Arms as strong as steel cables. She was suddenly conscious of the clean, salty, masculine smell of him, of his immense power and magnetism. It was as if he gave off some primitive aura of male dominance and arrogant self-assertion. And shamefully her whole body responded to that primal call. Tingling currents of excitement coursed through her limbs and she felt a throbbing warmth begin to uncoil deep inside her. She let out a faint gasp and stepped back a pace, breaking his hold.

'It's all right, Sarah,' he said in his low, husky voice. 'You're quite safe.'

'A-am I?' she faltered.

Something in the tone of her voice seemed to alert him to her feelings, for suddenly his eyes narrowed and he moved closer to her. In one swift movement he hauled her against him and kissed her with a violence which both enthralled and terrified her. A low whimper escaped her, half-protest, half-plea, and then she gave herself up to the rapture of his kisses. His lips were warm and urgent on hers and the virile power of his body against hers made her yearn for something more than mere kissing. Closing her eyes, she swayed in his hold, feeling as if her legs had turned to water beneath her. There was a roaring in her ears like the distant thunder of Niagara Falls and her heart seemed to be beating in the most erratic rhythm imaginable. The insane thought flashed into her mind that there was one thing she could feel intensely passionate about if she tried. Or even if she didn't try. Niall Morgan.

With a stifled gasp she pushed him away.

'Don't!' she begged, scarlet with mortification. 'I'm not like that, really I'm not. I don't kiss people I scarcely know. It shouldn't have happened.'

He looked down at her with an odd twisted smile.

'Who are you frightened of, Sarah?' he challenged. 'Me? Or yourself?'

She didn't answer. Couldn't. She was too preoccupied with fighting down the turbulent feelings of elation and panic that were hurtling through her.

'Look. About this party,' she began. 'I really don't think——'

But he cut her off ruthlessly.

'I'll pick you up at eight o'clock tomorrow morning,' he said.

CHAPTER TWO

THE first red glow of dawn was already spilling across the river when Sarah flung back the curtains at five forty-five the following morning. She had spent an abominable night tossing restlessly in the huge half-tester bed, trekking to the bathroom for unnecessary glasses of water and methodically torturing herself with the one unanswerable question: how could I have been such a fool as to get involved in all this?

It was a relief to pull on a tracksuit and go outside. Perhaps a run along the beach would clear the cobwebs out of her brain and magically reveal some avenue of escape. As she hurtled along the firm damp sand at the water's edge, Sarah felt the exhilarating pleasure of clean, salt air, sparkling blue water, bright sunshine and vigorous motion. But she didn't receive any inspiration. When at last she panted to a halt near the jetty at the end of Nutgrove Beach, her thoughts were as turbulent as ever. Only one possible explanation occurred to her.

'I must have been mad,' she muttered as she did some swift bending and stretching exercises. 'Temporary insanity, that's what it was. Brought on by stress.'

But would Niall Morgan accept that explanation and agree to release her from this crazy scheme? Somehow she doubted it. He didn't seem like the kind of man to give up easily once he had set his mind on something. No. Now that this outrageous deception had been suggested at all, the only thing to do was to present a united front and try to carry it off successfully. All the same, she couldn't help wondering how on earth she had ever let Niall run over her so dramatically. After all, she had never been the wimpish type. Howard, for instance, could never in a million years have persuaded her to do such a thing.

With a sudden jolt of dismay, she realised that she had barely thought about Howard all night. What kind of a woman was she? she wondered in horror. Hadn't she been involved with Howard for over a year? Hadn't she hoped and yearned to marry him? Then how could she possibly view his departure from her life with such indifference? She ought to be completely distraught. Instead, she realised guiltily that her main emotion was a slowly dawning sense of relief. I'll never have to put up with his childish sulks and tantrums again, she thought, never have to pander to his ego, never have to worry about whether he's cheating on me. I'm glad it's over! But that thought was quickly succeeded by another, less welcome one.

'Oh, dear,' muttered Sarah to herself. 'I wonder if my mother's right? She's always saying that I rush headlong into things without any thought for the consequences.'

A vivid image rose in her mind of that long, sensual kiss with Niall the previous evening. Her cheeks turned scarlet. That had certainly been rushing in without any thought of the consequences. Well, it would have to stop. It was bad enough to be committed to spending a weekend in Niall's company without giving in to this incomprehensible sexual chemistry that seemed to exist between them. I'll just have to keep things cool and reserved between us, she vowed. And was immediately tormented by the memory of being crushed against his warm, virile body. It appalled her that she could feel so strongly attracted to one man the very day after parting from another. With a low groan she sprinted back down the beach as if she could outrun her feelings.

A long, hot shower and a leisurely breakfast of orange juice, coffee and steaming blueberry muffins made her feel more in control of the situation. She dressed carefully in a lavender floral frock, brushed her unruly red hair back off her face and fixed it in place with two combs. Then she applied a discreet hint of red lipstick, grey eyeshadow, blusher and scent. Finally she fastened a single string of pearls around her neck.

'There!' she said with satisfaction. 'Now I even feel ready to face Niall Morgan.'

But it wasn't true and she knew it. Her stomach was fluttering with nerves and, as eight o'clock drew nearer and nearer, she found herself pacing the room with her heart beating unnaturally fast. I hope he doesn't do anything outrageous at the party, she thought. And then. . . No, I hope he does, so everyone will think it's a good thing when I get disengaged again. Oh, I wish I hadn't agreed to this. But perhaps he won't come. The doorbell rang.

She went to answer it on dragging feet. He was standing there in a pale grey lightweight suit, light blue shirt and darker blue tie, looking so suave and confident that she could have kicked him. Instead she gave him a wan smile.

'What's wrong?' he asked.

'I hoped you weren't coming,' she said bluntly.

His black eyebrows arched. 'Tough luck,' he replied cheerfully. 'Well, are you ready? Let's get going.'

His manners were impeccable, she thought grudgingly, as he helped her into the Mercedes and then carried her luggage to the back of the car. He may be an arrogant, overbearing swine, but he doesn't expect me to be a porter the way Howard did.

'Well, at least your grandparents have got a good day for their party,' Niall remarked, as he drove out on to the main road.

It was true. The fickle Tasmanian climate had turned on one of those glorious blue and gold days that made people think more of the Greek islands than the Roaring Forties. As they drove across the Tasman Bridge, the wide river was like a sheet of beaten silver under the glittering sun and the towering hills swam like dark blue mirages in a shimmer of heat.

'Well,' said Niall bracingly as they took the highway towards Sorrell, 'you're very quiet. What would you like to talk about? I can offer you Sydney theatre, Hobart restaurants, the history of hot-air balloons, the Australian Test Cricket team or our current balance of payment figures.'

'Oh, stop it!' begged Sarah. 'I feel far too churned up to talk about anything. Can't you see how awkward this situation is?'

'No,' said Niall in surprise.

Restlessly Sarah crossed one leg over the other and stared out of the windscreen of the car. But from the corner of her eye she saw the unmistakable flash of appreciation in Niall's glance.

'And don't look at my legs!' she added in a wobbly voice.

He swallowed a grin.

'So we're to spend a two-hour drive to Swansea in total silence, are we?' he asked mildly. 'Don't you think, now we're engaged, that we ought to be taking the chance to get to know each other?'

'We're not engaged!' cried Sarah. And then added reluctantly, 'But we'll have to convince my family that we are, won't we? Oh, help! I wish I'd never agreed to this. Look, do you think we should be swotting up on each other's backgrounds? You know, whether you had measles when you were five, what the first boy was called that I kissed behind the shearing shed when I was fourteen. That sort of thing?'

'No!' said Niall grandly. 'I know I've got all the major points under control and I'm sure we can improvise if there's anything desperately important.'

'All right,' agreed Sarah doubtfully.

'What was he called anyway?' asked Niall after a moment's pause.

'Who?'

'The boy you kissed behind the shearing shed.'

A reluctant flicker of amusement lit her face.

'Denis Cook.'

'Hmm. Was he any good?'

Sarah showed him the tip of her tongue. 'Oh, wouldn't you like to know?' she retorted with a provocative little shrug.

Niall darted her a forbidding look. 'Back in the days of our Scottish pioneering forebears, you would have been called a minx, my girl,' he told her. 'The sort of woman some strapping man would have taken in hand and tamed.'

'Oh? Like you, I suppose?' challenged Sarah.

'Yes,' said Niall through his teeth. 'Very probably.'

Something in his tone sent a delicious, shivering thrill down her spine, as if this were not a game, but a serious encounter. I wonder what it would be like to be tamed by Niall Morgan? she thought. And could not repress another quivering tingle of sensation deep inside her. Hastily she changed the subject.

'Well, I hope you know what you're doing,' she said. 'It seems to me we could both find ourselves in the soup if we aren't telling the same story.'

Niall frowned. 'There is one point we ought to clear up,' he admitted. 'Presumably your family must at least know your fiancé's name, don't they?'

Sarah chewed her lip. 'No. I don't think so,' she muttered.

'You don't think so?' roared Niall. 'What exactly does that mean?'

'Don't shout at me!' winced Sarah.

'Then kindly explain what you mean,' ordered Niall in clipped tones.

'Well, it was like this,' replied Sarah. 'I was living with Howard just minding my own business and my family didn't know anything about it. Until one morning my mother phoned about seven a.m. and wanted to speak to me. I wasn't even awake and Howard answered the phone. So that was how she found out he was living there.'

'Couldn't you have told her he had called in for an early morning jog or something?' asked Niall.

'Not really. You see, when she asked for her daughter Sarah, Howard, like a fool, said, "Oh, yes, she's right here. I'll just wake her for you." And then I came straight on the line, yawning and mumbling. I mean, it would have been obvious to a blind person. Anyway, my mother hit the roof and I panicked and told her we were engaged. She was so excited I don't think she even heard his name properly. Anyway, she hung up almost immediately so she could go and tell my father and I haven't spoken to her since.'

'I see,' said Niall evenly. 'Just let me get something straight, Sarah. Are you telling me that your engagement to Howard was all the result of a misunderstanding?'

Sarah swallowed hard.

'No!' she protested. 'I always wanted to marry him. At least I thought I did. And he said he was in love with me too.'

'Did he ever propose to you in earnest?' continued Niall relentlessly.

An aching sense of humiliation and sadness swept through her.

'Sort of,' she said huskily. 'After my mother telephoned, I was so worked up that we had an argument about what our relationship really meant and I told him I was going to move out. Then Howard said he would marry me, if it really mattered all that much.'

'Generous of him,' sneered Niall.

Sarah darted him a quick, unhappy look.

'Well, I didn't want it to be like that!' she cried. 'I wanted it to be a proper marriage. The real thing. And it would have been, if I'd had anything to do with it.'

She subsided miserably and stared out of the window, blinking two or three times and setting her lips.

'You little fool,' muttered Niall under his breath.

'Thank you,' snapped Sarah.

'You're welcome.'

They drove for the next thirty miles in silence. That was exactly what Sarah had thought she wanted, but now it no longer seemed quite so appealing, with Niall drumming his fingers on the steering-wheel and staring murderously through the windscreen at the golden fields and sunlit eucalypts that flashed past. It was not until they reached the coast that he spoke again, and it was clear from his tone that his disapproval was as strong as ever. Turning off the highway into a sandy parking area near a deserted beach, he brought the car to a halt.

'Get out,' he ordered. 'We'll take a ten-minute break to stretch our legs. And there's one other minor detail I need to sort out with you.'

Biting her lip, Sarah climbed out of the car. The beach was spectacularly beautiful. A smooth carpet of powdery white sand led down to a turquoise expanse of green water. Swooping cliffs curved around at both ends of the bay, protecting it from the wind, and the air was aromatic with the scent of eucalyptus. In any other part of the world such an idyllic spot would have been thronged with sun-worshippers. Here it was deserted, apart from a few seagulls gliding high above the cliffs and shrieking raucously. Yet something told her that Niall had not brought her here to admire the view. Taking her hand, he led her down a barely visible track through the undergrowth until they emerged on the sand.

'I don't suppose Howard bothered to buy you an engagement ring, then?' he challenged.

Sarah looked down at her bare left hand and flushed.

'No. He thought that sort of thing was a lot of bourgeois nonsense,' she admitted.

'Well, I like to do things properly,' growled Niall. 'You'd better see if this fits.'

Sarah gasped as Niall drew a blue velvet box out of his pocket and opened it to reveal a gold engagement ring set with five alternating diamonds and sapphires. He gave a crooked smile.

'I suppose it ought to be accompanied by a proposal, shouldn't it?' he demanded ironically. 'Will you marry me, Sarah?'

Sarah's hands flew to her face, as if to ward off a blow.

'Oh, don't!' she choked. 'It's awful. It makes such a mockery of something that ought to be. . .so special. So important.'

'No mockery intended,' Niall assured her curtly. 'But I have my own ideas of what a man owes a woman when he asks her to marry him. And, even if we are only pretending, I'll be damned if I'll do the thing shabbily. Now give me your hand.'

Flinching slightly, Sarah allowed him to draw her left hand down from her cheek and slide the ring on to it. It fitted perfectly, but she scarcely did more than glance at it, for Niall's rain-grey eyes held hers with an unreadable expression. For a moment, it was almost as if he gazed into the depths of her soul.

'All right,' he said abruptly. 'Consider yourself engaged. And now let's get moving.'

Shaken by that silent encounter, Sarah groped help-lessly for words.

'Th-this ring. . .' she stammered. 'It must be quite

valuable. I promise I'll give it back to you after. . .
after——'

Niall cut her off. Seizing her hand, he gave her an
ironic look and planted a kiss in her palm. Then,
folding her hand over it, he kissed her knuckle just
below the ring.

'Keep it, sweetheart,' he said mockingly. 'I doubt if
I'll find any further use for it.'

Sarah's emotions were in turmoil as she climbed
back into the car. Ever since she had first agreed to
this deception she had begun to regret it, but now the
regrets were taking on nightmare proportions. There
were so many things she simply hadn't considered—
like how it would feel to receive a proposal of marriage
from a devastatingly good-looking man who actually
had no intention of marrying her. Well, now she knew.
It felt rotten. Or how it would feel to show off a
beautiful engagement ring to her family, knowing full
well that she was deceiving them. Not that she had
actually done that yet, but she could make a good
guess about how that would feel too—rotten again.
She let out a long, shuddering sigh.

'What's turned you into such a misery?' demanded
Niall.

'Your proposal,' wailed Sarah.

'Oh. Didn't you like it?'

'No!'

'Pity. Why not?'

'Because it wasn't real. And I feel so mean for
cheating everyone. And. . .oh, Niall, can't we please
turn round and go back to Hobart?'

'No. Sorry. I don't believe in giving up on things.'

Sarah sucked in her breath.

'I can't go through with this!' she exclaimed unsteadily. 'This time yesterday morning I was in bed with Howard. If I start pretending that I'm in love you, I'm going to feel like an absolute——'

Niall cut her off with a warning gesture of his hand.

'Do me a favour,' he snarled. 'Don't ever remind me again that you used to share a bed with Howard. It does dangerous things to my blood-pressure.'

Sarah's heart began to pound violently. She wanted to ask Niall what he meant, but her mind reeled wildly away from the most obvious possibility. He couldn't be jealous; it was ridiculous even to think it. And yet, if he felt anything like the powerful physical attraction that she felt towards him, anything was possible. . . An odd breathlessness seized her.

'L-look, you will play it cool when we get there, won't you, Niall?' she stammered. 'I mean, I want my family to like you, but not too much. After all, we're going to be breaking this engagement off pretty smartly, so don't overdo the charm, will you?'

But it was useless. She might have known it would be. From the moment they drove up the long, poplar-lined driveway of Invergordon Farm and the whole clan turned out to meet them, Niall had everyone eating out of his hand. It was scorching hot on the gravel driveway in front of the long, low sandstone house, but all the Marlowes and McKenzies and Camerons were dressed to the eye-teeth as they stood waiting for the car to come to a halt.

'Stay there,' urged Niall and shot out to open the passenger door.

With a sinking feeling, Sarah let him help her out, observing as she did so the approving gleam in the blue eyes of the middle-aged woman who was hurrying to meet them. Damn Niall! So he was already chalking up Brownie points for good manners, was he?

'Mum, this is my. . .my fiancé, Niall Morgan,' muttered Sarah without enthusiasm.

'How do you do, Mrs Marlowe?' said Niall warmly. And, ignoring Helen Marlowe's outstretched hand, he kissed her on both cheeks.

'Now I can see where Sarah gets her beautiful eyes from,' he added in a matter-of-fact tone.

'Goodness,' murmured Mrs Marlowe, looking flustered but rather pleased as she patted her greying auburn hair into place. 'Well, now, Niall, you must meet everyone else. These are my mother and father, Mr and Mrs McKenzie, whose golden wedding anniversary we're celebrating; my husband Gordon; my son Tom and his wife Andrea; their three children Robert, Jenny and Susan; my daughter Fiona and her husband Jim Cameron and Baby Luke. And on my right here there's my brother John, his wife Robyn and their two children Emma and Dean. Then, last but not least, Gordon's brother Hugh, his wife Elizabeth and their sons Simon, Paul and James. There! Have you got all that?'

'Oh, I think so,' agreed Niall with a chuckle.

He probably has too with that elephantine memory of his, thought Sarah bitterly. Most people who had just been introduced to twenty-one total strangers would look at least a bit disconcerted, but Niall was busy shaking hands around the circle as if everyone were his closest friend. Yet he saved his warmest embrace for the frail Mrs McKenzie.

'Fifty years of marriage,' he murmured, kissing her withered cheek and taking both her hands in his.

'That's a wonderful achievement, Mrs McKenzie. And I'll be a proud and happy man if Sarah and I can do the same.'

'Oh, my dear,' replied Mrs McKenzie with a catch in her voice. 'I'm sure you will. And I hope every year of it will mean as much to you as my time with William has meant to me.'

Sarah felt tears rise in her eyes and had to swallow a lump in her throat. A huge wave of guilt engulfed her and she wondered despairingly if she ought to confess before this appalling charade went any further. Clearing her throat, she tried desperately to think of the right words.

'Gran,' she began in a strained voice. 'There's something——'

But she got no further. Niall's arm came round her in an apparently affectionate gesture and he gave her a sharp pinch on the side. She jumped.

'Yes, dear?' said her grandmother, peering at her over her spectacles.

'I was just going to say that I think we should go inside,' gabbled Sarah. 'You must be boiling out here, aren't you?'

'How thoughtful of you, dear. Yes, it is rather warm, isn't it? Now do you need help with anything from the car? I'm sure Hugh's boys will give you a hand, if you do.'

'No, we can manage, thanks,' said Niall. 'Sarah, do you just want the presents now or shall I bring the suitcases too?'

'Oh, I think Mum will expect us to stay at the smaller house where she and Dad live, won't you, Mum?' she replied, signalling frantically with her eyebrows at

Niall. 'Don't you remember, darling, Tom and Andrea and their family live here in the big house, Mum and Dad have the smaller house over the hill and Gran and Grandfather have the cottage? We're just having the party here because there's more room. I'm sure I told you about it all.'

Niall darted her a swift, murderous glance.

'Oh, yes. So you did,' he agreed in a tone that promised revenge.

Sarah gave a faint shudder as they followed the rest of the clan into the dark, panelled hallway that smelled of flowers and furniture polish. Something told her the difficulties were only going to get worse.

They did. Once inside the long living-room, Sarah's grandparents settled themselves comfortably on a chintz-covered sofa and beamed at the newly engaged pair.

'Now, do tell us something about how you two met and fell in love,' urged Mrs Marlowe with misty eyes. 'It's so nice to have another romance in the family, especially at such a time. It makes me feel as if William and I are passing on the torch to you young ones.'

'Well, let me give you your present first,' said Sarah hastily. 'Here it is. And a very happy anniversary to you.'

She kissed both old people on the cheek and thrust a parcel wrapped in gold paper into her grandmother's hands.

'Oh, look, William, how lovely! A pair of gold cuff-links for you and a gold brooch for me. They're exquisite, dear. Thank you so much.'

'It's from both of us,' added Sarah as a hasty afterthought.

'And this is a small extra present just from me,' added Niall. 'Sarah mentioned that you collected porcelain, so I thought this might appeal to you.'

Perhaps he's not so bad after all, thought Sarah unwillingly as she heard the soft gasp of pleasure from her grandmother. Niall's present was an old porcelain plate covered in gold and pink flowers. Obviously just the sort of thing one would pick up in a junk shop for a few dollars, but still precisely what her grandmother would cherish. Not an embarrassingly extravagant gift like Sarah's engagement ring, but gracious, thoughtful and exactly right for the occasion. Sarah slipped her hand impulsively through Niall's arm and smiled at him.

'That was nice of you, darling,' she murmured with hardly a trace of irony.

But then her grandmother spoiled everything.

'Oh, my dear young man,' she said in distress, turning the plate round and holding it up to the light. 'It's absolutely beautiful, but are you really aware of the value of what you are giving us? Unless I'm very much mistaken, this is a Swansea plate, probably dating back to about 1814 and likely to be very valuable. I couldn't accept such a gift, really I couldn't.'

Niall smiled lazily.

'Well, you can set your mind at rest,' he said. 'I found it in a junk shop for a few dollars and their loss is your gain. If it is what you say, I'm only too happy to hear it. It will make a worthy piece in your collection.'

Sarah glanced sideways at him sharply and knew in that instant that he was lying. With devastating certainty she realised that he had known the value of the piece all along, but his stern grey eyes trapped hers, daring her to reveal the truth. She felt suddenly suffocated by the crushing burden of Niall's generosity. Why? Why was he doing this? Laying such intolerable debts upon her that she could never repay? While her grandmother was still exclaiming joyfully over the plate, Sarah leapt to her feet.

'I suppose you'll need help in the kitchen, won't you, Andrea?' she asked. 'After all, lunch for twenty-three people is quite a chore. Can't I come and whip some cream for you or something?'

There was a mild buzz of astonishment at this.

'What? Sarah volunteering for KP duty?' exclaimed her father heartily. 'My word, you must have been a good influence on her, Niall! I never thought I'd live to see the day.'

Much to Sarah's relief, the group broke up then, but she soon found herself in the kitchen under a new form of attack. Her mother, her aunts Robyn and Elizabeth and her sister-in-law Andrea were all determined to extract every last detail of her romance with Niall and they went about the task with the zeal of newly qualified dentists. The only comfort was that her sister Fiona, the most ruthless gossip of all, had retired to a bedroom to feed Baby Luke. But no doubt she would soon reappear, fully equipped with a notebook, tape recorder and thumbscrews. With a sinking feeling, Sarah began to wish that Niall were there to help her out. But Niall had been dragged off to view Tom's prize merino ram and she was left to flounder alone.

'When did you meet Niall, dear?'

'What sort of family does he come from?'

'Can he sing or play the piano? We thought a little bit of entertainment after the lunch might be nice.'

'Does Niall eat asparagus, Sarah? What do you mean, you don't know? I know you live on TV dinners when you're alone, but you can't keep a man happy on that sort of rubbish!'

Sarah felt limp with relief when her father appeared after half an hour to forage for some cold beer in the fridge. But her relief didn't last long. As he set the glasses on a tray, he gave her a swift hug, almost lifting her off her feet.

'By gum, that chap of yours has got a head on his shoulders, Sarah,' he said approvingly. 'What he doesn't know about the superfine wool trade isn't worth knowing and he's already put me on to a few income tax deductions that will save me a packet. I reckon he'll be a real asset to the family.'

'Yes, you're right,' chipped in Sarah's mother. 'And I must admit he's absolutely charming.'

'He's got about as much charm as Attila the Hun,' muttered Sarah savagely, beneath the roar of the food processor. 'Or Genghis Khan.'

'What was that, dear?' asked her mother.

'Nothing.'

Yet somehow the whole ordeal seemed almost worthwhile when they all gathered in the dining-room for the formal lunch. Andrea had set the long mahogany table with a starched white tablecloth and all her best Wedgwood china, the old family silver and Waterford crystal. Sarah's mother had made a magnificent central flower arrangement of yellow roses and red gold azaleas, her aunt Robyn had baked a cake piped with yellow icing and Sarah herself had decorated the walls

with gold and white helium balloons. The look of
radiant joy on her grandmother's face as she entered
the room almost made Sarah burst into tears and she
was moved beyond measure when Niall suddenly
gripped her hand. For a moment she felt all the bitter-
sweet yearnings that would have been hers if she were
really going to be his wife. Then cold, hard reason
reasserted itself. He's just acting a part again, she
reminded herself despairingly. He thinks the whole
thing is a huge joke at my expense. Damn him!
Snatching her hand away from his, she wished the floor
would open and swallow her up.

Sarah barely tasted the pumpkin soup or the cold
duck with spiced apricots or the crème caramel pudding. All her thoughts were fixed now on simply
enduring the rest of the afternoon, getting back to her
parents' house and preferably barricading herself in
her room. Let her mother entertain Niall if she thought
he was so charming! she told herself wearily.

After the dinner was over there was a fresh ordeal
to face as the surprise engagement party swung into
action and she and Niall found themselves in the
spotlight. If she had been genuinely engaged, she
would have been thrilled at the way Niall's eyes lingered on her as the champagne toast was drunk. And
at the way he entered into the spirit of unwrapping
presents and exclaiming delightedly over them. As it
was, Sarah was appalled. How can he be so. . .so glib?
she wondered in dismay. And how can I possibly find
him so attractive when he's such a liar? Even when the
party finally did break up with her grandmother shed-
ding tears of joy and her grandfather blowing his nose

vigorously, it was still not the end of Sarah's agony.
Far from it.

As they sat in her parents' comfortable living-room
late in the evening, her father brought up the subject
she had been dreading.

'Well, now,' he said, fidgeting in his armchair and
looking ill at ease. 'Ah, Niall, will you have a drop of
this excellent Scotch you've so kindly brought?'

'Thanks, Gordon.'

Oh, so they're on to first names now, are they?
thought Sarah sourly. She sat bolt upright in the centre
of the leather chesterfield and only the insistent
pressure of Niall's arm around her shoulders kept her
anywhere within miles of him.

'Sarah, how about you? A glass of port, or one of
those Belgian chocolates that Niall gave your mother?'

'No, thanks, Dad.'

Sarah folded her arms and sat even more rigidly,
every line in her body radiating hostility and resentment of the false position she found herself in. Niall
gave her a mocking glance, poured her a glass of port
and handed it to her.

'Drink it, Sarah,' he ordered with a lazy smile. 'No
need to be nervous. I'm sure your dad just wants to
find out what sort of man he's entrusting his daughter
to. Is that right, Gordon?'

Sarah's father blew out his breath in a long sigh and
nodded.

Sarah gave a small, choking gasp of rage and
frustration.

'Don't mind her,' murmured Niall, patting her on
the arm indulgently. 'It's an emotional moment for
her.'

'You bet it is,' muttered Sarah into her port.

But she felt the small warning pressure of Niall's arm and did not dare say it any louder.

'Well, come on, then,' invited Niall. 'Fire away.'

Sarah's father scratched his head.

'Well, I don't know how to begin, son,' he confessed. 'But I reckon Helen and I would just like to know a bit more about your background—your family, your job, your prospects, that kind of thing. And your plans, of course—when the wedding is to be, where you'll be living, that sort of thing.'

Sarah felt cold with horror at this, but Niall seemed totally unfazed. Taking a casual sip of Scotch, he looked across at Gordon from under thick, dark brows.

'I'll give it to you straight,' he said. 'I don't have a family. I was illegitimate and I spent a good part of my youth in institutions, but that's not an issue—at least for me.'

Sarah's father stroked his chin.

'Well, a man can't choose his background,' he admitted. 'I always think it's what you are yourself that counts.'

'That's right,' agreed Niall. 'What's important is the fact that I'm in love with your daughter. And it's the family I'll have with her that really counts.'

'You're planning on children, then, are you?' asked Mr Marlowe.

'Oh, yes,' replied Niall with a sideways glance at Sarah. 'And the sooner the better.'

Sarah choked violently and a splash of port spilt all over the front of her frock.

'Oh, darling!' exclaimed Niall in a concerned voice. 'You must be more careful. Here, let me mop you up.'

As he drew out a large white handkerchief and dabbed vigorously at the bodice of her dress, Sarah's face was turned away from both her parents. Almost purple with rage, she mouthed her message to Niall: 'I'll kill you for this.'

He smiled serenly at her.

'And I love you too, sweetheart,' he announced, giving her a swift peck on the cheek.

'Well,' said Mrs Marlowe, 'what about your work, Niall? And your wedding plans? And where you're going to live?'

Niall's features took on the look of keen efficiency that they had worn the previous day in the restaurant.

'Well, I'm only in Tasmania on a short-term contract until the Van Diemen Festival finishes,' he replied. 'But I own a house in Sydney and that's where I normally make my base, so I think we'll live there, provided that suits Sarah. It's convenient for the stage design work that she wants to do, but you can rest assured that we'll come and visit you often.'

Sarah stared at him, aghast. She might be ready to murder him, but she had to admit that for sheer brass-faced effrontery nobody could come within miles of Niall Morgan. If she hadn't known that this was all a farce, she would have been perfectly convinced of his sincerity. He even wore the sleek, self-satisfied look of a man in love, and the glances he kept casting her were full of pride, affection and lingering desire.

'And the wedding?' prompted her mother. 'We'll have to start making plans for that, won't we?'

Niall took Sarah's hand and smiled winningly.

'Yes. Well, we thought February, didn't we, sweetheart?' he said. 'I don't approve of long engagements and, to tell you the truth, I can't wait to put my ring on Sarah's finger and know that she's all mine.'

Sarah's mother groped for her handkerchief and dabbed her eyes.

'Oh, that's the sweetest thing I've ever heard a man say,' she murmured, completely overcome. 'Well, I must say, Niall, you seem to have everything under control and I'm very, very happy to think that my daughter has found such a sincere and decent person to be her life's partner.'

Sarah shot to her feet, unable to bear another moment of it.

'If you'll excuse me,' she quavered on a half-hysterical note, 'it's been a long day and I think I'll go to bed now. Goodnight, everyone.'

'Wait, Sarah,' urged her mother.

Rising to her feet, Mrs Marlowe clasped her hands awkwardly in front of her and gazed from Sarah to Niall. Then she cleared her throat as if she was about to make an important announcement.

'As you know, Sarah,' she said, 'I really don't approve of all this modern permissiveness. Sleeping together and such. But since you're a grown woman and you're getting married soon anyway, I've decided to do what you're always asking me to do and be a bit more broad-minded. So I've put you and Niall together in the pink bedroom.'

CHAPTER THREE

'WHY didn't you say something?' wailed Sarah. 'Why
didn't you tell her the truth?'

She could hear her mother's footsteps receding down
the stairs and the walls of the pink bedroom seemed to
be closing in alarmingly around her. It was a pretty
room with swooping ceilings, sprigged floral wallpaper,
an ornately carved French wardrobe and a large brass
double bed covered in a patchwork quilt. The sort of
romantic retreat that would have thrilled any genuine
pair of lovers. But at this moment it looked more like
a prison cell than a love-nest to Sarah, particularly with
Niall Morgan standing carelessly in the lamplight,
loosening his tie.

'Why didn't you?' he retorted with a shrug. 'You've
got a tongue in your head.'

'Oh, yes!' snapped Sarah, twisting her hands
together in a despairing gesture. 'I'm sure! And let
them know that we've been making fools of them all
day?'

'Exactly,' agreed Niall, taking off his jacket. 'So now
you know why I didn't do it. If you didn't have the
heart to disillusion them, why should I?'

Sarah gave a strangled groan like the sound of air
running out of a punctured balloon.

'Heart?' she echoed. 'Heart? You don't have a heart,
Niall Morgan. I've known bulldozers with more heart
than you've got, I've painted canvas backdrops that

had more sensitivity! If you had any concern whatsoever for other people's feelings, you would never have
let this stupid hoax get so far out of hand.'

'Now don't get upset, Sarah,' murmured Niall, shifting her out of his path so that he could hang his jacket
in the wardrobe. 'I was only doing what you asked me
to do.'

The fact that there was some truth in this only made
Sarah feel worse. After all, it was her own unthinking
remark in the restaurant that had set the whole drama
in motion. But she had never really expected Niall to
take her up on her crazy suggestion. Nor to tell the
inevitable lies with such grace and style. And she
certainly hadn't expected herself to feel attracted to a
man who could deceive people so unscrupulously.

'Oh, go to hell!' she breathed. 'Don't you see you've
ruined everything? You've just come along and turned
my entire life upside-down. It wouldn't have been so
bad if you hadn't decided to worm your way into my
family's good books like that. But I think what you did
was utterly detestable.'

'Oh?' said Niall in a conversational tone, beginning
to unbutton the sleeve of his shirt. 'What did I do that
was so detestable?'

'You know very well what you did!' retorted Sarah
hotly. 'Bought all those gifts for everybody. The plate
for Gran, the chocolates for my mother, the Scotch for
my father——'

'Just normal social courtesy,' protested Niall.

'Yes, sure. If this had been a normal social visit, but
it wasn't, was it? And what I object to most is the way
you lied to everyone! You really laid it on with a
trowel, didn't you? All that guff about our wedding

plans and our children and where we'd live! It was
outrageous. And you were enjoying every minute of it!
I could see the glint in your eyes the whole time you
were talking. You thought it was really funny spinning
everyone a line like that, didn't you?'

Niall hauled his shirt over his head and dropped it
on the floor.

'Oh, now don't get so het up,' he urged soothingly,
as he took off his vest. 'The thing is, Sarah, if you're
going to do anything in life, you might as well do it
properly. Go the whole way. If you want people to
believe that you're in love, you have to act as if you
are.'

Sarah flung him a look of burning reproach.

'In love?' she said unsteadily. 'Don't talk to me
about love, Niall. This has nothing to do with love; it's
just your twisted idea of a huge joke. But I'll tell you
one thing. The minute I get back to Hobart, I'm
phoning my parents and telling them that this engagement is off. Do you hear me? Off!'

Niall's eyes held hers with unwavering intensity. For
a moment she felt a current of nameless emotion surge
between them so powerfully that she caught her breath.
She had the uncanny sense that Niall was playing a
game with her. A strange cat-and-mouse game that
made a tense exhilaration well up inside her. Until
Niall looked away indifferently.

'You can tell them whatever you like, Sarah,' he
replied. 'By all means say that the engagement is over,
if that's what you want. After all, that was the original
plan, wasn't it?'

Sarah felt an irrational pang of disappointment at
this simple statement. Yes, it had been the original

plan. So why should she object to it now? What did she want? Did she want Niall to argue with her, to insist that he really did want to marry her? With a flash of horrified insight, she realised that something very like that had been lurking at the back of her mind. She did want Niall to justify all the lies he had told today. But why? Was she simply afraid of her family finding out about the deception? Or did Niall awaken some deep primeval instinct that made her yearn for him as her mate?

Appalled by the thoughts that were flitting through her head, she glanced across at Niall and suddenly realised that he was unbuckling his belt.

'What do you think you're doing?' she cried on a note of panic.

'Getting undressed. What does it look as if I'm doing?' His hands paused on his buckle.

'But you can't!' she wailed. 'You can't just——'

Her voice cracked. Tears of anger and bewilderment sprang to her eyes.

'What are you afraid of, Sarah?' taunted Niall.

'I'm not afraid!' she blazed.

'Then why are you staring at me like that? Do you seriously think I'm going to rape you?'

He took a step closer to her and seized her shoulders. With agonising clarity she became aware of his half-naked, virile body so close to hers. Her gaze darted unsteadily over his wide shoulders, lean, flat stomach, narrow hips and taut muscles. She could smell the masculine odour of him, salty, wild and potently arousing, and her senses swam dizzily in response. However much she might resent him, her treacherous body did not seem on the same wavelength as her mind. With a

horrified thrill of dismay, she realised that her heart
was hammering in a staccato rhythm and her breath
was coming in shallow gulps. Worse still, a throbbing
warmth seemed to be uncoiling deep inside her, sending tingles of desire pulsing through every part of her.
She swallowed convulsively.

'Well?' he insisted.

'No,' she croaked. 'I don't think you're going to rape
me.'

'Then what's the problem?' he asked, touching her
cheek lightly with his fingertips. 'Nothing is going to
happen that you don't want.'

Sarah shut her eyes briefly.

'And what's that supposed to mean?' she demanded.
'That if I did want you, you'd make love to me?'

Niall's hand trailed slowly down her throat and came
to rest on her heaving bosom. A faint, stark smile
lurked around the corners of his mouth.

'No,' he said huskily. 'Not yet.'

Sarah's senses reeled. What on earth did he mean,
not yet? Was he implying that at some future time. . .?
She left the thought unfinished.

'W-well, you needn't think I'm sharing a bed with
you tonight!' she stammered, taking his hand and
removing it from her body with as much distaste as if it
were a tarantula.

Niall's lips quirked into a genuine smile. A sly,
mocking smile that made her more desperate than
ever.

'You'll find the floor rather hard, won't you?' he
demanded, gesturing at the polished boards.

Sarah ground her teeth.

'I'm not sleeping on the floor!' she exclaimed. 'You are!'

'Care to fight for it?' challenged Niall.

'You utter. . .! If you had the slightest shred of decency, you wouldn't behave like this,' stormed Sarah.

'Ah, but I haven't,' pointed out Niall with an amused glint in his grey eyes. 'We've already established that. I'm totally heartless. Now would a man like that pass up the chance to share your bed, Sarah?'

Sarah's only response was a strangled gasp of frustration. Then, picking up her overnight bag, she vanished into the small en-suite bathroom and slammed the door. When she returned ten minutes later, showered and changed into a lacy white nightdress, she was half afraid that she would find Niall naked. But he was lying sprawled on the bed, still dressed in his grey trousers and looking as casual and relaxed as if he really were a genuine member of the family. Unbelievably, he was actually reading a book, with one hand propped against his cheek. For some reason this infuriated Sarah even further. It was as if Niall was sending her the silent message that she was making a fuss about nothing.

'I've finished with the bathroom,' she said in glacial tones.

He looked up and smiled.

'Oh, good,' he replied pleasantly. 'I'll just read to the end of this chapter before I go in.'

Sarah stood drumming her fingers on her thighs and fuming silently. No way was she going to climb into that bed with Niall Morgan lying on the quilt, flaunting his naked chest at her. She stole a hasty glance at his taut, flat belly, the bronze sheen of his skin in the soft lamplight, the dark hairs that arrowed down beneath his belt. And looked desperately away. Damn him! How could she just wriggle in there beside him as casually as if she were climbing aboard a bus?

He looked up and smiled knowingly at her.

'Oh, now, don't be shy, Sarah,' he murmured in a husky baritone. 'I know there's a little awkwardness about the situation, but I can assure you I'm quite harmless.'

Sarah snorted.

'You're about as harmless as a white pointer shark!' she retorted bitterly. 'And I'm not getting into that bed with you.'

'Dear me,' murmured Niall, swinging his legs over the side of the bed, so that Sarah retreated hastily across the room. 'You are jumpy, aren't you, sweetheart? It's rather like a nineteenth-century wedding night, when you think about it. But that being the case, perhaps I'd better do the decent thing and retire to the bathroom while you get over your nerves. What do you say?'

What Sarah said was an extremely rude word, but apart from clicking his tongue sadly Niall made no response. The moment the bathroom door closed behind him, Sarah jumped into bed, huddled into a tight ball and wrapped the covers protectively around her like a suit of armour. She felt angry, confused, defensive. Her heart was thudding as violently as if she were running in a hundred-metre sprint and she had an overpowering urge to take some desperate action to escape from her present plight. But what?

She could tell her parents the truth, but the scene

which would inevitably follow would be almost as bad as being trapped for the night with Niall. And if she got dressed, crept downstairs and drove away into the night in his car. . . Oh, be serious, Sarah! she told herself furiously. It's just not an option. The only thing you can do now is wait it out—and stick a large ceremonial sword into Niall Morgan's ribs, if you ever get the opportunity! Still fuming, she reached out to switch off her bedside lamp and then paused. If she turned it off, mightn't Niall stumble in the dark? Naturally she would be only too delighted if he broke his neck, but if he fell on her that would be less enthralling. After a moment's indecision, she left the light on. From the bathroom, the sound of running water and exuberant singing suddenly ceased. Hastily Sarah screwed her eyes shut and buried herself under the covers. Perhaps Niall would think she was asleep.

Five minutes later he prowled softly into the bedroom, paused for a moment beside her and then walked around the bed. She felt the mattress plunge suddenly as he climbed in and her heart skipped a beat. But she concentrated on breathing slowly and rhythmically, until suddenly Niall's arm reached across her.

'Don't touch me!' she shrieked, shooting bolt upright.

He was staring down at her with a perplexed expression on his face.

'Sarah, Sarah,' he chided, shaking his head ruefully. 'I was only reaching across to switch off the lamp.'

'Oh.'

She slid down on the pillows, feeling intensely foolish. His grey eyes scanned hers with a glint of amusement. And perhaps something else. Picking up a strand of her hair, he held it up to the light, so that it glowed a rich, flaming red.

'Your hair is beautiful,' he said softly. 'Like barley sugar.'

'Barley sugar?'

It was so unexpected that it made her give a muffled gasp of laughter. His fingers tightened in her hair and he drew her towards him. The look on his face was so intent, so full of passionate, compelling need that her lips parted instinctively. But he did not claim her mouth. Instead he kissed her on the cheek. A feather-light kiss, full of controlled urgency.

'Goodnight, Sarah.'

As he snapped off the light, she was conscious of her heart beating a tumultuous tattoo inside her breast. It made her feel angry and oddly breathless. She distrusted him, didn't she? So why should she feel so urgently aroused by the brush of his lips, by the tantalising nearness of his body beside her? In the thick, velvety blackness, she lay flat on her back and tried not to think about Niall. But she could feel the warmth radiating out from his powerful frame beside her. Worse still, she found herself feverishly imagining what it would be like to reach out and slide her hand inside his pyjama-top. She could almost feel the coarse, wiry hair, the power of the tense muscles under the smooth skin. And if she ran her hand down further. . . She shuddered and turned her back on him, huddling herself into a tight ball. As she did so, her leg brushed accidentally against his.

'For heaven's sake, Sarah,' growled Niall. 'I don't know if you're doing it on purpose, but could you

please keep still? I really don't enjoy being driven out
of my mind.'

'S-sorry,' stammered Sarah. 'I only wanted——'

'This?' rasped Niall.

And, without giving her a moment to protest, he
dragged her into his arms and kissed her fiercely. The
room spun dizzily around her in the darkness and for a
moment she felt she would drown in sheer, sensual
rapture. His powerful, virile warmth loomed above her
and she found herself crushed into the pillows beneath
his weight. Uttering a small, protesting whimper, she
made a feeble attempt to push him away. But the truth
was that she wanted this as badly as he did. The
intoxicating scent of his skin, compounded of soap and
leather and primitive masculine hormones, roused her
to a fever-pitch of excitement. Winding her arms
around his neck, she drew down his head and kissed
him with open, trembling lips.

He made a low sound in the back of his throat and
his hands slipped inside the bodice of her nightdress
and cupped her warm, yielding breats. Fire tingled
through her veins at his touch and she felt her nipples
tauten into hard, aroused peaks. Arching her body
against him, she let herself yield to the urgent, clamor-
ous need that was building to a frenzy inside her.

'I want you, Sarah,' he groaned.

'I want you too, Niall.'

His hands darted down her body, wrenched furiously
at the nightdress that was bunched around her knees
and hauled it up with a sound of ripping cloth. Sarah
didn't care. She was in the grip of a roller-coaster
madness of desire that made every inch of her body
throb and blaze with need. And, as his merciless,

skilful fingers found the most secret part of her body and began to stroke it, every remnant of caution vanished. With a distant sense of shock, she heard her own faint, whimpering cries, felt her body thresh and quiver with a joy so intense it was almost pain, and wondered why love had never brought her such dizzying fulfilment before. Nothing in her relationship with Howard had ever prepared her for the rapturous, sensual torment that Niall was inflicting on her now, and she responded with joyful abandon. His breath tickled her cheek, his body was hot and urgent against her and she longed for only one thing—the natural climax of the ferment that was building inside her.

'Take me,' she whispered frantically in his ear. 'Take me.'

A shudder went through his muscular frame. Then with brutal suddenness he dragged himself off her and switched on the light. As he loomed beside her, she saw that his breath was still coming in long, dragging gulps, that his hair was wildly disordered and his eyes held a feverish gleam.

'No,' he rasped. 'I'm sorry, Sarah. I must have been insane to let it go this far.'

Her body was still on fire with longing and she could not comprehend this total change of direction.

'Why?' she whispered through trembling lips. 'Don't you want me?'

His laugh was a harsh, ugly sound. 'Want you?' he snarled. 'I'm half out of my mind with wanting you. But I can't let it happen like this.'

He sprang suddenly out of bed and stood glaring down at her.

'What do you mean?' she cried, reaching out to him. 'I don't understand.'

Shaking off her touch, he stepped back a pace.

'There's no need for you to understand,' he retorted with a return of his usual arrogance. 'Just accept it. If you'll give me one of those blankets, I'll sleep on the floor.'

'But Niall——'

'Leave it, Sarah!'

She felt shaken and almost sick as she watched him snatch a pillow, haul a blanket off the bed and toss together a makeshift resting-place in the far corner of the room. Nothing made sense to her. And the fire-storm of desire which had swept her along in such an amazing crescendo was rapidly giving way to an agony of regret and embarrassment. A feeling of hurt bewilderment surged through her. Snapping off the light, she lay down and buried her head under the covers. In the suffocating darkness, she choked back tears, determined not to yield to the final humiliation of weeping. I should never have done this, she thought. It's the worst mistake I've ever made in my life. And I must put an end to this farce the moment I get away. . .

It was shortly after lunch when they left Invergordon the following day. Sarah had been dreading the long drive home, but fortunately Niall seemed preoccupied and distant. At first she pretended to sleep, but with the hot sun and the motion of the car the pretence soon became a reality. When she finally woke, she found that they were in a driveway beside a garden. A cool sea breeze blew in from the beach and the late afternoon sun was gilding the shrubbery with a bright halo of light. The passenger door hung open and Niall was

crouched on his haunches beside her, shaking her
shoulder. As she swam up into consciousness, Sarah
saw the warmth in his eyes and smiled hesitantly at
him.

'Where are we?' she yawned.

'We're home, sweetheart.'

Sweetheart. Memory came storming back to assault
her and she tossed her head challengingly.

'This isn't my home and I'm not your sweetheart!'
she flashed back. 'Now, if you'll just let me inside to
collect my belongings, I'll find somewhere else to go.'

With a shrug, he marched up to the front door and
unlocked it. But once she was inside the cool dimness
of the house he laid one hand on her shoulder.

'There's no need to leave, Sarah,' he said mildly.
'There's plenty of room for two.'

'No doubt there's plenty of room for two in a lion's
cage,' she retorted scathingly. 'But I wouldn't accept
an invitation to stay there either.'

'Suit yourself,' murmured Niall. 'But I told your
mother that this was your new address and gave her
the phone number here.'

Sarah stared at him in disbelief.

'You think of everything, don't you?' she exclaimed.
'Well, I'll just have to ring her up and untell her!
Excuse me.'

She stalked across to the phone and punched in her
mother's number. After a single ring, the call was
answered.

'Mum? There's something I must tell you,' she said.

'Sarah, is that you? Oh, what a relief! I've been
trying to call you for the last fifteen minutes. Gran has
had an accident.'

'An accident?' echoed Sarah in a voice sharp with fear. 'What kind of accident? Is she badly hurt?'

'Badly enough,' replied her mother. 'She had a fall. Dr Wentworth says she's fractured her hip and there may be other injuries. He wants to send her down to Hobart by ambulance for X-rays and possible surgery. He's across at the big house right now getting her stabilised for the trip, but she wants me to come down with her. What I was wondering was whether you and Niall could possibly put me up for the night?'

'You want to stay here?' blurted out Sarah in horror.

But before she could say another word Niall nudged her aside and took control of the situation.

'Helen? Niall here. I overheard most of that and I'm very sorry about poor old Gran. Of course you must come and stay with us. And Grandfather too, if he wants to.'

There was a crackle of sound along the line and Sarah heard her mother's voice, faint and rather tinny, but quite distinct.

'Bless you, Niall, but my father won't be coming. He's diabetic, you know, and not up to coping with the journey. They're taking Gran to St Thomas's Hospital, so I'll call you the minute there's any news. Thank you so much for this. It's wonderful to have someone to count on in a crisis. I must fly now. Oh, but ask Sarah what she wanted to tell me, will you?'

Niall's dark eyebrows met in a frown and he held the receiver out to Sarah.

'Did you want to tell her something, Sarah?' he asked evenly.

Sarah bit her lip. 'It's not important, Mum,' she

gabbled. 'Just. . .love to you and Gran. And we'll see you soon.'

As she hung up, she gave Niall a defiant look. 'Well, I couldn't tell her now,' she muttered. 'Could I?'

'No, you couldn't,' agreed Niall. 'You did the right thing.'

Sarah let out a shaky sigh.

'Poor Gran!' she exclaimed. 'She's never been ill before, you know, and she'll absolutely hate it. She's always been so active. Oh, I hope it's not really serious!'

'Now look,' said Niall firmly, seizing her by the shoulders. 'You won't do her any good by worrying yourself into a state about it. What you need is something to keep you occupied. So why don't you get some sheets out of the linen cupboard, go upstairs and make your mother a bed in the spare room? At least that way you'll feel as if you're doing something useful.'

Sarah made a face.

'Look, this is ridiculous!' she exclaimed. 'Have you thought it through, Niall? If my mother stays here, she'll be expecting me to share a room with you again.'

'True,' agreed Niall serenly.

'Well, I won't!' cried Sarah. 'I'll never, ever share a bed with you again, so don't think it!'

'Never is a long time, Sarah,' Niall reminded her. 'But it's not important where I sleep. What's important is that we should put your mother's needs first and make her as comfortable as she can be at such a time. Right?'

Sarah's lips twisted wryly. Coming from anyone else,

she would have thought it a sensitive, tactful comment. But from Niall Morgan, the past master of deceit, it only made her deeply suspicious.

'I suppose so,' she said grudgingly.

'All right, then,' replied Niall, opening the wooden door of a recessed cupboard. 'Take these sheets and get to work. I'm going to be busy in my study for the next couple of hours on projects for the festival, but you can interrupt me if there's anything really urgent. And I'll be cooking dinner about seven, by the way.'

Finding herself casually but firmly dismissed, Sarah made her way up the stairs with an armful of lavender-scented linen. The spare room was a pleasant spot overlooking the river and she did her best to make it comfortable for her mother. Once the bed was made up, she went down to the garden and cut some sweet peas to put in a vase. Then she laid out clean towels, a box of tissues, a carafe of water and a couple of thick paperback family sagas. After that, unable to think of anything further to do, she sank into a chair by the window, and stared out at the water.

'I wonder if I'm going crazy,' she murmured to a seagull that was soaring effortlessly overhead. 'I've never had such a weird weekend in my life before.'

Her brain seemed to be seething with confused thoughts and emotions. Uppermost was her worry about her grandmother, but she could not help brooding about her present predicament with Niall. At any other time, she would have been glad to have her mother stay for a visit. They were very fond of each other and family loyalty among the Marlowes and McKenzies had always been strong. But there was no denying that Sarah and her mother were very different people. Where Sarah had always been adventurous, impulsive and free-thinking, Helen Marlowe was deeply conservative. Letting Niall and Sarah share a room had been a dramatic gesture of trust and liberalism on her part. If she ever found out that Sarah had met Niall only the day before and that the entire engagement was a hoax, all hell would break loose. Sarah shuddered at the thought. Her only chance was to keep up the pretence that she was in love with Niall, but how on earth could she bear it?

With a low groan, she tried to imagine how she would have to behave with Niall. Kisses on the cheek, lingering glances across the room, affectionate hand-holding would be bad enough. But if she had to share a bed with him again she would quite simply lose her mind. Her face grew warm at the thought of last night's fiasco. The worst of it was that, even though she didn't really trust Niall, he did seem to have an undeniable physical magnetism. In fact Sarah wondered bitterly whether any woman would be able to resist that husky baritone voice, those narrowed, silvery eyes, those sensual lips. And as for his body! He must have worked on a construction site or been a champion athlete to have such powerful, muscular shoulders, such a narrow waist, such amazing thighs. No woman could be crushed in the arms of a man like that and fail to feel an instinctive thrill at the experience.

Yet physical thrills were one thing and emotions were another matter entirely. After being so badly let down by Howard, Sarah had no intention of being hurt a second time. And everything she had seen of Niall Morgan made that danger seem very, very real. Hadn't he lied to her family with the utmost ease? Hadn't he manipulated her from the moment they first met? And was he likely to have the least scruple about seducing her? Of course not! She would have to be on guard at all times until her mother left and then she would have to leave pretty smartly herself. Oh, lord, what a mess it all was!

More to occupy herself than for any other reason, Sarah fetched a sketch-pad and some pencils from her bags and began to doodle idly. But before long she became interested in trying to capture the scene outside. She decided to treat it as if it were a stage backdrop and sketched in the Norfolk pines at the edge of the beach, using them as a frame for the panoramic sweep of the estuary and the rugged hills on the further shore. She was still working with total absorption when there was a knock at the door some time later.

'Come in,' she called.

Niall put his head around the door.

'Dinner,' he announced.

Sarah stretched and looked at her watch in disbelief.

'Seven twenty-five,' she said. 'Is it really that late? Oh, Niall, has there been any news about Gran?'

'No,' said Niall. 'And don't start looking so anxious. I'm sure your mother will phone you as soon as she can. Now come and eat.'

Sarah dropped her sketch-pad impatiently on the chair, from which it promptly slipped on to the floor. Niall picked it up and glanced at it. Then he gave a low whistle.

'This is very good work,' he said. 'Would you like me to arrange some interviews for you in the Sydney theatres? I have a lot of contacts there. It might help you get another job once the festival here is over.'

Sarah's mouth fell open.

'You mean go to Sydney and do set designing?' she asked.

'Yes, of course. You only stayed here to be with your ratbag boyfriend, didn't you? And, while the balloon business is enterprising and a lot of fun, it's not really your heart's desire, is it?'

Sarah was still staring at him in shock.

'I don't really know what my heart's desire is,' she admitted.

'Well, get a job in Sydney and maybe you'll find out. Let's see. . .Andy Lester could probably help you, or Graham Canning. I'll ring up tomorrow and see what's available.'

'I can't believe the speed you operate at,' complained Sarah as she followed Niall down the stairs. 'Do you always have to take action the moment you've thought of something?'

'Yes,' said Niall simply. 'It's the only way to get things done. Now I thought we'd eat on the back patio. Does that suit you?'

Sitting at a lavishly set table surrounded by a beautiful garden, Sarah found it hard to remember how much she distrusted Niall. An apple-green twilight was still lingering above the hill-tops and, although the sun had set, the brick paving still gave off a comforting warmth. The waves swished softly on the beach and a strong scent of honeysuckle and Mexican orange blossom drifted on the air.

'Isn't this nice?' said Sarah dreamily.

'Yes, it is,' agreed Niall. 'But wait until you see my

place in Vaucluse in Sydney. I bet you'll like that even more.'

That simple statement threw Sarah into a fresh flurry of misgivings. Was it just an idle remark or did Niall really expect to keep seeing her if she took a job in Sydney? And, if so, why? She picked up a glass of chilled Riesling and took a hasty gulp.

'This looks interesting,' she said, gazing at the colourful dishes on the table. 'What is it?'

'Spring rolls with minced pork filling. Steamed rice, shredded beef with ginger and baby corn, fresh prawns with mangetout peas and some scrambled eggs with ham and shallots.'

'Oh,' muttered Sarah, more impressed than she cared to admit. 'Are you fond of cooking?'

'Yes,' said Niall. 'Are you?'

'No,' admitted Sarah candidly. 'But I'm fond of eating.'

Niall chuckled.

'Then show me your talents,' he urged, handing her an empty rice bowl and a large serving spoon.

It was a delicious meal and, without the constraint of her family's presence, Sarah found it hard to resist Niall's effortless charm. He told her about Hong Kong, where he had spent three years, and she listened in fascination to his stories of travel in other parts of South East Asia. They were halfway through their pudding of strawberries and cream when the mobile phone rang. Sarah turned white and Niall reached out and squeezed her hand. Then he passed the phone to her.

'Hello. Niall Morgan's residence. This is Sarah Marlowe speaking.'

'Sarah. It's me. I just phoned to tell you we're at the hospital and Gran's gone into Theatre.'

There was an unsteady note in her mother's voice that Sarah had never heard before.

'Are you all right, Mum?' she asked. 'Can I come and join you? Is there anything I can bring you?'

'No. Just come,' breathed her mother. 'Please.'

And she rang off.

'Come on,' urged Niall, getting to his feet. 'Let's get moving.'

Sarah caught him up inside the kitchen.

'Are you coming too?' she asked in surprise.

'Of course. Bring that package off the bench. I thought your mother might appreciate a few sandwiches. And there's a Thermos of hot coffee too.'

When they reached the hospital it was clear that Helen Marlowe was near breaking-point. Sarah couldn't remember when she had last seen her mother cry, but she was sitting on a blue plush seat, dabbing furtively at her eyes when they entered the waiting-room.

'I'm so sorry,' Helen whispered. 'This is silly of me. A woman of forty-nine. But somehow, however old you are, you never think that your own parents might. . . might——'

It was Niall who sat down beside her and took her into his powerful embrace. Niall who made her drink the coffee and eat the sandwiches. Niall who kept her going until the good news came through—that the operation was safely over and Gran was doing well.

As they all reached home and Niall helped her mother out of the car and up to the front door, Sarah watched his face covertly in the moonlight. She could see nothing there but a genuine compassion and warmth. Was it possible that she had been wrong about Niall Morgan? And would she ever find out what his real nature was?

CHAPTER FOUR

'RISE and shine. We've got work to do!'

Sarah groaned her way up from the depths of sleep towards the reviving aroma of hot coffee. Yawning and blinking, she saw that Niall was holding a cup of steaming cappuccino just out of her reach. She also saw that the clock on the bedroom mantelpiece said 6.03 a.m.

'Three minutes past six,' she moaned in outrage, sinking back under the covers. 'I never get up that early.'

'You do now you're working for me,' retorted Niall. 'Come on. You've got five seconds to wake up properly or I'm drinking this cappuccino!'

'M-r-r-o-w,' grumbled Sarah, salvaging a couple of pillows from the floor and flopping back on them. 'All right, then.'

Niall grinned unsympathetically.

'You sound like a bad-tempered kitten,' he said, handing her the cup. 'But we do have a lot to do, so drink up and let's get moving.'

He sat down on the end of the bed and watched her for a moment with a thoughtful scowl. In his white towelling dressing-gown, he looked almost indecently virile. Sarah caught a hasty glimpse of muscular, tanned thighs and dark hair on a broad chest and then looked determinedly away. She had not been forced to share a bed with him as she had feared, for Niall had slept in the sunroom adjoining the main bedroom. But throughout a night of broken sleep she had been painfully conscious of his steady breathing only a few metres away. And now to have him sitting here sent the most shameful images rioting through her mind. Flushing uncomfortably, she stared at the froth on her coffee with earnest concentration.

'Can you ride a horse?' asked Niall abruptly.

It was so unexpected that Sarah choked on her coffee.

'Yes, but wh——?'

'Can you sing?'

'No.'

'Pity,' muttered Niall, pulling a notebook out of his dressing-gown pocket and jotting a couple of hasty scrawls in it. 'I need one more pioneering woman for the street pageant. But she has to be able to ride a horse and sing colonial ballads. And there are a few other skills that would be useful. Spinning, weaving, dancing Scottish reels, making butter by hand.'

'Are you sure you wouldn't like her to do a bit of brain surgery on the side?' asked Sarah tartly.

'Now there's a thought,' agreed Niall, his eyes glinting with amusement. 'Still, even if you don't have the skills of your forebears, I'm sure I can find plenty to occupy you. Come on, woman! Haven't you finished that coffee yet?'

Ten minutes later, after a breathless scramble to shower and get dressed, Sarah came downstairs in a jade-green skirt and blouse. She found her mother already up and looking immaculate, loading the dishwasher with the rice bowls and platters from the previous evening's Chinese meal.

'You don't have to do that, Mum,' said Sarah with a guilty expression. 'I would have done it after work tonight.'

Mrs Marlowe raised her eyebrows.

'Yes, I suppose you would!' she agreed despairingly. 'But I thought the least I could do was to leave the place tidy before I catch my bus this morning.'

'What? You're not leaving already, are you?' demanded Niall's deep voice from the doorway.

They both swung round to look at him. As usual, he was conservatively dressed and Sarah had never thought she liked men of that sort. But somehow, even in his superbly cut dark blue suit with a white shirt and Paisley tie, Niall had a quality of wildness about him that made him look like a pirate in disguise. His rugged features and fierce black eyebrows were at odds with his elegant clothes and the contrast was mysteriously alluring. As he leaned negligently against the architrave, Sarah felt a faint weakness in her knees at the sight of him. Her mother was more down-to-earth about it.

'You do look handsome, Niall,' said Helen. 'Goodness, I can't tell you what a relief it was when I first met you! I was so afraid Sarah was going to bring home some dreadful creature with his hair dyed purple and an earring in one ear.'

Niall's lips twitched.

'Yes, well, Sarah didn't have much taste in men until she met me, did she?' he agreed provocatively. 'But never mind that now. What were you saying when I came in? You surely can't be planning to leave us already?'

'Oh, I can't possibly keep imposing on you any longer,' said Helen.

'Rubbish!' growled Niall. 'We're delighted to have you, aren't we, Sarah?'

Sarah's mouth opened and closed silently like a goldfish's. If circumstances had been different, she would have agreed at once. As it was, she couldn't help feeling that it would be rather convenient if her mother went straight home.

'There! That's settled,' said Niall with satisfaction. 'Of course you must stay at least until Gran gets out of hospital. I'll order a hire car for you to spin around in and I'll get you festival tickets for the events next week. The break will do you good.'

It gave Sarah some satisfaction to see her outspoken mother dazzled into hypnotic submission by Niall just as easily as she herself had been. But not much. When they were alone together in the Mercedes a few minutes later, she tackled him about it.

'What on earth did you do that for?' she demanded crossly. 'Mum was all ready to catch the bus home.'

'I know,' said Niall. 'But it would have been heartless to let her. And you don't like me to be heartless, do you?'

Sarah clenched her fists in silent fury. Taking a deep breath, she counted up to ten.

'Don't you see,' she seethed, 'that now you've invited her to stay we'll have to keep up this ridiculous pretence of an engagement?'

Niall's eyes glinted with amusement.

'There is that,' he admitted.

'I won't do it!' stormed Sarah, folding her arms and setting her jaw. 'I don't know what kind of game you're playing, but I know you're up to something. And I won't be part of it. I won't!'

'Won't you?' drawled Niall lazily. 'But think how upset your mother will be if you tell her the truth right now. Not to mention your Gran. Some people would call that downright heartless.'

Sarah sucked in her breath. 'You——' she began.

'Language, language,' Niall reminded her.

For thirty seconds Sarah sounded like a lifesaver struggling to revive a drowned victim. Then at last she found her voice.

'One of these days I'm going to pay you back for all this,' she vowed.

'Is that a promise?' asked Niall, raising his eyebrows.

Sarah groaned. At least they would soon be at the festival office and, once they were in a normal working environment, Niall would have to behave like a rational human being instead of a bulldozer. Wouldn't he? But she was scarcely in the building for five minutes before that illusion was ruthlessly dispelled.

The festival office was on the fourth floor of one of the buildings directly overlooking the harbour. Niall was too impatient to wait for the lift and bounded up the stairs with his usual energy, so that Sarah arrived breathless and panting, ten paces behind him. He was already deep in conversation with a grey-haired woman behind a computer desk when Sarah staggered in. With obvious reluctance, he broke off his conversation to introduce them.

'Wendy—Sarah. Sarah—Wendy. Wendy's my secretary and I've hired Sarah as my personal assistant. She's doing a balloon release for the opening ceremony and any other artistic things that crop up. Is that clear? Good.'

And he vanished into his office with a brisk slam of the door. Sarah stared after him in horror.

'But where am I to work? What am I to do? How do I begin?' she wailed.

Wendy hid a smile.

'Don't worry,' she said, rising to her feet and laying a comforting hand on Sarah's shoulder. 'I felt exactly the same way on my first day, but it's amazing how quickly you get used to Niall's working methods. He's an extraordinary man, so dynamic and full of ideas, but he never explains what he's up to. You just have to tag along as best you can. Look, have a cup of coffee and a pastry and I'll show you next week's programme and what things we need help with.'

Sarah was halfway through her coffee when Niall emerged from his office. He pointed his finger at her.

'I'd like you to get me a whale,' he said.

'A. . .w-whale?' echoed Sarah on a rising note. 'What kind of a whale?'

'A big one,' replied Niall firmly.

Horrified visions flitted through her head of harpoons, fishing boats, turbulent seas and huge beasts blowing jets of water into the air.

'Th-they're protected now, aren't they?' she stammered.

'Oh, not a real one!' retorted Niall impatiently. 'Papier mâché or something. I'll leave it up to you. But I want it for the parade next Sunday.'

And he vanished back into his office. Sarah sat stunned for a moment and then reached for the telephone directory. The rest of the day passed in the same astonishing fashion. She had never been so busy in her life and yet, when the first shock dissipated, she realised she had never had so much fun either. It was seven o'clock before they left the office, but Sarah was riding high on a wave of exhilaration, bubbling over with new plans and feeling as if Niall's energy and drive were somehow contagious. After they had eaten dinner they drove to the hospital to visit Gran. Somehow it gave Sarah an uncomfortable, fluttery feeling in the pit of her stomach to learn that the beautiful roses in the ward had all been sent by Niall.

And that wasn't the only thing that made her feel uncomfortable in the days that followed. For Sarah soon found that it was impossible to share a man's house and wear his ring without wondering what it would really be like to be married to him. Particularly when her mother was breathing down her neck, chatting about bridesmaids' frocks and wedding marches at every opportunity. Yet what made Sarah more uncomfortable than anything else was the slow and horrified realisation that she was falling in love with Niall.

She was never sure exactly when it happened. Perhaps it was a result of working for him and seeing how he bulldozed everybody with complete impartiality. Somehow that made her feel better about giving in over the engagement hoax. After all, Niall obviously hadn't seen Sarah as unusually gullible and weakwilled. It was simply that he had thought the scheme a good idea. And once Niall Morgan thought something was a good idea the rest of the human race had better agree immediately. Or else. Yet, in the roller-coaster excitement of organising pageants and sausage sizzles and kayak races and poetry readings and fun runs and Morris dances, Sarah soon realised that Niall wasn't only a man with good ideas. He was also amusing, compassionate, provocative and as intoxicating as vintage champagne. With a wry sense of disbelief, Sarah found herself dreading the moment when they would have to part.

Two weeks after the accident, Sarah's grandmother was pronounced fit to travel home in an ambulance and Sarah's mother also prepared to leave. As Niall set down her suitcase in the bus depot, Helen embraced him warmly.

'Thank you for everything, Niall,' she said. 'You've been absolutely wonderful.'

'Don't be absurd,' replied Niall. 'We've loved having you. And what are families for anyway?'

Sarah flinched. However long it went on she could never feel comfortable with this deception. But her mother was speaking again, and what she said made Sarah go chill with horror.

'Well, I won't forget how generous you've been, Niall,' insisted Helen. 'And I hope you'll come up for a nice long stay at Christmas with Sarah.'

'I'd love to,' agreed Niall smoothly. 'Thank you very much.'

Sarah didn't have time to send any frantic Morse Code signals before her mother turned and kissed her too.

'Goodbye, dear,' she said. 'Do try and keep that kitchen a little tidier, won't you?'

But once they were outside, climbing into the car, Sarah raised the subject immediately.

'Why did you say that about Christmas-time?' she demanded furiously.

Niall smiled his lazy, mocking smile.

'I thought it was a good idea,' he replied. 'The festival will be over by then and we'll both need a bit of relaxation.'

'But you. . .but I. . .but they. . . Oh, help, what's the use? Look, Niall, don't you think it would be best if we call off the whole deception now? I can phone my mother when she gets home and tell her we've had a row or something. And I'll move out of your house and look for a flat.'

To her annoyance Sarah heard her voice wobble unsteadily as she said this. But she clamped her lips firmly together and shot a desperate glance at Niall. He frowned disapprovingly.

'No, I don't like the sound of that,' he said. 'I think you should stay.'

'Stay?' faltered Sarah. 'On what basis?'

'On the same basis as now,' replied Niall. 'You keep working for me and we keep sharing the house. It's simple.'

'Oh, is it?' retorted Sarah wrathfully, holding up her ring finger. 'And what about this? Is this simple too?'

'Yes, of course,' said Niall in surprise. 'Keep wearing it. It suits you.'

'But Niall, I don't underst——'

'Sarah, do you know anyone who owns a Swiss Alphorn that we could borrow?'

As she undressed for bed that night, Sarah wondered despairingly whether she had simply lost her sanity without even realising it. No woman in her right mind would stay in such an impossible situation, would she?

All her pleas to Niall to explain why he wanted their false engagement to continue had fallen on deaf ears. So why was she still in his house, doing exactly what he wanted? Because I love him, she thought miserably, brushing her long ginger curls until they crackled. He may be high-handed and infuriating, but he's the most magical, extraordinary man I've ever met in my life. And I can't bear to see it end.

Well, at least he hasn't tried to seduce me, she admitted as she climbed into bed. Yet somehow that thought did not bring her the comfort it ought to have done. With her mother's departure Niall had moved out of the dressing-room into one of the other bedrooms. Absurdly Sarah found herself wondering if he too was getting into bed at this moment. A vivid picture of his lean, muscular body and brooding grey eyes flashed into her mind and she had to swallow hard, turn on her side and think feverishly of Swiss Alphorns to make it vanish. But as she lay in the darkness she made a silent vow. Somehow she must find out what Niall really felt towards her.

In the next couple of weeks, she sometimes thought she had worked it out. There were moments when Niall's guard was down and the mockery vanished from his grey eyes. Moments when she was kneeling by the CD player at home or rummaging in a filing cabinet at work and glanced up suddenly. And each time she surprised a look of urgent, hungry longing in his face which disturbed her deeply. She felt her pulses racing and her breath coming in shallow flutters. More than once she moved towards him wistfully only to find herself rebuffed. He would ask her opinion about balloons for the gala ball or demand that some weird and impossible object be produced immediately. A giant apple pie twenty feet across or an antique stump-jump plough in full working order. Sarah felt certain that he was attracted to her, but had the unhappy feeling that he was deliberately fending her off. And she could not imagine why until the day Katherine Benson came into the festival office.

Mrs Benson was a small blonde woman with delicate features and a look of rather fragile grace. Wendy the secretary had been called away to investigate a faulty photocopier and Sarah was typing rather inexpertly at the computer when the newcomer arrived.

'Hello,' she said with a hesitant smile. 'My name's Katherine Benson. May I speak to Niall Morgan, please?'

Niall had been definite in his instructions. No phone calls, no visitors, no interruptions even if the building was on fire.

'I'm sorry,' replied Sarah. 'Mr Morgan is very busy at the moment. Can I help you in any way? Or may I take a message?'

'No, that won't do,' insisted Katherine, gripping her handbag tightly. 'I must see him. I know he'll see me. Please ask him.'

There was something about the urgency in the other woman's voice that overrode Sarah's reluctance. Picking up the phone, she buzzed Niall.

'Niall, I'm sorry to disturb you, but there's a. . .' she paused and saw a wedding-ring on the woman's hand '. . .a Mrs Katherine Benson here, asking to see you. Can you——?'

'Show her in at once, Sarah,' said Niall.

He appeared in the doorway of his office a moment later with a look of tense expectancy on his face.

'Well?' he asked.

Katherine gave a muffled gulp, half-laugh, half-sob, and flew into his arms.

'Oh, Niall. Oh, Niall! I'm so glad you were here!' she gasped.

As Sarah watched in fascinated horror, Niall crushed the other woman in his arms and held her tightly against him. She had never seen such intense emotion in his face before. For a long moment, he stood with his cheek pressed against the top of Katherine's head. Then he pushed her away with a deep, indrawn breath.

'Is everything all right, then?' he asked.

'Better than all right. It's wonderful!' replied Katherine, and burst into tears.

Niall put his arms around her and drew her inside.

'No calls, please, Sarah,' he said over his shoulder as he shut the door.

Sarah sat staring at the computer in baffled rage. What on earth was going on between that pair? Well, it didn't take much imagination to guess, she thought, twisting her lips bitterly. Anyone would have to be blind not to recognise the depth of feeling on Niall's face as he looked down at Katherine. A dull ache of misery and disbelief flooded through Sarah's entire body, but she struggled hard to be fair. There could be any number of reasons for Niall's behaviour, such as. . .such as. . .

She was still staring blindly at the computer terminal when the pair emerged ten minutes later. Niall's arm was wrapped firmly around Katherine's waist and her head was nestled into his shoulder.

'Shall I come and see you on Thursday next week, then?' asked Niall.

'Yes, do!' urged Katherine. 'Charles may come home early, but it's not likely. Anyway, we never let that stop us on Kiribati, did we?'

'No, we did not!' agreed Niall with a chuckle. 'When I think of the games we had. . . All right, Thursday it is.'

Katherine stood on tiptoe and kissed him warmly on the cheek.

'Take care,' she said with a catch in her voice.

'You too, sweetheart,' agreed Niall, keeping her hand in a lingering grip until she drew away.

Sarah could cheerfully have shot both of them. And she was still fuming when Niall drove her home at six o'clock that evening.

'What would you like for dinner?' he asked, as they came into the kitchen.

'Nothing,' said Sarah through her teeth.

'What's wrong? Would you rather go to a restaurant?'

'No, I would not rather go to a restaurant. Why don't you invite Katherine?'

'Katherine?' echoed Niall slowly. Then a look of dawning comprehension lit his face. 'I do believe you're jealous.'

'Don't flatter yourself!' snapped Sarah.

Niall advanced on her with an intent look in his grey eyes. Then he caught her by the wrist.

'There is nothing between Katherine Benson and me that need cause you a moment's worry,' he assured her.

'Worry?' sniffed Sarah. 'Why should I worry, whatever is between you?'

For once Niall did not change the subject or make a joke out of it. His rugged features were set in harsh, brooding lines. And, when he spoke, the words seemed to be forced out of him against his will.

'Perhaps because you're fallen for me just as badly as I've fallen for you?' he suggested hoarsely.

Sarah's heart gave a wild skip of disbelief. She could feel Niall's hand clenched around her wrist, warm and hard and powerful, could smell the spicy aroma of his cologne and see a pulse leaping spasmodically in his throat. But she could not believe what she was hearing.

'And what's that supposed to mean?' she demanded sharply.

He crushed her against him and caressed her cheeks with swift, sensual movements of his thumbs. A tremor of involuntary excitement went through her and Niall reacted at once. His arms came around her, trapping her against him so that her senses swam. She could feel the heat of arousal pulsing through him, the urgent, primitive need building inside him. Even the air between them seemed to throb with silent, unbearable tension.

'You know perfectly well what it means,' rasped Niall. 'It means that I've loved you from the first moment I saw you.'

Sarah swallowed convulsively.

'That's ridiculous!' she croaked.

'Is it?' he countered. 'Any more ridiculous than the way you've felt about me? I'm not blind, Sarah. I've seen the struggle you've had trying to deny that you wanted me, needed me, cared about me, just as I did about you. Maybe it would have been better if you'd had more time to get over that worthless young fool you were involved with before, but life doesn't always work like that. Love doesn't work like that. And I love you, Sarah. Believe me.'

Sarah took a long, unsteady breath and her eyes stung with tears.

'Don't say it if you don't mean it, Niall,' she choked. 'Please. I can bear anything else. But not that.'

'I do mean it,' growled Niall, dragging her recklessly against him. 'I intended to give you more time, Sarah, but I need you. I need you so badly. Will you trust yourself to me?'

His warm breath was fanning her ear, she could feel the rasp of his jaw against her cheek and a shudder of molten yearning went through her. He began to kiss her—small, unsatisfactory kisses that made her tremble with longing.

'Will you?' he whispered.

Another shudder went through her.

'Yes,' she breathed.

The room whirled around as he lifted her. She saw the walls of the kitchen flash by, then Niall was taking the stairs two at a time in his eagerness. When he set her down in the middle of the vast bed, she felt that her heart was beating even more violently than his. Reaching out, she touched his thick, dark hair and traced a line down his cheek to his jaw. A wave of emotion swept through her at the realisation of all she felt for him and she opened her mouth to try and say it. Her lips parted, but somehow the words remained caught in her throat. All she could do was look into his eyes and hope that he understood.

'Oh, Sarah, don't,' he begged hoarsely, catching her hand and kissing it. 'You look so innocent, so vulnerable. We don't have to do this yet if you're not ready.'

Sarah found her voice.

'I'm ready,' she said with pride. 'I'm a grown woman, Niall, and I want you just as much as you want me. More.'

And, leaning forward, she kissed him with lingering urgency on his open mouth.

'You little siren,' growled Niall, and sprang at her.

Sarah found herself pinioned on the bed with Niall astride her, trapping her wrists.

'Two can play at that game, sweetheart,' he said in a low, smoky voice.

Then he proceeded to show her how. Stretching out at full length, so that he crushed her soft curves beneath him, he began to kiss her with a ruthlessness that enthralled her. His mouth was warm and insistent and he knew every imaginable way of provoking her. At first he brushed her cheeks and lips and throat with small, tantalising kisses that teased and withdrew, leaving her increasingly frustrated. Trapped beneath his warm, hard body with her wrists imprisoned on the pillow above her, she could do nothing to ease the torment. But as her frustration increased Niall changed the rhythm of his kisses. They became deeper, longer, more demanding, until at last the two of them were strained together, breathing in long, disjointed gulps, thrusting deeper and deeper into each other's mouths until at last a complete firestorm of need overtook them.

Leaping to his feet, Niall tore off his clothes with wild abandon, flinging the correct, executive garb into every corner of the room. Sarah had never seen anything so magnificent as his proud, virile body as he stood stark naked, outlined against the light from the window. Then he prowled across to the bed, straddled her with his legs and insolently proceeded to undress her. Her whole body throbbed with a heated languor as he methodically unbuttoned her smart, tailored blouse and drew her upright so he could slip it off her. His lips moved in scorching trails across her shoulders, rousing her to a new dimension of excitement. When he met the obstruction of her bra, he unfastened it impatiently and threw it aside.

'You have the most beautiful breasts I could ever imagine,' he murmured. 'Let me kiss them.'

A tingling shaft of warmth shot through Sarah's body at the touch of Niall's warm mouth on her sensitive flesh. Arching her back and whimpering, she felt herself spin wildly out of control as he kept up his relentless, sensual exploration of her body. Only when she began to quiver and gasp did he pause and give her an odd, feral smile.

'You've had some pleasure, my darling,' he said hoarsely. 'But you'll have more, much more, before we've finished. I promise you.'

And, with that, he unzipped her skirt and feverishly pulled off every garment that she was wearing. When she lay naked beneath him, he gazed down at her with an intent, almost reverent look in his gleaming grey eyes.

'You're beautiful, Sarah,' he breathed. 'So beautiful. And I'm going to kiss every inch of you.'

Time lost all meaning as his merciless, expert hands and mouth drove her to a level of frenzy she had never guessed at. Yet amid all that pulsating, violent passion one thing remained clear and sharp in her mind—that she loved Niall Morgan. Loved him with her entire heart and soul. And when at last his urgent, virile need could wait no longer she welcomed him into her with a low gasp of delight and clung to him, whispering his name over and over. Never in her wildest dreams had Sarah imagined that love could bring such deep, intoxicating fulfilment. But as Niall thrust fiercely into her a strange, fluttering intensity began to grow and build inside her, sensation piling on sensation, till suddenly she took flight and soared over an invisible edge.

'Oh, Niall. Oh, Niall!' she gasped. 'I love you!'

She felt rather than heard the low sound he made in his throat. Felt too the sudden clenching of his arms around her and the shudder that shook him. His face was buried in her hair, his lips were on her throat.

'Sarah,' he whispered. Then he collapsed limply against her.

For a long time there was no sound but their harsh, uneven breathing. They lay slick with sweat and hopelessly entangled in the bedclothes but still strained in each other's arms. Sarah felt as if she were ready to die with happiness, but at last a numb, tingly feeling in her upper arm roused her to action. She giggled ruefully.

'Can you move, please? My arm's gone to sleep.'

With a protesting groan he rolled off her and then lay staring into her eyes.

'I love you,' he said firmly and leaned forward to kiss her.

'I love you too,' breathed Sarah joyfully.

'Your eyes are like stars,' he told her.

'And my arm is like pins and needles,' she retorted, making a face. 'Move so I can rub it, will you?'

'Shall I massage it for you?' he offered.

'Mmm. Yes. No! Ow, that tickles! Stop it, you beast, you're doing it on purpose!'

They both lay back, weak with laughter, and Niall drew her into his arms and rested his chin on her head.

'So, will you let me come home for Christmas?' he asked.

She hesitated briefly. Niall hadn't yet said anything about making their engagement a real one, but she didn't want to spoil this magical moment by nagging him. Anyway, she trusted him. Wasn't that good enough?

'Yes,' she agreed lazily.

'And are you still coming to the festival banquet and ball with me tomorrow night?'

'I wouldn't miss it for the world,' she assured him.

Snuggling dreamily into his arms, Sarah closed her eyes and let out a long sigh of pure bliss. Never in her entire life had she felt so happy before. For the first time all the conflicts that had troubled her seemed to be resolved. Niall might be unpredictable and infuriating at times, but she loved him with an intensity that overwhelmed her. Somehow he seemed to combine all the diverse qualities which she needed so badly. Along with passion, flamboyance and an exhilarating sense of fun, he had all the virtues her family admired: reliability, commitment, old-fashioned values. Things which Sarah had never appreciated until Howard let her down so badly.

'Are you happy?' asked Niall, kissing her closed eyelids.

Opening her eyes, she looked at him earnestly.

'I've never been so happy in my life,' she assured him.

The feeling of floating on air lasted until an hour before the ball was due to begin the following night. Sarah was in the ballroom of the big hotel on the waterfront, still frantically decorating the tables when a waiter approached her with a mobile phone.

'Telephone call for you, Miss Marlowe,' he said.

Sarah finished tying off a clear plastic balloon encasing three smaller coloured balloons, fastened it to a chair to prevent it from floating away and took the phone.

'Hello. Sarah? Niall here. Listen, sweetheart, I'm afraid there's a change of plans about the ball tonight. Something urgent's come up and I can't partner you. I've arranged for you to be with Wendy's party instead. Got it? Good. See you later.'

And he rang off before Sarah could even protest. How typical! thought Sarah in exasperation. I suppose he's got to fly off to Sydney on urgent business or something. Damn, damn, damn! Well, I've bought a new dress for this ball and I'm not sitting at home like Cinderella. I will go with Wendy's party.

The house was empty when she dashed home to get dressed fifteen minutes later, which strengthened her suspicion that Niall had shot off to the airport. So it came as a very unpleasant surprise when she arrived at the hotel shortly after eight o'clock to find him in the receiving line shaking hands with the guests, as if nothing had happened. But worse was to come. When everyone finally moved away to sit down, she saw that Niall was not alone at the official table. His partner was Katherine Benson.

Shaken to the core, Sarah tried to think of some good reason why Niall should have broken his date

with her in order to take Katherine to the ball, but
nothing occurred to her. And as the evening wore on she
grew steadily more miserable. She scarcely tasted her
smoked ham and honeydew melon or the soup or lobster mornay. Even when the raspberry parfait arrived,
she pushed away the tall glass after a couple of spoon-
fuls. It was impossible to concentrate on food when
Niall was leaning so attentively towards Katherine
Benson, making her laugh and pouring her wine. And
when Katherine gazed up at him with that radiant,
luminous look of joy on her face it was downright
unbearable. Not even Sarah with all her optimism
could pretend that this was just a business relationship.

She did not even wait for the dancing to begin, but
at the first possible moment when the banquet was over
she made her farewells and slipped away. Somehow
she kept her grief under control all the way home in
the taxi, but once she inserted her key into the front
door lock it was as if a dam had burst. Dropping her
evening bag and jacket on the hall carpet, she gave a
low, choking wail and rushed upstairs. She was still
kneeling on the floor in the main bedroom, weeping
and packing, when Niall arrived home nearly two hours
later.

'Sarah!' he exclaimed in consternation. 'What on
earth's wrong?'

She caught her breath on a convulsive sob and
scrubbed her eyes with an old T-shirt.

'If you don't know the answer to that, you're a
complete fool or a complete brute!' she gasped. 'Either
way, I hate you and I'm leaving!'

Niall heaved a long, exasperated sigh and sat down
on the bed.

'Don't be ridiculous!' he retorted.

'Don't you call me ridiculous, you low-down, two-timing, self-satisfied, manipulative swine!' cried Sarah.

'What is this all about?' demanded Niall.

'Why don't you ask Katherine?' raged Sarah. 'Maybe she can tell you!'

'I see,' said Niall curtly. 'You're a fool, Sarah. I would have thought better of your intelligence. And, in any case, I rang you up this evening and explained all that.'

'No, you didn't!' shouted Sarah in outrage. 'You explained nothing, absolutely nothing! As always. And I'm just supposed to trail along in the dark like the loyal camp follower, accepting everything you do without question. Well, I'm sick of it, do you hear me? Sick of it! I'm leaving.'

'No, you're not,' growled Niall.

'Oh, yes, I am! Now kindly move away from that suitcase.'

The open suitcase was on the bed, right next to Niall. Sarah ran to shut it, but found her wrists caught and held. There was an undignified tussle then Niall rose to his feet, holding her prisoner.

'You're not going anywhere, darling,' he said grimly. 'Except to bed. It's the middle of the night, you're overwrought and exhausted and I won't have you running out into the night like a prima donna. You'll stay here where you belong.'

His grip on her wrists was not actually hurting, but she was acutely conscious of the enormous power that he held in reserve. And even at that moment his closeness and warmth made her feel an unwilling shaft of desire. She stood swaying and panting, hating him. Hating herself.

'You can't make me!' she cried defiantly.

'Oh, yes, I can,' retorted Niall in a smouldering voice. 'Believe me.'

A reluctant tingle of excitement leapt through her body. He looked so stern in his black dinner-suit and white shirt with his eyebrows drawn into a forbidding scowl. Stern and yet heart-stoppingly desirable.

'You and I have things to discuss, Sarah,' he said. 'But this is neither the time nor the place. I want you up an hour before dawn tomorrow, dressed and ready for action. Trousers and a sweater should do. There's somewhere I want to take you.'

'I won't go!' cried Sarah.

Niall smiled thinly.

'Yes, you will,' he insisted. 'You've got a contract that says you have to obey me. Just think of it as one more festival stunt, if that makes it any easier. Now I'll say goodnight.'

And, with that, he left the room. A moment later Sarah heard the door of the neighbouring bedroom slam. She gave a low wail of frustration. How could you even have a quarrel with a man who wouldn't stay long enough to hear what you thought of him?

Next morning it was still dark when Niall tapped softly at her door. She emerged slowly, giving him a resentful, suspicious look. But he was as bland as ever while they ate their breakfast of croissants and coffee.

'By the way, I don't like to see those red eyes, Sarah,' he remarked as he poured his second cup of coffee. 'They spoil your looks. Pass the sugar, will you?'

I'd pass the cyanide if I could! thought Sarah furiously. But she had decided that dignified silence was her best line of defence. She kept it up throughout the twenty-minute drive to Blackman's Bay and thought it was having an effect until Niall helped her out of the car at a football ground.

'Oh, do stop sulking, Sarah!' he urged cheerfully.

Sarah gasped.

'Where are we going?' she demanded.

'Into the middle of the oval.'

Hunching her shoulders, she stalked indignantly across the grass and stopped dead. In the centre of the field several men were blowing up a huge hot-air balloon. As she stood entranced, it suddenly filled out into a vast dome of red, white and blue nylon. Forgetting her hostility, she turned to Niall who was marching across the grass with a bottle of champagne under his arm.

'What's this all about?' she demanded.

'We're going up in the balloon. You're not afraid of heights, are you?'

A fluttery feeling of excitement and speculation bubbled up inside her.

'No,' she said wonderingly. 'But what's the champagne for?'

Niall looked mysterious.

'Oh, it's an old tradition dating back to the early French hot balloonists,' he replied. 'They used to carry it to placate the peasants whose fields they landed in. It often saved them from being run through with a pitchfork, you know.'

His voice held so much meaning that Sarah pouted.

'I don't have a pitchfork!' she said rather tartly.

Niall's lips twitched.

'All the same, I think we'll take it with us,' he murmured. 'Now, come on. Climb aboard.'

It was fascinating to watch what happened next. The ground crew had already carried out the pre-flight safety checks, so all that Niall had to do was check the lines, do an instrument check and make sure that all the ropes and people were free. Then he climbed back aboard the gondola with Sarah.

'Clear!' he called.

That moment of floating up into the air was indescribable. All around them the sky was gold and scarlet with the glory of sunrise and, as they rose higher, they could see the full panorama of the estuary like a sheet of glittering glass. Sarah breathed in the cool, heady morning air and felt a sense of total exhilaration flood through her. Some of her pain and anger ebbed away and she looked warily at Niall.

'What are we doing up here?' she asked. 'Is it really another festival stunt?'

Niall shook his head slowly.

'No,' he said. 'It's something else. But before we discuss that I think I owe you an explanation about Katherine.'

Sarah's mouth fell open.

'An explanation?' she echoed. 'From you?'

'Mmm. Just this once,' he agreed with a smile. Then his craggy features grew serious. 'You were right about one thing, Sarah. I do love Katherine.'

Sarah caught her breath in anguish and gripped the side of the wicker gondola. Then Niall's fingers closed over hers.

'But not the way you imagined,' he continued. 'The Bensons were my neighbours on Kiribati ten years ago. I was director of an aid project and Charles was a volunteer doctor. There wasn't much entertainment there and Katherine and I often played games of chess together. Later on Charles qualified as a surgeon in Sydney and then they moved to Hobart. Last year Katherine was diagnosed as having acute lymphoblastic leukaemia.'

'Leukaemia?' echoed Sarah in horror.

Niall nodded grimly.

'She's been through a year of hell,' he said. 'Chemotherapy, lumbar punctures, the works. To be honest, nobody expected her to survive. But on Friday she had her first test that showed no cancer cells. That's what she came into the office to tell me.'

'Oh, lord!' groaned Sarah. 'And I thought——'

'Yes, you did rather jump the gun,' agreed Niall. 'Anyway, I gave her tickets so that she and Charles could go to the ball to celebrate. But at the last moment Charles was called out to an emergency operation so I took Katherine instead.'

Sarah's eyes filled with tears.

'I'm so sorry,' she muttered. 'I feel ashamed of myself.'

Niall's arm came around her.

'So you should be,' he growled. 'How could I look at another woman when I decided I was going to marry you the very first time I met you?'

'W-what?' stammered Sarah. 'You couldn't have!'

'But I did,' insisted Niall. 'I loved you from the first moment I met you.'

'Well, why didn't you tell me?' wailed Sarah.

'You would have thought I was crazy,' said Niall.

'I thought you were crazy anyway!' she retorted.

There was a long silence as the balloon floated silently upwards and Sarah digested this new information.

'Then all those lies you told my family. . .' she said slowly.

'Weren't lies at all,' finished Niall. 'But I must admit that my first proposal on the beach wasn't a resounding success, so I decided to do it properly this time. Look, Sarah! Can you see something down there?'

Sarah leaned out of the basket and followed Niall's pointing finger down to the empty football field from which they had ascended. Except that it was no longer empty. Against the green background of the grass, scores of huge red helium balloons now spelt out a message.

'MARRY ME, SARAH.'

'Well?' demanded Niall impatiently.

She gaped.

'How on earth did you do that?' she demanded.

'A hundred and fifty Boy Scouts and a natural talent for organisation. Come on, what's your answer?'

'Oh, Niall! What can I say?'

He took her in his arms and kissed her with a passion that enthralled her. Then he nudged her and pointed to the ground again. As if in response to Sarah's question the Scouts had reformed and this time their message was even simpler.

'SAY YES.'

Sarah burst out laughing and hugged Niall tightly.
'Yes,' she said.

The Proposal

By

Betty Neels

Betty Neels spent her childhood and youth in Devonshire before training as a nurse and midwife. She was an Army Nursing Sister during the war, married a Dutchman, and subsequently lived in Holland for fourteen years. She lives with her husband in Dorset, and has a daughter and grandson. Her hobbies are reading, animals—she owns a matronly Moggy—old buildings and writing. Betty started to write on retirement from nursing, incited by a lady in a library bemoaning the lack of romantic novels.

CHAPTER ONE

THE hazy early morning sun of September had very little warmth as yet, but it turned the trees and shrubs of the park to a tawny gold, encouraging the birds to sing too, so that even in the heart of London there was an illusion of the countryside.

The Green Park was almost empty so early in the day; indeed the only person visible was a girl, walking a Yorkshire terrier on a long lead. She was a tall girl with a tawny mane of hair and vivid blue eyes set in a pretty face, rather shabbily dressed; although her clothes were well cut they were not in the height of fashion.

She glanced at her watch; she had walked rather further than usual so Lady Mortimor, although she wouldn't be out of bed herself, would be sure to enquire of her maid if the early morning walk with Bobo had taken the exact time allowed for it. She could have walked for hours. . . She was on the point of turning on her heel when something large, heavy and furry cannoned into her from the back and she sat down suddenly and in a most unladylike fashion in a tangle of large dog, a hysterical Bobo and Bobo's lead. The dog put an enormous paw on her chest and grinned happily down at her before licking her cheek gently and then turning his attention to Bobo; possibly out of friendliness he kept his paw on her chest, which made getting to her feet a bit of a problem.

A problem solved by the arrival of the dog's owner—
it had to be its owner, she decided. . .only a giant
could control a beast of such size and this man, from
her horizontal position, justified the thought; he was
indeed large, dressed in trousers and a pullover and,
even from upside-down, handsome. What was more,
he was smiling. . .

He heaved her to her feet with one hand and began
to dust her down. 'I do apologise,' he told her in a
deep, rather slow voice. 'Brontes has a liking for very
small dogs. . .'

The voice had been grave, but the smile tugging at
the corners of his thin mouth annoyed her. 'If you
aren't able to control your dog you should keep him on
a lead,' she told him tartly, and then in sudden fright,
'Where's Bobo? If he's lost, I'll never——'

'Keep calm,' begged the man in a soothing voice
which set her teeth on edge, and whistled. His dog
bounded out from the bushes near by and his master
said, 'Fetch,' without raising his voice and the animal
bounded off again to reappear again very shortly with
Bobo's lead between his teeth and Bobo trotting obe-
diently at the other end of it.

'Good dog,' said the man quietly. 'Well, we must be
on our way. You are quite sure you are not hurt?' He
added kindly, 'It is often hard to tell when one is angry
as well.'

'I am not angry, nor am I hurt. It was lucky for you
that I wasn't an elderly dowager with a Peke.'

'Extremely lucky. Miss. . .?' He smiled again, studying her still cross face from under heavy lids. 'Renier
Pitt-Colwyn.' He offered a hand and engulfed hers in a
firm grasp.

'Francesca Haley. I—I have to go.' Curiosity got the better of good sense. 'Your dog—that's a strange name?'

'He has one eye. . .'

'Oh, one of the Cyclopes. Goodbye.'

'Goodbye, Miss Haley.' He stood watching her walking away towards the Piccadilly entrance to the park. She didn't look back, and presently she broke into an easy run and, when Bobo's little legs could no longer keep up, scooped him into her arms and ran harder as far as the gate. Here she put him down and walked briskly across the road into Berkeley Street, turned into one of the elegant, narrow side-streets and went down the area steps of one of the fine houses. One of Lady Mortimor's strict rules was that she and Bobo should use the tradesmen's entrance when going for their thrice-daily outings. The magnificent entrance hall was not to be sullied by dirty paws, or for that matter Francesca's dirty shoes.

The door opened on to a dark passage with white-washed walls and a worn lino on the floor; it smelled of damp, raincoats, dog and a trace of cooked food, and after the freshness of the early morning air in the park it caused Francesca's nose to wrinkle. She opened one of the doors in the passage, hung up the lead, dried Bobo's paws and went through to the kitchen.

Lady Mortimor's breakfast tray was being prepared and her maid, Ethel, was standing by the table, squeezing orange juice. She was an angular woman with eyes set too close together in a mean face, and she glanced at the clock as Francesca went in, Bobo under one arm. Francesca, with a few minutes to spare, wished her good morning, adding cheerfully, 'Let Lady

Mortimor know that Bobo has had a good run, will you, Ethel? I'm going over for my breakfast; I'll be back as usual.' She put the little dog down and the woman nodded surlily. Bobo always went to his mistress's room with her breakfast tray and that meant that Francesca had almost an hour to herself before she would begin her duties as secretary-companion to that lady. A title which hardly fitted the manifold odd jobs which filled her day.

She went back out of the side-door and round to the back of the house, past the elegant little garden to the gate which led to the mews behind the terrace of houses. Over the garage she had her rooms, rather grandly called by Lady Mortimor a flat, where she and her young sister lived. The flat was the reason for her taking the job in the first place, and she was intent on keeping it, for it made a home for the pair of them and, although Lady Mortimor made it an excuse for paying her a very small salary, at least they had a roof over their heads.

Lucy was up and dressed and getting their breakfast. She was very like her sister, although her hair was carroty instead of tawny and her nose turned up. Later on, in a few years' time, she would be as pretty as Francesca, although at fourteen she anguished over her appearance, her ambition being to grow up as quickly as possible, marry a very rich man and live in great comfort with Francesca sharing her home. An arrangement, Francesca had pointed out, which might not suit her husband. 'I hate you working for that horrid old woman,' Lucy had said fiercely.

'Well, love,' Francesca had been matter-of-fact about it, 'it's a job and we have a home of sorts and you're being educated. Only a few more years and you will have finished school and embarked on a career which will astonish the world and I shall retire.'

Now she took off her cardigan and set about laying the table in the small sitting-room with its minute alcove which housed the cooking stove and the sink.

'I had an adventure,' she said to her sister, and over the boiled eggs told her about it.

'What kind of a dog?' Lucy wanted to know.

'Well, hard to tell—he looked like a very large St Bernard from the front, but he sort of tapered off towards the tail, and that was long enough for two dogs. He was very obedient.'

'Was the man nice to him?' asked Lucy anxiously, having a soft spot for animals; indeed, at that very moment there was a stray mother cat and kittens living clandestinely in a big box under the table.

'Yes—he didn't shout and the dog looked happy. It had one eye—I didn't have time to ask why. It had a funny name, too—Brontes—that's——'

'I know—one of the Cyclops. Could you meet the man again and ask?'

Francesca thought about it. 'Well, no, not really. . .'

'Was he a nice man?'

'I suppose so.' She frowned. 'He thought it was funny, me falling over.'

'I expect it was,' said Lucy. 'I'd better go or I'll miss the bus.'

After Lucy had gone she cleared away the breakfast things, tidied the room and their bedroom, and made sure that she herself was tidy too, and then she went back to the house. She was expected to lunch off a tray at midday and she seldom got back until six o'clock each evening; she arranged food for the cat, made sure that the kittens were alive and well, and locked the door.

Her employer was still in bed, sitting up against lacy pillows, reading her letters. In her youth Lady Mortimor had been a handsome woman; now in her fifties, she spent a good part of her days struggling to retain her looks. A face-lift had helped; so had the expert services of one of the best hairdressers in London and the daily massage sessions and the strict diet, but they couldn't erase the lines of discontent and petulance.

Francesca said good morning and stood listening to the woman's high-pitched voice complaining of lack of sleep, the incompetence of servants and the tiresome bills which had come in the post. When she had finished Francesca said, as she nearly always did, 'Shall I attend to the bills first, Lady Mortimor, and write the cheques and leave them for you to sign? Are there any invitations you wish me to reply to?'

Lady Mortimor tossed the pile of letters at her. 'Oh, take the lot and endeavour to deal with them—is there anything that I should know about this morning?'

'The household wages,' began Francesca, and flushed at Lady Mortimor's snide,

'Oh, to be sure you won't forget those. . .'

'Dr Kennedy is coming to see you at eleven o'clock. Will you see him in the morning-room?'

'Yes, I suppose so; he really must do something about my palpitations—what else?'

'A fitting for two evening gowns at Estelle, lunch with Mrs Felliton.'

'While I am lunching you can get my social diary up

to date, do the flowers for the dining-room, and go along to the dry-cleaners for my suit. There will be some letters to type before you go, so don't idle away your time. Now send Ethel to me, have the cheques and wages book ready for me by half-past ten in the morning-room.' As Francesca went to the door she added, 'And don't forget little Bobo. . .'

'Thank you or please would be nice to hear from time to time,' muttered Francesca as she went to get the wages book, a weekly task which at least gave her the satisfaction of paying herself as well as the rest of the staff. She entered the amounts, got out the cash box from the wall safe and put it ready for Lady Mortimor, who liked to play Lady Bountiful on Fridays and pay everyone in cash. The bills took longer; she hadn't quite finished them when Maisie, the house-maid, brought her a cup of coffee. She got on well with the staff—with the exception of Ethel, of course; once they saw that she had no intention of encroaching on their ground, and was a lady to boot, with a quiet voice and manner, they accepted her for what she was.

Lady Mortimor came presently, signed the cheques, handed out the wages with the graciousness of royalty bestowing a favour and, fortified with a tray of coffee, received Dr Kennedy, which left Francesca free to tidy the muddled desk she had left behind her and take Bobo for his midday walk, a brisk twenty minutes or so before she went back to eat her lunch off a tray in the now deserted morning-room. Since the lady of the house was absent, Cook sent up what Maisie described as a nice little bit of hake with parsley sauce, and a good, wholesome baked custard to follow.

Francesca ate the lot, drank the strong tea which

went with it and got ready to go to the cleaners. It wasn't far; Lady Mortimor patronised a small shop in Old Bond Street and the walk was a pleasant one. The day had turned out fine as the early morning had indicated it might and she allowed her thoughts to roam, remembering wistfully the pleasant house in Hampstead Village where they had lived when her parents had been alive. That had been four years ago now; she winced at the memory of discovering that the house had been mortgaged and the debts so large that they had swallowed up almost all the money there was. The only consolation had been the trust set aside for Lucy's education so that she had been able to stay on as a day pupil at the same well-known school.

There had been other jobs of course, after learning typing and shorthand at night-school while they lived precariously with her mother's elderly housekeeper, but she had known that she would have to find a home of their own as quickly as possible. Two years ago she had answered Lady Mortimor's advertisement and since it offered a roof over their heads and there was no objection to Lucy, provided she never entered the house, she had accepted it, aware that her wages were rather less than Maisie's and knowing that she could never ask for a rise: Lady Mortimor would point out her free rooms and all the advantages of working in a well-run household and the pleasant work.

All of which sounded all right but in practice added up to ten hours a day of taking orders with Sundays free. Well, she was going to stay until Lucy had finished school—another four years. I'll be almost thirty, thought Francesca gloomily, hurrying back with the suit; there were still the flowers to arrange and the

diary to bring up to date, not to mention the letters
and a last walk for Bobo.

It was pouring with rain the next morning, but that
didn't stop Bobo, in a scarlet plastic coat, and
Francesca, in a well-worn Burberry, now in its tenth
year, going for their morning walk. With a scarf tied
over her head, she left Lucy getting dressed, and led the
reluctant little dog across Piccadilly and into the Green
Park. Being Saturday morning, there were very few
people about, only milkmen and postmen and some
over-enthusiastic joggers. She always went the same
way for if by any evil chance Bobo should run away and
get lost, he had more chance of staying around a part of
the park with which he was familiar. The park was even
emptier than the streets and, even if Francesca had
allowed herself to hope that she might meet the man
and his great dog, common sense told her that no one in
their right mind would do more than give a dog a quick
walk through neighbouring streets.

They were halfway across the park, on the point of
turning back, when she heard the beast's joyful barking
and a moment later he came bounding up. She had
prudently planted her feet firmly this time but he
stopped beside her, wagging his long tail and gently
nuzzling Bobo before butting her sleeve with his wet
head, his one eye gleaming with friendliness.

His master's good-morning was genial. 'Oh, hello,'
said Francesca. 'I didn't expect you to be here—the
weather's so awful.'

A remark she instantly wished unsaid; it sounded as
though she had hoped to meet him. She went pink and
looked away from him and didn't see his smile.

'Ah—but we are devoted dog owners, are we not?'

he asked easily. 'And this is a good place for them to run freely.'

'I don't own Bobo,' said Francesca, at pains not to mislead him. 'He belongs to Lady Mortimor; I'm her companion.'

He said, half laughing, 'You don't look in the least like a companion; are they not ladies who find library books and knitting and read aloud? Surely a dying race.'

If he only knew, she thought, but all she said cheerfully was, 'Oh, it's not as bad as all that, and I like walking here with Bobo. I must go.'

She smiled at him from her pretty, sopping-wet face. 'Goodbye, Mr Pitt-Colwyn.'

'*Tot ziens*, Miss Francesca Haley.'

She bent to pat Brontes. 'I wonder why he has only one eye?' she said to herself more than to him, and then walked briskly away, with Bobo walking backwards in an effort to return to his friend. Hurrying now, because she would be late back, she wondered what he had said instead of goodbye—something foreign and, now she came to think of it, he had a funny name too; it had sounded like Rainer, but she wasn't sure any more.

It took her quite a while to dry Bobo when they got back, and Ethel, on the point of carrying Lady Mortimor's tray upstairs, looked at the kitchen clock in triumph.

Francesca saw the look. 'Tell Lady Mortimor that I'm late back, by all means,' she said in a cool voice. 'You can tell her too that we stayed out for exactly the right time but, unless she wishes Bobo to spoil everything in her bedroom, he needs to be thoroughly dried. It is raining hard.'

Ethel sent her a look of dislike and Cook, watching from her stove, said comfortably, 'There's a nice hot cup of tea for you, Miss Haley; you drink it up before you go to your breakfast. I'm sure none of us wants to go out in such weather.'

Ethel flounced away, Bobo at her heels, and Francesca drank her tea while Cook repeated all the more lurid news from the more sensational Press. 'Don't you take any notice of that Ethel, likes upsetting people, she does.'

Francesca finished her tea. 'Well, she doesn't need to think she'll bother me, Cook, and thanks for the tea, it was lovely.'

Lucy would be home at midday since it was Saturday, and they made the shopping list together since she was the one who had to do it.

'Did you see him again?' asked Lucy.

'Who?' Francesca was counting out the housekeeping money. 'The man and his great dog? Yes, but just to say good morning.' She glanced up at her sister. 'Do you suppose I should go another way round the park? I mean, it might look as though I was wanting to meet him.'

'Well, don't you?'

'He laughs at me—oh, not out loud, but behind his face.'

'I shall come with you tomorrow and see him for myself.'

On Sundays Francesca took Bobo for his morning run before being allowed the rest of the day free. 'He's not likely to be there so early on a Sunday. . .'

'All the same, I'll come. What shall we do tomorrow? Could we go to Regent Street and look at the shops? And have something at McDonald's?'

'All right, love. You need a winter coat. . .'

'So do you. Perhaps we'll find a diamond ring or a string of pearls and get a reward.'

Francesca laughed. 'The moon could turn to cheese. My coat is good for another winter—I've stopped growing but you haven't. We'll have a good look around and when I've saved enough we'll buy you a coat.'

Lady Mortimor had friends to lunch which meant that Francesca had to do the flowers again and then hover discreetly in case her employer needed anything.

'You may pour the drinks,' said Lady Mortimor graciously, when the guests had settled themselves in the drawing-room, and then in a sharp aside, 'And make sure that everyone gets what she wants.'

So Francesca went to and fro with sherry and gin and tonic and, for two of the ladies, whisky. Cool and polite, aware of being watched by critical eyes, and disliking Lady Mortimor very much for making her do something which Crow the butler should be doing. Her employer had insisted that when she had guests for lunch it should be Francesca who saw to the drinks; it was one of the spiteful gestures she made from time to time in order, Francesca guessed, to keep her in her place. Fortunately Crow was nice about it; he had a poor opinion of his mistress, the widow of a wholesale textile manufacturer who had given away enough money to be knighted, and he knew a lady born and bred when he saw Francesca, as he informed Cook.

When the guests had gone, Lady Mortimor went out

herself. 'Be sure and have those letters ready for me—
I shall be back in time to dress,' she told Francesca.
'And be sure and make a note in the diary—Dr
Kennedy is bringing a specialist to see me on Tuesday
morning at ten o'clock. You will stay with me of
course—I shall probably feel poorly.'

Francesca thought that would be very likely. Eating
too much rich food and drinking a little too much as
well. . . She hoped the specialist would prescribe a
strict diet, although on second thoughts that might not
do—Lady Mortimor's uncertain temper might become
even more uncertain.

Sundays were wonderful days; once Bobo had been
taken for his walk she was free, and even the walk was
fun for Lucy went with her and they could talk. The
little dog handed over to a grumpy Ethel, they had
their breakfast and went out, to spend the rest of the
morning and a good deal of the afternoon looking at
the shops, choosing what they would buy if they had
the money, eating sparingly at McDonald's and walking
back in the late afternoon to tea in the little sitting-
room and an evening by the gas fire with the cat and
kittens in their box between them.

Monday always came too soon and this time there
was no Brontes to be seen, although the morning was
fine. Francesca went back to the house to find Lady
Mortimor in a bad temper so that by the end of the day
she wanted above all things to rush out of the house
and never go back again. Her ears rang with her
employer's orders for the next day. She was to be
earlier than usual—if Lady Mortimor was to be ready
to be seen by the specialist then she would need to get
up earlier than usual, which meant that the entire

household would have to get up earlier too. Francesca, getting sleepily from her bed, wished the man to Jericho.

Lady Mortimor set the scene with all the expertise of a stage manager; she had been dressed in a velvet housecoat over gossamer undies, Ethel had arranged her hair in artless curls and tied a ribbon in them, and she had made up carefully with a pale foundation. She had decided against being examined in her bedroom; the *chaise-longue* in the dressing-room adjoining would be both appropriate and convenient. By half-past nine she was lying, swathed in shawls, in an attitude of resigned long suffering.

There was no question of morning coffee, of course, and that meant that Francesca didn't get any either. She was kept busy fetching the aids Lady Mortimor considered vital to an invalid's comfort: eau-de-Cologne, smelling salts, a glass of water. . .

'Mind you pay attention,' said that lady. 'I shall need assistance from time to time and probably the specialist will require things held or fetched.'

Francesca occupied herself wondering what these things might be. Lady Mortimor kept talking about a specialist, but a specialist in what? She ventured to ask and had her head bitten off with, 'A heart consultant of course, who else? The best there is—I've never been one to grudge the best in illness. . .'

Francesca remembered Maisie and her scalded hand a few months previously. Lady Mortimer had dismissed the affair with a wave of the hand and told her to go to Out-patients during the hour she had off each afternoon. Her tongue, itching to give voice to her strong feelings, had to be held firmly between her teeth.

Ten o'clock came, with no sign of Dr Kennedy and his renowned colleague, and Lady Mortimer, rearranging herself once again, gave vent to a vexed tirade. 'And you, you stupid girl, might have had the sense to check with the consulting-rooms to make sure that this man has the time right. Really, you are completely useless. . .'

Francesca didn't say a word; she had lost her breath for the moment, for the door had opened and Dr Kennedy followed by Mr Pitt-Colwyn were standing there. They would have heard Lady Mortimor, she thought miserably, and would have labelled her as a useless female at everyone's beck and call.

'Well, can't you say something?' asked Lady Mortimor and at the same time became aware of the two men coming towards her, so that her cross face became all charm and smiles and her sharp voice softened to a gentle, 'Dr Kennedy, how good of you to come. Francesca, my dear, do go and see if Crow is bringing the coffee——'

'No coffee, thank you,' said Dr Kennedy. 'Here is Professor Pitt-Colwyn, Lady Mortimor. You insisted on the best heart specialist, and I have brought him to see you.'

Lady Mortimor put out a languid hand. 'Professor— how very kind of you to spare the time to see me. I'm sure you must be a very busy man.'

He hadn't looked at Francesca; now he said with grave courtesy, 'Yes, I am a busy man, Lady Mortimor.' He pulled up a chair and sat down. 'If you will tell me what is the trouble?'

'Oh, dear, it is so hard to begin—I have suffered poor health every day since my dear husband died. It

is hard to be left alone at my age—with so much life
ahead of me.' She waved a weak hand. 'I suffer from
palpitations, Professor, really alarmingly so; I am convinced that I have a weak heart. Dr Kennedy assures
me that I am mistaken, but you know what family
doctors are, only too anxious to reassure one if one is
suffering from some serious condition. . .'

Professor Pitt-Colwyn hadn't spoken, there was no
expression upon his handsome face and Francesca,
watching from her discreet corner, thought that he had
no intention of speaking, not at the moment at any
rate. He allowed his patient to ramble on in a faint
voice, still saying nothing when she paused to say in a
quite different tone, 'Get me some water, Francesca,
can't you see that I am feeling faint? And hurry up,
girl.'

The glass of water was within inches of her hand.
Francesca handed it, quelling a powerful desire to pour
its contents all over Lady Mortimor's massive bosom.

She went back to her corner from where she admired
the professor's beautiful tailored dark grey suit. He
had a nice head too, excellent hair—she considered
the sprinkling of grey in it was distinguished—and he
had nice hands. She became lost in her thoughts until
her employer's voice, raised in barely suppressed
temper, brought her back to her surroundings.

'My smelling salts—I pay you to look after me, not
stand there daydreaming——' She remembered suddenly that she had an audience and added in a quite
different voice, 'Do forgive me—I become so upset
when I have one of these turns, I hardly know what
I'm saying.'

Neither man answered. Francesca administered the

smelling salts and the professor got to his feet. 'I will take a look at your chest, Lady Mortimor,' and he stood aside while Francesca removed the shawls and the housecoat and laid a small rug discreetly over the patient's person.

The professor had drawn up a chair, adjusted his stethoscope and begun his examination. He was very thorough and when he had done what was necessary he took her blood-pressure, sat with Lady Mortimor's hand in his, his fingers on her pulse.

Finally he asked, 'What is your weight?'

Lady Mortimor's pale make-up turned pink. 'Well, really I'm not sure. . .' She looked at Francesca, who said nothing, although she could have pointed out that within the last few months a great many garments had been let out at the seams. . .

'You are overweight,' said the professor in measured tones, 'and that is the sole cause of your palpitations. You should lose at least two stone within the next six months, take plenty of exercise—regular walking is to be recommended—and small light meals and only moderate drinking. You will feel and look a different woman within that time, Lady Mortimor.'

'But my heart——'

'It is as sound as a bell; I can assure you that there is nothing wrong with you other than being overweight.'

He got up and shook her hand. 'If I may have a word with Dr Kennedy—perhaps this young lady can show us somewhere where we can be private.'

'You are hiding something from me,' declared Lady Mortimor. 'I am convinced that you are not telling me the whole truth.'

His eyes were cold. 'I am not in the habit of lying,

Lady Mortimor; I merely wish to discuss your diet with Dr Kennedy.'

Francesca had the door open and he went past her, followed by Dr Kennedy. 'The morning-room,' she told them. 'There won't be anyone there at this time in the morning.'

She led the way and ushered them inside. 'Would you like coffee?'

The professor glanced at his companion and politely declined, with a courteous uninterest which made her wonder if she had dreamed their meetings in the park. There was no reason why he shouldn't have made some acknowledgement of them—not in front of Lady Mortimor, of course. Perhaps now he had seen her here he had no further interest; he was, she gathered, an important man in his own sphere.

She went back to Lady Mortimor and endured that lady's peevish ill humour for the rest of the day. The next day would be even worse, for by then Dr Kennedy would have worked out a diet.

Of course, she told Lucy when at last she was free to go to her rooms.

'I say, what fun—was he pompous?'

'No, not in the least; you couldn't tell what he was thinking.'

'Oh, well, doctors are always poker-faced. He might have said hello.'

Francesca said crossly, 'Why should he? We haven't anything in common.' She added a little sadly, 'Only I thought he was rather nice.'

Lucy hugged her. 'Never mind, Fran, I'll find you a rich millionaire who'll adore you forever and you'll marry him and live happily ever after.'

Francesca laughed. 'Oh, what rubbish. Let's get the washing-up done.'

As she set out with Bobo the next morning, she wished that she could have taken a different route and gone at a different time, but Lady Mortimor, easy-going when it came to her own activities and indifferent as to whether they disrupted her household, prided herself on discipline among her staff; she explained this to her circle of friends as caring for their welfare, but what it actually meant was that they lived by a strict timetable and since, with the exception of Francesca, she paid them well and Cook saw to it that the food in the kitchen was good and plentiful, they abided by it. It was irksome to Francesca and she was aware that Lady Mortimor knew that; she also knew that she and Lucy needed a home and that not many people were prepared to offer one.

So Francesca wasn't surprised to see Brontes bound-ing to meet her, followed in a leisurely manner by his master. She was prepared for it, of course; as he drew level she wished him a cold good-morning and went on walking, towing Bobo and rather hampered by Brontes bouncing to and fro, intent on being friendly.

Professor Pitt-Colwyn kept pace with her. 'Before you go off in high dudgeon, be good enough to listen to me.' He sounded courteous; he also sounded as though he was in the habit of being listened to if he wished.

'Why?' asked Francesca.

'Don't be silly. You're bristling with indignation because I ignored you yesterday. Understandable, but typical of the female mind. No logic. Supposing I had come into the room exclaiming, "Ah, Miss Francesca

Haley, how delightful to meet you again"—and it was delightful, of course—how would your employer have reacted?' He glanced at her thoughtful face. 'Yes, exactly, I have no need to dot the Is or cross the Ts. Now that that slight misunderstanding is cleared up, tell me why you work for such a tiresome woman.'

She stood still the better to look at him. 'It is really none of your business. . .'

He brushed that aside. 'That is definitely something I will decide for myself.' He smiled down at her. 'I'm a complete stranger to you; you can say anything you like to me and I'll forget it at once if you wish me to——'

'Oh, the Hippocratic oath.'

His rather stern mouth twitched. 'And that too. You're not happy there, are you?'

She shook her head. 'No, and it's very kind of you to—to bother, but there is really nothing to be done about it.'

'No, there isn't if you refuse to tell me what is wrong.' He glanced at his watch. 'How long do you have before you have to report back?'

'Fifteen minutes.'

'A lot can be said in that time. Brontes and I will walk back with you as far as Piccadilly.'

'Oh, will you?'

'Did I not say so?' He turned her round smartly, and whistled to Brontes. 'Now consider me your favourite uncle,' he invited.

CHAPTER TWO

AFTERWARDS Francesca wondered what had possessed
her. She had told Professor Pitt-Colwyn everything.
She hadn't meant to, but once she got started she had
seemed unable to stop. She blushed with shame just
remembering it; he must have thought her a complete
fool, sorry for herself, moaning on and on about her
life. That this was a gross exaggeration had nothing to
do with it; she would never be able to look him in the
face again. The awful thing was that she would have to
unless he had the decency to walk his dog in another
part of the park.

She was barely in the park before he joined her.

'A splendid morning,' he said cheerfully. 'I enjoy the
autumn, don't you?' He took Bobo's lead from her and
unclipped it. 'Let the poor, pampered beast run free.
Brontes will look after him; he has a strong paternal
instinct.'

It was difficult to be stand-offish with him. 'He's a
nice dog, only he's—he's rather a mixture, isn't he?'

'Oh, decidedly so. Heaven knows where he got that
tail.'

For something to say, for she was feeling suddenly
shy, 'He must have been a delightful puppy.'

'I found him in a small town in Greece. Someone
had poked out his eye and beaten him almost to
death—he was about eight weeks old.'

'Oh, the poor lilttle beast—how old is he now?'

'Eight months old and still growing. He's a splendid fellow and strangely enough, considering his origin, very obedient.'

'I must get back.' She looked around for Bobo, who was nowhere in sight, but in answer to her companion's whistle Brontes came trotting up with Bobo scampering beside him. The professor fastened his lead and handed it to her. His goodbye was casually kind; never once, she reflected as she walked back to the house, had he uttered a word about her beastly job. She had been a great fool to blurt out all her worries and grumbles to a complete stranger who had no interest in her anyway. She wished most heartily that there was some way in which she could avoid meeting him ever again.

She thought up several schemes during the course of the day, none of which held water, and which caused her to get absent-minded so that Lady Mortimor had the pleasure of finding fault with her, insisting that she re-type several letters because the commas were in the wrong place. It was after seven o'clock by the time Francesca got back to her room over the garage and found Lucy at her homework.

'You've had a beastly day.' Lucy slammed her books shut and got out a cloth and cutlery. 'I put some potatoes in the oven to bake; they'll be ready by now. We can open a tin of beans, too. The kettle's boiling; I'll make a cup of tea.'

'Lovely, darling, I've had a tiresome day. How's school? Did you get an A for your essay?'

'Yes. Did you see him this morning?'

'Yes, just for a moment. . .'

'Didn't you talk at all?'

'Only about his dog.' Francesca poured them each a

cup of tea and then sat down to drink it. 'I wish I'd never told him——'

'Oh, pooh—I dare say he's forgotten already. He must have lots of patients to think about; his head must be full of people's life histories.'

Francesca opened the tin of beans. 'Yes, of course, only I wish I need never see him again.'

To her secret unacknowledged chagrin, it seemed that she was to have her wish. He wasn't there the following morning, nor for the rest of the week; she told herself that it was a great relief and said so to Lucy, who said, 'Rubbish, you know you want to see him again.'

'Well—yes, perhaps. It was nice to have someone to talk to.' Francesca went on briskly, 'I wonder if it would be a good idea to go to evening classes when they start next month?'

Lucy looked at her in horror. 'Darling, you must be crazy—you mean sit for two hours learning Spanish or how to upholster a chair? I won't let you. Don't you see the kind of people who go to evening classes are very likely like us—without friends and family? Even if you got to know any of them they'd probably moan about being lonely. . .'

Francesca laughed. 'You know that's not quite true,' she said, 'although I do see what you mean.'

'Good. No evening classes. Doesn't Lady Mortimor have men visitors? She's always giving dinner parties. . .'

Francesca mentally reviewed her employer's guests; they were all past their prime. Well-to-do, self-satisfied and loud-voiced. They either ignored her in the same way as they ignored Crow or Maisie, or they made

vapid remarks like, 'How are you today, little girl?'
Which, since she was all of five feet ten inches tall and
splendidly built, was an extremely silly thing to say.

She said, laughing, 'I can't say I've ever fancied any
of them. I shall wait until you are old enough and quite
grown-up, and when you've found yourself a millionaire I shall bask in your reflected glory.' She began to
clear the table. 'Let's get Mum fed while the kittens
are asleep—and that's another problem. . .'

September remained fine until the end of the month,
when wind and rain tore away the last vestiges of
summer. Francesca and Bobo tramped their allotted
routine each morning and returned, Bobo to be fussed
over once he had been dried and brushed, Francesca
to hurry to her rooms, gobble breakfast and dash back
again to start on the hundred and one jobs Lady
Mortimor found for her to do, which were never done
to that lady's satisfaction. The strict diet to which
Professor Pitt-Colwyn had restricted her might be
reducing her weight, but it had increased her ill
humour. Francesca, supervising the making of a salad-
dressing with lemon juice to accompany the thin slices
of chicken which constituted her employer's lunch,
wished that he had left well alone. Let the woman be
as fat as butter if she wished, she reflected savagely,
chopping a head of chicory while she listened to Cook
detailing the menu for the dinner party that evening.
A pity the professor couldn't hear that; it was dripping
with calories. . .

Because of the dinner party the staff lunch was cold
meat and potatoes in their jackets and Francesca,
knowing the extra work involved in one of Lady

Mortimor's large dinner parties, had hers in the kitchen and gave a hand with the preparations.

All the guests had arrived by the time she left the house that evening; Lady Mortimor, overpoweringly regal in purple velvet, had made her rearrange the flowers in the hall, polish the glasses again, much to Maisie's rage, and then go to the kitchen to make sure that Cook had remembered how to make sweet and sour sauce, which annoyed the talented woman so much that she threatened to curdle it.

'A good thing it's Sunday tomorrow,' said Francesca, eating toasted cheese while Lucy did her homework. 'And I must think of something for the kittens.' They peered at her, snug against their mother in the cardboard box, and the very idea of finding happy homes for them worried her. How was she to know if the homes were happy and what their mother would do without them?

They went to bed presently, and she dreamt of kittens and curdled sauce and Lady Mortimor in her purple, to wake unrefreshed. At least it wasn't raining, and Lucy would go with her and Bobo, and after breakfast they would go and look at the shops, have a snack somewhere and go to evensong at St Paul's.

The house was quiet as she let herself in through the side-entrance, fastened Bobo's lead and led the little dog outside to where Lucy was waiting. There was a nip in the air, but at least it wasn't raining; they set off at a good pace, crossed into the park and took the usual path. They had reached a small clump of trees where the path curved abruptly when Bobo began to bark, and a moment later Brontes came hurtling round the corner, to leap up to greet Francesca, sniff at Lucy and turn his delighted attention to Bobo, who was yapping his small head off. They had come to a halt, not wishing to be bowled over by the warmth of the big dog's attention, which gave his master ample time to join them.

'Hello—what a pleasant morning.' He sounded as though they had met recently. Francesca knew exactly how long it had been since they had last met—ten days. She bade him good-morning in a chilly voice, and when he looked at Lucy she was forced to add, 'This is my sister, Lucy. Professor Pitt-Colwyn, Lucy.'

Lucy offered a hand. 'I hoped I'd meet you one day,' she told him, 'but of course you've been away. What do you do with your dog? Does he go with you?'

'If it's possible; otherwise he stays at home and gets spoilt. You like him?'

'He's gorgeous. We've got a cat and kittens; I expect Francesca told you that—now the kittens are getting quite big we'll have to find homes for them.' She peeped at her sister's face; she looked cross. 'I'll take Bobo for a run—will Brontes come with me?'

'He'll be delighted. We'll stroll along to meet you.'

'We should be going back,' said Francesca, still very cool.

Lucy was already darting ahead and the professor appeared not to have heard her. 'I wish to talk to you, so don't be a silly girl and put on airs——'

'Well, really——' She stopped and looked up at his bland face. 'I am not putting on airs, and there is nothing for us to talk about.'

'You're very touchy—high time you left that job.' And at her indignant gasp he added, 'Just keep quiet and listen to me.'

He took her arm and began to walk after the fast retreating Lucy and the dogs. 'You would like to leave Lady Mortimor, would you not? I know of a job which might suit you. A close friend of mine died recently, leaving a widow and a small daughter. Eloise was an actress before she married—indeed, she has returned to the stage for short periods since their marriage— now she has the opportunity to go on tour with a play and is desperate to find someone to live in her house, run it for her and look after little Peggy while she is away. The tour is three or four months and then if it is successful they will go to a London theatre. You will have *carte blanche* and the services of a daily help in the house. No days off—but Peggy will be at school so that you should have a certain amount of free time. Peggy goes to a small day school, five minutes' walk from Cornel Mews——'

'That's near Lady Mortimor's——'

'Yes—don't interrupt. Eloise will come home for the very occasional weekend or day, but since the tour is largely in the north of England that isn't likely to be very often. The salary isn't bad. . .' He mentioned a sum which left Francesca's pretty mouth agape.

'That's—that's. . .just for a week? Are you sure? Lady Mortimor. . . I'm not properly trained.'

'You don't need to be.' He looked down his commanding nose at her. 'Will you consider it?'

'It's not permanent—and what about the cat and her kittens?'

He said smoothly, 'It will last for several months, probably longer, and you will find it easy to find another similar post once you have a good reference.'

'Lady Mortimor won't give me one.'

'I am an old friend of Eloise; I imagine that my word will carry sufficient weight. As for the cat and kittens, they may come and live in my house; Brontes will love to have them.'

'Oh, but won't your—that is, anyone, mind?'

'No. I shall be seeing Eloise later; may I tell her that you are willing to go and see her?'

'I would have liked time to think about it.'

'Well, you can have ten minutes while I round up the rest of the party.'

He had gone before she could protest, walking away from her with long, easy strides.

He had said 'ten minutes' and she suspected that he had meant what he had said. It sounded a nice job and the money was far beyond her wildest expectations, and she wouldn't be at anyone's beck and call.

Prudence told her that she was probably going out of the frying pan into the fire. On the other hand, nothing venture, nothing win. When he came back presently with Lucy chattering happily and a tired Bobo and a still lively Brontes in tow, she said at once, 'All right, I'll go and see this lady if you'll give me her address. Only it will have to be in the evening.'

'Seven o'clock tomorrow evening. Mrs Vincent, two, Cornel Mews. I'll let her know. I shan't be here tomorrow; I'll see you on Tuesday. You're free for the rest of the day?'

For one delighted moment she thought he was going to suggest that they should spend it together, but all he said was, 'Goodbye,' before he started to whistle to Brontes and turned on his heel, walking with the easy air of a man who had done what he had set out to do.

Lucy tucked an arm in hers. 'Now tell me everything—why are you going to see this Mrs Vincent?'

They started to walk back and by the time they had
reached the house Lucy knew all about it. They took
Bobo into the kitchen and went back to their rooms to
make some coffee and talk it over.

'It won't matter whether Mrs Vincent is nice or not
if she's not going to be there,' observed Lucy. 'Oh,
Fran, won't it be heavenly to have no one there but
us—and Peggy of course—I wonder how old she is?'

'I forgot to ask. . .'

'All that money,' said Lucy dreamily. 'Now we can
easily both get winter coats.'

'Well, I must save as much as I can. Supposing I
can't find another job?'

'Never cross your bridges until you get to them,' said
Lucy. 'Come on, let's go and look at the shops.' She
put the kittens back in their box with their mother.

'I'm glad they'll all have a good home,' Francesca
said.

'Yes. I wonder where it is?'

'Somewhere suitable for a professor,' said Francesca
snappily. It still rankled that he had taken leave of her
so abruptly. There was no reason why he shouldn't, of
course. He had done his good deed for the day: found
help for his friend and enabled her to leave Lady
Mortimor's house.

'I shall enjoy giving her my notice,' she told Lucy.

It seemed as though Monday would never end but it
did, tardily, after a day of Lady Mortimor's deep
displeasure vented upon anyone and anything which
came within her range, due to an early morning visit to

her hairdresser who had put the wrong coloured streaks
in her hair. Francesca had been ordered to make
another appointment immediately so that this might be
remedied at once, but unfortunately the hairdresser
had no cancellations. Francesca, relaying this unwelcome news, had the receiver snatched from her and
listened to her employer demanding the instant dismissal of the girl who had done her hair that morning,
a demand which was naturally enough refused and
added to Lady Mortimor's wrath.

'Why not get Ethel to shampoo your hair and re-set
it?' Francesca suggested, and was told not to be so
stupid, and after that there was no hope of doing
anything right. . . She was tired and a little cross by
the time she got to their rooms to find Lucy ready with
a pot of tea.

'You drink that up,' she told Francesca bracingly.
'Put on that brown jacket and skirt—I know they're
old, but they're elegant—and do do your face.' She
glanced at the clock. 'You've twenty minutes.'

It was exactly seven o'clock when she rang the bell
of the charming little cottage in Cornel Mews. Its door
was a rich dark red and there were bay trees in tubs on
either side of it, and its one downstairs window was
curtained in ruffled white net. She crossed her fingers
for luck and took a deep breath as the door was
opened.

The woman standing there was small and slim and as
pretty as a picture. Her dark hair was in a fashionable
tangle and she wore the kind of make-up it was difficult
to separate from natural colouring. She wore a loose
shirt over a very narrow short skirt and high-heeled

suede boots and she could have been any age between twenty and thirty. She was in fact thirty-five.

'Miss Haley—do come in, Renier has told me all about you. . .' She ushered Francesca into a narrow hall and opened a door into a surprisingly large living-room. 'Sit down and do have a drink while we get to know each other.'

Francesca sat, took the sherry she was offered and, since for the moment she had had no chance to say a word, she stayed silent.

'Did Renier explain?' asked Mrs Vincent. 'You know what men are, they never listen.'

It was time she said something, thought Francesca. 'He told me that you were going on tour and needed someone to look after your daughter and keep house for you.'

'Bless the darling, he had it right.' Mrs Vincent curled up in a vast armchair with her drink. 'It's just the details——'

'You don't know anything about me,' protested Francesca.

'Oh, but I do, my daily woman is sister to Lady Mortimor's cook; besides, Renier said you were a sensible young woman with a sense of responsibility, and that's good enough for me. When can you come? I'm off at the end of next week.' She didn't give Francesca a chance to speak. 'Is the money all right? All the bills will go to my solicitor, who'll deal with them, and he'll send you a weekly cheque to cover household expenses and your salary. If you need advice or anything he'll deal with it.'

Francesca got a word in at last. 'Your daughter—

how old is she? Can she meet me before I come? I
have a sister who would have to live here with me.'

'That's fine. She's up in the nursery; I'll get her
down.'

Mrs Vincent went out of the room and called up the
narrow stairs, and presently a small girl came into the
room. She was one of the plainest children Francesca
had ever set eyes on: lank, pale hair, a long, thin face,
small, dark eyes and an unhappy little mouth.

'She's six years old,' said Mrs Vincent in a detached
way. 'Goes to school of course—very bright, so I've
been told. Shake hands with Miss Haley, Peggy. She's
coming to stay with you while I'm away.'

The child shook hands with Francesca and Francesca
kept the small paw in her own for a moment. 'I shall
like coming here to live with you,' she said gently. 'I've
a sister, too. . .' She remembered something. 'Have
you a cat or a dog to look after?'

The child shook her head. Her mother answered for
her. 'My last nanny wouldn't have them in the house,
though it's all one to me.' She laughed. 'I'm not here
long enough to mind.'

'Then could I bring a kitten with me? Perhaps you
would like one of your very own to look after, Peggy?'

The child smiled for the first time; there was an
endearing gap in her teeth. 'For my own?' she asked.

'If your mother will allow that.'

'Oh, let the child have a pet if she wants.' Mrs
Vincent added unexpectedly, 'She takes after her
father.'

A remark which made everything clear to Francesca;
a lovely, fragile creature like Mrs Vincent would find
this plain, silent child a handicap now that she was

going back on the stage. Probably she loved her dearly, but she wasn't going to let her interfere with her career. She went pink when Mrs Vincent said, 'I've been left comfortably off, but I've no intention of dwindling into a lonely widowhood,' because she might have read her thoughts. She smiled suddenly. 'I shall wait for a decent interval and get married again.'

Francesca watched Peggy's small face; it was stony with misery. She said quickly, 'I'll bring the kitten when I come, shall I? And you can choose a name for it—it's a little boy cat; he's black and white with yellow eyes.'

Peggy slipped a small hand into hers. 'Really? Will he live here with us?'

'Of course, for this will be his home, won't it?'

Eloise poured herself another drink. 'You have no idea what a relief this is—may I call you Francesca? Now when can we expect you?'

'References?' ventured Francesca.

'Renier says you're OK. That's good enough for me; I told you that.'

'I shall have to give a week's notice to Lady Mortimor. I can do that tomorrow.'

'Good. I can expect you in a week's time. Give me a ring and let me know what time of day you'll be coming and I'll make a point of being in. Now have you time to go round the cottage with me?'

It was a small place, but very comfortably furnished with a well-planned kitchen and, on the ground floor, the living-room and, on the floor above, two good-sized bedrooms and a smaller room with a small bathroom leading from it. 'This is the nursery,' said

Mrs Vincent. 'Peggy plays here—she's got masses of toys; she's quite happy to amuse herself.'

Francesca wondered about that although she said nothing. 'How long will you be away?' she asked.

'Oh, my dear, how am I to know? The tour will last three months at least, and with luck will end up at a London theatre; if it doesn't I shall get my agent to find me something else.'

'Yes, of course. Has Peggy any grandparents or cousins who may want her to visit?'

'My parents are in America; Jeff's live in Wiltshire, almost Somerset, actually. We don't see much of them.' Something in her voice stopped Francesca from asking any more questions, and presently she bade Mrs Vincent goodbye, and bent to shake Peggy's hand.

'You won't forget the kitten?'

'No, I'll bring him with me, I promise.'

Back in her little sitting-room she told Lucy everything. 'It's a dear little house, you'll love it. I think Peggy is lonely—she's withdrawn—perhaps she misses her father; I don't know how long ago he died. I promised her a kitten—the black and white one. Mrs Vincent didn't mind.'

'You don't like her much, do you?' asked Lucy shrewdly.

'Well, she's charming and friendly and easy-going, but she didn't seem very interested in Peggy. Perhaps it's hard to stay at home quietly with a small child if you've been used to theatre friends, and perhaps when her husband was alive they went out a lot.'

'It'll be better than Lady Mortimor's, anyway. We had better start packing up tomorrow, and don't forget

Professor Pitt-Colwyn is going to take mother cat and the other kittens. Shall you meet him tomorrow?'

'He said he would be there.' She frowned. 'I must be careful what I say about Mrs Vincent; he said he was a close friend of her husband so I expect he is a close friend of hers as well.'

'Do you suppose she's got her eye on him?'

'Don't be vulgar, Lucy. I should think it was very likely, although for all we know he's married already.'

'You'd better ask him——'

'Indeed I will not.'

He was in the park, waiting for her when she got there the next morning with Bobo. It was a bright day with more than a hint of the coming winter's chill and Francesca, an elderly cardigan over her blouse and skirt, wished she had worn something warmer.

He wasted no time on good-mornings but said, 'You're cold; why didn't you wear something sensible? We had better walk briskly.'

He marched her off at a fine pace, with Bobo keeping up with difficulty and Brontes circling around them. 'Well? You saw Eloise Vincent? Are you going to take the job?'

'Yes, I'm going to give Lady Mortimor my notice this morning and let Mrs Vincent know when I'll be going to her.'

'You saw Peggy?'

'Yes.'

He looked down at her thoughtfully. 'And. . .?'

'She's a quiet little girl, isn't she? I said I would take one of our kittens there for her to look after; her mother said that I might. You will take the mother cat and the other kittens, won't you?'

'Certainly I will. When will it be convenient for me to collect them? One evening? Let me see, I'm free on Thursday after six o'clock. Where exactly do you live?'

'Well, over the garage at the back of the house. There's a side-door; there's no knocker or bell, you just have to thump.'

'Then shall we say between six o'clock and half-past six? Have you a basket?'

'No, I'll get a cardboard box from the kitchen.'

'No need. I'll bring a basket with me. You're quite happy about this job?'

'Yes, thank you. You see, it's much more money and it will be so nice not to be. . .that is, it will be nice to be on our own.'

'That I can well believe. Are you scared of Lady Mortimor?'

She gave his question careful thought. 'No, not in the least, but she is sometimes rather rude if anything has annoyed her. I have longed to shout back at her but I didn't dare—she would have given me the sack.'

'Well, now you can bawl her out as much as you like, though I don't suppose you will; you've been too well brought up.'

He had spoken lightly, but when she looked at him she saw the mocking little smile. He must think her a spineless creature, dwindling into a dull spinsterhood. He had been kind, but his pity angered her. After all, she hadn't asked him for help. She said in her quiet voice, 'I have to go. Thank you for your help, and we'll have mother cat and the kittens ready for you when you come.' She gave him a stiff smile. 'Goodbye, Professor Pitt-Colwyn.'

She would contrive to be out when he called on

Thursday evening, she decided as she made her way back to the house.

She couldn't have chosen a worse time in which to give in her notice. Lady Mortimor had been to a bridge party on the previous day and lost money, something she couldn't bear to do, and over and above that her dressmaker had telephoned to say that the dress she had wanted delivered that morning was not finished. Francesca went into the room in time to hear her employer declaring that it was no concern of hers if the girl working on it was ill, the dress was to be delivered by two o'clock that afternoon. She glanced up when she saw Francesca. 'Better still, I'll send round a girl to collect it and it had better be ready.

'You heard that,' she snapped. 'That stupid woman having the cheek to say I can't have the dress today. I intend to wear it to the Smithers' drinks party this evening. You'll fetch it after lunch.'

She sat down at the little writing-table and glanced through the letters there. 'Bills,' she said peevishly. 'These tradespeople always wanting their money. You'd better see to them, I suppose, Francesca.' She got up. 'I've a hair appointment—see that they're ready for me when I get back.'

Francesca picked up the letters. 'Lady Mortimor, I wish to give you a week's notice as from today.' She laid an envelope on the desk. 'I have put it in writing.'

Lady Mortimor looked as though she had been hit on the head. Her eyes popped from her head, her mouth gaped. When she had her breath she said, 'What nonsense is this? You must be mad, girl. A cushy job and a flat of your own. . . I won't hear of it.'

'There's nothing you can do about it,' Francesca

pointed out reasonably. 'It isn't a cushy job, it's very badly paid, and it surely isn't a flat—it's two small rooms with a minute kitchen and a shower which doesn't work half the time.'

'You'll have difficulty in getting work, I'll see to that. I'll not give you a reference.'

'That won't be necessary. I already have a job to go to and your reference won't be required.'

'Then you can go now, do you hear, you ungrateful girl?'

'Just as you say, Lady Mortimor. You will have to give me two weeks' wages, one in lieu of notice.' She watched her employer's complexion becoming alarmingly red. 'And whom shall I ask to arrange the dinner party for Saturday? And your lunch party on Sunday? Shall I let Ethel have the bills to check? And there will be the invitations for the charity tea party you are giving next week.'

Francesca paused for breath, astonished at herself. Really she had been most unpleasant and deserved to be thrown out of the house for rudeness. She realised that she wouldn't mind that in the least.

Lady Mortimor knew when she was worsted. 'You will remain until the following week.'

'Tuesday evening,' Francesca interpolated gently, ignoring the woman's glare.

'You will send an advertisement to the usual papers this morning. I require letters in the first instance; interviews can be arranged later to suit me.'

'Certainly, Lady Mortimor. Am I to state the salary?'

'No. The flat goes with the job, of course.' She swept to the door. 'It may interest you to know that you have ruined my day. Such ingratitude has cut me to the quick.'

Francesca forbore from saying that, for someone of Lady Mortimor's ample, corseted figure, the cut would have to be really deep.

Naturally a kind girl and seldom critical of other people, she felt guilty once she was alone. She had been most dreadfully rude; she felt thoroughly ashamed of herself. She had almost finished the bills when Maisie came in with her coffee.

'Cor, miss, what a lark—you going away. Mr Crow was just in the hall passing as you might say and 'eard it all. He said as 'ow you gave as good as you got and good luck to you, we all says—treated you something shameful, she 'as, and you a lady and all.'

'Why, Maisie, how very kind of you all. I'm afraid I was very rude. . .'

'A bit of plain speaking never 'urt no one, miss. I 'opes 'owever that 'oever takes yer place is capable of a bit of talking back.'

Francesca drank her coffee, feeling cheerful again. She wasn't going to apologise, but she would behave as she always had done, however unpleasant Lady Mortimor might choose to be.

She chose to be very unpleasant. It was a good thing that there were no signs of the professor the next morning for she might have burst into tears all over him and wallowed in self-pity, but by Thursday evening she didn't care any more and allowed Lady Mortimor's ill temper and spiteful remarks to flow over her head. Heedful of her decision, she took care not to get to the rooms until well after seven o'clock, only to find the professor sitting in comfort in the only easy-chair in the place, drinking tea from a mug while Brontes brooded in a fatherly fashion over mother cat and the kittens in their box.

'There you are,' said Lucy as Francesca went in. 'We thought you'd never come. There's still tea in the pot. But Renier's eaten all the biscuits; he didn't have time for lunch. Have you had a beastly day?'

'Well, a bit sticky. I say, isn't Brontes sweet?'

The professor had got up from his chair and pushed her gently into it, and had gone to sit on the small wooden chair which creaked under his weight. He said now, 'I shall be away for the next ten days or so; I hope you settle down with Peggy.' His hooded gaze swept over her tired face. 'It's time you had a change, and I think you will find she will be much nicer to live with than your Lady Mortimor.' He got up. 'I must be going.' He scooped the cat and kittens into the basket he had brought with him, while Lucy cuddled the other kitten on her lap. 'I'll take good care of them,' he said. He smiled at them both. '*Tot ziens*.' And when Francesca made an effort to rise he said, 'No, I'll see myself out.'

The room seemed very empty once he had gone.

CHAPTER THREE

THE week seemed never-ending, and Lady Mortimor was determined to get the last ounce of work out of Francesca before she left. There had been several answers to the advertisement, but so far the applicants had refused the job. They had turned up their noses at the so-called flat and two of them had exploded with laughter when they had been told their salary. They were, they had pointed out, secretary-companions, not dog minders or errand girls. Lady Mortimor actually had been shaken. 'You will have to remain until someone suitable can take your place,' she had said the day before Francesca was due to leave.

'That won't be possible,' said Francesca. 'I start my new job immediately I leave here. One of the agencies might have help for you, but only on a daily or weekly basis.'

Lady Mortimor glared at her. 'I am aware of that, but I have no intention of paying the exorbitant fees they ask.' She hesitated. 'I am prepared to overlook your rudeness, Francesca. I am sure that you could arrange to go to this new job, say, in a week's time?'

'I am very sorry, Lady Mortimor, but that is impossible.'

She watched her employer sweep out of the room in a towering rage, and went back to making out the last of the cheques for the tradesmen.

The last day was a nightmare she refused to dwell

245

upon. Lady Mortimor gave her not a moment to herself, and when six o'clock came declared that half the things she had told Francesca to do were still not done. Francesca listened quietly, allowing the tirade to flow over her head. 'There is nothing of importance left to do,' she pointed out. 'Whoever can come in place of me can deal with anything I've overlooked. Goodbye, Lady Mortimor.'

She closed the door quietly on her erstwhile employer's angry voice. She had a happier send-off from the staff, and Crow presented her with a potted plant from them all and wished her well. 'For we're all sure you deserve it, miss,' he said solemnly.

She went to join Lucy, and, after a meal, packed the last of their belongings. A taxi would take them the short distance to Cornel Mews in the morning.

Eloise Vincent was waiting for them when they arrived mid-morning. Peggy was at school, she told them. 'My daily woman will fetch her after lunch. I'm up to my eyes packing; I'm off this evening. I've written down all the names and addresses you might need and a phone number in case you should need me urgently, but for heaven's sake don't ring unless it's something dire.' She led the way upstairs. 'You each have a room; I'll leave you to unpack.' She glanced at the cat basket Lucy was holding. 'Is this the kitten? I dare say Peggy will like having him. There's coffee in the kitchen; help yourselves, will you? Lucy's bed is made up. I'm sorry I haven't put clean sheets on the other bed; the room's been turned out, but I had to empty cupboards and drawers—you won't mind doing it?'

She smiled charmingly and went downstairs, leaving them to inspect their new quarters. The rooms were prettily furnished and to have a room of one's own would be bliss. They unpacked and hung everything away and, with the kitten still in his basket, went downstairs. Mrs Wells, the daily cleaner, was in the kitchen. She was a pleasant-faced, middle-aged woman who poured coffee for them, found a saucer of milk for the kitten and offered to do anything to help. 'I've been here quite a while, before poor Dr Vincent died, so I know all there is to know about the place. I come in the mornings—eight o'clock—and go again after lunch,' she offered biscuits, 'though I said I'd fetch Peggy from school before I go home today.'

'Can't we do that?' asked Francesca. 'We have to get to know her, and it's a chance to see where the school is.'

'Well, now, that would be nice. It's at the end of Cornel Road, just round the corner in Sefton Park Street. Mrs Vincent hoped you wouldn't mind having a snack lunch—the fridge is well stocked and you can cook this evening. She is going out to lunch with a friend, but she'll be back by two o'clock, and aims to leave around six o'clock—being fetched by car.'

Francesca thought of the questions she wanted answered before Mrs Vincent left. She put down her coffee-cup. 'Perhaps I could talk to her now?'

Eloise Vincent was in the sitting-room, sitting at her desk, a telephone book before her, the receiver in her hand. She looked up and smiled as Francesca went in. 'Settling in?' she asked. 'Mrs Wells is a fount of knowledge if you've any questions.'

'Yes. She's been most helpful. Mrs Vincent, could you spare a moment? Just to tell me what time Peggy goes to bed, if there's anything she won't eat, which friends is she allowed to play with while you are away. . .?'

'Oh, dear, what a lot of questions. She goes to bed about seven o'clock, I suppose. She eats her dinner at school and I've been giving her tea about five o'clock. I don't know about her friends. My husband used to take her with him when he went to see his friends; they haven't been here, although on her birthday we had a party, of course——'

'May I have the names of your doctor and dentist?'

Mrs Vincent laughed. 'Oh, get Renier if anything is worrying you. He's Peggy's godfather; he's fond of her. She's never ill, anyway. Now, you really must excuse me—Mrs Wells can tell you anything else you may want to know.'

It was obvious to Francesca that Mrs Vincent had no more time for her. She went back to the kitchen and did a thorough tour of its cupboards and shelves, went through the linen cupboard with Mrs Wells and, when Mrs Vincent had left for her lunch appointment, sat down with Mrs Wells and Lucy to eat sandwiches and drink more coffee.

Peggy came out of school at three o'clock, and both of them went to fetch her since Mrs Vincent wasn't back. The children came out in twos and threes and Peggy was one of the last, walking slowly and alone.

They went to meet her and she seemed pleased to see them, walking between them, holding their hands, answering their cheerful questions about school politely. Only when Francesca said, 'The kitten's waiting for you,' did she brighten. They spent the rest of the short walk discussing suitable names for him.

Mrs Vincent was back and there was a car before the

door, which was being loaded with her luggage by a tall, middle-aged man. He said, 'Hello, Peggy,' without stopping what he was doing.

She said, 'Hello, Mr Seymour,' in a small wooden voice, all her animation gone again.

'You'd better go and say goodbye to your mother,' he told her over his shoulder. 'We're off in a few minutes.'

The three of them went inside and found Mrs Vincent in the sitting-room, making a last-minute phone-call. 'Darlings,' she cried in her light, pretty voice, 'I'm going now. Come and say goodbye to your old mother, Peggy, and promise to be a good girl while I'm away. I'll send you lots of postcards and when I can I will telephone to you.' She kissed her small daughter and turned to Francesca. 'I'll be trying to keep in touch,' she said. 'I'm sure you'll do a marvellous job. Let me know how you are getting on from time to time.'

She smiled, looking so pretty and appealing that Francesca smiled back, quelling the uneasy feeling that Eloise Vincent was only too delighted to be starting her theatrical career once more and couldn't wait to get away.

She was prepared for Peggy's tears once her mother had gone, but the child's face had remained impassive. 'May I have the kitten now?' she asked, almost before they were out of sight.

She and the small creature took to each other at once. She sat happily in the sitting-room with him on her small, bony knees, talking to him and stroking his head with a small, gentle hand. 'I shall call him Tom,' she told Francesca.

'That's a nice name.'

'Daddy used to read me a story about Tom Kitten. . .' The small voice quavered and Francesca said quickly, 'Shall we talk about your daddy? I'd like to know all about him.'

So that was the trouble, she reflected, listening to the child's rambling description of her father and the fun they had had together. Peggy had loved him dearly and there had been no one to talk to her about him. She let the child chat on, the small face animated, and then said gently, 'What nice things you have to remember about him, Peggy, and of course he'll never go away; he'll always be there inside your head.'

'I like you,' said Peggy.

It took a few days to settle into a routine. Lucy went to school each morning and Francesca took Peggy to her school shortly afterwards, going back to make the beds and shop and wash and iron while Mrs Wells gave the house what she called a good tidy up. Tom settled down without any nonsense, aware by now that he belonged to Peggy and no one else, sitting beside her chair at meals and sleeping at the foot of her bed.

There had been no news of Mrs Vincent. Francesca wasn't sure where she was, for the promised list of the various towns the company would be appearing in hadn't turned up. It was a relief that at the end of the week there was a cheque in the post with her salary and a housekeeping allowance.

It was two days later, after they had had tea and Francesca was on the floor in the kitchen, showing Peggy how to play marbles while Tom pranced around them both, that the front doorbell was rung.

'I'll go,' called Lucy, in the sitting-room with her

homework, and a moment later Professor Pitt-
Colwyn's voice sent Peggy flying to the kitchen door.
He caught her in his arms and kissed her soundly.
'Hello, love, I thought it was time I came to see how
you were getting on. . .'

He watched Francesca get up off the floor and brush
down her skirt. 'Marbles—am I in time for a game?'
and then he added, 'Good evening, Francesca.'

She was surprised at how glad she was to see him.
'Good evening, Professor.' She scanned his face and
saw that he was tired. 'Shall we go into the sitting-
room? I'll make a cup of coffee while you and Peggy
have a talk—she wants to show you Tom.'

He looked down at the small, earnest face staring up
at him. 'A splendid idea—shall we be disturbing Lucy?'

'I've just finished,' said Lucy. 'I'll help Fran get the
coffee——'

'A sandwich with it?' asked Francesca.

'That would be very nice.'

'Have you had no lunch or tea?'

'A rather busy day.' He smiled, and she could see
that he wasn't going to talk about it.

She made a pot of coffee, cut a plateful of cold beef
sandwiches and bore the tray into the sitting-room.
Peggy was sitting on the professor's knee and Tom had
curled up on her small lap. Francesca was astonished
to hear the child's happy voice, talking nineteen to the
dozen.

'We are talking about Peggy's father,' said the professor deliberately.

Francesca said at once, 'He must have been a
marvellous dad. Peggy has told us a little about him.'
She poured him a cup and gave it to him. 'You stay

there, darling. Here's your milk, and take care not to spill it over your godfather's trousers.'

She passed the sandwiches too, and watched him eat the lot. 'There's a cake I made this afternoon,' she suggested.

He ate several slices of that too, listening to Peggy's chatter, knowing just when to make some remark to make her giggle. Francesca let her bedtime go by, for the little girl was really happy. It was the professor who said at last, 'It's way past your bedtime, Peggy,' and when she wound her arms round his neck he said, 'If you go to bed like the good girl you are, I'll come and take you to the zoo on Saturday afternoon.'

'Fran and Lucy too?'

'Of course. Tom can mind the house and we'll come back here and have an enormous tea.'

She slid off his knee. Kissed him goodnight then, and went to stand by Francesca's chair. 'Will we?' she asked. 'Will we, really?'

'If your godfather says so, then of course we will, and I'll make a simply enormous cake and we'll have crumpets dripping with butter.'

'Could Lucy put her to bed?' asked the professor. 'We might have a chat?'

'Of course I can.' Lucy scooped up the kitten and handed him to Peggy. 'And Fran will come and tuck you up when you're in bed.'

Peggy went happily enough, her hand in Lucy's and the kitten tucked under one arm. Francesca, suddenly shy, offered more coffee.

'Any problems?' asked the professor.

She thought before she answered. 'No, I don't think so. I should have liked to have known a bit more about

Peggy before Mrs Vincent left, but there wasn't much time. Mrs Wells is a great help with things like shopping and so on. Peggy doesn't seem to have any friends. . .do you suppose it would be all right if I invited one or two children for tea one day? I think she is a very shy little girl.'

'She is a very unhappy little girl. She loved her father very much and she misses him; she likes to talk about him. I think that Eloise didn't understand that and the child is too small to carry so much hidden grief.' He glanced at her. 'She told me that she talks to you and Lucy about him.'

'Yes, he is still alive to her, isn't he? If you're sure that's the right thing to do?'

'Quite sure. By all means see if you can get some children round to play with her. Has she no friends at all at school?'

'Oh, one or two speak to her but she doesn't seem to have any special friends, but I'll do my best. She has masses of toys and it would be nice if she were to share them.'

'Have you heard from Eloise?'

'Me? No. She said she would be too busy rehearsing to write for a while.'

'I'm going to Cheltenham to see the opening show next week. If you think of anything you want to know about, let me know before then.'

'Thank you. She left everything beautifully organised. I expect she's a very good actress?'

He didn't answer, and she wondered uncomfortably if she had said something about Mrs Vincent which might have annoyed him. She couldn't think of anything but if he was in love with her, and she supposed that he was, he would be touchy about her. Lucy came in then.

'Peggy's bathed and in bed; she's waiting for you to say goodnight— both of you.'

The child wreathed her arms round Francesca's neck. 'I love you, Fran.'

'Thank you, darling. I love you too, and Tom of course. Now go to sleep quickly, won't you? Because he's asleep already.'

The professor was hugging in his turn, and he was reminded of his promise to take them to the zoo on Saturday, then he was kissed goodnight. 'Now tuck me in, please, Fran.'

So she was tucked in and he stood in the little room, leaning against the wall, watching, his eyes half closed.

Back in the sitting-room he said, 'I must be off. Thanks for the coffee and sandwiches.'

'It made Peggy very happy to see you,' Francesca said. The thought that it had made her very happy too was sternly dismissed. 'You will have a good meal before you go to bed, won't you?'

He looked as though he were going to laugh. 'Indeed I will.' He smiled at Lucy and dropped a large hand on Francesca's shoulder for a moment and went away. Lucy went to the window to watch him drive away, but Francesca busied herself with the cups and saucers.

'I shall enjoy the zoo,' said Lucy.

'Yes, it should be fun; Peggy will love it. Lucy, I must do something about finding her some friends. . .'

'Well, gossip around when you go to get her from school. I dare say our Eloise discouraged them— children are noisy and they make a mess. . .'

'You're probably right, but don't call her that,

dear—we might forget and say something—I mean, I
think he's in love with her, don't you? He's going all
the way to Cheltenham for the opening night.'

They were in the kitchen, washing up the coffee-
cups.

'That doesn't mean that he's in love with her. What
shall we have for supper? It's a bit late.'

The following day Francesca made a few tentative
overtures to the mothers and nannies taking the children to school. They were friendly enough, and she
made a point of letting them know that Mrs Vincent
had gone away for a time and that she was looking
after Peggy. She said no more than that, but it was, she
thought, the thin end of the wedge. . .

She wasn't sure, but she thought that maybe the
children had been discouraged from getting friendly
with Peggy, a child too shy to assert herself with the
making of friends. It might take some time, but it
would be nice if she could get to know a few children
while her mother was away, so that by the time she got
back home Peggy would have established a circle of
little friends. Already the child was livelier, learning to
play the games small children played, spending long
hours with Francesca or Lucy rearranging the elaborate
doll's house, planning new outfits for the expensive
dolls she had. 'Woollies for the winter,' explained
Francesca, getting knitting needles and wool and starting on miniature sweaters and cardigans.

They all went shopping the next day, and it was
apparent that Peggy had never been to Woolworth's.
They spent a long time there while she trotted from
one counter to the other, deciding how to spend the
pocket money Francesca had given her. After the

rigours of Lady Mortimor's household, life was very pleasant. Francesca, going about her chores in the little house, planning meals, playing wiith Peggy, sitting in the evenings sewing or knitting, with Lucy doing her homework at the table, felt that life was delightful. They had a home, well, not a permanent one, but still a home for the time being—enough money, the prospect of having some new clothes and of adding to their tiny capital at the bank. She was almost content.

The professor came for them after lunch on Saturday, bundled them briskly into his car, and drove to the zoo. It was a mild autumn day, unexpected after several days of chilly rain. Francesca, in her good suit, her burnished hair gleaming in the sunshine, sat beside him in the car making polite small talk, while Lucy and Peggy in the back giggled and chattered together. The professor, who had been up most of the night with a very ill patient, allowed the happy chatter from the back seat to flow over his tired head and listened to Francesca's pretty voice, not hearing a word she said but enjoying the sound of it.

The afternoon was a success; they wandered along, stopping to look at whatever caught their eyes, with Peggy skipping between them until she caught sight of the camels, who were padding along with their burden of small children.

The professor fished some money out of his pocket and gave it to Lucy. 'You two have a ride; Francesca and I are going to rest our feet. We'll be here when you get back.'

'You make me feel very elderly—bunions and dropped arches and arthritic knees,' protested Francesca, laughing as they sat down on an empty bench.

'You, my dear girl, will never be elderly. That is an attitude of mind.' He spoke lightly, not looking at her. 'You have settled down quite happily, I hope?'

'Oh, yes, and Lucy and Peggy get on famously.'

'So I have noticed. And you, Francesca, you mother them both.'

She was vexed to feel her cheeks grow hot. She asked stiffly, 'How is Brontes? And mother cat and the kittens?'

'He has adopted them. You must come and see them. The children are at school during the day? You will be free for lunch one day? I'll give you a ring.'

'Is that an invitation?' asked Francesca frostily.

'Certainly it is. You want to come, don't you?'

She had no intention of saying so. 'I shall be very glad to see mother cat and the kittens again.'

His stern mouth twitched a little. 'I shall be there too; I hope you will be glad to see me.'

'Well, of course.' She opened her handbag and looked inside and closed it again for something to do. She would be very glad to see him again, only he mustn't be allowed to know that. He was merely being friendly, filling in his days until Eloise Vincent should return. She wished that she knew more about him; she voiced the wish without meaning to and instantly wanted it unsaid.

'You flatter me.' He told her blandly, 'Really there is nothing much to tell. I work—as most men work. Perhaps I am fortunate in liking that work.'

'Do you go to a hospital every day or have a surgery?'

'I go to several hospitals and I have consulting-rooms.'

She persisted. 'If you are a professor, do you teach the students?'

'Yes. To the best of my ability!' He added gently, 'I examine them too, and from time to time I travel. Mostly to examine students in hospitals in other countries. I have a very competent secretary and a nurse to help me——'

'I'm sorry, I've been very rude; I can't think why I asked you about your work or—or anything.' She had gone pink again and she wouldn't look at him, so that the long, curling lashes, a shade darker than her hair, lay on her cheeks. She looked quite beautiful and he studied her with pleasure, saying nothing. It was a great relief to her when Lucy and Peggy came running towards them. Caught up in the excited chatter from Peggy, she forgot the awkward moment.

They went back to the little house in the Mews presently and had their tea: fairy cakes and a gingerbread, little sandwiches and chocolate biscuits. 'It's like my birthday,' said Peggy, her small, plain face wreathed in smiles.

The professor stayed for an hour after tea, playing ludo on the floor in front of the sitting-room fire. When he got to his feet, towering over them, he observed pleasantly, 'A very nice afternoon—we must do it again some time.' He kissed his small god-daughter, put a friendly arm around Lucy's shoulders, and went to the door with Francesca.

'I'll phone you,' was all he said, 'and thanks for the tea.'

It was several days later when she had a phone call. A rather prim voice enquired if she were Miss Haley and went on to ask if she would lunch with Professor Pitt-Colwyn in two days' time. 'If it wouldn't inconvenience you,' went on the voice, 'would you go to the Regent hospital at noon and ask for the professor?'

Francesca agreed. Were they going to eat at the hospital? she wondered, and what should she wear? It would have to be the brown suit again. Her winter coat was too shabby and although there was some money now Lucy needed a coat far more than she did. She would wash her hair and do her nails, she decided, and buy a new lipstick.

The Regent hospital was in the East End. It was a hideous building, heavily embellished with fancy brick-work of the Victorian era, brooding over a network of shabby streets. Francesca got off the bus opposite its entrance and presented herself at the reception desk inside the entrance hall.

The clerk appeared to know who she was, for she lifted the phone and spoke into it, and a moment later beckoned to one of the porters.

'If you would wait for a few minutes, Miss Haley, the porter will show you. . .'

Francesca followed the man, wishing that she hadn't come; she couldn't imagine the professor in this vast, echoing building. Probably he had forgotten that he had invited her and was deep in some highly urgent operation. Come to think of it, she didn't know if he was a surgeon or a physician. She sat down in a small room at the back of the entrance hall, facing a long corridor. It was empty and after a minute or two she was tempted to get up and go home, but all at once there were people in it, walking towards her: the professor, towering above the posse of people trying to keep up with him, a short, stout ward sister, two or three young men in short white coats, an older man in a long white coat, a tall, stern-looking woman with a pile of folders under one arm and, bringing up the rear, a worried-looking nurse carrying more folders.

The professor paused in the doorway of the room she was in, filling it entirely with his bulk. 'Ah, there you are,' he observed in a voice which suggested that she had been in hiding and he had just discovered her. 'Give me five minutes. . .'

He had gone and everyone else with him, jostling each other to keep up.

He reappeared not ten minutes later, elegant in a dark grey suit and a silk tie which had probably cost as much as her best shoes. They had been her best for some time now, and she hardly ever wore them for they pinched abominably.

'Kind of you to come here,' he told her breezily. 'I wasn't sure of the exact time at which I could be free. Shall we go?'

She walked beside him, out of the space reserved for consultants' cars, and got into the car, easing her feet surreptitiously out of her shoes. The professor, watching out of the corner of his eye, turned a chuckle into a cough and remarked upon the weather.

He drove west, weaving his way through the small side-streets until she, quite bewildered by the one-way traffic, saw that they were in Shaftesbury Avenue. But only briefly; he turned into side-streets again and ten minutes or so later turned yet again into a narrow street, its trees bare of leaves now, the houses on either side elegant Regency, each with a very small garden before it, steps leading up to doorways topped by

equally elegant fanlights. The professor stopped the
car and got out to open her door. 'I thought we might
lunch at home,' he told her. 'Brontes is anxious to see
you again.'

'You live here?' asked Francesca. A silly question,
but she had been surprised; it was, she guessed, five
minutes away from Mrs Vincent's cottage.

'Yes.' He took her arm and marched her up the steps
as the door was opened by a dignified middle-aged man
in a black jacket and pin-striped trousers.

'Ah, Peak. Francesca, this is Peak, who sees that
this place runs on oiled wheels. Mrs Peak is my
housekeeper. Peak, this is Miss Haley. Show her where
she can leave her coat, will you?' He picked up his bag.
'I'll be in the drawing-room, Francesca.'

In the charming little cloakroom concealed beneath
the curving staircase, she poked at her hair, added
more lipstick and deplored the suit; she had better take
off the jacket otherwise it might look as though she
were ready to dart out of the house again. Her blouse
wasn't new either, but it was ivory silk, laundered and
pressed with great care, and the belt around her slender
waist was soft leather. Her feet still hurt, but she would
be able to ease them out of her shoes again once they
were sitting at the table. She went back into the narrow
hall and the professor appeared at a half-open door.

'Come and have a drink before lunch.' He held the
door wide and Brontes stuck his great head round it,
delighted to see her.

The room was long and narrow, with a bay window
overlooking the street and a charming Adam fireplace.
The chairs were large and deep and well cushioned,
and there was a scattering of small lamp tables as well

as a handsome bow-fronted display cabinet embellished with marquetry, its shelves filled with silver and porcelain. The professor went to the rent table under the window. He asked, 'Sherry for you? And do sit down.'

She sat, and was aware that mother cat and her kittens were cosily curled up together in one of the easy chairs. She said, 'Oh, they seem very much at home.'

He handed her the sherry. 'Brontes has seen to that; he is their devoted guardian angel.'

She sipped her sherry, very aware of him sitting opposite her, Brontes pressed up against him, both of them watching her. Her tongue, as it sometimes did, ran away with her. 'Do you want to tell me something? Is that why you asked me to lunch?'

'Yes, to both your questions, but it can wait.' He settled back in his great chair. 'Your sister is a bright child; has she any ideas about the future?' It was a casual question and she answered readily enough.

'She's clever; she's set her heart on GCSEs, A levels, and a university.'

'Some discerning young man will snap her up long before then.' He smiled at her. 'And why aren't you married?'

It was unexpected. 'Well, I—I. . .that is, they weren't the right ones. None of them the right man.'

This muddled statement he received with a gentle smile. 'Have you any messages for Eloise?'

'If you would tell her that Peggy seems happy and is doing well at school and that everything is fine. She hasn't written or phoned, but I expect she's very busy.'

'Undoubtedly,' he agreed gravely. Peak came then to tell them that lunch was ready, and she went with the professor to a smaller room at the back of the house, which overlooked a surprisingly large garden. 'You've got trees, how lovely,' she exclaimed. 'It must look beautiful in the spring.'

They lunched off iced melon, baked salmon in a pastry case and a coffee *bavarois* and, while they ate, the professor kept the conversation quite firmly in his hands; impersonal topics, the kind of talk one might have had with a stranger sharing one's table in a restaurant, thought Francesca peevishly. Back in the drawing-room, drinking coffee from paper-thin cups, she said suddenly, 'I wish you would talk about your work—you looked different at the hospital; it's a side of you that I know nothing about.' She put down her cup. 'I'm sorry, I'm being nosy again.' She looked at her feet, aching in the shoes she longed to kick off. 'Only I'm interested,' she mumbled.

'I have an appointment at half-past two,' he told her. 'I'll drive you back as I go to my rooms, which means that we have half an hour. Do take off those shoes and curl up comfortably.'

'Oh, how did you know? I don't wear them very often and they're a bit tight. You don't mind?'

'Not in the least. What do you want to know about my work, Francesca?'

'Well, I know that you're a professor and a consultant, but are you a surgeon or a physician? You said you went to other hospitals and that you travelled. Why?'

'I'm a surgeon, open-heart surgery valve replacements, by-passes, transplants. Most of my work is at Regent's, but I operate at all the big provincial hospitals if I'm needed. I have a private practice and an out-patients clinic twice a week. I work in Leiden too, occasionally in Germany and the States, and from time to time in the Middle East.'

'Leiden,' said Francesca. 'You said "*tot ziens*" one morning in the park; we looked it up—it's Dutch.'

'My mother is a Dutchwoman; she lives just outside Leiden. I spend a good deal of time there. My father was British; he died two years ago.'

He looked at her, half smiling, one eyebrow raised in a gentle way. The half-smile widened and she thought it was mocking, and went red. He must think her a half-wit with no manners. She plunged into a muddled speech. 'I don't know why I had to be so rude, I do apologise, I have no excuse, if I were you I wouldn't want to speak to me again——'

He said gently, 'But I'm not you, and fortunately I see no reason why I shouldn't speak to you again. For one thing, it may be necessary from time to time. I did tell Eloise that I would keep an eye on Peggy.'

'Yes, of course. I—I expect that you would like to go now.' She sat up straight and crammed her feet back into her shoes and then stood up. 'Thank you for my lunch—it was delicious.'

He appeared not to notice how awkward she felt. Only as he stopped in Cornel Mews and got out to take the key from her and open the door of the cottage did he say, 'We must have another talk some time, Francesca,' and he bent to kiss her cheek as she went past him into the hall.

CHAPTER FOUR

FRANCESCA was sitting by the fire, reading to Peggy, when Lucy came in. 'Well, did you have a good lunch? What did you eat?'

Francesca recited the menu.

'Nice—to think I was chewing on liver and bacon. . . Where did you go?'

'To his house; it's quite close by.'

Lucy flung down her school books and knelt down by the fire. 'Tell me everything,' she demanded.

When Francesca had finished she said, 'He must be very rich. I expect he's clever too. I wonder what his mum's like.'

'How's school?'

'OK.' Lucy dug into a pocket. 'There's a letter for you, but don't take any notice of it; I don't want to go. . .'

The words were bravely said but palpably not true. A party of pupils was being organised to go skiing two weeks before Christmas. Two weeks in Switzerland with proper tuition and accompanied by teachers. The fare and the expenses totalled a sum which Francesca had no hope of finding.

'Oh, Lucy, I'm so sorry. If it's any consolation I'll get the money by hook or by crook for next winter.' She glanced at her sister's resolutely cheerful face. 'All your friends are going?'

'Well, most of them, but I really don't mind, Fran.

We can have a lovely time here, getting ready for Christmas.'

So nothing more was said about it, although Francesca sat up late, doing sums which, however hard she tried, never added up to enough money to pay for Lucy's skiing holiday. There was enough money set aside for her school fees, of course, but that wasn't to be touched. She went to bed finally with a headache.

There was no postcard from Mrs Vincent; nor was there a phone call. Francesca reminded herself that the professor would be with her, and most likely he would bring back something for Peggy when he returned. The child showed no concern at the absence of news from her mother, although it seemed to Francesca that she was looking pale and seemed listless; even Tom's antics were met with only a half-hearted response. Francesca consulted Mrs Wells. 'I think she should see a doctor. She isn't eating much either. I wonder if she's missing her mother. . .'

Mrs Wells gave her an old-fashioned look. 'I'm not one for telling tales out of school, but 'er mum never 'as had no time for 'er. Disappointed she was; she so pretty and charming and Peggy as plain as a pikestaff. No, you don't need to fret yerself about that, Miss Haley; little Peggy don't love 'er mum all that much. She was 'appier when her granny and grandpa came to visit. That was when Dr Vincent was alive—loved the child they did, and she loved them.'

So Francesca had done nothing for a few more days, although Peggy didn't seem any better. She had made up her mind to get a doctor by now. If only the professor had phoned, she could have asked his advice, but he, of course, would be wherever Mrs Vincent was. She fetched Peggy from school, gave her her tea which she didn't want and, as soon as Lucy came home, took the child upstairs to bed. Peggy felt hot and she wished she could take her temperature, but there was a singular lack of first-aid equipment in the house, and she blamed herself for not having attended to that. She sat the child on her lap and started to undress her, and as she took off her clothes she saw the rash. The small, thin back was covered with red spots. She finished the undressing, washed the pale little face, and brushed the mousy hair and tucked the child up in bed. 'A nice glass of cold milk,' she suggested, 'and Lucy shall bring it up to you.'

'Tom—I want Tom,' said Peggy in a small voice. 'I've got a pain in my head.'

'You shall have Tom, my dear,' said Francesca and sped downstairs, told Lucy, and went to the phone. Even if the professor were still away, surely that nice man Peak would have a phone number or, failing that, know of a local doctor.

She dialled the number Mrs Vincent had left in her desk and Peak answered.

'Peak, did Professor Pitt-Colwyn leave a phone number? I need to speak to him—Peggy's ill.'

'A moment, Miss Haley,' and a second later the professor's voice, very calm, sounded in her ear.

'Francesca?'

'Oh, so you are there,' she said fiercely. 'Peggy's ill; there's a rash all over her back and she feels sick and listless. She's feverish, but I can't find a thermometer anywhere and I don't know where there's a doctor and I've not heard a word since Mrs Vincent went away——'

'Peggy's in bed? Good. I'll be with you in about ten minutes.' He rang off and she spent a moment with the unhappy thought that she had been anything but calm and sensible; she had even been rather rude. . .and he had sounded impassive and impersonal, as though she were a patient to be dealt with efficiently. Though I'm not the patient, she thought in a muddled way as she went back to Peggy and sent Lucy downstairs to open the door for the professor, and then sat down on the side of the bed to hold the tearful child in her arms.

She didn't hear him come in; for such a big man he was both quick and silent. She was only aware of him when he put two hands on her shoulders and eased her away from Peggy and took her place.

He was unhurried and perfectly calm and apparently unworried and it was several minutes before he examined the child, took her temperature and then sat back while Francesca made her comfortable again. 'Have you had chicken-pox?' He glanced at Francesca.

'Me? Oh, yes, years ago; so has Lucy.'

'And so have I, and now so has Peggy.' He took the small, limp hand in his. 'You'll feel better very soon, Peggy. Everyone has chicken-pox, you know, but it only lasts a few days. You will take the medicine Francesca will give you and then you'll sleep as soundly as Tom and in the morning I'll come and see you again.'

'I don't want Mummy to come home——'

'Well, love, there really is no need. Francesca will look after you, and as soon as you feel better we'll decide what is to happen next, shall we?' He kissed the hot little head. 'Lucy will come and sit with you until Francesca brings your medicine. *Tot ziens.*'

Peggy managed a watery smile and said, '*Tot ziens*.'

In the sitting-room Francesca asked anxiously, 'She's not ill, is she? I mean, ill enough to let her mother know? She said she didn't want to be—that is, there was no need to ring her unless there was something serious.'

When he didn't answer she added, 'I'm sorry if I was rude on the phone; I was worried and I thought you were away.'

'Now why should you think that?'

'You said you were going to Cheltenham.'

'As indeed I did go.' He was writing a prescription as he spoke. 'Don't worry, Peggy is quite all right. She has a temperature but, having chicken-pox, that is only to be expected. Get this tomorrow morning and see that she takes it three times a day.' He took a bottle from his bag and shook out a tablet. 'This will dissolve in hot milk; it will make her more comfortable and she should sleep.'

He closed his bag and stood up. 'I'll call in on my way to the hospital in the morning, but if you're worried don't hesitate to phone me; I'll come at once.' At the door he turned. 'And don't worry about her mother. I'll be seeing her again in a day or so and then I can reassure her.'

Francesca saw him to the door and wished him a polite goodnight. If it hadn't been imperative that she should see to Peggy at once, she would have gone somewhere quiet and had a good cry. She wasn't sure why she wanted to do this and there really wasn't time to think about it.

Peggy slept all night and Francesca was up and dressed and giving the little girl a drink of lemonade when the professor arrived. He was in flannels and a thick sweater and he hadn't shaved, and she said at once, 'You've been up all night.'

'Not quite all of it. How is Peggy?'

They went to look at her together and he pronounced himself content with her progress. There were more spots now, of course, but her temperature was down a little and she greeted him cheerfully enough. 'Anything in moderation if she's hungry,' he told Francesca, 'and get the elixir started as soon as you can.'

'Thank you for coming. Lucy's made tea—we haven't had our breakfast yet. You'll have a cup?'

He refused pleasantly. 'I must get home and shower and change; I've an out-patients clinic at ten o'clock.'

She opened the door on to a chilly morning.

'I'll look in some time this evening.' He was gone with a casual nod.

It was late in the afternoon when Francesca had a phone call from Peggy's grandmother in Wiltshire. It was a nice, motherly voice with no hint of fussing. 'Renier telephoned. Poor little Peggy, but we are so glad to know that she is being so well looked after. I suppose you haven't heard from her mother?'

'Well, no, the professor said that he would be seeing her and that there was no need to let her know. Peggy is feeling much better and he is looking after her so well, so please don't be anxious.'

'She's our only grandchild and so like our son. He was Renier's friend, you know. They were at university together and school together—he was best man at their wedding and is godfather to Peggy.'

'Would you like to speak to Peggy? She's awake. I'll

carry her across to the other bedroom; there's a phone
there. . .'

'That would be delightful. Shall I ring off or wait?'

'If you would wait—I'll be very quick. . .'

The conversation went on for some time, with Peggy
on Francesca's lap, talking non-stop and getting too
excited. Presently Francesca whispered, 'Look, Peggy,
ask Granny if you can telephone her each day about
teatime, and if she says "yes" say goodbye now.'

A satisfactory arrangement for all parties.

The professor came in the evening, once more the
epitome of the well-dressed gentleman. He was coolly
polite to Francesca, spent ten minutes with Peggy, who
was tired and a little peevish now, pronounced himself
satisfied and, after only the briefest of conversations,
went away again.

'No need to come in the morning,' he observed, 'but
I'll take a look about this time tomorrow.'

The next day he told Francesca that Peggy might get
up in her dressing-gown and roam the house. 'Keep
her warm, she needs a week or so before she goes back
to school. You're dealing with the spots, aren't you?
She mustn't scratch.'

The next day he told her that he would be seeing
Eloise on the following day.

'How nice,' said Francesca tartly. 'I'm sure you will
be able to reassure her. Peggy's granny has been
phoning each afternoon; she sounds just like a
granny. . .' A silly remark, she realised, but she went
on, 'Peggy's very fond of her.'

'Yes, I know. I shall do my best to persuade Eloise
to let her go and stay with her for a few days. You will
have to go too, of course.'

'But what about Lucy?'

'I imagine that it could be arranged for her to board for a week or so? Eloise will pay, of course. Would Lucy mind?'

'I think she would love it. . .but it will be quite an expense.'

'Not for Eloise, and Peggy will need someone with her.'

'What about Tom?'

'I'm sure that her grandmother will make him welcome. I'll let you know.'

He made his usual abrupt departure.

'Most unsatisfactory,' said Francesca to the empty room. She told Lucy, of course, who found it a marvellous idea. 'They have such fun, the boarders— and almost all of my friends are boarders. Do you suppose Mrs Vincent will pay for me?'

'Professor Pitt-Colwyn seemed to think she would. He's going to let me know. . .'

'Well, of course,' said Lucy airily. 'If they're in love they'll do anything to please each other. I bet you anything that he'll be back in a few days with everything arranged.'

She was right. Several days later he arrived at teatime, just as they were sitting on the floor in front of the fire, toasting crumpets.

Peggy, no longer spotty but decidedly pasty-faced, rushed to meet him.

'Where have you been? I missed you. Francesca and Lucy missed you too.'

He picked her up and kissed her. 'Well, now I'm here, may I have a cup of tea and one of those crumpets? There's a parcel in the hall for you, too.' He put her down. 'Run and get it; it's from your mother.'

'Will you have a cup of tea?' asked Francesca in a hostess voice and, at his mocking smile and nod, went on, 'Peggy seems to be quite well again, no temperature for three days, but she's so pale. . .'

She came into the room then with the parcel and began to unwrap it without much enthusiasm. A doll—a magnificent creature, elaborately dressed.

'How very beautiful,' said Francesca. 'You must give her a name. What a lovely present from Mummy.'

'She's like all my other dolls and I don't like any of them. I like my teddy and Tom.' Peggy put the doll carefully on a chair and climbed on to the professor's lap. 'I had a crumpet,' she told him, 'but I can have some of yours, can't I?'

'Provided you don't drip butter all over me and Francesca allows it.'

Francesca passed a large paper serviette over without a word, and poured the fresh tea Lucy had made. That young lady settled herself on the rug before the fire once again and sank her teeth into a crumpet.

'Do tell,' she said. 'Is——?' She caught the professor's eye. 'Oh, yes, of course,' and went on airily, 'Did you have a nice time wherever you went?'

The professor, who had spent exactly twenty-four hours in Birmingham—a city he disliked—only four of which had been in Eloise's company, replied blandly that indeed he had had a most interesting time, as he had a flying visit to Edinburgh and, since heart transplants had often to be dealt with at the most awkward of hours, an all-night session there and, upon his return, another operation in the early hours of the morning at Regent's. Francesca, unaware of this, of course, allowed her imagination to run riot.

She said waspishly, 'I expect a man in your position can take a holiday more or less when he likes. Have another crumpet?'

He took one and allowed Peggy to bite from it before demolishing it.

'There are no more crumpets, I'm afraid,' said Francesca coldly, 'but there is plenty of bread. I can make toast. . .'

He was sitting back with his eyes closed. 'Delicious— well buttered and spread with Marmite. You know the way to a man's heart, Francesca.'

He opened one eye and smiled at her, but she pretended not to see that and went away to fetch some bread and a pot of Marmite. She put the kettle on again too, foreseeing yet another pot of tea.

The other three were talking about Christmas and laughing a great deal when she got back, and it wasn't until he had at last eaten everything he had been offered that he exchanged a glance with Lucy, who got up at once. 'Peggy! Help me take everything into the kitchen, will you, and we'll wash up? You can have an apron and do the washing; I'll dry.'

Peggy scrambled off the professor's knee. 'You'll not go away?'

'No. What is more, if I'm allowed to, I'll stay until you're in your bed.'

Left alone with him, Francesca cast around in her head for a suitable topic of conversation and came up with, 'Did Mrs Vincent give you any messages for me?'

'None. She thinks it a splendid idea that Peggy should go to her grandmother's for a week or so and

that you will go with her. She is quite willing to pay for
Lucy to stay at school during that time since she is
inconveniencing you. She has asked me to make the
arrangements and deal with the travelling and payment
of bills and so forth. Oh, and she wishes Mrs Wells to
come each day as usual while you're away.'

'Tom Kitten. . .?'

'He can surely go with you; I can't imagine that
Peggy will go without him.'

'No. I'm sure she wouldn't. You reassured Mrs
Vincent about Peggy not being well? She's not
worried?'

The professor had a brief memory of Eloise's pretty
face turning petulant at the threat of her new, exciting
life being disrupted. 'No,' he said quietly. 'She is
content to leave Peggy in your charge.'

'When are we to go?'

'Sunday morning. That gives you three days in which
to pack and leave everything as you would wish it here.
I'll telephone Mrs Vincent and talk to her about it; I
know that she will be delighted.'

'It won't be too much work for her?'

'She and Mr Vincent have plenty of help. Besides,
they love Peggy.'

'Am I to ask Lucy's headmistress if she can board
for a week or two?'

'I'll attend to that as well.'

Lucy and Peggy came back then. 'I've washed up,'
piped Peggy importantly, 'and now I'm going to have a
bath and go to bed. I'll be so very very quick and if
you like you can see where my spots were.'

'I look forward to that,' he assured her gravely. 'In
ten minutes' time.'

He went as soon as Peggy, bathed and in her nightgown, had solemnly shown him the faint scars from her spots and then bidden him a sleepy goodnight.

His goodbyes were brief, with the remark that he would telephone some time on Saturday to make final arrangements for Sunday.

Lucy was over the moon; she was popular at school and had many friends and, although she have never said so, Francesca was aware that she would like to have been a boarder, and, as for Peggy, when she was told there was no containing her excitement. Something of their pleasure rubbed off on to Francesca and she found herself looking forward to the visit. The future seemed uncertain: there was still no word from Mrs Vincent, although Peggy had had a postcard from Carlisle. There had been no message on it, merely a scrawled, 'Hope you are being a good girl, love Mummy'.

Francesca's efforts to get Peggy to make a crayon drawing for her mother or buy a postcard to send to her came to nought. She wrote to Mrs Vincent's solicitor, enclosing a letter to her and asking him to forward it. She gave a faithful account of Peggy's progress and enclosed an accurate rendering of the money she had spent from the housekeeping allowance, assured her that the little girl was quite well again and asked her to let her know if there was anything special she wished done. The solicitor replied immediately; he understood from Mrs Vincent that it was most unlikely that she would be returning home for some time and Miss Haley was to do whatever she thought was best for Peggy. It wasn't very satisfactory, but Francesca realised that she would have to make the best of it. At least she could call upon the professor again if anything went wrong, and, now that they were going to stay with Peggy's grandparents for a while, they would surely accept responsibility for the child.

The professor telephoned quite early on Saturday morning; he would take Lucy to her school and at the same time have a word with the headmistress. 'Just to make sure that everything is in order,' he explained in what Francesca described to herself as his soothing voice.

'Should I go with you?' she wanted to know.

'No need. I dare say you've already had a few words with her.'

Francesca, feeling guilty, said that yes, she had. 'Just about her clothes and so on,' she said placatingly, and was answered by a mocking grunt.

He arrived on the doorstep in the afternoon with Brontes sitting on the back seat, greeted her with casual civility, assured Peggy that he would take her to her granny's in the morning, waited while Lucy bade Francesca goodbye at some length and then drove her away, refusing politely to return for tea. 'I'm expecting a call from Eloise,' he explained, watching Francesca's face.

Lucy telephoned in the evening; she sounded happy and any doubts that Francesca might have had about her sister's feeling homesick were swept away. She promised to phone herself when they arrived at Peggy's grandparents' house and went away to finish packing.

The professor arrived in time for coffee which Mrs Wells, who had popped round to take the keys and lock up, had ready. He was in an affable mood, answering Peggy's questions with patience while

Brontes brooded in a kindly fashion over Tom. Francesca drank her coffee and had nothing to say, conscious that just having the professor there was all she wanted; he annoyed her excessively at times and she didn't think that he liked her overmuch but, all the same, when he was around she felt that there was no need for her to worry about anything. The future was vague—once Mrs Vincent came home she would be out of work again—but then in the meantime she was saving almost every penny of her wages and she liked her job. Moreover, she had become very fond of Peggy.

Rather to her surprise, she was told to sit in the front of the car. 'Brontes will take care of Peggy,' said the professor. 'Tom can sit in the middle in his basket.'

She stayed prudently silent until they joined the M4 where he put a large, well-shod foot down and allowed the car to slide past everything else in the fast lane. 'Just where are we going?' she asked a shade tartly.

'Oh, dear, did I not tell you? But you do know Wiltshire?' When she nodded he added, 'Just on the other side of the Berkshire border. Marlborough is the nearest town. The village is called Nether Tawscombe. They live in the Old Rectory, a charming old place.'

'You've been there before?'

He laughed shortly. 'I spent a number of school holidays there with Jeff and later, when we were at Cambridge and medical school, we spent a good deal of time there.'

'Then he got married,' prompted Francesca.

'Yes. Eloise was never happy there; she dislikes the country.'

Something in his voice stopped her from saying

anything more; she turned round to see how the occupants of the back seat were getting on. Peggy had an arm round Brontes's great neck, she had stuck the fingers of her other hand through the mesh in front of Tom's basket and wore an expression of happiness which turned her plain little face into near prettiness. Francesca, who had had secret doubts about the visit, knew that she had been mistaken.

They arrived at Nether Tawscombe in time for lunch. The one village street was empty under the thin, wintry sunshine, but the houses which lined it looked charming. They got larger as the street went uphill until it reached the church, surrounded by a churchyard and ringed around by fair-sized houses. The Old Rectory was close by; an open gate led to a low, rambling house with diamond-paned windows and a solid front door.

As the professor stopped before it, it was opened and an elderly man came to meet them. She stood a little on one side until Peggy's excited greetings were over and the two men had shaken hands. She was led indoors while the professor saw to their baggage. The hall was stone-flagged, long and narrow, with a door opening on to the garden at the back of the house at its end. Brontes had made straight for it and had been joined by a black Labrador, who had rushed out of an open doorway as a grey-haired lady, cosily plump, had come into the hall.

Peggy screamed with delight and flung herself at her grandmother, and Mr Vincent said to Francesca, 'Always had a soft spot for each other—haven't had her to stay for a long time. This is delightful, Miss—er. . .?'

'Would you call me Francesca, please? Peggy does.'

Mrs Vincent came to take her hand then, with a warmth which caused sudden tears to prick her eyelids, for the last few years she had been without that kindly warmth. . .

That the professor was an old friend and welcome guest was evident: he hugged Mrs Vincent, asked which rooms the bags were to go to, and went up the wide staircase with the air of a man who knew his way about blindfold.

Mrs Vincent saw Francesca's eyes follow him and said comfortably, 'We've known Renier for many years. He and our son were friends; he spent many a school holiday here and Jeff went over to Holland. He's a good man, but I suspect you've discovered that for yourself, Miss. . .may I call you Francesca?'

'Oh, yes, please. What would you like me to do? Take Peggy upstairs and tidy her for lunch? She's so happy and excited.'

'Yes, dear. You do exactly what you've been doing. We know so little about her day-to-day life now that her father is dead—he brought her here very often, you see.'

No mention of Eloise, reflected Francesca. It wasn't her business, of course. She bore Peggy away upstairs to a couple of low-ceilinged rooms with a communicating door and windows overlooking the wintry garden beyond. After London, even the elegant part of London, it was sheer bliss.

The professor stayed to lunch and she was mystified to hear him say that no, he wasn't going back to London.

'Having a quiet weekend at Pomfritt Cleeve? Splendid,' observed Mr Vincent, and most annoyingly said no more about it.

Renier took his leave soon after lunch, saying good-bye to Francesca last of all, patting her shoulder in an avuncular fashion and remarking casually that he would probably see her at some time. She stood in the hall with everyone else, wishing with all her heart that she were going with him. For that was where she wanted to be, she realised with breathtaking surprise, with him all the time, forever and ever, and, now she came to think about it, she had been in love with him for quite some time, only she had never allowed herself to think about it. Now he was going; not that that would make any difference—he had always treated her at best with friendliness, more often than not with an uninterested politeness. She looked away so that she didn't see him go through the door.

However sad the state of her heart, she had little time to brood over it. Peggy was a different child, behaving like any normal six-year-old would behave, playing endless games with the Labrador and Tom, racing around the large garden with Francesca in laughing pursuit, going for rides on the elderly donkey who lived in the paddock behind the house, going to the shops in Marlborough with her grandmother and Francesca. She had quickly acquired a splendid appetite and slept the moment her small head touched the pillow. A good thing too, thought Francesca, for by bedtime she was tired herself. She loved her days in the quiet village and Mr and Mrs Vincent treated her like a daughter. Sometimes she felt guilty that she should be living so comfortably while Lucy was in London, although she thought that her sister, from all accounts, was as happy as she was herself. They missed each other, but Francesca had the sense to see that it was good for Lucy to learn independence. She tried not to think of the professor too often and she felt that she was succeeding, until after a week or so Lucy wrote her usual letter and mentioned that he had been to see her at the school and had taken her out to tea. 'To the Ritz, no less!' scrawled Lucy, with a lot of exclamation marks.

The professor, having returned Lucy to her school, went to his home and sat down in his great chair by the fire with Brontes pressed against his knee and mother cat and the kittens asleep in their basket to keep him company. Tea with Lucy had been rewarding and he had made no bones about asking questions, although he had put them in such a way that she hadn't been aware of how much she was telling him. Indeed, she had confided in him that her headmistress had offered her a place in a group of girls from her class going to Switzerland for a skiing holiday. 'But of course I can't go,' she had told him. 'It's a lot of money and Fran couldn't possibly afford it—I mean, we both have to have new winter coats, and if Mrs Vincent comes back we'll have to move again, won't we?'

He had agreed with her gravely, at the same time prising out as much information about the trip as he could. He stroked Brontes's great head. 'I shall have to pay another visit to Eloise,' he told the dog. 'Now how can I fit that in next week?'

Presently he picked up the telephone on the table beside him and dialled a number.

A week, ten days went by. Peggy was so happy that Francesca began to worry about their return; she saw that the child loved her grandparents and they in turn loved her. They didn't spoil her, but she was treated with a real affection which Francesca felt she had never had from her mother. One morning when Peggy had gone off with her grandfather, leaving Francesca to catch up on the washing and ironing of the child's wardrobe, Mrs Vincent came to sit with her in the little room behind the kitchen where the ironing was done. 'You must be wondering why we don't mention Peggy's mother. Oh, I know we talk about her because Peggy must not forget her mother, but you see Eloise never wanted her and when she was born she turned against her—you see she takes after my son, and Eloise was so pretty. She said that her friends would laugh at such an ugly child. It upset Jeff, but she was fortunate—he was a loyal husband; he took Peggy around with him as much as possible and they adored each other. It was a pity that Peggy overheard her mother telling someone one day that she wished the child had not been born. She never told her father, bless the child, but she did tell Mrs Wells, who told me. There is nothing I would like better than to have Peggy to live with us always.'

'Have you suggested it to Eloise?'

'No; you see she will probably marry again and he might like to have Peggy for a daughter.'

Francesca thought Mrs Vincent was talking about the professor. She said woodenly, 'Yes, I dare say that would be very likely.'

It seemed as though it might be true, for the very next day he arrived just as they were sitting down to lunch.

Francesca, going out to the kitchen to ask Bertha, the housekeeper, if she could grill another few chops for their unexpected guest, was glad of her errand: it gave her time to assume the politely cool manner she could hide behind. It was difficult to maintain it, though, for when she got back to the dining-room it was to hear him telling the Vincents that he was on his way to see Eloise. 'I shall be glad of a word with you, sir,' he told Mr Vincent, 'as my visit concerns Peggy, and I think you should know why I am going.'

Francesca ate her chop—sawdust and ashes in her mouth. Afterwards she couldn't remember eating it; nor could she remember what part she took in the conversation during the meal. It must have been normal, for no one looked at her in surprise. She couldn't wait for the professor to be gone, and as though he knew that he sat over coffee, teasing Peggy and having a perfectly unnecessary conversation with Mrs Vincent about the uses of the old-fashioned remedies she used for minor ailments.

He got up at length and went away with Mr Vincent to the study, to emerge half an hour later and, amid a great chorus of goodbyes, take his leave.

This time Francesca watched him go; when next she saw him he would most likely be engaged to Eloise— even married. She was vague about special licences but, the professor being the man he was, she had no doubt that if he wished to procure one at a moment's notice he would find a way to do so.

It was three days later when Mr Vincent remarked to his wife, 'Renier phoned. He has got his way. He's back in London, but too busy to come down and see us for a few days.'

Mrs Vincent beamed. 'Tell me later—how delightful; he must be very happy.' Francesca, making a

Plasticine cat for Peggy, did her best to feel happy, because he was happy, and one should be glad to know that someone one loved was happy, shouldn't one? She found it hard work.

He came at the end of the week, walking in unannounced during a wet afternoon. He looked tired; he worked too hard, thought Francesca lovingly, scanning the weary lines on his handsome face. He also looked smug—something she found hard to understand.

CHAPTER FIVE

RENIER had had lunch, he assured Mrs Vincent, before going with Mr Vincent to the study again. When they came back into the sitting-room the older man said, 'Well, my dear, it's all settled. Which of us shall tell Peggy?'

'What?' asked Peggy, all ears. 'Is—is it something nice? Like I can stay here forever?'

'You clever girl to guess,' said Mrs Vincent, and gave her a hug. 'That's exactly what you are going to do—live here with Grandpa and me and go to school every day.'

Peggy flung herself at her grandfather. 'Really, truly? I may stay here with you? I won't have to go back to Mummy? She doesn't want me, you know.'

'Well, darling, your mummy is a very busy person and being on stage is very hard work. You can go and see her whenever you want to,' said Mrs Vincent.

'Shan't want to. Where will Francesca go?'

Francesca went on fixing a tail to another cat and didn't look up. 'If there is no objection, I think it might be a good idea if I took her somewhere quiet and explained everything to her,' said the professor.

He added gently, 'Get your coat, Francesca, and come with me.'

'Now that is a good idea,' said Mrs Vincent. 'Run along, dear; Renier will explain everything to you so much better than we can.'

There was no point in refusing; she fetched her old
Burberry and went out to the car with him, to be
greeted with pleasure by Brontes, who was roaming
the garden. The professor opened the door and stuffed
her gently into her seat, got in beside her and, with
Brontes's great head wedged between their shoulders,
drove off.

'Where am I going?' asked Francesca coldly.

'Pomfritt Cleeve. I have a cottage there. We can talk
quietly.'

'What about? Surely you could have told me at Mrs
Vincent's house?'

'No, this concerns you as well as Peggy.'

He had turned off the main road into a narrow, high-
hedged lane going downhill, and presently she saw a
cluster of lights through the gathering dusk. A minute
or so later they had reached the village—one street
with a church halfway along, a shop or two, and small,
old cottages, well maintained—before he turned into
another narrow lane, and after a hundred yards or so
drove through a propped-open gate and stopped before
a thatched cottage of some size. There were lights in
the windows and the door was thrown open as she got
out of the car, hesitating for a moment, giving Brontes
time to rush through the door with a delighted bark,
almost knocking down the stout little lady standing
there. She said, 'Good doggie,' in a soft, West Country
voice and then added, 'Come on in out of the cold, sir,
and the young lady. There's a good fire in the sitting-
room and tea in ten minutes.'

The professor flung an arm around her cosy person
and kissed her soundly. 'Blossom, how very nice to see
you again—and something smells delicious.'

He caught Francesca gently by the arm. 'Francesca, this is Blossom, who lives here and looks after the cottage for me. Blossom, this is Miss Haley. Take her away so that she can tidy herself if she wants to, and we'll have tea in ten minutes, just as you say.'

The cottage, decided Francesca, wasn't a cottage really. It might look like one, but it was far too big to warrant such a name, although there was nothing grand about it. The sitting-room to which she was presently shown was low-ceilinged with comfortable chairs and tables dotted around on the polished floor. There was a low table before the fire and sofas on either side of it. She sat opposite her host, pouring tea into delicate china cups and eating scones warm from the oven and, having been well brought up, made light conversation.

However, not for long. 'Let us dispense with the small talk,' said the professor, 'and get down to facts. Eloise is quite happy to allow Peggy to live with her grandparents. She will of course be free to see the child whenever she wishes, but she will remarry very shortly and intends to stay on the stage, so it isn't likely that she will visit Peggy more than once in a while. Mrs Vincent will employ her old nanny's daughter to look after Peggy, so you may expect to leave as soon as she arrives.' Francesca gave a gasp, but he went on, 'Don't interrupt, I have not yet finished. Lucy has been told that she may join a school party going to Switzerland to ski—I have seen her headmistress and she will join the party.'

'Now look here,' said Francesca, and was hushed once more.

'I haven't said anything to you, for I knew that you would refuse to do anything about it. The child deserves a holiday and, as for the costs, you can repay me when you are able.'

'But I haven't got a job,' said Francesca wildly. 'I never heard such arrogance—going behind my back and making plans and arranging things——'

'Ah, yes, as to arrangements for yourself, Eloise is quite agreeable to your remaining at the cottage for a few days so that you can pack your things.'

She goggled at him, bereft of words. That she loved him dearly went without saying, but at the moment she wished for something solid to throw at him. 'You have been busy, haven't you?' she said nastily.

'Yes, indeed I have. I shall drive Lucy over to Zeebrugge to meet the school party there; you would like to come with us, no doubt.'

'How can I? I'll have to look for a job——'

'Well, as to that, I have a proposal to make.' He was sitting back, watching her, smiling faintly.

'Well, I don't want to hear it,' she declared roundly. 'I shan't listen to anything more you may say——'

'Perhaps this isn't the right time, after all. You are cross, are you not? But there is really nothing you can do about it, is there? You will break young Lucy's heart if you refuse to let her go to Switzerland——'

'She had no skiing clothes.'

'Now she has all she needs—a Christmas present.'

She all but ground her teeth. 'And I suppose you're going to get married?'

'That is my intention.'

Rage and despair almost choked her, and she allowed rage to take over.

'I hope you will be very happy.' Her voice was icy and not quite steady.

'I am certain of that.'

'I'd like to go back.' He agreed at once, which was a good thing—otherwise she might have burst into tears. Where was she to go? And there was Lucy to think of when she got back from Switzerland. Would she have time to get a job by then? And would her small hoard of money be sufficient to keep them until she had found work again? There were so many questions to be answered. Perhaps she should have listened to this proposal he had mentioned—it could have been another job—but pride wouldn't allow her to utter another word. She bade Blossom goodbye, complimented her on the scones and got into the car; it smelled comfortingly of leather and, very faintly, of Brontes.

Strangely enough, the great bulk of the professor beside her was comforting too, although she could think of no good reason why it should be.

Back at the Vincents' house after a silent drive, he bade them goodbye, bent his great height to Peggy's hug, observed cheerfully to Francesca that he would be in touch, and left.

She had no idea what he had said to the Vincents, but from what they said she gathered that they understood her to have a settled future, and there seemed no point in enlightening them. Peggy, chattering excitedly as Francesca put her to bed, seemed to think that she would see her as often as she wanted, and Francesca said nothing to disillusion her. The future was her own problem.

She left the Vincents two days later, and was driven back to the mews cottage by Mr Vincent. She hated leaving the quiet village. Moreover, she had grown very fond of Peggy who, even while bidding her a tearful goodbye, was full of plans to see her again, which were seconded by her grandmother. She had responded suitably and kept up a cheerful conversation with her companion as they drove but, once he had left her at the empty house, with the observation that they would be seeing each other shortly, she sat down in the kitchen and had a good cry. She felt better after that, made a cup of tea, and unpacked before starting on the task of re-packing Lucy's cases as well as her own. There had been a brief letter for her before she left the Vincents', telling her that they would be crossing over to Zeebrugge in two days' time, and would she be ready to leave by nine o'clock in the morning and not a minute later?

Mrs Wells had kept the place spotless, and there was a note on the kitchen table saying that she would come in the morning; there was a little ironing and nothing else to do but pack. She was halfway through that when Lucy phoned.

'You're back. Isn't it exciting? I can't believe it's true. I'm coming home tomorrow afternoon. The bus leaves here in the evening, but Renier says he'll take us to Zeebrugge early the next day and I can join the others there. Isn't he a darling?' She didn't wait for Francesca's answer, which was just as well. 'Oh, Fran, I do love being a boarder. I know I can't be, but you have no idea what fun it is. I've been asked to lots of parties at Christmas, too.'

Francesca let her talk. There was time enough to worry over the problem of Christmas; she still had almost three weeks to find a job and somewhere for them to live, too.

'You're very quiet,' said Lucy suddenly.

'I've had a busy day; I'm packing for us both now—I'll do the rest tomorrow. I've got to talk to Mrs Wells, too.'

'I'll help you. You are looking forward to the trip, aren't you?'

'Tremendously,' said Francesca with her fingers crossed. 'See you tomorrow, Lucy.'

By the time Lucy arrived, she had done everything that was necessary. Mrs Wells had been more than helpful, arranging to come early in the morning to take the keys and lock up. The solicitor had been dealt with, she had been to the bank and taken out as much money as she dared, found their passports—unused since they had been on holiday in France with their parents—and, finally, written a letter to Mrs Vincent which she had enclosed in a letter to the solicitor. There was nothing more to do but have a good gossip and go to bed.

The Bentley purred to a halt outside the cottage at precisely nine o'clock, then the professor got out, wished them an affable good-morning, put Francesca's overnight bag and Lucy's case in the boot, enquired as to what had been done with the rest of their luggage—safely with Mrs Wells—and urged them to get in. 'You go in front, Lucy,' said Francesca and nipped into the back seat, not seeing his smile, and resolutely looked out of the window all the way to Dover, trying not to listen to the cheerful talk between the other two.

Five hours later they were in Zeebrugge, driving to the hotel where the rest of the party had spent the night, and it was only then that she realised that she had no idea what was to happen next. There wasn't

any time to think about it; the bus was ready to leave.
It was only after a hasty goodbye to Lucy, when she
was watching the party drive away, that the full awkwardness of the situation dawned upon her. 'Whatever
am I going to do?' She had turned on the professor,
her voice shrill with sudden fright. 'When is there a
boat back?'

He took her arm. 'We are going to my home in
Holland for the night. My mother will be delighted to
meet you.'

'I must get back—I have to find a job.'

He took no notice, merely urged her gently into the
car, got in beside her and drove off.

'This is ridiculous. . . I've been a fool—I thought we
would be going straight back. I'm to spend the night at
Mrs Wells's house.'

'We will telephone her.' His voice was soothing as
well as matter-of-fact. 'We shall soon be home.'

They were already through Brugge and on the motor-
way, bypassing Antwerp, crossing into Holland, and
racing up the Dutch motorways to Tilburg, Nijmegen
and on past Arnhem. The wintry afternoon was turning
to an early dusk and, save for a brief halt for coffee
and sandwiches, they hadn't stopped. Francesca, trying
to make sense of the situation, sat silent, her mind
addled with tiredness and worry and a deep-seated
misery, because once they were back in England there
would be no reason to see the professor ever again.
The thought cast her in such deep gloom that she
barely noticed the country had changed: the road ran
through trees and thick shrubbery with a light
glimpsed here and there. The professor turned off the
road through a gateway, slowed along a narrow, sanded

drive and stopped before the house at its end. He leaned over, undid her safety belt, got out and helped her out too, and she stood for a moment, looking at the dark bulk of the house. It was square and solid, its big windows lighted, frost sparkling on the iron balcony above the porch.

She said in a forlorn voice, 'I should never have come with you. I should never have let you take over my life, and Lucy's, too. I'm very grateful for your help; you have been kind and I expect it suited you and Eloise. I can't think why you've brought me here.'

'You wouldn't listen to my proposal at Pomfritt Cleeve,' the professor had come very close, 'I can see that I shall have to try again.' He put his arms around her and held her very close. 'You are a stubborn, proud girl with a beautiful head full of muddled thoughts, and I love you to distraction. I fell in love with you the first time I saw you, and what is all this nonsense about Eloise? I don't even like the woman, but something had to be done about Peggy. Now you will listen, my darling, while I make you a proposal. Will you marry me?'

What with his great arms around her and her heart thumping against her ribs, Francesca hadn't much breath—only just enough to say, 'Yes, oh, yes, Renier,' before he bent to kiss her.

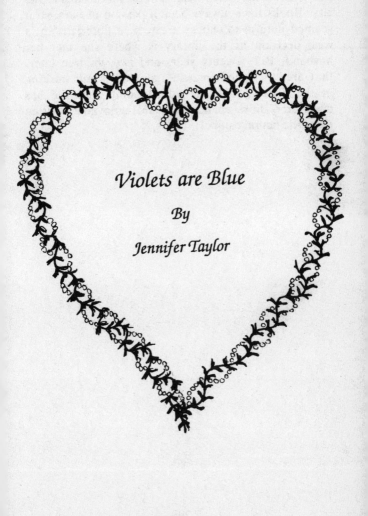

Violets are Blue

By

Jennifer Taylor

Jennifer Taylor was born in Liverpool, England, and still lives in the north-west, several miles outside the city. Books have always been a passion of hers, so it seemed natural to choose a career in librarianship, a wise decision as the library is where she met her husband, Bill. Twenty years and two children later, they are still happily married, and she is still working in the library, with the added bonus that she has discovered how challenging and enjoyable writing romantic fiction can be!

CHAPTER ONE

HE HADN'T changed. Oh, there were traces of silver in the black hair at his temples, a few more lines around those light green eyes which made such a startling contrast to the darkness of his tanned skin, but basically he hadn't changed.

Michael Callan had walked out of that very door almost three years before but as he stood there now, tall and arrogant, staring around the assembled group, Claire experienced again that familiar, disturbing surge of awareness—only this time she ruthlessly suppressed it. He might not have changed, but she had! She was no longer the foolish, trusting girl who had worn her heart on her sleeve. This time her relationship with Michael Callan was going to be strictly business!

'Cal! Good to see you. How was the flight?' Tom Jackson, manager of the store, hurried forwards, a beaming smile barely concealing the anxiety they all shared. Michael Callan had built himself the reputation of a hard taskmaster in the past few years and he wouldn't be pleased about recent events. The fact that he had come himself from New York to sort out the problems at Hadley's London store, flagship of the worldwide chain his family had built its fortune on, was proof of that.

'Tom.' He shook the man's hand then walked past him to take the seat behind the desk as though it was his right, and Claire felt her blood start to boil at the deliberate slight to Tom. Without a word she got up and fetched another chair, setting it next to hers in the row lined up in front of the huge mahogany desk.

'Thanks.' Tom sat down and smiled nervously around the room at the rest of the staff, who were starting to look uneasy. 'I think you know everyone here, don't you, Cal? I'd just like to say on behalf of us all what a pleasure it is——'

'Let's cut the formalities, shall we, Tom, and get right down to business?' Cal opened the case he'd set on top of the desk and drew out a folder before glancing along the row. Claire steeled herself for that moment when his eyes would meet hers, for that first hint of recognition, but he did no more than skim a cool glance over her face before his gaze travelled on. 'You all know why I am here. What I want to hear now is an explanation as to why this branch is losing money. We are at present in the position of making a loss of some seventeen per cent each month. That is totally unacceptable and unless we can find some way to reverse the situation fast then I'm afraid this store will have to close.'

'Close? But Cal, you can't really mean that. . .?' Tom tailed off, looking helplessly around at all the other stunned faces.

'I rarely say things I don't mean. Right, I asked that you should all prepare a report on the state of your departments, outlining your plans for the future. Let's start with you, shall we, Graham? Electrical is just about holding its own thanks to the Christmas trade but it still isn't doing the sort of turnover we expect. Let's hear your views.'

He sat back in the leather swivel chair, loosening his

tie and unbuttoning the collar of his white shirt in a gesture that was achingly familiar to Claire. He had always hated the restriction of formal clothing, pulling off his tie and unbuttoning the collar of his shirt as soon as he'd got home to the flat they had shared so briefly. So many memories, so many fragments of a past they had once shared, all the love, all the laughter, held at bay these past years, yet suddenly they came rushing back and the room and the steady drone of Graham's voice faded.

'Claire!' She jumped when Tom dug her hard in the ribs, colouring as she caught sight of all the faces turned her way.

'Sorry,' she said quickly. 'I missed that.'

'I asked if you would like to give your report next, Claire. If it isn't too much trouble, that is.'

The sarcasm in his deep voice stung. Claire lifted her head, meeting the frosty green stare across the desk with an equally cool one of her own. 'Of course, Mr Callan.'

His jaw tightened at the deliberate, mocking formality, his hand contracting around the folder of notes, and just for a second Claire regretted what she'd said, before tossing the silky blonde bob of hair back from her flushed face in a gesture of defiance. It was about time that someone pricked that damnable composure of his! He'd got too used to being the one to cut people down, but, still, it wouldn't be wise to antagonise him too much.

Conscious of the icy atmosphere, she gave her report, keeping her eyes centred on her notes until she came to the end. 'In the absence of Miss Jones, our departmental head, I didn't feel it appropriate that I should put forward any plans for the future. I am sure that she must have her own ideas and would prefer to discuss them with you herself.'

'Perhaps she would; however, as Miss Jones is absent yet again through sickness, that isn't possible. The directive I issued was quite straightforward, Claire. I asked that each and every department head or his assistant should prepare a report stating why turnover is down and what improvements can be made in the future.' He glanced down at the notes he'd spread on the desk, his face uncompromising as he looked back at her. 'Over recent months Greetings Cards and Gifts is one of the departments that has shown the greatest losses. So may I suggest that you take yourself into the outer office and start putting a few ideas down on paper—that is if you can manage to keep your mind fully on the business at hand? Now, David, how about——?'

'Just a minute! Who do you think you are to speak to me like that? I am not some schoolgirl whom you can tell off for not doing her homework! I didn't outline any plans for the department because I felt it wasn't my place to do so!' She was so angry that she could hardly see straight, lights flashing across her blurred vision. How she loathed him! Loathed him for his arrogance, his cold, unremitting use of authority, his total lack of any human feelings. He had always had a tendency towards high-handedness when they had lived together and she had foolishly gone along with it, too blinded by her love for him to want to argue. He had meant everything to her then. She had lived just to hear him laugh, to see him smile at her as though she was someone special in his life, but no more. She'd had a cruel awakening to the fact that it had all been a lie. He had taken what he'd wanted from her then tossed her aside, too intent on pursuing his own driving ambitions to care about her.

'No, you aren't a schoolgirl, Claire, even though it appears you intend to act like one. You are an employee of this company. . .remember?' He sat back, flexing his shoulders as though he was tired, but there was no weariness about the grim set of his face as he stared at her then looked around at the rest of the group. 'I want to make one thing clear here and now to everyone in this room and that is that I am not interested in hurt pride, injured feelings or any other such emotions. All I'm concerned about is getting this store back on its feet, or, if that proves impossible, in closing it down while causing the least damage possible to the rest of the chain.' He studied each person in turn before his gaze returned to Claire's flushed face. 'If that causes a problem for any one of you then I expect you to tell me now.'

'I'm sure we are all with you on this, Cal.' Tom broke the tense silence that had fallen over the room. 'We are all committed to bringing the London branch back to the top of the league.'

'That's all I wanted to hear.' He turned away, ignoring Claire, who quietly gathered up her notes and left the room. She closed the door, shutting out the sound of his deep voice, wishing it were as easy to shut him completely out of her mind. She'd been dreading their meeting ever since she'd heard that he was coming back, but nothing could have prepared her for that confrontation.

She went and sat down at the desk, spreading her

notes in front of her, but her mind was far away. All she could think of was Cal's voice, so cold and impersonal as he'd reminded her that she was an employee. She had to remember that that was all she was to him now and lock the memories of those golden days when they had loved and laughed together deep in the back of her mind. It was over and they'd both moved on; she'd rebuilt her life, made new friends, and she wouldn't allow any feelings of bitterness to destroy all that she'd worked so hard to achieve. She was an employee, and that suited her just fine!

With a sigh, she forced herself to concentrate on drawing up the plans he wanted. Not that it was a difficult task. She had plenty of ideas, most of them firmly squashed by Miss Jones at one time or another. The elderly head of department had her own fixed ideas on how things should be run, and didn't welcome interference. Now, however, Claire allowed her imagination free rein.

When the connecting door between the offices opened, she didn't glance up, assuming that Tom had been sent to fetch her back into the meeting. 'Just give me a second. I'd better make sure that our dear boss has everything he wants otherwise I shall be well and truly in the doghouse——' She broke off, horrified to see Cal when she finally glanced around. 'I. . .I didn't realise it was you. I thought it was Tom.'

'Obviously. How are you getting along? Have you managed to put some ideas down on paper?' The cool, dismissive note in his voice hurt. This man had held her, kissed her, made love to her, yet now he spoke to her as though she were a stranger!

She stood up, tidying the papers into a pile, her blue

eyes bright as glass as they met his. 'I have plenty of
ideas. Did you think I hadn't? Were you using this as
some sort of test to see if I can cope?' She shook her
head, the silky pale hair swinging back and forth.
'Sorry to disappoint you, Mr Callan, but I am not
lacking in ability to do my job!'

'I never imagined that you were. You wouldn't be
working here if that was the case. I have kept track of
your progress, Claire, and I have to admit that I've
been impressed with your achievements so far. You've
gone from a junior sales position to assistant departmental head in less than three years. That proves that
you have the ability as long as you don't allow personal
feelings to interfere.'

He turned to go but Claire caught his arm, her
fingers closing around the hard muscles under the
smooth, fine wool of his grey suit. 'And that isn't
something anyone can ever accuse you of doing, is it,
Cal? You never allow personal feelings to interfere in
business.' She laughed, a hollow sound that held a note
of scorn. 'Don't I know that! You were quite happy to
use me for your own ends while you were maintaining
that masquerade of being just an ordinary employee
but once you'd assumed your rightful position as one
of the Hadley family then you couldn't wait to get rid
of me, could you? You didn't want me then.'

'That's where you're wrong.' With a speed that was
alarming, he swung her round and caught her hand as
she tried to draw it away from his arm. 'I wanted you a
lot, sweet, seductive little Claire.' He pulled her closer,
his fingers hard around hers. 'I could still want you
now, in fact. Is that what this is all about? Is that why
you're trying to provoke my anger—to see if there

is still that same marvellous sexual chemistry between us?' He hauled her to him, his arms closing around her body. 'Let's test it out, shall we?'

'No! Cal, stop it! Stop——!' His mouth closed over hers, his lips bruising as he kissed her with a deliberate passion. Claire tried to turn her head away to escape the kiss, but his finger burrowed under her long, pale hair, forcing her to stay where she was. She moaned softly, hating the rough assault of his mouth on hers, and felt him still for a moment before slowly the bruising pressure eased and he began to kiss her in a way that sent a sudden fierce sensation of heat along her veins. This time his lips weren't trying to punish— they were seducing, warm and mobile, awakening memories of other times when he had kissed her just this way. Time seemed to be suspended, the past rolling into the present, then Cal put her from him and everything shot back into bitter, sharp focus.

'So now we know the spark is still there if and when we ever choose to rekindle it. But I'm afraid we shall have to leave any further discussions, tempting though they may be, until later. There are more pressing matters to attend to now.'

'There won't be any later!' She rubbed her mouth, feeling shaken to the core by what had happened. She'd convinced herself that she was over him, but how could she be when one deliberate kiss could light this fire inside her again?

'Oh, I think there will. There has to be, and you know that, Claire. However, everyone is waiting for your report right now.'

He went back through to the inner office, leaving the door open for her to follow. Claire took a shaky breath then smoothed her ruffled hair back from her hot face. How she hated him, now more than ever! She would cling to that thought to get through the rest of the day. After all, in a few hours' time he would be back in New York and that would be the end of it all.

She was aware of the speculative looks cast her way as she walked back into the meeting but she ignored them, focusing all her attention on Cal, unwilling to give him the chance to take her to task again after the last disturbing occasion.

'Right, then, Claire, let's hear your plans.' He looked down at his notes to check some figures, his tone cool and quite impersonal once more. 'Greetings Cards has been steadily declining for some time now, apart from a small upsurge at Christmas. So what do you propose to do to rectify the situation?'

Claire glanced at what she'd written, hesitant now about putting her ideas forward, but that upsurge in business he'd mentioned had been the result of her planning when Miss Jones had first gone off sick. Maybe she wasn't so way off track after all. 'It seems to me that the real problem lies in the fact that there has always been a tendency to let greetings cards sell themselves. People need a card for birthdays, Christmas and so on. There's never been much promotional work done in the past.' She paused for a moment, but Cal's face was totally impassive so she hurried on. 'It will be cutting things fine as we're already into January but I would like to do a big promotion centred around St Valentine's Day. Oh, I know we always do a display of the cards, but I want to do more than that. I want to really push the idea of sending a valentine this year, make the public feel that it is something they *must* do.'

'And how do you intend to do that?' Cal straightened, his eyes narrowing on her with interest in their green depths. How she'd used to love looking into those eyes, used to thrill at the way the colour would change from palest clear green to a stormy jade as he'd been aroused to passion. Now just the memory was enough to make her breathless so that it was an effort to remember where she was and what had just happened between them. She was more vulnerable around Cal than she cared to admit.

'I was hoping that we could run some sort of a competition as a draw, perhaps offer a weekend in Paris for the winner, with champagne for the runners-up. The whole store can be involved even if it's just by carrying the entry forms, but we could decorate selected departments with hearts, flowers and devote window space to the theme. Fashion, lingerie, the flowershop, all can contribute something, I'm sure, but obviously Greeting Cards will be the central point of the promotion, offering a gift-wrap service, balloons, maybe even handwritten valentines. We could hope to increase turnover by around fifty per cent during the weeks running up to Valentine's Day itself.'

'I see. Interesting.' He tapped his fingers on the desk. 'We've had Christmas, we're in the middle of the sales, so it would mean a lot of hard work for everyone.'

'I'm sure none of us would mind that, Cal.' Tom leant forwards, an earnest expression on his pleasant face. 'We are all very anxious about the store's future and not just because of our jobs. This shop is an

institution: it would be a crying shame to see it forced
to close. We want it back at the top!'

'And this along with the rest of the ideas you've all
put forward today could help achieve that. Good.
That's what I wanted to hear. I had reservations when
I came over on the plane as to whether the commitment
was still as strong as it used to be, but obviously it is. If
we work together then I'm sure we can keep this store
open.'

There was a collective sigh of relief as he stopped
speaking. Cal smiled suddenly, looking so much more
like the man she had once fallen in love with that
Claire felt her heart start to ache. How different would
her life have been if Cal had been what she'd thought
he was—a young man working his way to the top? She
had no idea, just the cold certainty of knowing that it
was pointless to speculate now.

'I can see you're all relieved. I know it hasn't been
easy for any of you recently. My uncle was unwell for
some time before he retired and didn't keep the control
he should have done over the business. However, that
is in the past. Now I have a few suggestions I want to
put to you—nothing earth-shattering, mind, just a few
ideas to prove that I am prepared to do my share of
the work.' He looked round, his gaze lingering almost
deliberately on Claire so that she had the strangest
feeling that he knew she wasn't going to like what he
was about to say.

'The American end of the business is very healthy at
present. So much so that I feel I can safely leave it in
other capable hands while I come back to England and
concentrate on getting this branch back up to standard.
I won't be usurping Tom's position as manager. I shall

be working in an advisory capacity with each department in turn and in view of what I've just heard I propose that the first department I shall turn my attention on is Greetings Cards and Gifts. Claire and I shall be working together on the valentine project.'

Proposal? That wasn't a proposal! The word proposal implied a degree of flexibility, a chance to consider the facts and *then* make a decision. This was all cut and dried. Michael Callan was coming back to England to work in the store. . .to work with *her*. . . and there wasn't a thing she could do or say to make him change his mind!

CHAPTER TWO

'I'D LIKE a word with you before you go, Claire.'

Claire glanced after the rest of the group, a trace of desperation in her eyes as Tom closed the door to leave her and Cal alone in the office. 'I really have to get back. What do you want?'

He glanced at his watch then slipped the folder into the case as he came round the desk. 'Just a few words in private. I have to catch the afternoon flight back to New York but I have a couple of hours before I need to be at the airport. We may as well have some lunch.'

'I don't want any lunch, thank you. Look, Cal, I have nothing whatsoever to say to you of a private nature. Now, if you'll excuse me, I must go. We're short-staffed with Miss Jones being off.'

'And that's what I want to talk to you about.' He steered her out of the office and along the corridor to the lift before she had time to draw breath to object again. 'Sorry if I made it sound as though I had something personal to say to you. It's purely business, I can assure you, but something I don't want spreading around until all the details are finalised.'

He summoned the lift, raising a quizzical brow when she hovered uncertainly at his side, not sure if she should believe him or not. 'Scout's honour, Claire. This is business. And don't go worrying about the department. I had a word with Tom earlier and he's arranged cover over the lunchtime period.'

'I doubt very much if you were ever a Scout and as for honour. . .!' She smiled waspishly at him. 'I don't think you have much idea what that word means.'

He laughed slowly, standing aside for her to precede him into the lift. 'What a little firebrand you've turned into, Claire. You used to be a whole lot more amenable three years ago.'

'I was a lot of things three years ago, but I've grown up now, Cal. I'm not some gullible young girl now!'

'No, you're not.' He slid a gaze over her, his eyes lingering on her slender figure in a way that sent heat rushing along her veins. 'You're how old now—twenty-three. . .four? And a very beautiful woman who obviously knows what she wants from life and intends to have it. Yes, Claire, you have changed.'

'Well, you haven't! You always were arrogant and self-opinionated. It may surprise you to learn that I don't give a toss what you think of me now!'

'No?' He studied her flushed face in silence, then let his eyes meet hers and linger for a heartbeat. 'Then why are you getting so upset?'

'I am not getting upset!' She drew in a deep breath, forcing the anger down, willing herself to stay calm. 'Look, Cal, this is ridiculous. We are two adults who once shared. . .well, shared a relationship, but it's all in the past and I'd be grateful if you wouldn't keep on trying to remind me of it all the time. Frankly, it isn't something I want to remember all that much!'

'Yet you were the one who started it this morning at the meeting. Be honest with yourself, Claire, and admit that you would never have dreamt of challenging me that way if we hadn't shared that. . .relationship.'

His eyes bored into hers, brilliant green, searching. . .

for what? An admission that he was right? They both knew that he was. 'No, I wouldn't, but nor would you have spoken to me in that tone either, Michael Callan. You want honesty, do you? Well, then, I'll be honest and tell you straight that the thought of having to work with you for the next few weeks isn't pleasant!'

'Why not? Surely you've worked with other men you've dated? You aren't trying to tell me that you've led the life of a nun for almost three years, or that all the men in the store are blind to your obvious attractions?' His tone was mocking, bringing a flush of colour to her face. When the lift stopped at the ground floor she could hardly wait to get out, hurrying ahead of him towards the taxi he pointed out that was waiting in the car park, using the few minutes it took to get in to gather her composure around her.

Yes, she had dated several of the men who worked at the store, and was still on friendly terms with them, but then none had touched her emotions as Cal had done. He had been the yardstick she had unconsciously measured them against and each one had fallen short. It was easy to work with them now, but it wouldn't be easy to work with Cal and that bothered her. If she were really over him then it shouldn't have mattered, should it?

The thought held her silent on the short drive to the small, exclusive restaurant down by the river. Claire stepped out on to the pavement, jumping nervously when Cal slid a hand under her elbow to guide her in through the door. She moved away from him, looking round the room, studying the subdued lighting, the crisp white tablecloths, the clientele whose very appearance spoke of wealth, then turned to smile coldly at Cal.

'Showing your true colours now, I see.' She indicated the subtle opulence of the restaurant with a dismissive sweep of her hand, icy scorn ringing in her voice. 'I don't recall us visiting places like this before, but then, of course, you were keeping up that pretence of being just another Hadley employee.'

His brows lowered, his face grim and remote as he studied her in silence for a moment. 'And I don't recall us *wanting* to come to places like this. We were happy with the simple things in life, remember? However, I brought you here today not to impress upon you how things have changed but to reassure you. I use this place for business whenever I'm in town.'

As though to emphasise the point the head waiter came over, greeting Cal by name as he led them to a table in the far corner of the room. Claire sat down, smoothing the linen napkin across her knees, wishing she'd held her tongue. She *did* remember how things had been, how a simple picnic in the park had meant more than any expensive gourmet meal. The magical ingredient had been love and that had turned even the most ordinary outing into something special.

'You never did answer my question.' His voice drew her out of her reverie. Claire sat up straighter, forcing herself to meet his eyes across the table and ignore the echoes of the past.

'What question?'

'About who you've dated in the store.' He put the menu down, leaning back in the gilt-framed chair, his expression both cool and mocking, instantly kindling her temper again.

'I don't see that it's any of your business, do you?'

'Maybe not, but I can't help but be curious as to what you've been doing since we broke up.'

'Well, I haven't been sitting around pining for you!' she snapped.

'I never imagined that you would have. So come on, then, Claire, tell me who the man in your life is at present. Is it anyone from the store or someone with no connections there at all?'

What should she say? How could she admit that there was no one special in her life and hadn't been since he'd left? That was the one thing she had no intention of admitting!

'Not that I see what business it is of yours, but Tom and I have been seeing each other recently.' It was such a small lie but she crossed her fingers anyway as she uttered it. She had been out with Tom on several occasions but both had soon realised that the relationship would go no further than friendship.

'Tom? Now that does surprise me.' He steepled his fingers, staring at her over the top in a way that made her want to wriggle in the seat, but she curbed the urge.

'Yes! We enjoy each other's company. Is that a crime?'

He ignored the sarcasm, smiling calmly back at her. 'No. Tom is a nice enough guy but he's hardly your type, Claire.'

'Is that right? And what makes you such an expert on the type of man I need?' She let her eyes drift over him, clasping her hands tightly together on the napkin, afraid that she would be sorely tempted to reach over and slap his arrogant face. 'I don't really think that you have any idea of my taste in men.'

'Haven't I indeed?' He leant forwards suddenly, pinning her with a glance. 'Let's not play games, Claire. We both know the type of man you need.'

'Meaning you, I suppose?' Sensations were rushing through her, threatening to destroy her composure, but she fought against them with a steely determination that stemmed from fear of letting him see how she really felt. 'Sorry, Cal, but I think not. A few years ago maybe, but now the type of man who attracts me isn't the least like you. He's warm, caring, a man who puts relationships before the demands of business.' She smiled bitterly back at him, feeling her heart aching with a sharp, fresh pain. 'I'm afraid that you don't fit that bill at all.'

'No?' He reached out and caught her chin, smoothing the pad of his thumb across her mouth, watching the way her lips parted almost helplessly under the evocative caress. 'I'm sure I could make you change your mind about that.'

'I. . .' It was hard to think while he was touching her like this but she had to try, had to break this spell he was casting over her again. She jerked her head away, running her hand across her mouth to wipe away the lingering sensation of heat. 'I don't want you to change my mind. I'm perfectly happy with my life the way it is. Now I believe that you said you had something you wanted to discuss with me, something to do with work, that is?'

It was an effort to keep her voice level but she managed it. She couldn't afford to let him see how shaken she felt. It would give him an advantage she couldn't afford to lose. Michael Callan was a worthy opponent no matter what game he chose to play. Why he should choose to play this one now was beyond her but she had to keep her head and remember how dangerous he could be.

He sat back, smiling faintly as he studied the warmth in her smooth cheeks. 'I shall have to take your word for it that you are happy, then, Claire, but I have my doubts. However, now isn't the time to debate the point. . .not in such a public place, at least——' He broke off as the waiter came to take their order. Claire opted for the chef's salad, knowing she couldn't manage anything more substantial. Her stomach was a churning mass of nerves thanks to Cal. She had no intention of letting him walk all over her but it would be foolish to start an argument. She had to stay calm and let him believe that she didn't care what he thought. After all it wasn't a lie: she *did* like her life the way it was now, neat and ordered, uncluttered by any deep emotional entanglements. If she occasionally yearned for the excitement and passion that had been such an integral part of their relationship then she had learned to keep such feelings locked at the very back of her mind.

'Right, we'd better get down to business, then.' Cal glanced at his watch then back at her, his expression coolly impersonal once more. 'Over the past few months I have become increasingly concerned about Miss Jones's frequent absences. It is a situation that I feel cannot be allowed to continue.'

'What do you mean?' Claire stared back at him in consternation. 'I know she's been sick a lot recently but surely you can't be planning on dismissing her?

She's been with the firm over thirty years! That should count for something even with you!'

His mouth thinned with displeasure. 'I am well aware of how long she has worked for us, and *no*, I am not planning on dismissing her. I have a very strong sense of loyalty towards Hadley's employees, especially those who have given the sort of devotion to the company that Miss Jones has.'

Claire had the grace to blush at the rebuke but she wouldn't apologise for what she'd said until he'd made it clear what he intended. 'Then what are you planning on doing about it?'

'I have already started the ball rolling. I asked Tom to visit her at home and find out if she would be interested in taking early retirement.' He shrugged. 'It's a benefit I've been keen to introduce for some time and now seems like the ideal opportunity.'

'I see, and what did she say about the idea?'

'Once she discovered that financially she would lose very little, she was delighted to accept. It seems that work has become increasingly stressful for her of late and I think she was just relieved to discover that she could retire earlier than she'd planned.'

His consideration shouldn't have surprised her. The Cal she remembered had always been a caring man who had willingly helped others less able than himself. Yet somehow over the years they'd been apart she'd built up this picture in her mind of a cold, ruthless despot, storing the rumours about his tough business deals as evidence of the fact. Had it been a deliberate attempt on her part to find things to dislike about him? She had the uncomfortable and disturbing feeling it had.

Guilt made her smile warmly at him. 'I think it's a marvellous idea. I know she finds it hard to cope but she's just tried to carry on.'

'Well, this should solve her problems and ours as well. We need people in this store who are open to fresh ideas, Claire. Staff who aren't so deeply rooted in traditions that they won't try something different. With that in mind I have decided to offer you the position of head of department when Miss Jones leaves. What do you say?'

'Me? I. . . Well. . . Why me, Cal?' She shook her head, trying to clear the jumble of thoughts, and felt a cold wave of sickness envelop her as a sudden unpalatable thought struck her. 'There are many others who have worked for the firm longer than I have and who are better qualified to take over the job, so why offer it to me? It isn't meant to be some sort of a sweetener, is it?'

His eyes narrowed at the sharpness of her tone but he spoke calmly. 'No, it isn't. What a suspicious little mind you have, Claire.'

'Is it any wonder?' She drew in a slow breath but it was hard to stay unemotional. 'I've not had much reason to trust you, Cal, so is it any wonder if I view this offer with more than a trace of scepticism?'

'This is business, Claire. You above anyone should know that I never put personal feelings before business decisions. His eyes held hers, cold, glacial, so remote that she felt a sharp stab of pain and wished for a moment that she hadn't voiced her concerns before she realised that she was doing it again, allowing him to manipulate her emotions. She couldn't afford to soften.

She had to find out exactly what was behind this offer of promotion.

'I still don't accept that I'm the best person for the job, not because I don't feel that I can cope with it but because of the mere fact that I have only been assistant departmental head for less than a year. There are others who've been waiting for promotion far longer than that.'

'There are, but that doesn't mean that they are ready to handle it. As far as I'm concerned, Claire, you are the one person who can put that department back on its feet. The ideas that you outlined this morning only serve to emphasise that. All I want to know is if you are willing to accept.'

'I. . .' What should she say? It was a golden opportunity, something she'd been working towards, but could she trust him? Yet on the other hand why should she throw all her hard work away? As he'd just said, she knew that business always came first in his life.

'Come on, Claire. What's the problem? Yes or no?' There was mockery in his deep voice and she glared at him. He was the problem and he knew it! Knew that her reluctance stemmed from a fear of being drawn back into his life. But she was her own woman now: he couldn't make her do anything that she didn't want to. The days when she had hung on to Michael Callan's every word and rushed to fulfil his every whim were long past!

'Yes. Thank you, I shall accept.'

'Good. I was hoping that you would.' He smiled at her, his eyes so warm that a shiver raced down her spine. He picked up the bottle of wine and filled their glasses, then raised his in a toast. 'Here's to us, Claire. To our new. . .alliance.'

Claire picked up her glass, her hand trembling as she touched it lightly against his then set it down again. Had she done the right thing? Or had she just made the biggest mistake of her life? She had the uncomfortable feeling that only time would tell.

'There's a few phone calls I need to make. I'll be upstairs if you need me, Claire. Just phone through. Oh, and leave the rest of that display until I get back.'

Claire stiffened at the sound of the slow, deep voice. She should have become used to having Cal around by now but she hadn't. He'd been working in the department for over a week yet she still hadn't found a way to quell this instant surge of awareness every time he spoke. She glanced over her shoulder to where he stood, immaculate in a dark grey suit and pale blue shirt that did all the right things for his tall, leanly muscled body, and sighed. Why did he have to come back?

'All right? Can you manage, then?'

Did he *mean* to make it sound as though she couldn't? Claire didn't bother giving him the benefit of the doubt as she stared coldly back. 'I shall try my best, but don't worry, Mr Callan, I shall phone you up if I find that I can't!'

His face tightened, his green eyes frosty. 'Feel free.' He turned away, walking briskly towards the escalator without a backward glance. Claire watched him go, ruing the fact that she had let her temper get the better of her again. It had kept happening all the time this past week and it was starting to worry her. She wasn't normally so quick-tempered, but there again the situation wasn't exactly normal, was it?

Annoyed with both herself and him, she glanced round at the silk hearts and gilt cupids that decorated the department. Everyone had worked so hard getting the promotion off the ground and it was nearly finished, just another few items to be set in place. She'd be damned if she'd stand about wasting time until Cal chose to come back. She would finish it off herself.

Hadley's was an old building, with elegant wooden panelling stretching up to high ornate ceilings, but it was only when she reached the top of the ladder that Claire fully realised just how high they were. She stopped to catch her breath then reached over to hang the last gilt cupid into place, gasping when the ladder slipped a fraction so that she was forced to grab hold of the cupid to steady herself, then found to her horror that she couldn't seem to persuade herself to let it go again. She seemed to be frozen in place, one hand clutching the shiny gilt cupid, the other clinging to the ladder.

'Claire! What the hell are you doing? Get down at once!' There was no mistaking the anger in Cal's voice but she found it as impossible to answer as she did to move. Grimly, she hung on then gave a tiny scream when the ladder shook.

'It's all right. I'm just coming up there to get you.' His voice was soft, soothing; it seemed to break the spell and she looked round, eyes widening when she saw him climbing up to stand just beneath her.

'Now I want you to move your foot slowly down to the next rung. Can you do that for me, Claire?'

'Y-yes.' She inched her foot off the tread to feel for

the one below. Cal's fingers closed gently around her ankle, warm and firmly reassuring as he positioned her foot in place.

'Good. And again, just another step. Slowly now. There's no need to rush.' His fingers brushed the back of her leg as he moved down a rung and prepared to help her again and Claire shuddered, finding far more danger in that disturbing touch than in being stuck twenty feet off the ground!

'I can manage now. You don't need to help me any more,' she said faintly.

'I'm sure you can but let's do this my way.' Once again his fingers found the slim curve of her ankle, then slid up her calf to steady her as she stepped down. Claire bit her lip, feeling shivers of fire fanning out from where his hand rested on her leg. Without another word she let him help her, gasping when he lifted her the last few feet then slowly let her slide to the ground. She moved away from him at once, conscious of the fact that her pulse was racing, and not just from fear. What was it about him that affected her so? She wished she knew, then maybe she could find some way to cure this awareness she always felt when he was near.

'Thank you,' she said stiffly. 'But I could have managed.'

'Could you indeed? It didn't look that way to me! What a stupid thing to do. What were you trying to prove, Claire? Just how well you can do everything by yourself? Well, I'm afraid it misfired this time, my sweet!'

'Don't you "my sweet" me! And I wasn't trying to prove anything. I just wanted to get the display finished.'

'And that was more important than your safety?'

'Of course not! I was perfectly safe. It just startled me when the ladder slipped but I could have got down without your help.'

'Oh, come on!' He shook his head, a lock of dark hair falling rakishly across his brow when she started to protest. 'Save your breath. We both know that you were too scared to move. It was pure stubbornness that made you climb up there in the first place instead of waiting for me to do it.'

'I *could* have got down! However, if you choose to see yourself as my rescuer, then feel free. As for my being stubborn, well, I have no idea why you should think that.' She went to walk away, incensed by his high-handedness and his perceptive reading of the situation, but he caught her arm and stopped her, an expression on his face that sent an immediate *frisson* down her spine.

'You seem to forget how well I know you, Claire.' His hand slid down her arm, his fingers burning through the thin silk of her white blouse as they laced around her wrist. 'I remember just how stubborn you can be at times.'

'So what do you expect me to say? Should I feel flattered that you remember so much about me?' She dragged her arm away, rubbing her wrist to erase the burning touch, wishing she could wipe away the pain she felt at the coldly arrogant assertion. 'I'm sorry to disappoint you but I don't give a damn what you do or don't remember! That's all in the past and that's where it is going to remain!'

'Is that right? Somehow it doesn't seem so simple to separate the past and the present any longer.' He stared down at her in silence. 'It would be easy to pick up the threads again, wouldn't it, Claire? There's still a lot of feeling left between us.'

'Don't be ridiculous! My heaven, but I never fully realised before just how huge your ego is! You can't bear to think that I've got over you.'

He shrugged. 'I'm a realist. But if you want to carry on fooling yourself then be my guest. However, this does need talking through, though not here. Perhaps over dinner tonight if you're free?'

'I won't ever be free for you! Do you really imagine that I would be fool enough to fall for that?' She laughed hoarsely, her face paper-white. 'There is no way that you are manoeuvring me into another affair! If you need female companionship then find someone else, because I am not interested! The only thing we have in common is business.'

'Is it?' He moved suddenly, trapping her against the shelves, shielding her from any curious eyes as he stood in front of her so close that she could feel the heat from his body. For a silent moment he stared into her eyes then smiled slowly as his gaze dropped deliberately to her mouth in a look she could feel. 'You say that with such fervour, Claire, yet I find it difficult to believe it.' He ran a finger softly down her cheek, triumph gleaming in his eyes when he heard her swift intake of breath.

Claire closed her eyes then pushed him away, her heart aching at the deliberate way he was trying to torment her. 'Then I suggest you try harder. I'm not interested in anything you have to say unless it's related to business.'

'I see. In that case I'd better tell you what I came to

before I got side-tracked.' He leant easily against the wooden panelling, composed, assured, unperturbed by what had happened and her obvious anger, and that more than anything enabled Claire to get a grip on her emotions.

'And that was?' she asked.

'That I've been making arrangements for you to fly to the New York store next week.'

'New York? But. . .I don't understand. Why do you want me to go there?' It was hard to follow this sudden switch in conversation from personal to business.

'Experience. You will be taking over the department soon so now seems like the ideal opportunity for you to get some idea of how our other branches operate. One of the major failings here has been the lack of any ongoing training programme. I mean to rectify that. New York has been directed to undertake a valentine project too so that it would be invaluable experience for you to compare their ideas with your own at first hand.'

'I see. But when would you want me to go?' She glanced round uncertainly. 'I want to get this under way first.'

'Naturally, but it should be up and running by next week. I can't claim that all the American sales techniques would work here but we can all learn a lot from them. So what do you say?'

'Well, yes. Obviously I would love to go.' Her mind was working overtime. What a marvellous opportunity it would be not only to learn about the other store but to get away from Cal for a time and give herself a breathing-space. That was all she needed, of course— a few days to get herself back in hand. He was no longer a part of her life and she accepted that; it was just the fact that he was always around that had been proving so difficult to handle lately.

'Good.' He turned to go then stopped, glancing back at her, something about his expression that made her new-found optimism waver. 'I forgot to mention that I shall be flying out there with you.'

'You will?' It was impossible to hide her shock. It felt as though the ground had just fallen away beneath her, leaving her teetering on the edge of some vast chasm.

'Mmm, there's a few problems that need my attention so I thought we may as well make the journey together. It isn't a problem, is it?'

The mockery in his eyes told her that he knew that it was, but she'd be damned if she'd admit it! 'No.'

'Well, that's settled, then. I'll let you have all the details.'

Claire murmured a response then turned away, making a great performance out of clearing up the mess from the display. He had sounded so businesslike as he'd explained his reasons for this trip but that glint in his eyes warned her that he might have other, different ideas. Well, if he had then he was going to be sorely disappointed! Oh, she wasn't fool enough to imagine that he had been harbouring thoughts of turning back the clock because he *cared* about her. Far from it. From what she could see, Michael Callan's ego was the only thing suffering here. He didn't like to think that she was no longer interested in him, and that made him dangerous, but she'd be prepared. This was a business trip and by heaven it was going to stay a business trip. She'd make certain of that!

CHAPTER THREE

'CHAMPAGNE, madam. . .sir?'

'Just coffee, black, please. Claire?'

'I'll have the champagne, thank you.' Claire accepted the glass, wrinkling her nose as she took a sip of the wine. She didn't really like champagne but maybe it would do the trick of quieting her nerves. She set the glass down on the lap-top table and glanced at Cal, who was engrossed in his paperwork. This was probably all old hat to him but for her it was a whole new experience. She'd never dreamt that they would fly Concorde to New York!

He looked up, smiling at the shimmer of excitement in her eyes. 'Not sorry that you agreed to come?'

'Of course not!' She bit her lip, realising she had responded instinctively to the warmth in his deep voice. 'I'm looking forward to learning all I can from the trip.'

'Of course.' Mockery gleamed in the depths of his green eyes as he put down his pen and lifted the cup to his lips. 'That is the only reason why you've come, isn't it?'

'Yes!' She picked up her glass, annoyed that he could stir these feelings inside her so easily. Was she being overly sensitive or had that note of warmth been deliberate?

She glanced back at him, her temper rising when she saw the expression on his face. 'Stop that! I don't know what's going on inside your head and frankly I don't want to, but I only agreed to come for the sake of business!'

'Did I say anything to imply otherwise? I'm hurt, Claire, that you seem to have this low opinion of my motives. Why do you feel like that?'

'Why?' She laughed shortly. 'I imagine it owes something to what happened three years ago!'

'It might surprise you to learn that I did what I did with the best of intentions.' The mockery faded abruptly, his eyes level as they met hers. Claire could see herself reflected in their clear green depths, as though he was drawing her inside him, sapping her will as he had done once before, but she was older now and wiser. She wouldn't allow him to trick her with soft words.

'You expect me to believe that?' She shook her head. 'Sorry, Cal, but I gave up believing in fairy-stories some time back, around the time that you decided to end our relationship. . .for the very best of intentions, of course.'

He sighed softly as he set the cup back down. 'I never intended for you to get hurt, Claire.'

'How did you imagine that I would feel? Grateful that you'd suddenly decided to tell me the truth? We were living together, Cal. I thought that implied a degree of commitment, not to mention honesty on both sides. Yet I go home to find you with your bags packed, calmly announcing that you were a member of the Hadley family and that our relationship was finished!' She was shaking with anger and pain. This was the last thing she had wanted to happen but there was no way she could let it pass. 'I would feel more respect for you if you just told the truth instead of making up these stories about doing it for my benefit.'

'And the plain truth is that I never wanted to hurt you.' There was anger in his voice now. 'You don't understand the circumstances, so don't be so hasty to pass judgement.'

'Hasty? I've hardly been that. I've had three years to form my opinion of you, three years to work out how any decent human being could treat another the way you treated me! Oh, it was slickly done, obviously well planned and just as well executed. You had your bags packed and were gone almost before I knew what was happening, avoiding any unpleasant scenes. You must have had a lot of practice at doing it, Cal. Or is it just that you are a born bast——?'

'Don't!' He gripped her arm, his fingers bruising. 'You aren't doing yourself any favours by talking like this.'

'Is that a threat?' She laughed hoarsely, twisting her arm free of his grasp. 'What do you intend to do, Mr Callan—dismiss me for impertinence? Well, for your information I could quite easily get another job! I did toy with the idea three years ago, even went as far as accepting an interview at another store, but then I thought, Why should I? Why should I leave and have to start afresh, make new friends, work from the bottom again? *I* hadn't done anything wrong!' She smoothed her hair back, her eyes skimming his face with contempt. 'But perhaps you were merely threatening to withhold this promotion from me. Surely that would mean a lot of awkward explanations for you?'

'I think not.' He sat back, his face cold. 'You seem to forget that I control this company. No one would question a decision I made about the future of an employee, although they might wonder what you had done to deserve it. You might find it a lot harder to get another job than you imagine. However, I wasn't making any threats. I can't make you believe me, Claire, I can only repeat that you don't understand the circumstances behind what happened.' He picked up his pen, his glance impersonal now. 'There is a board meeting today so we shall be going directly to the store once we land.'

He turned back to his work and Claire sank back in her seat, closing her eyes against the sudden sting of tears. She'd been so determined to handle this trip coolly and professionally, yet look what had happened now.

'Don't brood, Claire. It doesn't help anything.'

She blinked back the tears. 'It's difficult not to brood, Cal. The past seems to be at the root of all our disagreements recently. Not very professional, is it?' She made a shaky attempt at a laugh, freezing as he leant over and gently wiped a tear from her cheek.

'You're only human, Claire. You can't help your feelings.'

'Not even when they get in the way of business? That doesn't sound like the Michael Callan who's built himself the reputation of being a ruthless businessman who *never* allows emotion to influence his decisions.' She moved away, wiping her eyes with her hands.

'Perhaps I haven't had the time to be anything else. When I took over control of Hadley's it was about to go under. It took all my time and all my concentration to save it. Emotion hasn't been a luxury I've been able to afford, but that doesn't mean that I am unfeeling.' His eyes drifted softly over her face, darkening to a smoky green as they met hers. 'I remember what we had, Claire. Breaking up was the hardest decision I've ever had to make.'

His low, deep voice was lighting fires inside her again, flames that threatened what little composure she had left. She drew in a shuddering breath, her eyes filled with pain. 'But you still made that decision, Cal. You say that I don't understand; I say that's just an excuse. I no longer fitted in with your plans so end of story, and end of our relationship. Oh, I'll admit that I was devastated, but I've got over it now. So don't worry about me, not when you have more important things to think about.'

'Does anyone really get over a lost love-affair? Isn't it more accurate to say that it lingers at the back of one's mind, a tantalising memory full of regrets?' He smiled almost sadly. 'The problem is that in this case no amount of regrets could have changed the outcome. I was forced to make a decision, but that doesn't mean that I don't remember what we had and often wish things could have turned out differently.'

'But they didn't so there seems little point in dwelling on it.' She beckoned to the flight attendant to refill her glass, effectively putting an end to the disturbing conversation, but it wasn't easy to put it out of her mind. Had Cal been telling the truth about being forced to end their relationship? If he had then it opened up a floodgate of possibilities that kept her busy until they came in to land.

She sighed as she watched him pack up his papers. What did it matter now? What they'd once had was all in the past.

*   *   *

'And best and last is my department. Not that I'm biased, of course, Claire!'

Claire laughed. She'd taken an immediate liking to Brandon White, her opposite number at the New York store. He had taken her on a full tour of the huge building and now her head was reeling with impressions of vastness and luxury. She turned slowly on her heel, admiring the huge crystal chandeliers that hung from the ceiling, waterfalls of sculptured glass that reflected rainbows of light on to the smoked-glass mirrored columns.

'I've never seen anything like this! It's so vast, so luxurious. It makes the London store look like something from the Dark Ages!'

Brandon smiled, running a hand over his perfectly cut brown hair. 'It might surprise you to learn that a lot of our customers would love to shop at the London store. I've seen photographs of it and I must say that I find all that elegant old wood and sense of history far more attractive than all this gloss.' He shook his head. 'Don't get me wrong. This is a great store and Cal has done a fantastic job over the past few years, but London! It has to be my dream to work there.'

Claire laughed again, ruefully. 'I suppose it's just a case of familiarity breeding contempt. You're right, there is a timeless elegance about the London branch, but that doesn't mean that I don't enjoy a bit of "gloss" now and then. And as for your valentine promotion— well, it's lovely.'

'The original idea was yours, I believe.' Brandon led the way to where a small garden had been laid, complete with trees and miniature waterfall and flower-decked gazebo. 'We were planning on doing something but went to town after we'd received Cal's directive. I'm particularly pleased with this display of valentine cards on loan from one of our museums. Take a look at this one designed by the British artist Kate Greenaway. It was printed around the 1880s. Then there's this from the Civil War period, around 1861. I doubt anyone would find a tent romantic nowadays but when you lift those tent flaps you can see a Union soldier kneeling by a table writing to his sweetheart back home. Here, let me unlock the case so that you can see it properly.'

He opened the glass case, watching as Claire gently raised the tent flaps on the card. 'It's lovely. So touching that even in wartime men and women still sent their cards. And look at this one. The satin is still so fresh, and is that real lace the frame is made from?'

'It is. That's one of my favourites also. It dates from around 1850 and was produced by Esther A. Howland, one of the first US valentine manufacturers. It uses a theme that was popular then, a couple in an idealised country setting, plus the obligatory heart, of course.'

'It's a pity that no one makes cards like this today.' Claire stood aside while Brandon re-locked the case.

'They do. We have a display of them right over here.' He led her to the counter, lifting a card out of the glass display front. 'There are several artists making cards for us during the promotion but this must be one of the best.'

Claire took it carefully, inspecting the delicate arrangement of pressed flowers and lace, the exquisite penmanship inside. 'It's beautiful. Is it expensive?'

'Depends what you call expensive.' He named a

sum, laughing at her expression as she converted the
dollars into sterling.

'That's expensive! Surely you don't sell that many of
them?'

'You'd be surprised. The type of customer who shops
here not only has the money but the need to spend it.
We sold over a hundred similar cards yesterday and
expect to sell several thousand during the promotion,
all at a tidy profit.'

'And that is why I thought you should come here,
Claire. The London store has been in danger of letting
its standards drop but that isn't what a Hadley's
customer wants. There are plenty of run-of-the-mill
shops around but few high-class ones.'

She stiffened as she heard Cal's voice. They'd come
straight to the store, where he had handed her over to
Brandon before he had left for his meeting. Now just
the sound of his voice sent all those unsettling quivers
of awareness racing up and down her spine again,
putting her instantly on the defensive.

'I understand that, but I doubt if our customers in
London would pay so much for a card.' There was a
note of challenge in her voice and she felt Brandon
look at her in surprise.

'And that is the heart of the problem. Not the
customer's unwillingness to pay, but the staff's blink-
ered attitude. Hopefully this trip will help you overcome that, Claire.'

There was no mistaking the rebuke and she flushed,
staring coldly back at him. 'I am willing to learn if it
will improve my effectiveness in the job. However, I
think you too have things to learn, Cal. American
marketing techniques won't always work in England.'

'We shall see.'

He moved away, his face set as he walked over to the garden area. Claire let out a shuddering sigh, smiling with embarrassment when Brandon said softly, 'I never thought I'd live to see the day when that guy lost his cool. What is it with you two, Claire? You could have cut the atmosphere with a knife just now!'

'We. . .we just rub each other up the wrong way occasionally.'

'And that's all it is?' He held his hand up to stave off her protests. 'OK, I believe you. I'm just glad that's the way things are. It means I can safely ask you out tonight without stepping on any toes. So how about it, Claire? Dinner, maybe a club, just to welcome you to the Big Apple, you understand?'

His brown eyes were filled with warmth and Claire smiled. 'I'd like that very much, thank——'

'But unfortunately you will have to pass up the invitation. I've already made plans for the evening, Claire.'

Twin spots of colour burned in her cheeks at the arrogant statement. 'I hadn't realised that dining with you was part of the schedule?'

Cal smiled tauntingly, obviously amused by her anger. 'It isn't. However, I've made arrangements for you to meet with a couple of buyers from our Miami branch who are in town at the moment. Naturally I expect you to fall in with the arrangements. I'm sure Brandon can alter his plans accordingly.'

It was an order, not a request and they all knew it. For a second Claire was tempted to argue, but what was the point? She was here on business and if he chose to fill her every waking moment with work then she had to go along with him. 'Whatever you say. However, I shall need to get changed. Can you call me a cab to take me to my hotel, please?'

She directed the request at Brandon, but it was Cal who answered. 'You don't need a cab. You'll be staying here in the penthouse suite. Show her where it is when you're through here, Brandon.'

He walked away, mingling with the crowd of elegant shoppers. Claire counted to ten, unwilling to make a fool of herself, but there was no way she could leave unasked the question that was nagging inside her head. 'Who usually uses the penthouse suite?'

There was a faint but marked hesitation before Brandon replied, speculation in the look he gave her now. 'Cal. He lives there. It appears that you two will be sharing.'

Claire clenched her hands. Abruptly she turned away to avoid the man's gaze, staring after Cal with desperation in her eyes. What was he up to now? What?

CHAPTER FOUR

THE knock came at the door just as she was putting the finishing touches to her make-up. Claire stepped back from the mirror then paused to study her reflection.

The black velvet suit had been wickedly expensive, an impulsive purchase made only that morning before they had left for the airport. Now she was glad that she had bought it. It emphasised her slender figure and served as the perfect foil for her blonde hair, lending her a cool sophistication she was grateful for. She would need every bit of help she could get to last through the coming evening in Cal's company.

'Are you ready yet, Claire?'

As ready as she was ever going to be! With one last, confidence-boosting glance in the mirror she went over to the door and opened it. 'Yes. Do we have to leave now?'

'In a few minutes or so. They'll ring through when the car arrives. Would you like a drink before we go?'

She shook her head, moving past him into the huge central sitting area that separated the two bedrooms with their en-suite bathrooms. Cal hadn't been in when she'd arrived at the penthouse and she'd taken time to explore the apartment, trying to convince herself that it would be less intimate sharing this vast space than sharing adjoining hotel bedrooms, but it hadn't worked. At least in a hotel there would be other people about while here they were completely alone.

'No, thank you, not after that champagne I had earlier.'

He followed her into the room, the thick palest grey carpet absorbing his footsteps as he walked over to the bar. 'Please yourself, but I doubt if a couple of glasses of wine will have had a lingering effect.'

'Probably not, but I prefer to keep a clear head for a business meeting.' She sat down on one of the huge dusky blue sofas, crossing her sheer-clad legs as she watched him pour whisky into a cut-glass tumbler. Everything in the apartment was the best that money could buy and at any other time Claire would have enjoyed staying in such luxurious surroundings, but now she was too tense to relax.

'Ah, yes, business. Of course.' He took a swallow of the whisky then swirled it around the glass. He was wearing a dark lounge suit and white shirt with a discreetly patterned silk tie, clothes that bore all the hallmarks of civilisation, but when he looked up suddenly there was nothing civilised about the expression in his glittering green eyes.

Claire's heart leapt in an instinctive response. She stood up abruptly and walked to the window, willing herself to stay calm, but it was impossible to stem the shudder that ran through her when she heard him put down the glass.

He came to stand behind her, his reflection merging with hers in the mirror-dark glass. It was like a flashback to the past to see them standing there like that, and she felt her heart ache with a fresh grief. She had loved him so much, but in the end it hadn't been enough to hold him.

'It isn't easy, is it, Claire?'

His voice was deep, warmly intimate, making her tingle with a heady longing. She closed her eyes, trying desperately not to respond to the seductive quality, but that was like asking a flower not to open to the sun or a bee not to search for nectar. There was no way that she could ignore him and pretend that she didn't understand what he meant.

'No, it isn't easy.' She shrugged lightly, her shoulder-blades brushing the hard wall of his chest. 'But then who said that life should be easy?'

'And who said that it should be this difficult? There is an answer to this, Claire.' He turned her slowly to stare intently into her face.

'Is there? From where I'm standing I can't seem to see one.' She laughed shakily, more disturbed by the glitter in his darkening green eyes than she cared to admit.

'That's because you aren't thinking logically.' He smiled almost tenderly at her, his hand moving to her cheek to stroke the smooth fine skin. 'It's really quite straightforward.'

The touch of his hand was making her dizzy. It seemed to be drawing the strength from her limbs and the ability to think from her mind. Every bit of her seemed to be centred on that one small area where his hand smoothed so slowly, so insistently across her flesh. 'I. . .I don't understand, Cal.'

'Then let me explain. We take up where we left off.' His hand stilled against the underside of her jaw where a pulse was beating rapidly in mute betrayal of her vulnerability. It seemed to please him because he smiled with a touch of arrogance. 'There is still some-thing there between us, Claire—that's obvious, so why

keep on pretending there isn't? It was good between us
once and I see no reason why it shouldn't be so again.'

'And what if it doesn't work out? What then?'
Coldness was stealing through her, a coldness born out
of horror. She couldn't believe what she was hearing,
couldn't believe that he would suggest such a thing!

He must have caught an echo of it in her voice
because he bent closer. 'Then we call it a day. We
aren't two young kids any more. We're two adults who
can decide what we want from life and if we make
mistakes then we can rectify them. Surely it isn't a
crime to see if we can enjoy the same sort of happiness
we once shared?'

'No, it isn't a crime. It's the crassest suggestion I've
ever heard! Do you really imagine that I would willingly start another affair with you after last time?' She
swatted his hand away, her blue eyes filled with fire.
'Thank you but no, thank you. I'm not interested!'

His face tightened, his eyes narrowing to glittering
pin-points of ice. 'That isn't the impression you've been
handing out!' He dragged her into his arms, his hand
moving over the soft folds of velvet to close over her
breasts, triumph on his face when he felt her rigid
nipple pushing into his palm. 'You can lie all you like,
sweet Claire, but your body can't. See how it responds
to me, see how it still longs for my touch?'

He caressed her through the soft fabric, teasing the
nipple into a throbbing peak of desire that sent waves
of bitter-sweet longing flooding through her. This was
the very thing she had been dreading might happen,
betraying how easily he could make her respond to his
touch, but she would never admit it to him!

'You flatter yourself, Cal. As you just said, neither

of us is inexperienced now. Naturally I respond to your touch as I would to any attractive man. Passion once awoken is hard to subdue, so why try?' She forced a hint of cool amusement to her expression as she stared back at him. 'You were my first lover, Cal, but don't make the mistake of thinking you are the only one. That could lead to a great deal of disappointment. Now if you have quite finished practising your seduction techniques, would you mind letting me go? I don't want to waste time re-doing my make-up.'

Had she gone too far? She held her breath as she watched the expressions that crossed his face, ranging from disbelief to anger, to finally a wry acceptance. With a mocking bow he let her go, watching silently as she sat down on the sofa again.

Claire steeled herself to meet his gaze, feeling the pain gnawing inside her. She had sworn never to let him hurt her again but what he'd just suggested had almost torn her heart in two. When he made no attempt to speak, she raised a delicate golden brow, keeping the hurt out of her voice. 'Don't tell me that I have actually managed to take the wind out of your sails?'

He laughed deeply, walking over to the bar to pick up his glass. 'Not quite, although I do confess to feeling a trifle surprised.'

'At what? That I should refuse your tempting offer?' She smoothed her hand over the velvet skirt, making furrows in the pile with her fingertips.

'No. Contrary to your opinion of me I'm not that vain. What surprises me, Claire, is that you should show such little outward sign of all those lovers.' He let his gaze skim over her, openly assessing her slender curves in a look that brought the colour to her face.

'You still look as untouched and innocent as I remember you, but it just goes to show how deceptive appearances can be, because now it seems you are a woman of the world.'

He didn't believe her? Her heart turned over at the thought and she stood up abruptly. 'Frankly, Cal, that is the most sexist statement I've ever heard! Why should I *look* any different?' Her eyes skimmed his face but she found it impossible to hold that glittering green gaze for longer than a heartbeat. 'If you want the truth then neither do you look any different, but I doubt if you've led a monk-like existence these past three years!'

She hadn't meant it to come out that way, not with jealousy echoing in her voice. He smiled slowly, putting down the glass with a deliberation that set her nerves on edge before he moved towards her. 'No, I can't claim to have been a monk, but neither can I claim to have been living the life of a rake either. You, Claire, were a hard act to follow and I found that when I did have time to spare from keeping the business afloat I didn't have much inclination. It's difficult to make love to a woman when your head is full of pictures of another.'

He bent and brushed her lips with his in a kiss so brief that it was over before Claire had a chance to object. She touched a finger to her mouth, staring up at him with confusion in her eyes, and saw him smile in a way that made everything inside her flare to life. Emotion flowed between them, touching him, touching her, joining them with an invisible bond, and she half raised her hand to reach out to him when the telephone rang.

She drew in a tiny, shuddering breath, watching as

Cal went to answer it. Saved by the bell, but saved from what? From making a complete and utter fool of herself by giving him what he wanted? Had he been telling the truth just now or had it been a way of manipulating her again? She wished she knew, because it was becoming increasingly difficult to fight not just him but herself as well.

The restaurant was elegant and expensive, situated in New York's Little Italy district and filled with the cream of society. Claire studied the other well-dressed diners then let her eyes drift back to the man at her side, her heart leaping when she found that he was watching her. It had kept happening all night long— she would look up to find Cal's eyes on her—and now her nerves were raw.

The coffee-cup rattled against the saucer as she set it down and she felt rather than saw the smile Cal gave. He knew how she was feeling, knew that she was dreading the time when they would have to return to the apartment for the night. Had he been planning this all along, right from the moment he had suggested this trip? Frankly, she wouldn't put it past him!

'I'm going to the rest-room, Claire. Would you like to come?'

The softly voiced question broke into her disturbing thoughts. Claire turned to smile in relief at Cathy Davies, one of the buyers from Miami. 'Oh, yes, please. Lead the way.'

The rest-room was empty when they walked in. Claire set her bag down then took out her lipstick, cursing as she smudged lipstick on her upper lip because her hands were shaking.

'Here.' Cathy handed her a tissue from the box set on the marble counter, smiling faintly. 'Not that it's any wonder your hands are shaking. You could cut the atmosphere between you and Cal with a knife. Forgive me for being nosy, but are you *really* here to learn about American marketing techniques?'

Claire's hand slipped again, setting another peach-tinted smear on her upper lip. Deliberately, she wiped it away, using the few seconds it took to find some dismissive answer to the question, but it was impossible to think up a convincing lie. 'I thought I was.'

'But now you're starting to wonder if the game-plan has altered?' Cathy laughed as she opened her bag and took out a compact. 'I never thought I would live to see the day when the Ice Man started to melt.'

'What do you mean? Are you referring to Cal?' There was no way that Claire could hide her surprise and Cathy laughed again.

'Of course! And the fact that you have never thought of him that way only serves to emphasise the very point I'm making.' She snapped the compact shut then looked at Claire. 'I am just one of many women who have done their utmost to attract Cal's attention, one of the many *disappointed* women, to be precise. He's been polite, friendly, charming in that coolly British way, but never once has he shown a single ounce of real emotion. . .until tonight! I tell you, honey, the air fairly sizzles when he looks at you. Tell me what your secret is and I'll have it patented.'

Claire laughed, unable to take offence at such friendly teasing. 'There's no secret. Cal—well, Cal and I did have something going for us once but it's past history. All we have in common now is business.'

'If that's business then where have I gone wrong? That man looks at you in a way that makes my toes curl. Take it from one who would dearly love to step in your shoes that the last thing he has on his mind is business!'

Claire's face went pale. 'I don't care what he has on his mind. No power on earth would make me get involved with him again on a personal level!'

'You still love him that much, huh? Never mind, honey, I'm sure it will work out in the end.' She patted Claire's hand kindly then headed out of the door, missing the shock etched on Claire's pale face. The door swung to but Claire stayed where she was, listening to the drumming beat of her heart, the echo of Cathy's words beating inside her head.

She loved Cal. That was why she had been so afraid since he'd come back into her life, and it had taken the perception of a stranger to make her face the fact. Now all she could do was make sure that he never found out how she felt.

The wind was bitter, gusting along the street, knifing through the soft folds of the velvet suit. Claire shivered as she hurried towards the door while Cal finished speaking to the driver. The limousine drove away and he turned to follow her, digging the key out of his pocket to unlock the side-door. The wind blew his hair back from his forehead, leaving his face stark in the cold glow of the security lights, and just for a weak moment Claire allowed her eyes to feast on the sight of him before hurriedly dropping her gaze as he turned to her.

'Let's get inside. You look half frozen. I should have

warned you to wear a coat. New York in February is one of the coldest places I know.'

He put a hand to the small of her back to guide her ahead of him into the small private hallway that gave access to the lift that went solely to the penthouse suite. Claire moved away as soon as they were inside, ignoring the mocking tilt to his mouth. She didn't care what he thought; there was still tonight to get through, and all the other nights until she returned to London. She had to make it clear that, no matter what he had planned, she had no intention of sleeping with him!

'Don't look so worried, Claire. I don't intend to pounce on you once we're upstairs.' He leant against the wall, his hands pushed into his trouser pockets, his tie hanging loosely, his black hair mussed from the wind, looking so devastatingly attractive that Claire could have wept. It took all her strength to stare coldly back at him.

'I never imagined that you would. *Pouncing* isn't your style, Cal!'

He laughed at the stinging retort. 'You know me too well, Claire. It takes all the surprise out of what I do.'

'Oh, I expect you can still surprise me if you really think it worth trying, but let's lay our cards on the table. I will not sleep with you. So save your breath and my time because nothing you can do or say will make me change my mind.'

'Nothing?' He straightened slowly, his eyes holding hers for a moment that hummed with tension. 'Is it wise to issue a challenge like that? I could find it tempting to take you up on it.'

'It wasn't meant to be a challenge! I just wanted you to understand how I feel.' Anger rippled through her, anger that was intensified by a strange, disturbing excitement which she tried her hardest to suppress. 'I resent the fact that you've placed me in this position. You know I only agreed to this trip because I believed it to be purely for business! I didn't come to provide you with a few hours' amusement. Even Cathy noticed the——' She broke off, her face colouring as she realised how it would sound.

'Cathy noticed. . .what?' He spoke quietly but there was a steely note of authority in his voice. 'Has she been saying something to upset you, Claire?'

'No. Forget it.'

'But I don't want to forget it. Obviously she's said something about me and I want to know what it is.'

'Why?' She glared back at him. 'Afraid that she might have said something to damage your reputation? Don't worry, Cal. Cathy is a fan of yours even though she does find that cool composure of yours hard to swallow. What was it that she called you?' She pretended to think for a moment, enjoying the mounting annoyance on his face. 'Ah, yes, that's it: the Ice Man. Mmm, she could be right. There is something decidedly cold and calculating about you, Michael Callan, as I know better than most.'

'Do you? But when was I ever cold with you, Claire?' He moved suddenly, trapping her against the wall as he stood in front of her. 'Our relationship was red-hot from the word go, from what I remember of it. Don't tell me that time has dimmed your memory? Maybe it could do with a refresher, my sweet.'

He bent towards her, intent written all over his face, but Claire turned her head away to avoid the kiss. 'I don't need any refreshers, thank you. I recall exactly how it was between us, and how it ended: coldly, calculatedly, the Ice Man at his best!'

The lift hummed to a stop and she slid away from him to step inside, feeling her heart pounding. She shouldn't let him goad her like that but she'd always found it impossible to ignore him. He had this knack of arousing her to anger just as easily as he'd always aroused her to passion.

'Seems to me that you and I need to talk. It's about time I explained why I had to end our relationship so abruptly.'

'I'm not interested! The time for explanations is long past, Cal. Nothing is going to change the past, especially not talking about it, not when we can barely manage to say half a dozen civil words to one another before we end up arguing.'

'We always did argue, Claire.' He turned the key to set the lift in motion, leaning casually against the panelled wall as he watched her. 'But making up afterwards made all those arguments worthwhile. Perhaps that's what this is leading up to right now—a quarrel that we can patch up in that highly satisfactory way?'

He was so smugly self-assured that she could have hit him! 'No way! You might have tricked me into staying in the apartment with you but that's as far as it goes. There won't be any attempts at making up!'

'I didn't trick you into staying here. I just didn't relish the thought of you being alone in some hotel. New York is a dangerous place for a woman alone. I wouldn't have been able to rest wondering what might be happening to you.'

There was no doubting his sincerity. Claire felt

warmed by his concern even though that was the last way she wanted to feel. No matter what she really felt for Cal she couldn't blind herself to the truth that he would use any vulnerability she displayed to get what he wanted. And in this case it seemed that he wanted her!

'How sweet! I suppose I should feel flattered, Cal, that you show such concern for an employee, but then I expect it's really because you don't want all the inconvenience if anything did happen to me. Isn't that right?' There was a nice ring of scorn in her voice which she felt proud of until she saw the anger that flashed across his face.

'One of these days, lady, that sharp little tongue of yours is going to get you into trouble.' He smiled wolfishly, moving slowly and deliberately towards her so that she backed hurriedly against the wall.

'Look, Cal, don't you think this is——?'

'Trying to talk your way out of it now, are you, my love?' He shook his head, his hand sliding around the back of her neck as he pulled her towards him. 'Don't bother. It's far too late for that now!'

His lips were hot and demanding as they met hers in a kiss that seemed to shake her to the very depths of her soul. For a moment, Claire resisted, but it was merely a token resistance when everything inside her was urging her to kiss him back. With a tiny, helpless moan she opened her mouth, feeling his body surge against hers as he deepened the kiss until she was breathless and clinging to him. This was what it had all been leading to, all the arguments, all the tension—to this moment when Cal held her and kissed her as though nothing else in the world mattered.

When the ground suddenly shuddered beneath their feet it seemed right, as though nature was as affected by the moment as they were. It was only when Cal lifted his head and swore softly that Claire realised something was wrong. She stared round in confusion, suddenly aware that they were no longer moving.

'Why have we stopped? We can't have reached the penthouse yet, surely?' She glanced at the indicator panel, but there were no lights gleaming to show which level they were at.

Cal punched a button on the controls, his face grim when nothing happened. 'No. We appear to be stuck halfway.'

'Halfway. . .you mean that the lift has broken down? But Cal. . . Oh!' She gasped as the lights went out, plunging them into darkness.

'It's all right. The emergency lighting will come on in a second. There.' He smiled reassuringly at her as dim lights glowed in the ceiling and Claire fought down the momentary panic.

'So what do we do now?' she asked quietly.

'Not a lot. We shall have to wait for someone to sort the trouble out.' He loosened his tie and unbuttoned the neck of his shirt then sat down on the floor. 'You may as well make yourself comfortable, Claire. This could turn out to be a long night.'

Claire stared at him for a long, silent moment then looked round the confines of the small lift and swallowed. There was no 'could' about it. This was going to be a very long night indeed!

CHAPTER FIVE

IT WAS so hot.

Claire ran a hand over her face, wiping the perspiration from her upper lip before resting her head back and closing her eyes.

'Are you all right? You look very pale.'

Cal spoke softly, his voice barely disturbing the silence, but she still jumped nervously. She looked over at where he was sitting, his back propped against the lift wall. He had stripped off his jacket and shirt and now she could see beads of perspiration caught in the thick tangle of black hair that covered his muscular chest, evidence that he was feeling just as hot and uncomfortable as she was; but that was the only outward sign. Resting easily against the wall, his long legs taking up most of the small floor space, he looked totally relaxed. Did nothing dent his iron-clad composure?

Panic rose inside her all at once and she forced herself to concentrate on answering the question to keep it at bay. 'I'm fine. Just rather hot, that's all.'

His eyes narrowed assessingly on the black velvet suit before returning to her pale, strained face. 'You'd feel a whole lot more comfortable if you took that jacket off, Claire. It's stifling in here and it will probably get worse before too long. The heating system isn't linked to the power so it won't switch off.'

She shook her head, brushing away a damp strand of

hair that clung to her cheek. 'I'll be fine. It can't be much longer before they fix it, surely? How long have we been stuck here now?'

Cal glanced at the wafer-thin gold watch strapped to his wrist. 'A little over an hour, but you have to face facts, Claire. There's no saying if anyone even knows that we're here seeing as the alarm doesn't seem to be working.'

'But somebody *must* know that the lift is stuck between floors!'

There was desperation in her voice and Cal stood up, his face set as he pressed the red alarm button again. 'We can only hope that they do, but this lift is solely for the use of anyone staying in the penthouse. The security staff don't need to come into this part of the building when they know I'm here.'

'That's ridiculous!' The strain was making her edgy, ready to snap at the least provocation. 'I would have thought it was common sense to keep a check on what was going on here.'

'When I'm away obviously that is what happens but when I'm using the apartment I prefer not to have people intruding on my privacy.'

Especially not when it might prove a shade awkward! 'I see. What a pity that you can't find some place else to entertain your ladyfriends! Then maybe we wouldn't be in this situation. Routine security checks would be merely a sensible precaution, not an invasion of your precious privacy!'

He laughed deeply, moving over to sit on the floor beside her. 'I thought *I* was the one with green eyes!' He tapped her cheek gently with a long finger, smiling into her angry face. 'Not that I'm objecting. I find your jealousy rather flattering if you'd like the truth.'

'I am not jealous! You can get that out of your head right away. I was merely making an observation, a wholly justifiable one in the circumstances.'

'Mmm, so you say. I'd debate that with you if I didn't know it would be a sheer waste of effort. I get the impression lately that you'd call black white if it would promote an argument with me. You really should try to keep a rein on your temper, Claire.'

He was mocking her quite deliberately and, while Claire knew it, it seemed impossible to stem the angry flood of words. 'I have never had any trouble with my temper before! It's just you, Michael Callan. You seem to be deliberately trying to annoy me!'

'Do I?' His expression altered subtly, his eyes darkening as they traced her face. 'And have you asked yourself why that could be?'

'I. . . No!' The way he was looking at her made her feel suddenly afraid. She scrambled to her feet and crossed the lift to press the alarm bell, slamming her hand against the panel when it remained silent. 'Oh, why won't it work? Can't you do something?'

'Such as?' He looked up at the ceiling, squinting against the yellow glow from the emergency lighting. 'We're stuck somewhere between the fifteenth and sixteenth floors, I'd guess. I suppose it might be possible for me to get out into the shaft and see if I can climb to the next floor.' He stood up and flexed the heavy muscles in his shoulders as he started to reach for the trapdoor set in the lift roof.

'No!' She caught his arm, her hands fastening around the warm, faintly damp flesh, feeling sick with fear at the thought of him taking such a risk. 'You could get hurt, Cal. I won't let you do it!'

'I didn't think you cared one way or the other what happens to me, Claire.' There was a note in his deep voice that sent a warning *frisson* racing down her spine, but for some strange reason she chose not to heed it.

'Of course I care.' She took a slow, deep breath, fighting to keep the pictures of him lying hurt and helpless from her mind, but it was impossible to drive them away. Her hands clung to him, tightening around the firm flesh of his upper arm, feeling the warmth of his skin, the hard outline of muscle over bone.

'Do you, Claire? Do you really care?'

What was there in his voice that made her heart start to beat like crazy? She didn't know and suddenly didn't care as she looked up straight into his eyes. It was like drowning in a sea of darkening green, like being drawn deeper and deeper into fathomless depths. She looked away, willing herself to fight this attraction she felt for him, but when she looked back at him she knew it was impossible.

'Yes, I. . .I care.' Her voice was little more than a thready whisper, reluctant, hesitant, and he smiled with gentle understanding.

'The same as I care what happens to you, Claire. I always have and I always will.'

How she wanted to believe him, but there was no way she could blind herself to the truth. 'No. If you had cared then you would never have left me the way you did.'

There was a wealth of sadness in her voice and his face filled with pain. He drew her into his arms, nestling her head against the hard strength of his chest. 'I can't change what happened, Claire, just as I can't make you believe that I did it *because* I cared.'

That made no sense. She wanted desperately to ask him to explain but before she could speak he slid his hand under her chin and lifted her face, his mouth burning as he took hers in a kiss of such passion that a shudder ran through her body. For one brief moment she resisted, terrified of what would happen if she gave him the response he sought, but as his lips parted hers and his tongue slid inside her mouth to tangle with hers she knew that she was lost. If it had just been Cal she'd been fighting then maybe she could have resisted the seductive spell he was casting over her, but how could she fight against something she wanted so much herself?

'Claire, oh, Claire!' His voice was hot and rough with desire yet his hands were gentle as they dropped to the silk-covered buttons on her jacket and started to work them loose. Claire lifted her arms, running her fingers through the cool, silky dark hair at the back of his head, feathering kisses up the slanting curve of his jaw to tease the lobe of his ear. He swore softly, his impatience growing as the buttons defeated his attempts to unfasten them and she laughed gently, rubbing her lips around the curve of his ear as she stood on tiptoe, feeling the deep shudder that ran through him with a flare of heady excitement.

'Think it's funny, do you, you little witch? Teasing me like that?' There was just the faintest hint of a threat in his deep voice and she shivered delicately, wondering what form the reprisals might take.

'Mmm, you never used to have so much trouble with a few buttons, Cal.' Her mouth moved again, leaving his ear to skim along his cheekbone, her lips parting as she pressed tiny fleeting kisses to his skin. He drew in a heavy breath, his hands lifting to catch her face and hold it while he kissed her hard until she was the one who shuddered with longing. He smiled in satisfaction, his gaze scorching as it lingered on the swollen fullness of her mouth, the haze of desire that darkened her eyes almost to black.

'Do it for me, Claire. Take your jacket off.'

Such simple words, but the message in them made her shake with longing. For a moment she held his gaze then slowly let her hands drop to the buttons, watching the way his face tightened and his whole body stilled. Slowly, one by one, she worked them free, feeling the blood thundering through her veins as his eyes followed every movement of her fingers. When at last her hands dropped to her sides, he reached out, his fingers warm and gentle against her skin as he traced so lightly, so delicately down from her collarbone to her waist that she had to bite her lip to stop herself from crying out.

'Take it off, Claire. . .please.'

He tried to phrase it as a request but it came out as an order, the tension evident in the deepening timbre of his voice. Claire hesitated for a second then slowly slid the jacket down her arms, colour flowing into her face as she heard his swift indrawn breath as she finally stood in front of him clad only in the pearl-grey camisole which did little to conceal the thrusting fullness of her breasts.

'So beautiful, Claire, so very beautiful. I'd almost forgotten.' His eyes were as dark as a stormy sea as they lingered on her then lifted to meet hers in a moment that seemed to hold the whole world suspended.

Claire shuddered, more affected by the look than she could say. 'Cal, I. . .' There was just the faintest hint of fear in her soft voice, a fear not of him but of what she was doing. Would she come to regret this moment of madness all too soon? Was this really heaven within her grasp or a bitter hell?

He pressed a finger gently to her lips, his face full of understanding. 'Don't, Claire. You know you want this as much as I do.'

Tears filled her eyes and she bowed her head, unable to look at him then. 'Yes, I do, but that doesn't make it right, Cal.'

'Neither does it make it wrong.' He ran his hands lightly down her arms from shoulder to wrist, his touch so light that it felt like the brush of wings, the caress of a warm breeze, and she shivered. 'I want you, Claire. I want you more than I have ever wanted any woman, but it's your choice what happens next. Yours.'

Her choice, but which one should she make? How did one choose between heaven and heartache? She stared helplessly at him, torn in two by her needs and this fear of being hurt again as she'd been hurt before. 'Help me, Cal,' she whispered brokenly. 'Help me decide what to do!'

His face contorted and he dragged her into her arms, holding her so close that she could feel the heavy pounding of his heart against her breast, feel the evidence of his aroused body, and suddenly there was no choice to make any longer. When his hand slid up to cover her breast through the thin silk, she moaned softly, glorying in the touch of his fingers, which sent sweet waves of desire piercing through her body. Each sweep of his fingers against her flesh was driving her crazy, making her ache with a need she could no longer deny.

'Cal. . .Cal!' She whispered his name like a prayer, uncaring that he must hear her need of him in the urgency of her tone. When his head came down as he plundered her mouth with a raw, almost primitive desire, she kissed him back just as fiercely, just as demandingly. A groan tore from his lips and he moved his mouth to run a fireline of kisses across her cheek to the soft curve of her jaw, lingering on the spot at the base of her neck where a pulse was beating so desperately.

His tongue snaked out, tracing the throbbing, pulsating spot, making it beat even harder until Claire felt dizzy with the fast hammer of blood that surged along her veins. She clung to him, her fingers biting into the hardness of muscles in his shoulders, then gasped when she felt herself being lifted from the ground by strong arms wrapped around her waist. Her eyes opened straight into his, all her emotions naked to him at that moment, before he bent his head and opened his mouth over her breast, drawing the rigid nipple with its fine silk covering between his teeth.

Claire cried out, her nails biting into his flesh, her head thrown back as a sudden fierce spasm of ecstasy claimed her. The rasping feel of his tongue against the silk was lighting fires inside her, fires that burned higher and higher as he turned his attentions to her other breast, moistening the silk so that it clung to her nipple and heightened the sensations.

She was shivering when he slowly let her slide down

so that her feet touched the floor once more, every
nerve raw, aching, wanting. He held her to him, his
hips pressed against hers as he moved her in a rhythm
that sent a flashfire of desire into the pit of her stomach.
She arched against him, pressing her soft curves against
the hard tautness of his body, hearing his breathing
quicken.

When his hand went to the zip of her skirt she helped
him, just as eager as he was to rid herself of the
restriction of clothing. The skirt slid to the floor,
whispering softly as it slipped over the pearl-grey silk
panties, the fine mesh of her sheer stockings. Cal's
hands followed its downward movement, sliding tantalisingly over her hips to stroke down her thighs, lingering on the smooth flesh above the tops of her stockings
before he drew back a fraction and let his eyes enjoy
what his fingers had only hinted at.

'My God, Claire, what an outfit. It's enough to drive
a man wild!'

She laughed shakily, smoothing her hands across the
warm roughness of his chest, letting her nails lightly
graze his skin. 'I'm glad you like it.'

'I do, but I think I'd like it even more if you weren't
wearing anything.' He slid his fingertips under the thin
strap on her shoulder, watching her the whole time as
he started to push it down so that the camisole dipped
to expose one hard-tipped breast to his gaze. Claire
closed her eyes, quaking shudders of longing surging
inside her as she felt his knuckles brush over her bare
flesh, back and forth until her breasts were throbbing
and she was clinging helplessly to him.

'Cal, please. . .'

'Please what? Hold you? Kiss you?' His mouth

brushed hers as his hand moved again in another slow, deliberate sweep. 'Make love to you? That's exactly what I intend to do, my sweet.'

His hands went to his belt as he started to unbuckle it, then cursed roughly when the lift gave a sudden jolt and started to move. Claire blinked, blinded by the glare from the lights, dazed by the abrupt, shocking departure from passion.

'You'd better get these back on in case there's a reception committee waiting for us.' Cal handed her her clothes, pushing her fumbling hands aside as he helped her step into the skirt and zip it up then buttoned the jacket for her. Swiftly, he pulled his shirt on and tucked it into the waistband of his trousers just as the lift came to a halt and the doors slid open.

With a hand at her waist he guided her ahead of him, his voice icy with displeasure as he spoke to the two men waiting nervously by the lift doors. 'I shall expect a full report on this tomorrow. Now get the hell out of here.'

They went without a word, barely sparing Claire a glance, but she still felt her face start to burn with embarrassment. If Cal hadn't acted so quickly, or if the lift had restarted just a few minutes later, then there was no knowing what they might have seen!

She glanced at Cal, wondering if he too realised what a narrow escape they'd had, and felt her heart turn over when she saw the cold fury on his set face. Who was he so angry with, those men or her? Was he suddenly regretting what had happened between them and maybe blaming her for it?

Shame kept her silent as he let them into the penthouse. She walked slowly to the sitting-room and crossed to the window, resting her hot cheek against the cool glass, wishing that he would say something.

'I suggest you get to bed. It's late already thanks to that fiasco with the lift. There's a staff meeting at eight in the morning that I want you to sit in on. Goodnight.'

Was that it? Did he really think that he could walk away like that after what had happened? Claire spun round, her face pale, her eyes glittering with anger. 'Just wait a minute! Is that all you have to say, Cal?'

He stopped at once, his face devoid of emotion as he glanced back at her. 'What else is there to say? I imagine that untimely interruption has spoiled the mood for you just as it has for me, Claire.'

'That wasn't what I meant!' Her face flamed at the cold sarcasm but she faced him proudly.

'Then what do you want me to say? That I'm sorry for what happened before? That I was wrong to instigate it?' He shook his head, arrogantly male and unbending as he stood there. 'I'm afraid you'll have a long, disappointing wait if you're hoping for that. I am not in the least bit sorry. I didn't force you into anything, Claire. It was your choice, your willing choice.'

She looked away, staring down at the pale grey carpet, looking anywhere but at his cold, set face. 'I know that. I'm not trying to blame you, although I imagine you had something of the sort planned when you decided that I would stay here.'

'I explained why I wanted you here. I didn't plan anything. Now, as I said, it's very late. I suggest we leave any further discussions until tomorrow. Things often look entirely different in the clear light of day.'

He was so cold and aloof that she wanted to shake

him, wanted just once to make a dent in that damnable composure of his. 'Do they indeed? So you think that I'll wake up in the morning and realise that it was all a mistake, that I didn't *really* want to make love with you?'

A muscle ticked in his jaw but that was the only sign that she might have succeeded. 'Perhaps. It has been known to happen. We were both placed in an unusual situation tonight. It isn't surprising that things got slightly out of hand.'

Was that the way he viewed it now, as a situation that had got out of hand through circumstances? Her heart ached at the cold dismissal of what they'd shared, those tender, wonderful moments of magic, but she hid it behind a veil of anger. 'Yes, they did, but it isn't going to happen again, Cal! Understand? I didn't come here to be a. . .a plaything for you!'

'Nobody said that you did.' His eyes narrowed as he stared at her flushed face. 'You're the one jumping to conclusions, Claire.'

'Am I indeed? Well, silly me. Why on earth should I do such a thing?'

'I have no idea.'

'No? Maybe it has something to do with the way *you* have been acting, Cal.' She laughed bitterly. 'So much for this being a business trip! I think that you got me here so that you could prove just how much I still want you. Isn't that right? Your ego couldn't take the thought that I might not find you attractive any longer!'

She tossed the challenge at him, her whole body humming with tension as she waited to hear what he would say, but he said nothing, merely gave her a level look as he walked over to the bar and poured himself a brandy. He sipped it in silence then slowly set the glass down and turned back to her, and Claire felt herself grow cold at the total lack of emotion on his face.

'I asked you to come on this trip, Claire, to enhance your knowledge of the business. Personal feelings never entered into it. However, it's obvious that it is going to be a total waste of time unless we come to some sort of an agreement.'

Business, always business. It had come before everything else in the past and it came before everything now, putting their relationship exactly into the context he wanted. It made her suddenly realise what a fool she'd been to imagine it could ever change. Now all that was left to her was pride, pride not to let him see how hurt she felt.

'What sort of agreement?' she asked.

'That we forget what happened tonight and get on with the job at hand.' He picked up the glass again then took another sip of the brandy, cradling the glass in one lean hand. Claire found her eyes drawn to his hand, remembering how it had felt when he had touched her, caressed her, but she had to put such thoughts from her mind. Cal was her employer, not her lover: he might have been tempted before for whatever reason, but that didn't alter the fact that the smooth running of the business took precedence over everything else.

'That sounds perfectly all right to me. In fact I'd be only too glad to forget about it!'

'Good.' He set his glass down with a sharp clatter that might have made her think he was annoyed if she hadn't known him better. However, there was nothing in his tone to betray such feelings as he continued levelly, 'I want you to carry on here as we planned with one slight alteration.'

'And that is?' She strove to match his tone, keeping her voice as neutral as she could make it.

'That I won't be here to supervise your training. There are a few problems I need to attend to at the Miami store. I shall go down there tomorrow and I doubt if I'll be back before you return to England. However, I'm sure Brandon will be able to answer any of your queries. I shall have a word with him in the morning.'

So that was it, all cut and dried, planned out nice and neatly. She would carry on with her training while Cal would go and sort out more problems with his beloved business and both of them would forget all about what had happened tonight in the lift. Only could they? Could she forget that she loved him? Could she go back home and pretend to live a life that was in reality merely an existence? Didn't she owe it to them both to tell the truth?

'Cal, I——'

He cut her off abruptly, his face hard. 'I hope you aren't going to come up with any objections, Claire. Frankly, this seems to me the best solution to all our problems.'

Had he somehow guessed what she'd been about to say? Did he imagine that she wanted some kind of commitment from him, the same commitment he had walked away from once before? She loved him, but did she have the right to tell him that when it might be something he wouldn't want to hear?

The words died on her lips and she turned away to

walk to the door, terrified of breaking down and causing them both a great deal of embarrassment.

'Claire.'

She stopped but she didn't turn. She couldn't trust herself to turn back to him and hide what she felt. 'What is it?'

'I'm sorry.' His voice was soft and deep as it carried across the room to where she stood. Her fingers curled into her palms, digging into the soft flesh as she strove to control the instinctive response her body gave to those rich, velvet tones.

'For what?' Her own voice was thready, breathless, filled with a note of longing that echoed in the silence like a prayer. There was a moment when he seemed to hesitate, a moment when her heart stopped and her whole body stilled on a sudden surge of sweetly glorious hope, then he continued and all that sweet hope crumbled around her feet.

'For disrupting your schedule, of course.'

Her breath caught on a sob and she closed her eyes, calling herself every kind of a fool. What had she expected? That he was apologising for throwing away her love and leaving her, for putting business before all else? Would a few words of apology really have made up for all that? She didn't know. All she knew was that if any dreams had lingered in her heart they had now fled.

The pain was raw but she welcomed it. It gave her the strength to turn and look at him then for the first time with eyes that held no echoes of the past, no secret hopes for the future, just the cold reality of the present.

'It doesn't matter, Cal,' she said quietly. 'It really doesn't matter at all.'

CHAPTER SIX

'IT's good to have you back, Claire. We've missed you. This valentine promotion of yours has really taken off!'

'I'm glad to hear it, Tom. I'd better get down to work, then, hadn't I? Maybe I'll see you later.'

'Of course. You can give me a run-down on what happened in New York.' He walked away but not before Claire had seen the fleeting disappointment on his face at her rather obvious dismissal. She sighed, wondering if she should call him back, but what was the point of doing that? She would never feel anything more for Tom than friendship. Michael Callan had ruined her chances of falling in love with anyone else.

The morning was hectic. With only two days left before St Valentine's Day, Claire had lost count of the number of cards she'd sold. She should have felt proud that the promotion was such a huge success but it was hard to feel anything apart from this icy numbness that had filled her ever since that night at the penthouse. She'd not spoken to Cal since, not that she'd wanted to. He had said all that needed to be said then.

When lunchtime came she carried on working, only stopping late in the afternoon to make a cup of coffee in the office. Wearily she closed the door on the throng of shoppers and picked up the kettle, then stopped abruptly when she saw the sheaf of roses lying on her desk. For a moment she stood and stared at them in surprise, then she put the kettle down and picked them

up, searching through the wrapping paper for a card to
say who had sent them, but there was nothing apart
from a slip of paper with her name on it stapled to the
Cellophane. They were beautiful, deep red and velvety, their perfume filling the air, but who could have
sent them? Unless. . .

She dialled Tom's office, her voice warm when he
answered. 'It's Claire. I just wanted to say thank you.
They're gorgeous.'

There was a moment's silence then Tom spoke.
'Sorry, but I've no idea what you are talking about,
Claire.'

'You mean you didn't send me the roses?' Her
bewilderment was obvious and he laughed with a trace
of embarrassment.

'I'm afraid not. I wish I had done, though. It was a
nice way to welcome you back.'

'Oh, I see. Sorry. I expect I shall find out who they
are from soon enough.' She replaced the receiver and
stared at the flowers as though they could supply the
answer to the mystery, but it eluded her for the rest of
the day.

The following morning it was violets, a huge, hand-
painted china bowl of them standing on the filing
cabinet. Claire slowly closed the door and walked over
to touch a gentle finger to the velvety petals. Once
again there was no card, just a slip of paper bearing
her name taped to the bowl. She stood in silence then
reached for the phone before abruptly putting it down
again. Was it wise to phone Tom and thank him again
for something he might not have sent? Logically, they
must be from him, prompted by guilt after yesterday,

but she didn't want to make any more embarrassing mistakes.

When the box appeared on her desk the next day she'd just got back from lunch. Tom had made no mention of the violets and short of asking him outright she'd been unable to get to the bottom of the mystery. Now as she spotted the gaily wrapped parcel she felt her stomach churn. Slowly she closed the door and walked across the room but it was several minutes before she could make herself unwrap the parcel, and she gasped in astonishment at what she found inside.

Sugar mice, a dozen of them, perfectly sculpted in pink and white, nestling in a bed of crackling black paper inside a silver-filigree box that bore the now familiar slip of paper with her name printed on it. What on earth was going on? Was it some sort of a joke? Because if it was she failed to see the funny side of it!

The questions whirled around her head all afternoon long until she felt quite dizzy with them, her whole body consumed with tension, her nerves quite raw. When the message came for her to go up to the office just as she was ready to leave that evening, it seemed like the final straw. All she wanted was to get home to the quiet safety of her flat and think through what had happened, find some sort of sensible answer to it all. This delay seemed almost more than she could bear. She marched upstairs and into the office after only the most cursory of knocks, then stopped dead when she found it empty.

For a moment she stood irresolutely then turned to leave, feeling her heart pounding sickeningly when she suddenly spotted the envelope propped up on the desk

with her name printed on it. Tension hummed along
her veins and she clenched her hands into fists, staring
almost wildly at the plain white envelope, knowing that
there was no power on earth that would make her pick
it up and see what it contained.

'Why don't you open it, Claire?'

His voice was deep and quiet in the silence. It filled
her head and sent quaking shudders racing through her
body. She pressed a fist to her lips and closed her eyes,
praying that her imagination was playing tricks, but
when he spoke again she knew it had been no mistake.

'Open it, Claire. Go on.'

She shook her head, her face as white as the envelope, her eyes huge and haunted. 'No.'

He smiled gently, drawing her gaze as he moved
across the room from where he'd been standing in the
shadows by the window and picked up the envelope
and held it out to her. 'Trust me, Claire. Open it.'

'Trust you?' The pain was stark and unadorned as it
echoed in her voice. She made no attempt to hide it,
nor did she try to disguise the contempt that was
shimmering in her eyes as she stared back at him. 'I
would sooner trust a rattlesnake than trust you,
Michael Callan!'

Red ran along his cheekbones in a thin, angry line
but his gaze was level, his voice steady. 'I know I've
hurt you, Claire, but I am asking you to give me one
last chance, and I promise that I won't ever hurt you
again.'

'Why should I? Why should I give you anything?
Frankly, Cal, you've had all I'm prepared to give. . .
ever!' She pushed past him, wanting only to get out of
the room and away from this fresh nightmare, but he

caught her arm and stopped her, swinging her round to face him so that she was forced to look straight into his eyes.

'Why, Claire? Because you love me.' His voice was deep, filled with something that seemed to cut straight through to her heart. Just for a moment Claire allowed herself to imagine that he meant what those soft, seductive tones implied, then deliberately pushed such foolish ideas from her head.

'Yes, I love you. But that doesn't mean that I'm willing to let you walk all over me again! You made it very clear what you wanted from me in New York, Cal, so don't insult me now by pretending anything else. I know exactly where I stand with you now, and what I feel for you has no bearing whatsoever on our business dealings!'

'And you really think that you can separate your emotions into neat little compartments like that?' There was disbelief in the question and she glared at him, more hurt that he should do this to her than she could admit.

'Yes! You do it all the time, so why should it be so different for me?' She laughed harshly, tossing her head so that her hair swirled back from her face. 'You are a true master of your emotions, Cal. You can turn them on and off at will, and I've used you as a role model!'

He sighed, his eyes sweeping over her face with gentle patience before he reached out to smooth a stray wisp of hair back from her cheek. 'I thought I could control my emotions, Claire, but that was before you came back into my life. 'You've always been my Achilles' heel.' He picked up the envelope and ripped it open, smiling in a way that made her heart thunder as he held her gaze and spoke softly, words that seemed to make no sense at first. '"Roses are red, violets are blue, sugar is sweet, and. . ." Well, I think this says it all for me.'

He held the card out to her, but Claire made no attempt to take it. She couldn't. She felt as though she'd just been pole-axed. Red roses, blue violets, sugar mice. . .

'It was you? You sent all those things!'

He laughed deeply, taking her hands to draw her to him. 'Yes, and you need one last very important item to complete the list. Here you are, Claire. Won't you take it?'

He handed her the card, his eyes filled with an expression that made her feel hot and dizzy and breathless all at the same time. Claire stared down at the card, her hands shaking so much that she could barely open it, and read the message written beneath the red satin heart.

'I do, Claire. I love you. I've written it there and I'm telling you it now. I love you with all my heart and all I want is to hear if you love me, as I hope and pray that you still do.'

'I. . .I. . . Oh, Cal!' The card fell from her hands as she hurled herself into his arms, burying her face into the curve of his neck as she held him close. He closed his eyes, a deep shudder running through him as his arms tightened around her.

'Thank God! I've been so afraid that I'd destroyed everything you felt for me. I don't deserve you to love me, Claire.'

There was anguish in his deep voice and she looked

up, smoothing a hand lovingly down his cheek, trembling when he turned his head and pressed his lips to her palm. 'It isn't that easy to destroy love, Cal.' She laughed almost sadly. 'Although I must confess that I tried to do it many times during these past years, and tried even harder since that night in New York. But you're in my heart, in my blood, in my soul. If I destroyed what I feel for you then I would be destroying part of myself as well.'

He bent and kissed her fiercely, his mouth possessive as it took hers in a kiss of naked passion. 'I can't make up for what I've done but I shall try, Claire. I shall try my hardest!'

She shook her head, glorying in the feel of his lips on hers, the sheer possessiveness of his hold. 'The past is over and done with, Cal. Let's not dwell on it.' She stopped uncertainly, her eyes clouding. 'You're sure that you mean what you say? I don't think I could bear to go through another break-up.'

'I'm sure. I've never been more certain of anything in my life. I knew that night in the lift how I really felt about you, and it shook me!'

She laughed at the wry admission, moving closer as she slid her arms around him under the soft folds of his jacket. 'Is that why you acted so coldly afterwards? Because you didn't want to face up to how you felt?'

'Yes, dammit! It was madness, Claire, but such delicious madness. It's haunted my dreams, I can tell you, remembering how you looked standing there in that lift!'

She laughed shakily, her blood heating at the note of desire in his voice. 'And that's when you finally realised you still loved me?'

'No. That's when I finally *admitted* it.' He tilted her face up to his, his expression very grave. 'I have always loved you, Claire. I never stopped loving you. I just tried to bury it at the back of my mind because I couldn't afford such feelings.'

'I wish you'd told me, Cal. I wish you'd explained instead of leaving with barely a word spoken.' She looked away, not wanting to mar this sudden gift of happiness yet all too aware that it wasn't easy to ignore the past. 'You couldn't have loved me that much, I don't think.'

He framed her face with his hands. 'I did. I ended our relationship because I had no choice but to do so.' He let her go and walked over to the window, his face etched with pain. Claire wanted to run to him and hold him, tell him that it didn't matter, but in her heart she knew it must all be sorted out before they could think about the future.

'Why not?' she asked quietly. 'Why didn't you tell me who you really were right from the beginning, Cal?'

'Because I'd promised my uncle that I wouldn't say anything to anyone at the store. The plan was that I would gain some much needed practical experience before moving into a management position.' He shrugged. 'I'd never been interested in working in the family business, if you want the truth, but felt beholden to after my parents were killed. My mother was a Hadley before her marriage and it's through her that I inherited my stock in the company. When my uncle suggested that I should take an interest in it I agreed mainly because I knew that was what she would have wanted. However, I never imagined that I would be thrust in at the deep end so quickly.'

He ran a hand almost wearily through his hair, his eyes softening as they went back to her. 'Has anyone ever told you how beautiful you are, Miss Parkinson?'

Her blood ran thick and she shivered delicately, feeling the look like a caress. 'Hundreds!' She smiled as his face darkened. 'But never anyone who mattered. . . apart from you.'

He smiled arrogantly, not missing the slight huskiness in her voice. 'Good. But before I get side-tracked I had better finish my story, hadn't I?'

'Only if you want to tell me, Cal,' she said softly, her eyes adoring him openly.

'I do. I want this out of the way now, Claire. It's way past time I explained anyway.' He seemed to gather himself, then continued firmly, as though he had thought often about what he would say. 'I wanted to tell you the truth about who I was many times, even discussed it with my uncle, but although he left the final decision up to me I never did it, and then it was too late.'

'Why? Did you think it would make a difference, Cal?'

He shrugged. 'Maybe. I liked what we had, Claire. I valued it. I didn't want it to change. I'd had experience of how attitudes change in direct response to the amount of money a person has and I didn't want that to happen with us.'

Her eyes flashed and she stared back at him hotly. 'I don't give a damn how much money you have or haven't got, Michael Callan! That doesn't influence my feelings one iota!'

'I know, I know. But it might have put a constraint on our relationship and that was something I wasn't willing to risk. Also there was the very real chance that other people would find out who I was once I started telling the truth, and that was something I didn't want to happen. I needed to learn the business from the ground up, not be treated differently because I was one of the Hadley family.'

'I suppose I can understand that.'

'I hope you can, Claire.' He smiled lovingly at her. 'It's very important to me that you try to understand how I felt and why I acted the way I did.

'Well, things were going along quite well until fate took a hand in it all. My uncle had his first heart attack and found that he couldn't keep the control he should over the business. There was an attempted take-over at the American end which would have meant the breakdown of the whole chain. Uncle John was too sick to fly over and sort it out so it was suddenly down to me. I had just two days to get things under control again and convince the shareholders that Hadley's was still a good investment. That's why I left so abruptly.'

'But you could have explained that to me, Cal!'

He shook his head, his face set and uncompromising. 'I didn't have enough time, Claire. It was touch-and-go as to whether I could get the support I needed to retain control.'

'I could have gone with you, helped you in any way I could!'

'No one could help me. It was down to me, the whole future of Hadley's. I worked twenty-hour days for that first year and not much less after that. I knew it would be hard. I knew that I wouldn't have time for a personal life, Claire. The business had to come first and foremost if it was to survive. It wasn't fair to ask you to go with me then desert you. It would have ended in bitterness and heartache and I couldn't do that to you because I care too much. I convinced myself that it was better to make the break swift than let what we had die a painful death.' He shrugged. 'Perhaps I was wrong but I don't think so. I still believe that it was the only thing to do in the circumstances.'

Was he right? Would the pressure have been too great for them to have sustained their relationship? With the hindsight of maturity, Claire could see that it might have been. She had grown up a lot these past three years, changed from a girl into a woman. That made a world of difference to her outlook.

Suddenly the pain that had lain in her heart for so long faded, leaving her filled with joy. Cal hadn't left her because he no longer cared about her, but because he had cared too much!

She went to him, slipping her hands into his in a gesture of trust that made him draw in a slow, deep breath as his fingers tightened around hers. 'I love you,' she said softly. 'I never stopped loving you and I never shall.'

He pulled her to him, holding her so close that she could feel his heart thundering against the swell of her breast. 'My God, Claire, but you can't have any idea how I've longed to hear you say that! I thought I'd ruined everything, but thank heavens I haven't!' He smoothed kisses across her eyelids, her cheeks, fleeting tokens of love and tenderness that made her ache. 'I knew I still felt attracted to you as soon as I saw you again but you seemed so determined to keep our dealings on a business footing.' His eyes gleamed wickedly as he brushed her mouth with his then drew back tormentingly with a seductive smile that seemed to melt her backbone so that she had to cling to him. 'And *that* made me determined to alter things. But it was only after what happened in the lift that I faced the fact I was still in love with you, that it wasn't just desire I felt.'

Claire pressed against him, loving the feel of his body hard and taut against hers. 'So what happens now?'

'Oh, that's up to you.'

'Me? What do you mean?' She drew back a fraction, confusion on her face as she stared up at him.

'Well, I've been the one making all the proposals of late, so now I think it's your turn.'

'Proposals?' She sounded like a parrot, repeating every word, but it was hard to follow what he meant.

'Yes, proposals. I mean, you do want to make an honest man of me, Claire, don't you? After almost compromising me in that lift?'

'Me compromise you? Huh! And as for making an honest man of you, I've no idea what you. . .' She stopped short, suddenly realising what he was saying. 'This isn't. . .isn't leap year, Cal,' she whispered huskily.

'I won't tell if you won't.' He feathered a kiss across her parted lips, drawing tantalisingly away just out of reach when she started to respond.

'Cal!' Frustration echoed in the sound of his name and he smiled tormentingly as he ran a finger across the soft, ripe fullness of her lower lip, teasing the warm flesh until she gave a little moan, part-protest, part-desire.

'You know the answer, Claire. You want me, don't

you, my sweet? But I am a man of principles. I need to know that this is going to be a permanent commitment.'

'I. . .' Desire was making her dizzy and she closed her eyes then opened them again slowly to look up into his handsome face. She loved him so much; to think of having the right to love him for the rest of her life suddenly gave her courage.

'I love you, Cal. Will you marry me?'

His whole body stilled then abruptly his mouth came down and he kissed her hard before he drew back to look straight into her eyes. 'Yes. I love you too, Claire, probably more than you can ever imagine. Now let's get out of here!'

He started across the room, taking her with him, making her breathless with his haste. Claire laughed, pulling back to make him slow down.

'Hey, stop a minute. What's the rush?'

He turned and caught both her hands in his, raising them to his lips to kiss them. 'The rush is because I can't wait a minute longer than strictly necessary to make love to you.'

'Oh!'

'Oh, indeed.' He laughed as he ran a finger along the soft flush of colour that stained her cheeks then led her out of the office and into the lift, taking her into his arms as soon as the doors had closed. His kiss was hot and tender, demanding and giving, everything she'd ever longed for and dreamt about. It seemed to draw the very essence from her, wrapping her deep in its magical spell so that it was several minutes before she realised that the lift had stopped.

She drew back, staring round in confusion. 'We seem to have stopped again.'

'There's no "seem" about it.' He held up the key he had taken from the control panel then slipped it into his pocket and let the jacket drop to the floor. 'This time, Claire, I'm taking no chances on being interrupted, so if you have any objections then voice them now.'

She smiled seductively, her hands going to the buttons on her blouse, her eyes loving him as she worked them loose. 'I've no objections, Cal. After all, this is St Valentine's Day, the one day in the year just meant for lovers!' And stepped back into his arms.

THE PERFECT GIFT FOR MOTHER'S DAY

Accept 4 FREE Romances and 2 FREE gifts

FROM READER SERVICE

An irresistible invitation from
Mills & Boon Reader Service. Please
accept our offer of 4 free Romances,
a CUDDLY TEDDY and a special
MYSTERY GIFT... Then, if you choose,
go on to enjoy 6 captivating
Romances every month for just £1.70
each, postage and packing free.
Plus our FREE Newsletter with author
news, competitions and much more.

Send the coupon below to:
Reader Service, FREEPOST,
PO Box 236, Croydon,
Surrey CR9 9EL.

NO STAMP REQUIRED

Yes! Please rush me 4 Free Romances and 2 free gifts!
Please also reserve me a Reader Service Subscription. If I decide to subscribe I
can look forward to receiving 6 brand new Romances each month for just
£10.20, post and packing free.
If I choose not to subscribe I shall write to you within 10 days - I can keep the
books and gifts whatever I decide. I may cancel or suspend my subscription
at any time. I am over 18 years of age.

Ms/Mrs/Miss/Mr ————————————————————— EP30R

Address ————————————————————————

————————————————————————

Postcode——————————Signature ——————————

Offer expires 31st May 1993. The right is reserved to refuse an application and
change the terms of this offer. Readers overseas and in Eire please send for details.
Southern Africa write to Book Services International Ltd, P.O. Box 42654, Craighall,
Transvaal 2024.
You may be mailed with offers from other reputable companies as a result of this
application. If you would prefer not to share in this opportunity, please tick box ☐

Next Month's Romances

Each month you can choose from a wide variety of romance with Mills & Boon. Below are the new titles to look out for next month, why not ask either Mills & Boon Reader Service or your Newsagent to reserve you a copy of the titles you want to buy – just tick the titles you would like and either post to Reader Service or take it to any Newsagent and ask them to order your books.

Please save me the following titles:	Please tick	√
AN OUTRAGEOUS PROPOSAL	Miranda Lee	
RICH AS SIN	Anne Mather	
ELUSIVE OBSESSION	Carole Mortimer	
AN OLD-FASHIONED GIRL	Betty Neels	
DIAMOND HEART	Susanne McCarthy	
DANCE WITH ME	Sophie Weston	
BY LOVE ALONE	Kathryn Ross	
ELEGANT BARBARIAN	Catherine Spencer	
FOOTPRINTS IN THE SAND	Anne Weale	
FAR HORIZONS	Yvonne Whittal	
HOSTILE INHERITANCE	Rosalie Ash	
THE WATERS OF EDEN	Joanna Neil	
FATEFUL DESIRE	Carol Gregor	
HIS COUSIN'S KEEPER	Miriam Macgregor	
SOMETHING WORTH FIGHTING FOR	Kristy McCallum	
LOVE'S UNEXPECTED TURN	Barbara McMahon	

If you would like to order these books in addition to your regular subscription from Mills & Boon Reader Service please send £1.70 per title to: Mills & Boon Reader Service, P.O. Box 236, Croydon, Surrey, CR9 3RU, quote your Subscriber No:..................................... (If applicable) and complete the name and address details below. Alternatively, these books are available from many local Newsagents including W.H.Smith, J.Menzies, Martins and other paperback stockists from 12th February 1993.

Name:..

Address:..

....Post Code:.........................

To Retailer: If you would like to stock M&B books please contact your regular book/magazine wholesaler for details.

You may be mailed with offers from other reputable companies as a result of this application. If you would rather not take advantage of these opportunities please tick box ☐